Waterball

A. SCOTT HOWE

Fifth Revision 2024
Plug-in Creations, Beaverton, Oregon, USA

ISBN: 098507650X
ISBN-13: 978-0985076504

DEDICATION

This book is dedicated to the fine crews and support teams of the NASA mission analogs programs, including the NASA Desert Research and Technology Studies (D-RATS) field analogs and the undersea NASA Extreme Environment Missions Operations (NEEMO) programs that have propelled so many fine space exploration concepts forward in their development. I also dedicate this book to the Wrightwood Ward Young Men program with whom we've shared so many adventures in extreme places, and the instructors and students of the Orange County Regional Occupational Program (NOCROP) diving program.

ACKNOWLEDGMENTS

I would like to acknowledge the hard work and dedication of my wife Ingping Chia Howe for her patience and encouragement when very few others could see the potential of this work. Thanks to my children and adventuresome brothers.

WATERBALL

PROLOGUE

It happened long ago. A small fleet of submarines drifted in the serene green ocean. The vessels were so near the surface the crews could almost feel the chaotic churning of monstrous waves above them. The communications officer of one of the vessels looked up through the clear bubble cockpit at the frothy surface and was glad he was safe underwater. *Out there the eternal winds would rip our boat apart*, he thought. In fact, he had never been above the surface, nor had his father, or his father's father. It was unthinkable.

Suddenly there was movement out on the periphery.

"What was that?" one of his colleagues exclaimed.

The communications officer peered out into the green gloom, but all he could see was one of the other submarines some distance away.

Then it was upon them -- a wall of seething creatures stretching all the way to the horizon.

"The thrash tide!" someone shouted.

The officer watched as untold millions of raging bodies came at them. The whole ocean seemed to boil over and the chaotic surface bulged into a wall of water. *Must get a warning out*, he thought, but he couldn't take his eyes off the approaching storm.

The companion sub was hit first and tumbled like a toy tossed about by a raging stream of storm runoff. Quickly the officer tapped out the clicks but it was too late.

Some distance away an officer on a third submarine listened to the unfinished message and understood. He clicked out his own message that carried from vessel to vessel until the warning reached headquarters deep in the foundations of the floating city.

'*The Continent*', a massive structure whose main bulk stretched out deep in the serene, peaceful green ocean could be shattered by the thrash tide. Even in good times armies of salvage crews canvassed its forgotten corridors trying to shore up wave-torn towers and buoyancy tanks -- it was a way of life for generations. Orders went out via runners to redouble their efforts -- and find a place to hide.

At that moment two men stood in a ruined part of the city and calmly examined a stretch of wall.

"Take a look at this," the young Nux began, indicating the solid obstacle, "What do you make of it?"

The older Hancho brought his own lantern closer to the uneven barrier, the illumination barely penetrating the darkness. The surface was rough and aged, having accumulated a few hundred seasons of growth. But it was unmistakable -- there was a slight depression there. Holding the lantern in his teeth, the older man used his hands to gently scrape away the layers and reveal the underlying plaster.

"This was definitely done later. It looks like a patch job, but cleaner, done by a skillful master -- notice how the newer part blends into the original material," Hancho thought the repairs could have been even older than the time his people came to occupy the city.

The two men scraped away at the wall, tracing the outline of what could have been a plastered-over doorway.

"It's almost as if they were trying to hide something from the casual passersby." Hancho muttered almost as an afterthought.

Both men paused and looked at each other, two faces partially concealed by respirator masks that helped them breath when the air was thin. *Are you thinking what I'm thinking*, the eyes seemed to say. It wasn't usual that one found a sealed chamber out in the ruins -- perhaps there was some hidden cache of treasure, perhaps even something from those mysterious inhabitants 'Those Who Went Before' who left unknown machinery and other belongings scattered throughout *The Continent* before disappearing forever.

Both men brought out their tools and greedily tore into the wall. Every swing brought down large pieces of the gray-crusted wall until one thrust embedded the tool all the way to the handle. Faster and faster they attacked the wall. The hole widened until Hancho was able to pass his lantern inside, and they could barely see answering glints of reflected light off shiny surfaces. The possibility of a hidden room full of ancient artifacts only excited them more -- in no time they had widened the opening enough to crawl through.

Had the men known the thrash tide was coming, one wonders if they would have tried to seek shelter, or if they would have gone after the loot anyway.

Nux went first, squeezing through the hole with his lantern out in front of him. As Hancho moved to follow, he heard the younger man whoop and holler in excitement. The older man quickly pushed through and craned his neck around to see -- and involuntarily gasped in surprise. Three massive metallic vaults stuffed a narrow undisturbed chamber. The two men found themselves side-by-side eyeing three large reinforced metal doors built into the gleaming curved sides. Vaults could only mean one thing, they thought -- hidden treasure.

One by one they opened up the three vaults. Vault One and Vault Two had stacks of polished cases containing thousands of blocks of crystals.

"What are they?" Nux seemed disappointed.

Hancho had no idea. Case after case held the same thing -- all he could think of was how they could dump the crystals and sell the beautiful precision-made cases. The crystals might fetch a price as trinkets, but they couldn't possibly get all those heavily loaded cases out by themselves -- empty cases would be easier to carry.

"There's some sort of filing system, I think." Nux exclaimed.

Hancho could see dividers with ancient symbols on them, "I think you're right. Can you read them?"

Nux shook his head.

But it was the contents of the third vault that the men found the most intriguing -- shelves full of gadgets, small machines, and unidentifiable objects. And right inside the door was a console apparently meant to catch the attention of any visitor who entered, with a large screen or monitor beyond. Hancho recognized right away one of the crystal blocks inserted into a slot on the top of the console.

Nux walked over and pulled out the crystal block, eyeing it more closely than before. "Do you suppose this could be some sort of data storage system?" he asked.

The realization hit Hancho like a wall of bricks. All those cases -- he had heard of the theoretical density of information, and how data storage could someday be recorded on impurities embedded in crystal. If each of those blocks were to hold that much data, the thought boggled his mind -- added together the vaults might house a library of astronomical proportions, perhaps revealing the secrets of Those Who Went Before.

"I think the Third Vault is the key to everything." Hancho realized.

Nux frowned, "We've got to get help. One of us is going to have to make a run back to tell the others."

The men looked at each other -- neither one wanted to leave behind the greatest find of all time, but they both knew the runner would have to be Nux. The elder would never be able to keep up. Nux dropped everything and rushed to the ragged opening that led out of the chamber. The glowing illumination from his lantern faded as his running feet echoed down the dark passage. Hancho listened as the footfalls faded away and began to set up generators and light stanchions in the vault room.

Unfortunately it was too late. The thrash tide slammed into the city and the men had not been warned. A rumbling began under his feet and Hancho could hear the sound of water down distant passageways. Beyond the chamber walls he heard a muffled crash as structure gave way, and he gasped as the whole room tilted at an angle. Somewhere below he could hear water rushing in as bulkheads collapsed.

"Nux, wherever you are, the whole place is sinking!" he cried out.

Down slope a part of the floor buckled and dark liquid began bubbling up from below. Hancho grew alarmed when he realized the frothy seawater was only a few armlengths from the gaping door of Vault One. Avoiding falling debris, the old man made his way from handhold to handhold until he got to the massive circular hatch just as the water reached the threshold. He swung it shut and spun the handle to engage the locking bars, then splashed through the liquid to the second vault.

Still holding the lantern in his teeth, Hancho looked around and realized the water was rising too fast. By the time he reached Vault Two and closed the door, some of the liquid had spilled in. The shaking continued, making it hard for the old man to make any progress. When he got to Vault Three, one of his generators and a mess of cables had lodged itself in the doorway and salty water began pouring over the threshold. He tugged at the cables but could not get them free. Finally, he lifted the whole mess and shoved the generator inside the opening.

Hancho started to swing the door closed but stopped.

What do I do next? he asked himself as he watched the chamber crumble about him.

Without further hesitation he jumped onto the mesh deck and shut himself up inside the vault. It was the safest place he could think of for the moment. But just as the locking bars engaged the whole world broke loose. A massive force somewhere outside slammed the entire vault off its foundations. All he could think was that the terrible monster of the deep had found him at last -- it was time for the final judgment.

The trauma of tumbling about, of knowing his tentative sanctuary was being irretrievably washed out to sea, proved too much. Somehow Hancho knew his sanctuary was no longer buoyed up by city walls -- the vault was sinking into the bottomless void. He began to hear wrenching sounds of the strained metal hull and recognized the first signs of a pressure vessel approaching crush depth. *Not much longer*, he thought.

The lantern flickered briefly taking away its feeble illumination. Not wanting to be left alone in the dark, he recalled seeing ancient electrical light fixtures above the shelving and remembered he had tossed the generator into the vault before sealing himself in. Could it be possible after all these eons that some of the fixtures would still work?

The oxygen in the vault was getting thin. Hancho struggled for breath and looked over to where the generator had come to rest after tumbling about. He reached over and sorted out the cables, detaching a smashed light stand. He had no idea how to switch on the old lights, or even if the voltage or current matched, but under the deck a junction box caught his eye -- if only he could get that open he may be able to supply power into the long-dead system. He pulled out a tool and began prying at the metal floor mesh.

It wasn't long before he was able to lift the deck plate out of the way and connect the cables to the old junction box. When he powered up the generator there was an answering flicker from one of the ancient light fixtures that immediately shorted out, sending sparks flying. At the same time the lantern died.

No light and no air...

As the man stared wide-eyed into the nether recesses of the dark vault, suddenly he became aware of a light on the console. The crystal block was glowing as a light emanated from the slot underneath it. Behind the console, muted colors flashed across the screen as if some image was trying to form.

While Hancho stared at the screen, other parts of the ancient installation began to come to life, drawing power from the borrowed generator. The open place in front of the hatch brightened, and a shape began to form seemingly in midair. He momentarily forgot his struggle for breath, and stared in astonishment. The form resolved itself into an image that seemed three dimensional, but not entirely solid -- a digital projection maintained by ancient technology.

"What the -- ?" Hancho exclaimed.

A crescendo of electronic video images from Those Who Went Before flashed before his oxygen-starved mind -- wonders he could not have imagined, and secrets...

Hancho involuntarily gasped. Reality melted away and he could see the thrash tide rush in from the periphery. The teeming mass of swimming creatures hid something deep below. *What the hell -- what is THAT doing down there?*

As the projection ended, his mind slowly slipped into the dark abyss. He desperately tried to hang on -- his people must know the truth! In one final act of desperation he willed himself to hold onto reality. *Perhaps there was a way.* The corners of his vision darkened as he asphyxiated. He recalled the shadowy line of tanks under the grille-like deck as he crawled toward the valves. Must...open...the valve... But Vault Three and the dimly lit room faded away, and the shelves, and the crumpled body lying on the deck, and the greatest secret of all time receded into nothingness...

CHAPTER 1

The instant Mox laid eyes on the place he knew it would provide endless entertainment for he and his friends. It was in an abandoned part of the city, perhaps from the time of Those Who Went Before. The cylindrical space stretched way up overhead without a single deck to interrupt its volume -- it must have been at least ten stories high and chocked full of stairs, ladders, catwalks, ducts, and pipes cascading all the way down to where he believed was sea level. But the most interesting part was that none of it stopped there -- all those conduits and ladders continued down below sea level another five levels, ending in a deep pool of clear, clean liquid. The node tower volume must have provided plenty of buoyancy for that whole section of the great floating city.

On top of all his objections, his brother Ix had brought a girl along -- someone from the ward whom they had met at Young Men / Young Women activities. The three of them stood on a narrow expanded metal deck and stared up at the space in awe. Rainwater dripped down in places and fed streams that flowed down half-pipe culverts. They each had respirator masks on their faces, since the forecast had been for thin air.

Holina asked, "What's all that noise up there?"

"I think the top of the tower way up there is right in the storms. There's probably a hole in the ceiling." Mox answered. *Silly girl*, he thought, *what fun would it be without a hole opening up to the storms?*

The girl suddenly realized the expanded metal floor they were standing on had the effect of being somewhat transparent, and backed against the wall -- they could see all the way down into the dark depths.

Mox pointed to a fat pipe almost lost among the others and said, "Ix, do you see what I see?"

His brother, who had been staring wide-eyed since they had entered the space replied, "I see water, air, a huge drop, and no rules. I must be in heaven!"

Where else in their confined world could a guy just drop stuff from so high, without any obstruction -- and into water no less? And the air pipes -- they could hear pressure rushing through all sorts of tubes. Think of what an enterprising fellow could do with all that force and no one around. The boys could tap into that and run all sorts of homemade contraptions.

"No look deeper -- there's a drop chute!" Mox exclaimed.

Ix turned to Mox with a big grin on his face, and each of the twins knew exactly what the other was thinking. Leaving poor Holina behind, both of them rushed over to any structure they could find with a semblance of hand and foot holds and began to race each other to the top. Mox found a large culvert full of rainwater and shimmied up its sides until it became too slick to grasp, then switched over to an air pipe that had braces spaced along its height. He looked over and saw Ix climbing the cross bracing under a series of cascading catwalks. He barely noticed the girl trying to find a more normal route up ladders and stairs.

In no time the brothers were laying on their backs on the top-most platform, panting away in the respirators, trying to catch their breath. Holina wasn't far behind them, and timidly topped the highest tread, trying not to look down.

It was a terrible racket. Just above their heads a small ragged opening only about a handwidth in diameter opened up to the incessant storms just as Mox had suspected. Occasionally debris would come shooting through as the ferocious winds propelled it downward. There was rain pouring in too, and long ago someone had constructed a catchment basin below that fed a small culvert. The boys watched in awe, rarely getting a chance to be exposed to such raw, unharnessed power.

After a while Mox watched as Ix got up and picked up a beam discarded on the deck. Ix looked back at him with an impish grin.

"Don't do it. It's too dangerous!" Holina implored.

But Ix was unstoppable and Mox encouraged him with his eyes as he also jumped up and approached the hole.

"It will take two of us, bro." he said, and held out the beam, one end pointed upward.

Mox stared into his brother's eyes and grasped the end of the beam. Four hands held on tightly and they slowly raised the end of the beam up to the hole. The girl held up her hands and covered her face, not bearing to look.

"Ready… now!" Ix yelled over the din.

The young men quickly braced themselves and thrust the beam up through the hole, holding it tightly. Suddenly a massive force wrenched the beam to one side and lifted them both off the floor. Mox, even though he had been expecting it, almost let go but held on tight. The brothers were pulled against the ceiling. Mox twisted himself around in an inverted position and pushed the ceiling with his feet, fighting against that unseen power that tried to yank the beam up through the hole.

Just as suddenly, the force dissipated and the two boys were sent tumbling to the floor. Mox couldn't hold back a thrill of pure pleasure, and the two rolled across the deck laughing their bowels out. Holina slowly lowered her hands from her face and timidly began to join in the merriment. Mox howled until he spotted the beam that had been completely shredded except where the boys had been holding it. Ix and Holina also stopped laughing as a somber mood caught hold.

"Whoa!" Ix expressed a greater reverence for the wild tempests outside, then picked up the mangled beam and looked back and forth between it and the hole.

The three of them stood silently, trying to imagine all that power.

Then without warning Ix walked over, took the remains of the beam, and shoved it up the hole. A great sucking noise could be heard and the beam disappeared with a 'whump'. He looked back and smiled, and the twins had another moment of mutual understanding. They canvassed the place, collecting any bit of loose debris they could find and one by one fed them up the hole, each one making its own 'whump' sound.

"Whoa, that was a good one!" Mox said as one of the pieces seemed to spiral around the edge of the hole a bit before meeting its demise.

Ix found an object that couldn't quite fit in the hole, but they shrieked in pleasure as the storms outside tore it to pieces a little at a time. It went on and on until Mox accidently dropped one of the pieces over the edge. The three listened as the object bounced around between pipes and ladders until it made a distant splash. Then they entertained themselves by throwing things over the edge for a while. The girl joined in too.

While searching around for things to drop into the liquid far below, Mox found an abandoned toolbox. It appeared almost shiny and new, so he thought it might have been lost in the ruins quite recently. However, when he opened it up, even though most of the tools were in seemingly pristine condition, some were heavily cankered in rust.

"Mox, those are *really* old! I think they may be something from Those Who Went Before." Ix said when he realized what his brother had found.

Mox looked down at the tools and didn't see anything special about them -- they could have been a cheap set that anyone in the core city might have possessed. He tried to imagine old god-like wise ones, with one of the tools in each of the multiple arms, fixing several machines simultaneously, but the glistening objects didn't seem to fit the image.

He looked at his brother with an incredulous expression, "No way! Look how new these things are! It's like they're shiny plated resin."

Ix shrugged in agreement, and Mox dumped the whole thing down the abyss. The boys peered over the edge and listened as all the metal pieces bounced around the countless pipes and conduits and finally made a splash far below. He would later regret the rash move, and it would forever haunt him that he might have had genuine ancient artifacts on his hands. But at the time, they were having so much fun that such thoughts didn't tarry for long.

When they got bored of throwing things off the high platform, the three made little boats and set them loose in the culverts, racing down the streams that forked and merged on a dozen paths downward. They followed the progress of the little vessels, descending stairs and ladders until the floating objects were deposited in the pool down at the bottom. The dropped items were there, buoyed on the surface and could be carried back up to start all over again. They dove in and swam around between boat races, howling in laughter.

At one point the three of them found themselves back at the top again all at the same time. Mox had found a spherical object and was playing with it, thinking about tossing it down, when he spied the drop chute. The interesting thing about drop chutes was that they were large in diameter, and didn't descend straight down, but leveled out a bit each time they approached a catwalk. The fat pipe went down at a steep angle, then leveled off, then descended steeply again in a pattern that wound its way down fifteen stories to the level of the pool. In some places the pipe turned into a half-opened trough, presumably to allow workers at various levels to add material into the chute, which would take it away. Mox peered down the hole and started hatching a plan.

"No bro, you can't be serious!" Ix came up behind him and also peered down the hole.

Mox turned around and looked at his brother but was in deep thought, and the appearance of the other may not have even registered.

"What if it has a damper in there somewhere? What if there's junk clogging it up?" Ix persisted.

Again Mox turned and looked at the other boy for a brief instant, and promptly dropped the ball down the hole. The two of them listened as the ball rolled quickly down the steep parts, slowed down at the shallow descents, and wound its way around the room. The drone went on and on then ended with the telltale splash at the bottom. The brothers looked at each other with wide grins. Ix immediately lifted one leg over the edge and was about to slide down when his brother stopped him.

"Wait! It gets better." Mox said.

He went over to the catch basin and eyed the makeshift culvert. Ix caught on and the two, assisted by the girl, got to work rerouting the stream to flow into the chute. In no time they stood around admiring the brilliant creation, and listened as the rushing water gurgled down the curves to fall finally into the clear, deep pool far below.

Ix went first, jumping feet first down the hole. Mox could hear his brother whoop and holler as he was carried quickly down the steep parts and around curves, finally to end in a big splash fifteen stories down. Mox followed right on the other boy's tail. The roller coaster chute turned out to be the most amazing rush either of them had found *ever*! They spent the rest of the wake period going down forward, backward, feet first, head first, and in tandem. They even got Holina to do it with them a couple of times, overcoming her better judgment.

Late in the wake period the three of them lay exhausted on the top level, smiles on their faces. How would they ever be able to beat that?

There were still the air tubes.

As he lay there, Mox noted that the main branch of the air pipe penetrated the ceiling above their heads. There must have been a working scoop out there, channeling in the force of the storms. Were those pipes abandoned like all the other amazing structures they had found in the tower?

Mox got up and examined the pipe, walking around its girth as the others stared on. On the opposite side, he found a small maintenance door in the side of the duct. He had seen these before -- if one opened the door, a cleverly designed airlock on the inside prevented the tremendous volume of air from rushing out through the opening. A maintenance worker could then insert a burnisher ball and close the door, whereupon the lock would be exposed to the flow and the ball would be whisked along the air stream, cleaning pipes as it went.

You guessed it -- Mox began to hatch another idea. He searched his pockets for something soft and found a handkerchief. Opening the little door, Mox placed the kerchief into the little chamber and shut it again. Immediately they could hear the swish of fabric bouncing through the pipe system. It was over in an instant. Somewhere below the kerchief 'plunked' as it presumably deposited itself in another lock far below. If the fabric piece were a burnisher ball, and if Mox were a repair worker, he could just go down and retrieve the ball and either run it through again or send it to some other part of the network.

But Mox was not a repair worker, and there were no rules...

Ix was quickly by his side, searching his own pockets. But besides a handkerchief or two, boys only carried around hard objects like knives, bones, coins, ball bearings, bolts, and such. In unison the brothers turned to Holina.

"Oh no! You guys are NOT putting my bonnet in there!"

Too late. Ix had wrenched the bonnet from her head and in a well-timed maneuver Mox had the little door open and ready to receive it. The bonnet made a bigger swishing sound as it was whisked through the network, this time going down a different pipe, 'plunking' into a different lock. The boys begged and coaxed the poor girl into giving them a steady stream of soft feminine articles and delighted as the objects found their way to various parts of the network. Holina would quickly descend the ladders and go search for whichever lock the article ended up in, only to be robbed of it once more when she got back up to the platform. Finally, after all the items had been recovered for the last time, all three of them stood around bored again, wondering what to do next.

It was at this point that Ix brought out a spherical object with a mischievous grin on his face. He had discovered the object in his pocket earlier when he had been searching for soft things to put into the lock.

"A stink-bomb!" Mox exclaimed.

The stink bomb was sulfur-based and could be manufactured by any boy from the city. The bomb disintegrated on impact giving off smelly fumes. Unfortunately sulfur was hard to get and expensive -- the boys had to sneak into the labs and manufacturing sections and collect what they could off the floor before it was recycled -- and before they were shooed away.

"Where did you get that?" Mox asked.

"I traded Drand for it. His dad works for Lord Jirt."

Mox had heard of Jirt, who was one of the Manufacturing Lords in the city.

"What are you going to do with that?" Holina asked.

Ix and Mox both smiled at her, and without saying a word turned and popped it into the airlock. Immediately the wind caught the heavy object and carried it along. They could hear the thing banging along a bit slower than the soft items owing to its increased weight. Mox imagined the bomb coming apart little by little as it impacted the walls of the duct, slowly releasing more and more of its terrible fumes. They wouldn't want to be around when it finally impacted the lock!

"Quick, we've got to get out of here before it goes off!" Ix exclaimed.

The three of them rushed down the stairs and ladders to reach sea level, following the progress of the bomb as it bounced and rattled through the airways.

Unfortunately, probably due to its heaviness, the bomb didn't end up in any of the locks they had found -- instead it headed down a new pipe off on a side passage. It was on its way toward core city!

Alarmed, Mox and Ix looked at each other, wondering what to do. They couldn't just go away now -- somehow they had to stop it! Quickly they ran down the passageway eyeing the pipe up above as the rattling continued along.

It was apparent that the air pipe was in use, and it powered the lights along the ceiling. The rush of air would branch off to each of the light elements and excite the mechanism, causing it to glow. But with the bomb slowing down the upstream airflow, all the downstream light elements dimmed and it began to get a little dark. As soon as the bomb rattled past and air could get through, the element would brighten up again.

The twins left poor Holina, who was a bit younger than they, and shot off ahead following the progress of the bomb. Folks walking up ahead would look up in confusion, wondering why the lights had dimmed, then would hear the object rattling through the pipe overhead. If Mox hadn't been so distraught over trying to stop the thing, he would have thoroughly enjoyed watching peoples' reactions to it.

The boys ran from node tower to node tower, passing gradually into the more populated parts of the floating city as the overhead air pipe branched and divided to supply pressure energy to the sectors it ran through. Mox thought, *what did we get ourselves into this time?*

The bomb continued toward the restaurant district. Without warning, the pipe branched so small that Mox could hear the bomb obliterate itself at the intersection. He imagined all those smelly fumes rushing down the pipe right into all those restaurants.

Ix who had been slightly ahead stopped, causing Mox to run into his brother's back.

"What are you doing?" Mox yelled.

But Ix just calmly turned around and looked at Mox.

"We're going that way." he said, and began to drag Mox off in the opposite direction.

Mox tried to protest but realized there was nothing they could do, and just followed his brother. Behind them they could hear screams as people rushed to get out of the enclosed spaces. The twins just ran and ran, trying to get as far from that place as they could. A stream of people, all running with handkerchiefs over their noses, merged into the passageway behind them. One woman was flailing her arms about as she screamed, as if the world as she knew it had come to an end. Mox and his brother didn't look out of place at all as they sped ahead of the crowd.

At length the boys finally arrived in their own neighborhood and fell about the place laughing their heads off. Mox even lost his respirator at one point and had to scramble for it to catch his breath.

"Did you see..." Ix began, trying to get the words out between bouts of laughter, "Did you see the man with the red nose? He was waddling along as if he had messed his pants!"

Mox laughed anew, "And the two little girls that kept banging into the lady's rear end!"

Ix laughed so hard his eyes got bloodshot.

After a while the brothers picked themselves up and walked toward their apartment, talking about how splendid an experience it all had been. But as they turned the corner they ran into their father. The boys stood up straight at attention and looked down at the deck, hoping their little prank wouldn't show on their faces. Mox wondered if the fun would be cut short with another training exercise with the salvage & repair teams that their father had often arranged.

"I just got back from the School for Technicians and have both good news and bad news," father began.

Mox wondered what it could have been. Both he and his brother had recently taken the coveted examinations to enter the Technicians' Guild. Had their father heard something?

"Congratulations Ix. You've been accepted into the Technicians! They're going to train you to work on one of the submarines."

Mox looked at his brother who was beaming. Ix would go away for a few seasons as he learned the Technician trades, and would be able to go out on one of those fabulous underwater machines!

But that meant the bad news was for him.

"I'm sorry Mox," father began, but didn't finish the thought -- he would have to follow his father into the ranks of the salvage teams.

But his father was still smiling. There was something else...

Father continued, "Congratulations Mox! The Salvage Lord wants you to serve as a diver."

A diver! He would be able to swim in that endless ocean. The boys smiled at each other and followed their father home. It was a splendid time indeed.

CHAPTER 2

Far away from the floating city a girl was dealing with the challenges of her own world. Though she soared through the forest at blinding speeds, she was still barely able to keep up with the other two Wardens. There was just too much to see along the way. Sometimes a flier would pass in front of her with its big floppy wings. Below her the usual velvet green carpet sped by, dotted with occasional flowers. *It would feel so good to just lie down there and do nothing,* she thought. She spied a small group of cuddlers dancing on a limb and slowed down to watch. Little puffs of fuzz with the cutest eyes. Oh how she longed to hold one in her own arms! The fat puffs danced and waddled high above the ground. How long had it been since this part of the Database was renewed? She could never tell whether she was looking at a real cuddler family or just a cleverly crafted loop from a hundred seasons before.

Up ahead, one of the others turned around in midair and called back to where she flew, "Come on Miss Blujic. You always get lost in the forest."

Blujic said good-byes to the little cuddlers. She could almost see them waving back, but knew no such thing would happen. A slight throw of her arms toward the others set her body in motion. She tipped into a prone position with her head cocked back. The farther she stretched her toes and stuck out her chest the faster she would move. Tossing her arms this way and that kept her steered in the right direction. It was almost like swimming, but she was not affecting her own propulsion.

Her friends swerved behind the bole of a great moss-covered tree. When Blujic reached the tree, she tucked up her legs and swung her torso to the right to do a sharp turn. It was one of those maneuvers that she prided herself in, but the only problem was that when she performed those power turns, her feet often got caught on the frame of her rocker. Ha! *Rockers were made for stiff-bodied people*, she thought. Passing between two trees, she saw her friends cruising low over a crystal-clear pond. It was beautiful -- Blujic was glad they had convinced her to take this new route to the *Origin*.

Blujic called out to the others, "Are you sure you haven't told anyone about this place?"

"I just found it two days ago." Miss Tarroc momentarily twisted herself around to face Blujic while she talked. The motion didn't slow her much, for the body nuance indicating that she intended momentary backward travel came automatically. As soon as the words came out of her mouth she righted herself again and faced forward.

"Miss Tarroc brought me here yesterday while you were diving in the Great Ocean." added the second Warden girl.

"Let's keep this place a secret, just the three of us." Blujic said.

On the far side of the pond was a pristine meadow sheltered by huge trees. The eyes of all three of them caught a slight scurrying motion there, and they watched another family of cuddlers tiptoe from the base of one tree to that of another.

Miss Pollic looked at the meadow and said, "We can form a castle over there and have it all to ourselves."

Blujic flashed angry eyes at her friend, "Let's don't do anything imaginary here, it's so beautiful the way it is. We can come here and play with the cuddlers."

Miss Pollic replied, "Oh Miss Blujic, you and that Flesh kick. What difference does it make? Besides, maybe someone imagined this place long ago. How would we ever know?"

"Well, we didn't imagine it. It seems real that way. We can form a place like this somewhere else and make a castle. If no one knows about this then why not keep it untouched?" Blujic prevailed on her friends this time, but it was obvious they weren't convinced of the logic of her reasoning.

A thin tree protruded from the surface of the pond in front of them. As they passed by, Blujic reached out her hand and whacked it just for the fun of it. There was a certain tactile response from her suit, but not enough to prevent her hand from passing right through it. Blujic laughed in delight due to the lightheadedness of the moment. Reaching the other side of the pond, Miss Tarroc and Miss Pollic alighted on the ground and began walking around the meadow. Blujic hated walking in the rockers; the tactile feedback to the bottom of her feet was realistic to a certain extent, but still seemed too contrived for her liking. She continued to hover alongside her friends.

"I wonder if the Inmates ever get this far?" Blujic thought out loud.

"We haven't seen any of the armies down this way."

"At least nothing in the Database, right?"

"What difference does it make? If the Inmates don't show up in this part of the Database then we'll never run into them."

Blujic knew that that might be true, but just the thought of them being there in the Flesh bothered her. Warden boys, who enjoyed playing multi-player war games, loved to run into Inmates in the Database, because usually the games required them to do battle to achieve some status of bravery or obtain treasure. Girls rarely had patience for that sort of activity, and for Blujic it was that Flesh thing she always seemed to worry about. Of course, even if there were Inmates in the area they wouldn't be able to see her. It was just that they always made unpleasant noises and were continually distracting.

The grass and moss of the meadow looked so soft; oh how she longed to run around barefoot and feel that moss between her toes. Her *real* toes. Blujic split with her friends and followed a cuddler across the meadow. The cute waddle was more than she could stand. She reached out and gently grabbed at the little creature. The cuddler didn't stop its waddle, nor was its motion affected by her attempts to catch it. Her hands passed back and forth right through the creature. The tactile system of her suit gave her a vague sensation that she was touching something wispy, but not solid.

"Hey, let's hurry up and go to the *Origin*, and then come back here afterwards on our way home."

All three agreed, and they each took off. They first had to find the coastal forest wall that they could follow along until they found landmarks they could recognize. Blujic spiraled higher and higher hoping to get above the tops of the younger trees. She suddenly broke out of the under forest into a wide-open space broken only occasionally by the massive older trees. It was from this altitude that they were able to do their visual navigation simply because they could see so far. Blujic had flown much higher than that before, but trying to fly above the tops of the larger trees was pointless because the Database there soon faded into nothing. She could soar out into the grayness and turn around to look at the brilliant bubble that was her world. The same could be said about the Great Ocean, where coastlines were represented well enough but faded to grayness beyond.

Casting her eyes about, Blujic recognized the coastal forest wall and headed in its direction. The forest wall was tightly packed with many older trees. It was dense enough to separate this serene land from the raging storms covering the ocean.

Blujic carefully noted the features of the area so she would be able to recognize it later. It only took a moment to reach the wall with her friends and slip into the flow of the throughway. There were dozens of other Wardens in the throughway going this way and that attending to their own respective business. The throughway wasn't a thing or an object, but the zone or area along the coastal wall that afforded the Wardens with easy passage. It was a trunk line of sorts that allowed them to travel to different parts of the country.

The three friends followed the wall for a while until they began to see signs indicating the *Origin* was nearby. The forest had almost completely disappeared below them, leaving endless expanses of rolling hills and meadows with occasional dense groves of old trees. In this part of the country the hills were so steep that the gnarled wood and fiber understructure broke through the soil in some places. The best way to approach the *Origin* was along the ground, so the three girls lowered their altitude to just above the meadow floor. They swung around a particularly high hill that everyone called The Sentinel and found themselves in the upper reaches of a wide valley sprinkled with many lakes. From their end of the valley, a long depression in the valley floor stretched all the way to the other side. The depression became deeper as one moved along it, until it actually got deep enough to have filled with liquid over time and become an elongated reflecting pool. At the other end of that deep swath was their destination: the *Origin*.

The *Origin* protruded from the valley floor. It was huge, rounded like a hill, but was perfect in its hemispherical shape. Seeing the long depression in the valley floor and the hemispherical *Origin* resting at its end, Blujic often felt that it reminded her of a gigantic ball that rolled along soft clay and sunk in at the end after it lost its momentum. The *Origin* had been made of some metallic substance, but over the eons had become mostly overgrown with the plants of the valley. In addition, there were fissures and cracks in its surface that opened up to blackness. Foliage spilled out of the fissures, and in some cases a very young tree or two had taken root therein.

The girls floated gently over the reflecting pond as they reverently approached the *Origin*. There were several other Wardens around, praying or meditating in the sacred setting. Blujic and the others took their places at various spots around the dome and did their own meditation in individual solitude. Blujic's thoughts went back to a topic that filled her with intense curiosity: what was inside the *Origin*? No one was allowed to approach those fissures and cracks in order to take a peek inside. Only the few ministers who continually watched over the *Origin* were allowed to approach it, but Blujic had never actually seen anyone do so. Once she had visited the sacred structure and, seeing no one around, had gotten close enough to knock on its aged, corroded skin -- but collision detection in the Database kept her from passing through its surface and she had been reprimanded at the time. Was the *Origin* real, or did someone form it eons ago? If Blujic came here in the Flesh, would there be an *Origin*, and would the ministers be guarding it?

Blujic considered the scenery of the sacred valley. Bright green foliage and moss covered the ground underfoot, and blanketed the surrounding hills as well. Around the edge of the valley occasional towering clumps of massive trees bundled together as a backdrop that made the *Origin* look puny in comparison. Suddenly an all too familiar feeling passed over her. Blujic had to get outside and walk around in the Flesh. The desire was so strong it wouldn't leave her the rest of the day. Even when the girls stopped at the forest pond on the way home she couldn't shake the feeling.

By the time the girls were on their way home along the throughway it had already started to get dark. Up ahead they could see the crystal palaces towering into the skies, all their lights glittering over the landscape. Blujic and her friends approached their own tower and flew to the great rocker port. Blujic hovered above the approach apron and spun around to look at the city. The many towers were incredibly beautiful; a forest of core supports rooted in the city fabric below reached up into the sky above her head. The cores each had concentrations of decks, balconies, floors, and roofs cantilevering out from them at many places along their height. Between the towers were great halls and many-floored building entities floating in the air. Only thin wispy bridges attached the entities to the towers. There were a thousand wonderful activities a young girl could get involved in out there. Her favorite place was the floating building just barely visible six towers over. She spent most of her days there, playing games and finding newly formed objects on display. She even spent lots of time forming things herself.

Blujic wondered; without the formed things everyone has contributed over the eons, what was that tower like? She had tried to find her way to it without a rocker but was always unsuccessful. So far she was only able to get out there through the Database by mounting a rocker and flying out of the rocker port. She could not locate the hallway from the Flesh.

Blujic suddenly had a strange thought -- what if all the towers were separated in the Flesh? In order to get there she would have to go outside of her own building into the real world to walk between the buildings. On impulse Blujic leaped from the rocker port apron and spiraled down to the ground. Slowly she made her way around the base of the building and searched for a door or some other opening. If she were able to find such on the outside, she might be able to look for it from the inside later.

She had almost made a full circle before she found what she had been looking for. It was a large door almost twice her height and was shut solid. There were two types of doors in the city: manual and automated. If it were a manual door she would have to open it by hand from the Flesh, but if it were automatic, simple voice commands would suffice. Hovering in front of the door, Blujic voiced the common commands that opened most automated doors in the city. There was no response. The next thing she could do was to simply pass through the wall. Even though the Database caused most walls and floors to be solid seeming with collision detection, some were not. Passing through walls was a little unpleasant because of the tactile feedback from the rockers, but it was done occasionally nevertheless. Blujic charged the wall only to be repulsed by a tangible barrier that denied penetration. The force of the rebound sent her into a spin, and she had to swing her arms in a controlled countermeasure in order to recover.

Gaining her composure, she sat back for a while and tried to think through it. There didn't appear to be any access from the rockers, so that left the Flesh as the only route she could take; she would have to find the door from the inside without the rocker and open it manually.

Blujic looked up at the magnificent towers. Hundreds of Wardens scattered across the sky as they flew back and forth on their various errands. Blujic threw her arms up into the sky that set her in motion on a trajectory that would bring her close to the rocker port. As she slowly glided toward the apron, her body started to shake uncontrollably. It was true she had thought about it before many times, but this time she had made up her mind and was about to really do it. She crept toward the black hole of the rocker port that gaped in front of her. The activity and commotion of the city behind her began to fade out when the tunnel corridor engulfed her, and Blujic began to notice faint markings on the walls and floors indicating the proper direction. She turned a corner into almost complete darkness, which the commotion of the city could not penetrate.

Blujic knew this corridor well. She turned another corner and suddenly emerged high above the floor of an immense darkened hall. Looking down, she could barely make out large spherical objects on the floor, nicely laid out in rows as far as the eye could see. Some of the spheres were darkened and lifeless, but a strange sort of dynamic faint light radiated from the interiors of most of the others. There were figures barely visible within each of those, wriggling and struggling like embryos within giant translucent eggs. These spherical contraptions were the 'rockers'.

In truth, Blujic knew that she was one of those very figures in the Flesh and that the Database only gave the illusion of her floating above the hall like this. Each of the Wardens in the rockers below was busy experiencing their own part of the Database, moving about to navigate through some unknown obstacles. Ahead, glowing markers indicated the direction Blujic was to go. She floated atop the translucent eggs and passively followed the markers until they led her to the only empty socket in the entire hall. She thought it strange how the Database worked: with all the rows and rows of rockers, the only break in the pattern without a sphere in place was the spot where her own rocker was to land. Of course her own rocker was there in place all the time, and the Database only gave the illusion that she was about to land.

Blujic slowly sank down into the empty socket. The bars and framework of her rocker began to materialize around her, and the translucent skin of the sphere blocked the outside scene by degrees. The framework consisted of three independent concentric circular frame structures, each hinged within the next ring in a nested hierarchy in such a way as to affect three degrees of freedom in rotation. When in action, their combined range of rotation traced out a sphere. Powered actuators attached to the harness simulated displacement. When the rocker had fully settled, Blujic looked down at her own body, fully covered with the tactile suit. The cross beams of the rocker ingeniously connected to a harness which suspended her in the middle of the sphere. Her arms and legs were free to move about as she saw fit, without the possibility of hitting the crossbeams. Only on the power turns did her feet manage to twist up enough to get caught on the cables if she weren't careful.

The rocker shut down completely leaving her fully in the Flesh. Blujic reached up with her gloved hands and removed her goggles and facemask. A narrow platform disengaged itself from the bottom of the rocker and moved up to meet the bottom of her booted feet. She disconnected the cables first, and then released the attachment of the rocker to her harness. With her full weight resting on it, the platform slowly sank back down into the floor. It didn't stop at floor level, but continued to sink below. Standing on the lift, the floor of the rocker appeared to rise higher and higher until she passed entirely underneath it. When the lift stopped, Blujic found herself in a small chamber barely larger than the platform containing a few lockers, and changed into her Flesh clothes. She pushed on a panel that opened onto a long, brightly lit corridor.

In the Flesh again! All of her friends despised the Flesh. One felt heavy and uncoordinated; it was necessary to use one's feet to go from place to place. Blujic was different. She liked the way it felt to walk and really touch things. Stepping out into the corridor she blinked at the bright light. Several other Wardens were trudging about, obviously reluctant to use their legs that way. One of the men cast his arms down the corridor and tripped flat on his face. Obviously he was trying to float down along the way and forgot he was off his rocker (that kind of thing happened quite often so no one gave it a second thought). The corridor was lined with panels similar to the one she had just emerged from. Occasionally a Warden would emerge from one of the panels; it was getting late and most of the cafeterias were already open for the evening. Another thing Blujic loved about the Flesh was eating. The Database could not replace that joy!

After leaving the locker room, Blujic went and met Miss Tarroc and Miss Pollic at the Cafeteria Orange. As they lined up at the dispensing machine, Miss Tarroc and Miss Pollic were excitedly talking about their plans later on in the evening. Blujic barely noticed that they talked about meeting some boys in the tower. She took some manufactured meat and vegetable blocks along with processed chocolate and absentmindedly followed her friends to the sterile tables. Her hands shook as she went over and over in her mind what she was going to do.

"...Well, Miss Blujic?" suddenly she looked up and realized that her friends had been trying to talk to her.

"Wha... what?"

"Are you going with us to the tower? Is something the matter? You don't look too good."

"No, I think I'll stay in this evening."

The girls started to make a fuss but she didn't seem to notice. The rest of the evening passed in a daze. Some time or other Miss Tarroc and Miss Pollic went on their way and left Blujic to herself. She wandered about and found herself in front of a door in a dimly lit corridor with scarcely a memory of how she got there. Pushing hard on the surface, the door slowly crept open. There was a vast dimly lit room beyond filled with all kinds of machinery with blinking lights humming at full capacity. As Blujic closed the door behind her and strode to the middle of a wide-open area, an automaton swerved to give her wide berth. There were many of them wandering about doing maintenance on the machinery, and none of them noticed she was there unless she actually stood in their path. It was not really a place Wardens should go, but she had seen automatons round and about before.

Blujic made some quick calculations in her head. The machine room was two floors below the cafeteria, which meant that the ground level would be another five or six floors below that. The corridor she had just come from was the lowest she had ever been able to find, so she suspected that any stairway to lower levels (should one exist) might be accessible from this vast machine chamber.

The automatons probably didn't need any room lights to function, but there were enough readouts and displays about to somewhat illuminate the floor for her. Blujic worked her way to the right of some particularly frightening machinery that made an awful racket, and found her way to a wall beyond. She slipped along the wall hoping to use it as a guide. At one point the pools of light ceased and the wall was bathed in darkness. Blujic paused in a moment of uncertainty, wondering whether her curiosity was really worth bumping around in the dark of that scary place. Nevertheless she began to feel her way into the dark reaches.

After what seemed like an awful long time, Blujic's hands felt a depression in the wall to her right. There was quite a draft of air flowing in and the sound of electric motors. She moved in front of the opening and felt the steady breeze blow into her face and ruffle her hair. There was a very weak ambient light that seemed to flicker from the end of a long tunnel. The passage was large in section, perhaps twice her height. Blujic moved into the breeze and made her way down the tunnel. She didn't need to go too far before she realized that the flickering was caused by huge electric fans. There were three of them side by side across the tunnel, but one of them was stilled. It was what lay beyond the fans that made her stop and gasp. The ambient light was coming in from the outside.

Blujic moved over to the stilled fan and squeezed between the massive blades. On the other side was a narrow space between the fans and a grille that spanned the entire tunnel. Blujic stood in the narrow space and held onto the grillwork as she looked through to the other side. The tunnel continued beyond the grille for a while and opened into the night air. There were vines and plants almost completely covering the opening, but not thick enough to block the view. Blujic could not hold in her excitement as she realized that those were real plants that she would soon be able to touch with her own hands in the Flesh.

Quickly she looked over the grille and found a hinged gate. It didn't take long before she figured out how to work the mechanism and successfully opened the gate a crack, as far as it would go. There was some kind of debris blocking the way. In fact, she began to notice that the whole inside of the tunnel beyond was scattered with all sorts of debris, arranged in piles. Blujic looked closely and began feeling a little uneasy. The stuff lying on the floor looked like the type of things people collect: utensils for eating, stacks of material, various artificial objects, and items that appeared to be used as furniture of sorts. Suddenly a frightening thought entered her mind. What if this was a place the Inmates came to regularly? She was not here in the rocker but in the Flesh; what would those terrible armies do with her if they found her?

Somehow the thought only pushed her further. There was something grandly adventurous about the idea that she could actually be in danger in the Flesh. She reached through the open crack and grabbed a long rod that had been propped up against the other side of the grille. With the rod she worked at prying away the debris immediately blocking the panel and finally succeeded in opening the gate enough to let her through. Blujic tiptoed through the stacks of things like one in a dream. She couldn't believe this was happening to her!

As she approached the tunnel opening, her interest in what lie scattered about faded and she gave all her attention to the vines and the outside. Something seemed odd. She never descended any stairs after she entered the machinery room. If she were standing five or six floors above ground level, why would there be plants? Blujic could see dark rolling hills in the distance bathed in an ambient light. She knew that any moment she would be able to see the lights of the other towers. She reached out and grasped one of the vines and pulled some leaves from the stem. They felt so good in her fingers; nice and supple, the leaves were almost as large as the palm of her hand. Instinctively she carefully broke one free and inserted it in the front of her blouse to protect it.

From where she stood, there were no towers to be seen. *This tunnel must be facing away from the city*, she thought. Blujic stared in disbelief. The tunnel opening was not five floors high but was at ground level. Cautiously she stepped out into the night for the first time in her life. Instead of the crisp evening she was familiar with from flying about, there was a steady amount of precipitation falling from an overcast sky. Undaunted, she walked right out into the rain and began to thrill as all of her senses were filled with wonderful nature. Immediately outside, the ground sloped down to a low meadow. Blujic suddenly could not contain herself as she let out a cry and ran down the hill on her uneasy legs. In the meadow she danced around until the excitement wore off a bit.

It was out on that meadow that she finally realized the truth that she had never even remotely suspected; something was terribly wrong. In spite of the beauty before her under the ambient illumination of the overcast sky, she suddenly felt very alone. She stood up straight and looked back toward the tunnel opening from which she had come. There were rivulets of water streaming down her face as she stared in utter disbelief. The building from which she had come, to which the tunnel connected, was no tower at all; it was a rather low pyramidal structure mostly enclosed in enveloping berms, almost hidden from view with a healthy selection of plants growing on the roof. Indeed, the rocker port was probably on the highest level.

Still, the shock of seeing that low building was nothing compared to what she saw beyond it. There was nothing at all! No towers, no floating buildings, not even other low bermed buildings. The only thing in the world under that sky was that little bermed structure on the vast landscape, soaked in rain. They were all alone. What of all the shops and museums and halls that gave life meaning? The structures were all imaginary; the city was just a creation of generations of Wardens -- it only existed in the Database.

Dejectedly, Blujic went home. In the Flesh.

CHAPTER 3

Ix swayed and held on as the submarine rolled slightly, then dipped and cut through the liquid depths. The men were all staring at him, smiling. He looked around, and appreciated the camaraderie that contrasted with the cold pipes, conduits, and equipment that framed the small space. It seemed like a lifetime had passed since his training began and those carefree times with his brother Mox had come to an end. In reality it had only been a couple of seasons packed with an unbelievable rush of hands-on equipment operation, classroom study, fabrication, number crunching, and wrench work. And there he was, beginning his first voyage to the open sea, and these old submariners somehow thought *he* was the expert going to teach *them* what to do.

Ix was about to demonstrate a new piece of equipment he had been trained on, all freshly installed in the bridge. He reached up to turn the instrument on, and the men watched as a cool glow answered on the scopes. A faint line swept around each scope and illuminated bright splotches of pattern every time it passed. There was a strange repetitive sound echoing through the hull.

The men applauded.

Ix looked back with a big grin and said, "These bright patterns are probably small groups of fish swimmers. The sonar bursts bounce off the fish and come back to our detectors."

The captain, whom they called 'sencho', was awestruck. "Do you mean this tool shows where they are even beyond our headlights?"

Ix thought for a moment. Behind the men he could see the dark green 'Mother's Plasma' -- their name for the ocean -- through the thick transparent bubble cockpit. Thin pencils of light shot out from their vessel and illuminated floating particulates until they faded into the darkness.

Ix replied, "Probably more than ten times as far."

Sencho's eyes got wide as saucers. Ix was pleased at the positive reception the crew were giving the new piece of equipment. He had worked hard trying to arrange for its test installation in their vessel, and was sure they would be able to find more swimmers quicker than the other submarine pods in the fleet.

He looked back and forth at the three scopes, over the shoulder of the tracking officer who was just learning how to interpret the patterns in a useful way. Two of the round monitors had peculiar shaded regions near the bottom of the screen, prompting Ix to go back and adjust the knobs again. He wasn't sure if the stain-like patterns were real, or artifacts from the new electronics as they warmed up. Ix couldn't have known that those unknown patterns would haunt him in the seasons that followed.

Ix wondered if there might have been a connection between the unpredicted patterns and the compass needles. He let his gaze follow the navigator across the cabin as the men broke up and went to their separate workstations. The officer, whose name was Mag, tapped at the compasses and shrugged in frustration -- the needles had gradually begun to misbehave at the beginning of the voyage and were now spinning wildly. Apparently it was a phenomenon that occurred every time the fleets approached the thrash tide and the massive cloud of fish, but no one could explain why. Indeed, their people had been using the compass trick for countless generations -- when the needles began to behave oddly, they knew the swimmers would be riding the thrash tide in. And Ix could tell each of the men were nervous, not looking forward to getting too close to that huge seething entity. What would it do to their pod if they were careless and allowed themselves to be swallowed by the tide? No one wanted to find out.

The knobs didn't seem to help any so he let off for a while to see if the splotches would go away during the operation. Ix looked around and thought about all the hacked together instruments and the long list of malfunctions that kept him busy. Though he was trained for it, and knew the inner workings of the submarine fairly well, this was his first extended tour -- until now it had been only short hops out of the submarine base that they called the 'pod port'. Back at home, he and his fellow freshman technicians had taken the training pod apart and reassembled it to full working order over sixteen times. They had taken it on test runs and learned how each piece of equipment worked. In addition, each of them had learned manufacturing processes of at least one of the instruments. Ix tried to avoid looking directly at any of the machines, afraid he might jinx the mechanisms.

As if to confirm his worries, suddenly all the lights went out. The sencho began trying a few of his controls, which for the most part were dead. He ordered over his shoulder, "Ix, hurry and get that circuit back up again."

Ix carefully pulled out a tool from his bag and began removing an access panel. He had to get down on his back and slide under the unit in order to reach the faulty equipment. Unfortunately the floor wasn't entirely dry -- the resin hulls of their vessels were mostly sound, but some of them had developed numerous small squirts that pooled up now and then. Ix ended up lying in a shallow puddle of salty, mineral-rich sea water that had not yet reached the bilge pumps, trying to reach up to replace a part deep inside the console. He sensed that the sencho was pacing a small area of deck in his impatience to get started again so he quickly wrapped up the job and buttoned up the unit. As he got up onto his feet, he watched the others power up their instruments.

The communicator that had been only marginally active during the entire exercise suddenly began amplifying a flood of clicking noises coming from the other craft. The com officer quickly turned to his hand set and began translating the messages and sending off replies. The crew called the man by the nickname 'Smash', because of the peculiar heavy-handed way he clicked out the endings to his messages. Apparently, each craft's communication had its own feel to it, and each operator had his own signature, but Ix couldn't tell the difference. With the rush of clicks their submarine was back in working order again and the communications were mostly an attempt to recover a coordination of actions.

As the crew settled back in, Ix wandered over to the sonar scopes again to check on the anomaly. The tracking officer was judging the swimmer clumps correctly, and calling out positions to be relayed by the communicator. One scope showed a horizontal cross-section out to the nether horizons. The other two showed vertical views -- one could make out the hard barrier at the top where the roiling Plasma ocean met the relentless storms, and mountainous waves mercilessly beat objects to smithereens. But where the scopes should have faded into the depths below, the unknown patterns persisted -- ghostly curves that remained fixed over time, in contrast to the shifting outlines of the swimmer groups. Ix was puzzled -- they were definitely secondary signals coming up from underneath and didn't have anything to do with the unit's electronics.

When Ix's responsibility ended he made his way back to his bunk, pondering the meaning of the shadowy feedback. There was a view port there in the cabin, where he could kick back and watch himself to sleep with the calming powers of Mother's endless deep. Ix tried to look downward but knew nothing would be visible in those dark depths besides an occasional swimmer. He also knew that somewhere down there was the dense liquid Mineral Strata that his people painstakingly mined for its metals, alkali, halogens, and carbons. Were the strange echoes a product of all that stuff suspended in the Plasma?

He recalled early in the mission when they had briefly visited an underwater mining and processing outpost to obtain supplies. Great conduits reached down where no pod could go, beyond the deepest crush limit. He recalled the throbbing pipes, and imagined untold volumes of mineral-laden liquid sucked up from below and run through Plasma distillers only to yield a meager output. The supply his people gleaned from the Mineral Strata was the only source of raw materials available to them. Mother gave them all they needed, but with great effort and price.

And below the Mineral Strata -- as far as they could tell it was bottomless. Ix always wondered the meaning of it -- where did it all end? And above the surface he knew that up in the storms nothing could survive, but would be ripped apart after a few moments of exposure. There seemed to be only a narrow hospitable zone of serene calm, bounded above and below by the violent storms and crushing pressures. Mother was their entire world, enveloping their city and machines like a liquid womb. There should not have been anything big enough down there to set off the sonar.

Suddenly Ix had a horrifying thought. He didn't think they were near the swarming fish yet -- was it possible that some huge branch of the swimmer cloud stretched *underneath* them? Could they at that moment be in danger of being engulfed, *from below*? Or worse, were there larger, more fearsome creatures down there?

Ix must have drifted off to sleep, because the next thing he knew was that one of the crewmen was trying to wake him. The man was leaning over him, shaking him with an outstretched arm. Ix still didn't know all the crew's names. They were a tight-knit group from hereditary pod crew families. He himself was born into a salvage and repair clan, but had passed the examination to become a technician and thus was privileged to have an opportunity to serve among the pod crews.

"Sencho needs some work done on the thruster controls." The crewman explained.

Ix looked out the port and realized they were moving at a healthy clip. Floating particles and occasional swimmers whizzed past the port with dizzying speed. Small changes in direction caused sensations of lightness, heaviness, and sideways roll. He got up and followed the crewman back to the control cabin, using the wall-mounted handgrips along the way.

"You're Sal, right?" Ix asked.

"You remembered." Sal acknowledged with a smile.

Passing through the open hatch, the room presented itself with a flurry of activity. The banks of controls and instruments on both sides were monitored by a full complement, as apparently everyone on board was at their posts.

Straight ahead Ix saw Hord the pilot silhouetted against the large clear bubble of the cockpit, operating the joysticks and casting them all about with every slight direction change. Suspended particles, debris, and swimming creatures came at them at a terrific speed. Hord couldn't take a perfectly straight shot but was required to maneuver through the clearest parts of the Plasma to prevent the clogging of the thruster jets.

Piloting was one of the things little boys dreamed of. When they were little, Ix and his twin brother Mox had often played as though they were pilots speeding through the blue-green void. They constructed rafts out of debris and floated them through flooded passages, pretending they were pod pilots. Once the brothers went as far as to cobble together a hack pod that could actually submerge itself for a short period of time, including working valves, ballast tanks, and human pedal power. And now Ix was finally stationed on a real one.

The sencho was standing at the chart table directly behind the pilot. Logs and record book-films were opened up there, clamped into place by narrow metal spring bands, and large sheets of drawing film. The captain often doodled on the film, making notes of areas of thicker density, currents, or high concentrations of suspended minerals. The sencho kept track of these things with utmost dedication. The amount of common-sense information the pod captains had stocked up in their brains was astounding. Any one of the senchos of the pod fleet could circle their floating city entirely without the use of a single thruster jet, based on the knowledge of currents, waves, and undertow generated by the submerged portions of the city. This is what the yacht racers did, spreading their sails and catching the currents rushing through narrow passes in the great foundations of the city.

"The controls are a bit sluggish." Sencho indicated.

Ix wondered about whether that huge arm of the thrash tide could still be underneath them and began to get worried again. As he passed behind the tracking officer he did a double take -- the scopes were normal.

“Ix, the echo is gone. All we are seeing are signals from the straggling swimmer clusters.” The officer explained.

“When did the anomaly go away?” Ix asked.

“It happened suddenly, as if there was a floor below us one moment, that dropped out of sight the next.”

Ix began tinkering with the thruster controls, but his mind was on the now non-existent echo. He crawled under the unit and found himself lying in another puddle of Plasma, trying to poke around in his tool bag.

He called over to the tracker from his awkward position below the machinery, “How long ago was it?”

“It was just a while ago, before you walked in.”

Ix continued checking over the problem thruster controls but couldn't seem to find anything wrong. He took apart some of the subassemblies and put them back together again, using spares in place of the parts that appeared the most worn.

He turned to the sencho and said, "I've replaced this relay just in case -- let's see what happens. If this doesn't solve the problem we may have to wait till we return to port and check the outboard connections."

He got up and took an empty chair next to the sencho, wiping himself with a small cloth.

"I'm going to do some test maneuvers," Hord announced. He powered up the front thruster set and began testing their response with a series of pitches and semi-roll movements.

Ix thought about the echo. “Can you run your maneuvers back to the point where the sonar became clear?”

The Sencho agreed, and the pilot did a sharp bank that almost turned into a quarter roll. As Ix monitored the motor response, he was also distracted by the tracker scopes. Then, as if they passed over an invisible threshold, the echo suddenly came up again. *It couldn’t have been the thrash tide*, he thought. The swimmer cloud characteristically would have had rough, undefined boundaries. He did some quick thinking and turned to the pilot, “It's got a clear edge. Like there's something down there. Can you circle around and see if we can follow it?”

Hord did a spiral pattern and the trackers found that the echo traced a distinct crisp line. He set a course that followed the line, but did a weave to make sure they stayed over the boundary. The trackers continued to translate their readings for the hunter fleets, but kept a curious eye on the anomalous signal.

This continued well into the sleep period. Their course over the boundary mapped out a wide curve that could not possibly have been either the thrash tide nor caused by anomalous artifacts in the system -- it was an object of immense proportions. The young technician and the others looked at each other nervously, not knowing what to think of it.

Ix had a fitful sleep, worrying about what sort of massive thing could be lurking below the cloud of swimmers. It was still on his mind the next wake period as he stumbled into the control room on the heels of Mag the navigator. There was a different atmosphere from before -- the deck was quiet, since most of the crew hadn't woken up yet. But more striking was the view out the bubble cockpit -- the Plasma up ahead was seething with fish.

Sal was sitting at the tracker station, standing in for the regular officer.

"Ix, I think we found the main tide," Sal nervously pointed at the scope, which was almost entirely solid in front of them as the line swept around, "I'm surprised you were able to sleep through all that turbulence."

The sonar scopes were overwhelmed. If there was something down underneath them besides the swimmers, no one could tell. Ix hoped they had the thrusters primed, ready to bolt if the seething mass got too close. *So this is the thrash tide*, Ix thought. He could see how it got its name with all those fish thrashing about. But in spite of all their numbers, the creatures were just small animals -- too large to fit through the grilles of the thruster intakes, but too small to cause any damage. It didn't seem like they could affect the submarine at all -- wouldn't the swimming bodies just gently press against the view ports and then move on?

Ix thought out loud, "How could these little creatures be dangerous?"

Sal wasn't sure. "I suppose just their large numbers may combine and cause trouble."

"And the hunting fleets are mopping up now?" Ix supposed. He imagined the large vessels tentatively approaching the boundaries of the cloud and reaching out with their nets to try and capture as many stragglers as they could without getting surrounded.

Both Smash and the sencho were still aft, and Hord, who had the command, was slowly steering through the straggling creatures out on the boundaries.

Sal returned, "No, not all of them. I think some pods haven't responded yet."

Ix knew their primary mission was now over. They had found the thrash tide, and would now see if they could get an indication of how far out it spread, and the general direction the swimmers were heading. All that information would go out to the hunter fleet for hopefully many wake periods of prosperous fishing.

The other officers wandered in one by one, and Ix was soon busy with maintenance tasks. The sencho ordered their vessel on a slow, time-consuming orbit around the mass of swimming creatures to map the edges of the swarm.

Ix was still agitated about the anomalous readings, and kept his eyes on the sonar scopes, even though all the readings were still saturated by the wall of living creatures. If they could only go down there and explore, he thought.

As he passed the scopes for the umpteenth time, Ix got an idea. "Sencho, what if we got up on top of the tide? We could find the extents quickly."

Almost in unison, all the men looked in his direction, concerned looks on their faces.

Sencho shook his head, "I don’t think the thrash tide goes up as far as the surface. We'll only see stragglers up there."

Ix knew it was more than that. Sencho and the others were worried that the seething creatures might surround their vessel -- should anything go wrong they would be trapped between that teeming mass and the violent surface strata that could wrench a submarine apart.

Ix pointed to the new tracking system, "We don't need to see anything, sir. We can keep our distance and still measure the whole mass of them."

The sencho thought for a moment, and then, realizing how much time it would save, tentatively agreed, "Pilot, be very careful -- I want to be able to retreat at any sign of danger."

Hord flushed Plasma from the ballast tanks and, gingerly pampering the thrusters, skillfully powered their craft upward.

The eyes of all were facing forward, peering out the bubble cockpit.

Ix could see a marked change as the solid mass of swimming creatures broke up into isolated groups and stragglers. The pitch black of the deep Plasma gave way to a dark green hue as light filtering in from the great storms illuminated the suspended particles around them.

Mag called out, "We're down thirty, sir."

Ix rushed over to a side view port and peered upward. There he could see the underside of the mountainous waves as they boiled and churned in violent agitation. The view port produced a strange fish-eye effect that made it look as though the horizons were gathered inward like the surface of a sphere.

"I'm getting great readings now! I can see the whole lot of them almost." Sal called out, "Forward ho! Just a few passes and we could wrap this up."

Ix wandered over to the tracker scopes. The great mass of swimmers below them gave a healthy echo that showed up clear and crisp on the two vertical screens. Somewhere below that, the swarm masked a secret that Ix was determined to uncover. Was the unknown thing related to the swimmers somehow?

When he looked at the third screen Ix was surprised to see that a wall of color surrounded their vessel. What should have been clear Plasma out to the horizons showed a glowing halo that reached saturation at the edges of the screen. Puzzled, he looked over at Sal, but the other had his attention riveted elsewhere. In fact, as Ix looked up he saw the sencho and the others staring wide-eyed out the front of the craft.

Still unable to see clearly what was going on, Ix followed the other men as they crowded around the bubble cockpit. When he finally jostled into a good position he was astounded by what he saw. The fish-eye lensing effect he thought he had observed earlier through the view port was not a result of light refraction through the thick material -- it was real! The entire boiling surface of Mother's Plasma mounded up such that their craft hovered near the apex of a mountain of liquid. The uplift included the entire surface out to the limits of their visibility.

"Do you see that?" Hord asked. "I've never seen anything like it."

"What do you suppose it is?" Mag said in a small voice.

Sal commented, "A bulge pushed up directly over the thrash tide."

Ix connected the uplift with what he saw on the scope, "The sonar is sending back a echo from all around us -- it's bouncing off the underside of the Plasma. Are we inside a giant wave?"

Mag responded, "It can't be a wave -- it's moving too slowly."

The group sat and stared for a while, wondering if the mound of Plasma might suddenly collapse and lose its shape. But the sencho ordered them back to their workstations. Soon Hord had them crossing the bulge, taking measurements of the curvature as they did soundings of the swimmers in the thrash tide below them. The fear of getting trapped in the middle of the swarm proved unfounded, since there was plenty of clear, serene liquid just below the waves in which to maneuver.

The uplift persisted, though not as noticeable the further one got from the center. It wasn't long before the survey was finished -- in record time. They had mapped the size of the tide and knew where it was headed. Ix listened as the data went out in a rush of clicks to be passed on to the hunter submarine fleet.

The quickness of their work might have improved the efficiency of the hunt, but Ix wasn't very enthusiastic. As he analyzed the data he found the results quite sobering. The uplift coincided with the swimmers in the thrash tide, as if the strength of the swimmers alone could cause the Plasma to rise with all their agitation. And perhaps the compasses were affected by it too. But Ix was most alarmed by that shadowy edge below -- whatever it was he had no idea, but it was huge, deep, and it was moving steadily in a straight line -- right in the direction of their floating city!

CHAPTER 4

News of the approaching thrash tide reached the floating city -- *The Continent* -- early the next wake period. Ix's twin brother Mox had no idea anything had changed as he slowly strolled along a remote stretch of pavement. He looked up at the crisscrossing walkways high in the node tower and saw the usual foot traffic in and out of small shops and galleries. Ducts and vents characterized the tall cylindrical space, producing a cacophony of hissing sounds where air captured from the storms outside passed swiftly through narrow openings and drove a myriad of machines and generators.

Off to the side he found a small workstation illuminated from above, containing rows of green-tinged cylinders exposed to the light. He paused a moment to look at his own respirator, and remembered that he hadn't changed the cylinders in a while. He removed the unhealthy-looking canisters from around his neck and hovered over the rows of brightly lit modules until he found a few that had had longer exposure than the others. He took the new ones from the rack, connected them to his own respirator, and replaced them with the old dull green ones he had been carrying. That started the clock for regeneration of the algae inside, and after a period of time the old ones would be just as good as new. He put the mask to his face and breathed in a quick breath of refreshing oxygen before continuing on his way.

Mox saw nothing unusual about the people he passed as he entered the tunnel leading to the next tower. The passageway constricted to a narrow track, and air rushing through a small pipe overhead excited the light elements into bright luminosity. Ahead small jets of wind leaked out of the pipe and messed at women's hair when they passed under it. When Mox walked through the stray breeze, he paused and took off his respirator, letting the air pressure fill his lungs in a moment of pleasure.

It was when he strode into the next tower that he began to get a hint that something was different. That particular node had three archways around the perimeter that Mox recalled were dark most of the time. But as he exited the tunnel, he noticed the halls behind the arches were brightly lit, and groups of workers were cleaning and polishing the giant cannery machines. *Ix and the fleet must have found the swimmers*, he thought. His people had maintained the machines for countless generations.

He only spent a few moments eyeing the big machines as a naturally curious boy working through his own mind how the fish would be dumped in one end and sliced and processed until neatly sealed resin canisters emerged from the other. His mind wandered elsewhere, and before he knew it he had already moved on and walked three-quarters of the way home. As he overheard the conversations along the way, Mox started to suspect this season would be like no other he had ever experienced before. It appeared to him that people were getting more and more agitated the closer he got to home. Rather than being excited about a replenished food supply, they were concerned about the walls falling down.

"The swimmers will pass right near us." Mox heard someone say in a nervous voice.

Why would that bother anyone?

By the time he got to his own neighborhood, the general alarm was almost palpable. Shops began to close early, and folks with respirator masks were running around carrying equipment. Mox paused at the pond at the bottom of the circular stair that led to the family residence and watched the people scurry about. Puzzled, he slowly made his way up the spiral as it curled around the rainwater falls.

From the landing Mox could see across several interconnecting plazas. *The Continent* consisted of hundreds of node towers -- tall cylinders standing at the intersections of a vast triangular network of passageways. Catwalks and connector tubes bridged between the towers at multiple levels to form an impossibly complex lattice. The triangular bays in between were filled with homes, plazas, gardens, shops, and civic spaces. He could see air ducts and waterfalls that cascaded down and flowed into streams, canals, troughs, and ponds. It was beautiful! He had beheld the scene all his life, but never had there been so much urgency in the air.

Mox watched a group of workers rush across the deck below, then turned around and stepped inside the apartment. There was no one home. Everything was quiet except for the sound of gurgling water troughs, hissing pipes, and the air-powered fan blades. *That's strange*, he thought -- usually his mother was around at this time. He stood at the threshold and surveyed the place, which looked like a disaster had struck. Clothes were strewn all over, and the portable tool kits that usually lined the wall had been carried away. In the middle of the room was a neatly folded bundle with a note on top.

Mox smiled as he read his mother's words, "I packed your things dear. All the trainees are to report to the Outer Hex right away. We've gone to the library to help secure the readings."

This was it, the call he had been waiting for. He and his colleagues would be sent away for a long work detail. But the note left him in confusion -- things were starting to get interesting and now this? It was typical of his mother to leave out the most important part -- what was everyone so concerned about? Mox quickly went to his room and grabbed some pages from grandpa's journal that he had been reading, then lifted the heavy pack and headed right back out the door. He had been training with the salvage crews in order to follow in the footsteps of his fathers. After his failure to follow Ix into the ranks of the technicians, his one consolation was that he had finished his diver qualifications and had gotten himself outfitted only a few wake periods earlier -- and that heavy equipment weighed on his back as he walked along. If they were being called to duty already, then there might be a chance that he could do some diving sooner than he had thought.

Mox carefully avoided the frenzied crowds and headed for the Outer Hex. Passing through several narrow streets, the wide, six-walled plaza opened up suddenly and he found himself in the middle of a crowd of workers rushing back and forth carrying supplies to unknown destinations. After a little search he found his fellow trainees and the sensei-teacher who had been looking for him. Apparently Mox was the last to arrive from their class.

The sensei wasted no time.

"Alright let's go. We've got work at the perimeter." he called out as he eyed each of the young men in turn.

The 'perimeter' was the part of *The Continent* that made up the vast ruin between the brightly lit core city and the surrounding storms. No one lived out there, where the pounding waves incessantly battered the remote, forgotten towers. Mox thrilled in excitement that he might finally live some of the adventures his grandfather had wrote about -- exploring old chambers and finding ancient machines as part of a work detail.

"It's the darnedest thing," the sensei began, "Have you ever heard of a mini tower?"

All the recruits looked at each other in confusion.

The sensei explained, with a puzzled look on his face, "They say we will be fixing up a mini tower -- the only mini tower ever found."

They all lifted their packs and hastily followed the sensei through the crowd down a dim alley. As they walked Mox worked his way toward the front of the line until he was in earshot of the teacher.

"What's happening? Why is everyone so afraid of the swimmers?" he asked.

Sensei paused and looked back for a moment, then began to explain as they marched along. "Quakes." he said.

Apparently every skilled worker that could be found had already been sent out to help shore up the outer barrier, and now the Salvage Lords were scrambling to reinforce the teams with new recruits.

"This one's going to be a big one," the teacher explained, "think of how big the quakes are when the thrash tide passes out on the horizon. Can you imagine what will happen if the swimmers were nearby?"

Mox half recalled hearing that the swimmers brought quakes, but no one could explain why small creatures could cause so much damage when they never even got close. He remembered back to the time when he was young, and his room shuddered and felt as though it would collapse. He hadn't understood at the time, but it was certainly terrifying.

"How can that be?"

The teacher shrugged, "No one knows. But somehow it happens."

Around them the mark of civilization gave way to signs of decay. They passed into dimmer, less-traveled alleyways, and Mox soon realized they were in the dark ruins of the perimeter. Each time they moved into another node tower he peered into blackened doorways and wondered how many countless generations had passed since civilization had touched those ancient walls. Mox drifted toward the back of the line as curiosity captured his attention.

Above his head someone had strung a makeshift hose that tied into a still-functioning storm scoop somewhere. The rush of air through the hose stimulated widely spaced dim light elements that defined a path up ahead. The ruins didn't have clean pavement to walk on, since flooding in the past had brought in all sorts of silt that had built up on the floor. The silt was so deep in one tunnel that they had to crouch to keep their packs from hitting the ceiling. In another tunnel, a rainwater stream freely flowed knee-deep, and each of them had to take careful steps to avoid losing their footing. At times old broken furniture or unidentifiable remains of rusting equipment had been hastily cleared to one side to create a narrow path through the debris.

Finally one of the figures toward the front stopped in the middle of a particularly dark tunnel and the whole line came to a halt.

"We must be near the perimeter," he said in a muffled voice that failed to resonate along the corridor, "I feel the waves."

Silhouetted against a distant path light, his outstretched hand lay flat against the moist wall and strained to pick up traces of a distant disturbance. Mox reached out and thought he could feel mountains of Plasma ramming against the outer walls.

When the team got moving again he fell into step behind a large fellow named Oke, and the group continued on. He began to hear a muffled shouting ahead that got louder as they approached the *genba.* 'Genba' was an older term in their language meaning 'work site' that still had wide use among the salvage and repair teams. Because of the big fellow's massive silhouette Mox didn't realize they had reached the work area until they had already exited the tunnel and a busy scene unfolded around them. Laborers were rushing in and out of nearby doorways carrying equipment and supplies that appeared to have been stockpiled in nearby rooms. Mox saw a gaping hole in the middle of the tower floor that opened into the depths below. Peering over the edge, he saw that the hole went down several stories, and a series of platforms and crude scaffolding filled the cavity. Generators, hoppers, carriers and a myriad of other tools were scattered across the platforms, and skilled workers were down there patching the cracked walls with a crude paste.

The age of the place settled on him, but if it weren't for the unkempt conditions the towers could have been identical to any of those he knew in the core city. It was sobering to think that those ancient beings could have lived and died nearby eons before. He had spent time in the ruins, always thinking that old things were worthless and needed to be gotten rid of. But since he had begun his training, he had developed a keen interest in the old ones. It was one time of many that he would think back on his younger days and regret having dumped those ancient tools into the pool in that moment of pleasure. He remembered back to Grandpa Nux who was a legendry salvager that would go out to patch up the perimeter. No one knew how many generations it had been going on -- when did the first salvager crews frantically try to shore up their floating city from the relentless pounding of the storms? Grandpa used to talk about his discovery of the three vaults in the Defender Zone and the fabled metal man from Vault Three. There had been containers made of metal or unknown, ageless materials that had been sitting in the vaults for hundreds if not thousands of seasons, without the slightest sign of decay. The mysterious Those Who Went Before that lived long ago had left behind cubes of data crystal that still hadn't been deciphered after all these seasons. Unfortunately, the most exciting finds had been in the Third Vault that was lost at sea when the quake struck. He must have heard those stories a hundred times since childhood, but this time something piqued his curiosity -- what did Those Who Went Before look like? Grandpa had sketched a cartoon of a strange humanoid with a long beard, fierce expression, and six arms, but Mox realized no one had ever seen a likeness of the ancient wise beings before. Who were they? Did they walk and talk and have families like his people?

As Mox peered down into the hole, something didn't seem right about the cylindrical volume. Like other towers, it must have been carefully balanced to provide buoyancy for the sector, but for some reason it appeared to be a smaller diameter than he had seen before. Weren't all towers the same?

"I've never seen a mini tower before," the sensei pointed down to the shrunken hole.

Curious, Mox thought. Soon he was assigned a job below Plasma line, mixing plaster for a veteran patcher. It was down in the pit, deep in the bowels of the tower on one of the scaffolding platforms. Mox would hike up a series of ladders to where the yeast and resin blocks were kept and would carry appropriate amounts of each down to the hopper sitting by the side of his assigned veteran salvager. The patcher was troweling the plaster at merely one level on the whole height of the curved wall. The newer stuff just didn't seem as refined as the original wall material. It was slow going, with plenty of time to talk.

"There's a creature down there I tell ya," the old patcher insisted, "That's what they used to say."

Mox was perplexed, "A creature hiding in the thrash tide?"

"It comes around and shakes the foundations. We're done for this time."

Mox wasn't sure what to think. He was in a new situation, and his world seemed to be coming undone -- first he was thrust out on his own suddenly, then there was the thrash tide coming, perhaps hiding something huge and unpleasant. By the middle of the wake period his excitement to be filling Grandpa Nux's shoes had somewhat worn off and he was feeling the reality of things. It was directly related to the number of resin-blocks he had hauled down those precarious ladders. On top of that the tower was too narrow and it made him nervous.

The patch job wasn't without interruptions. Unfortunately, about three quarters through the wake period the wall developed some diagonal cracks and began leaking. Numerous small squirts shot out of the wall and sprayed the workers with liquid. Mox and the others frantically worked to repair the leaks but to no avail. Without warning a small section of the wall broke free and a jet of Plasma began shooting straight out from the wall. The fissure was between sixty to seventy arm-lengths below Plasma level, so the depth pressure caused a stream so strong that every time one of the men ventured in its way in attempt to block it he was knocked down. Mox and the others were brushed aside when a team climbed down carrying props and supports. The Plasma began to rise, and soon the men below were sloshing around in knee-deep liquid trying to get the props and supports against the hole in a fluid gate of sorts.

Mox and the other workers frantically began to remove all their equipment up to safer ground just as a pumping team arrived, and the thick hose was lowered into the fast-rising pool. Immediately the hose began to stiffen while the liquid gradually rose up its length. Two of the pump salvagers were struggling with the now heavy hose to fasten it at several points along the scaffolding. The Plasma level below had gotten just above the men's waist but appeared to be lowering slowly.

Mox understood the danger. Hundreds of node towers were balanced just right to provide buoyancy for the city. If one of them had too much liquid, it would become a burden on the others around it and cause strain in the connecting passages.

Suddenly there was a loud creaking noise and a muffled pop. Before the men had a chance to finish the gate another big chunk had broken loose adjacent to the first one more than doubling the size of the hole. Again the fluid level began to rise as before. One of the pumping crew who had been handling the hose was staggering around with his arms over his face. Some of the debris from the fissure had hit him in the head and a fair amount of blood began to ooze onto his shoulder and upper chest. Two of the other men stepped up to his side and the three of them sloshed over to the ladder in order to get him out. At the same time the others worked frantically to finish the fluid gate before more gave way.

Soon the entire work force was set to evacuate the leaky tower. All the men were busy clearing out equipment and supplies from the hole, in case the break gave in a major way. There was even a demolition team bringing in explosives and inspecting all the passageway connection points in case they were called on to recalculate the buoyancy of the neighboring volumes so they could blow the structure and drop the tower. Mox was put to work hauling equipment into the next node as part of a chain gang. He was startled when a group of black-clad veterans came rushing into the node. They were divers!

"Are there any recruits with diving qualifications?" one of them called out.

Mox lifted his head up and looked around the room. The other recruit, Oke, who also carried a suit into the genba, was nowhere to be seen. Reluctantly he stood to his feet and raised his right hand. In a hoarse voice he stuttered, "I...I have qualifications."

The veteran who had made the request came straight over to him and began asking a few questions, "Have you ever dove outside of the pod port?"

"No, except in some swimming pools and water tanks."

"Well, that will do. Get suited up immediately. Meet me over at the hole." Then he turned and walked out.

Mox hurried back to where his personal effects were stacked and proceeded to strip off the respirator and boots. The diving suit was folded neatly, just as he had stashed it after he had used it last. Loosening two straps as he picked it up, the entire suit unrolled and the leggings slapped the floor. He quickly stepped through the leggings and slung the webbed fins over his shoulder.

As he went through the process of fastening and sealing the suit, a feeling of excitement welled within him. He hadn't really expected to actually dive on his first trip, even if he was required to keep his suit with him. And another thing, like the veteran said, he had never swum outside the pod port. Everyone in *The Continent* swam. There were rainwater streams, ponds, and plasma filled tanks galore in the core city.

Most of the time it was only a few arm-lengths of depth in the bottom of some node tower (enough to be insignificant in the overall buoyancy) under the family dwelling areas. As to swimming ability, any of his fellow recruits could swim as well as he, and perhaps some could swim circles around him.

The big difference was the qualifications course. Not everyone was willing to swim out in the terrifying open sea where there were no walls to define the boundaries of your world. The qualifications course included learning how to wear and service the suits, and how to swim in open Plasma. The suits when worn were completely sealed from head to foot and had built-in gills. A series of exposed electrodes covered the entire suit and let out a mild shock when activated, to ward off the larger sea predators.

Mox sealed the entire suit except for the hood, which he allowed to hang back on his shoulders. He went directly to the hole where the collapse had been and immediately recognized the group he was to be with, for they were all suited up as well. There were three of them, all veteran salvage divers. Their hoods were also hanging back, but there was something more professional about how the fasteners were open at just the right spot and exposed the right amount of neck. These guys were tough. Mox suddenly realized that his own fastener was zipped up too high at the neck and he probably looked like a greenhorn. He looked around to see if anyone had noticed, and quickly attempted to slide the fastener down a bit in order to look as much like the pros as possible. He tried to dampen a feeling of pride that swelled up when he noticed three of his fellow recruits eyeing him with envy from across the node.

As soon as he walked up the diving team's hancho motioned for the other two to go on ahead and began to explain the procedure they would follow. 'Hancho' was their name for team leader -- the ones who hired fresh-outs and directed the work teams.

He pointed at the ragged fissure jetting water and said, "On the outside, we're going to try to gum up the hole with as much underwater plaster as we can get to stick. That should give them a chance to block up the hole from the inside. Understood?"

Mox nodded in the affirmative.

The hancho continued, "A small pod fleet has arrived and will be there for protection. Don't worry; you'll be all right. Let's go."

Mox followed him down the same dark tunnel into which the pump hose disappeared. The whining noise of the main pump got louder as they continued on, and since this particular passage had a build-up of the same old muck their diving boots made great sucking noises. Passing one node and continuing to the next tunnel, ahead they saw a pool of light from a single light element. In the sphere of illumination sat a generator and main pump casing. When they arrived at the spot Mox suddenly realized that a hole had been opened in the wall of the tower to the outside. From the light of the pump, he could see a boiling cauldron of Plasma only a few arm-lengths below them. Since they were a node or two away from the sea, it was somewhat protected from the ferocious storms, but still enough waves got through to make him nervous. As he watched, huge waves would bust against the towers beyond and bounce around among the foundations of the city until sizable swells slapped against the wall and attached ladder below him. At the same time, volumes of foamy liquid would splash down from above between the cracks of bridges and towers. A constant drizzle from overhead and a strange howling sound continually reminded Mox of the awesome power unleashed just above those structures.

A pipe from the main pump was spewing forth liquid to the outside. The hancho motioned for him to follow and leaped into the Plasma feet first after sealing his hood and adjusting his mask. Mox felt his heart go to his throat as he realized that he also must jump in. He slipped on the webbed fins and only hesitated a moment before taking the same position as the hancho had and tossed himself out the opening. Making a leap into Plasma was not so much a novelty as the fact of where he actually was. He immediately went under and started using his gills by kicking and waving limbs. The gills were collectors attached to the arms and legs of the suit that separated free oxygen out of the rich Plasma -- as long as the diver kept moving enough oxygen could be extracted for the diver's needs.

The Plasma was clear and colorless. The first thing he noticed was the incredible vast openness. Looking straight down he could discover no obstacle for as far as the eye could see, extending into darkness below. He imagined something huge and terrible just beyond the visual range that could reach up and snatch him without a moment's warning. For someone who had never ventured out of narrow passages and chambers, sudden feelings of acrophobia and agoraphobia seized him momentarily until he raised his gaze to the level of the great foundations of *The Continent.*

As he hesitated in those moments, a strange thought came to him. How had Those Who Went Before protected and shored up the city? Had they also sent out divers with four or six arms, or whatever, to patch up the towers when they began to fail? The curiosity burned within him -- what did they look like? *He had to know*!

Immediately in the area where he entered the Plasma, he could see four or five pods drifting nearby, with spotlights moving back and forth. Mox could see other divers as well, each carrying a light and anti-corpuscle equipment. Fear gripped his chest when he realized there was nothing between him and the creatures swimming just beyond the line. Corpuscles were hideous amoeba-like organisms that could dissolve the flesh off a man's bones. They often found loose objects and absorbed them into their bellies, perhaps using the hard items like borrowed bones. He imagined the terrible shapeless flesh forming around the objects, rerouting veins, muscles, and growing tendons to leverage the compressive strength and allow them to swim faster or even walk and crawl. Though none of them were allowed to get close, he could see the dark shadows here and there undulating and oozing around. What if one of them broke through? Mox cleared his mind of the thought and swam over to where the hancho was waiting.

Together they headed for the crippled node. As they progressed the natural lighting increased and more of the surfaces of the towers and supports could be seen. The underside of the Plasma surface began to show much more turbulence the closer they swam to the perimeter. Wave after wave splashed through the structural elements and bounced around until dissipated only after moving well into the cracks and crevices leading into *The Continent*'s interior. Watching the difference of heights of the wave crests and troughs as they moved up and down the curved wall was sobering.

The rift was on the other side of the tower, on the wall facing open Plasma. As Mox began to swim out of the protection of the jumble of *The Continent*'s foundation, the acute feelings of agoraphobia increased. Here was open Plasma; beyond this point *The Continent* didn't exist, but only an empty, harsh nothingness filled with corpuscles stretching to all eternity. And now something massive was approaching that could doom their whole city. Instinctively he rushed over to the nearest crossbeam and clung on for a few desperate moments until he regained his sanity. Apparently the hancho was expecting this, for he waited patiently until Mox detached himself and again joined him at his side. The embarrassed recruit forced himself to remain calm.

It wasn't long before Mox became aware of a strange visual effect. The leaky tower, from the outside, seemed to be normal in diameter -- wasn't it supposed to be a mini tower? As he looked from foundation to foundation, all of the structures appeared to be the same. Had they gone in the wrong direction? But the hancho resolutely continued swimming around the curve, to a point where the other two salvage divers he had seen earlier were making ready submersible plaster packs. They were in the right place, so Mox assumed the underwater distortions were playing tricks on his vision.

The hancho first took Mox over to where the hole could be seen, and motioned that he should stay clear of the opening. Unfortunately things didn't go entirely according to plan. They started to apply submersible plaster packs, working up from the bottom. The two other divers were at either side while Mox worked from the top in an inverted position, applying packs as he went. The hancho was just behind Mox observing the work. The patching job progressed quite smoothly up to the big hole, and Mox was so engrossed in the work that he forgot about his agoraphobia, or the corpuscles, or the terrible imaginings from the deep.

That's when it happened. The big hole had been filled in and almost completely hardened when suddenly the entire wall area above the leak gave way. The two other salvage divers were able to hold on to irregularities in the wall enough to protect themselves, but since the collapse occurred right where Mox had been working, he was immediately sucked in. The last thing he remembered was suddenly looking up with a shocked expression on his face at a grinning hancho. He thought the terrible great creature lurking deep below had finally snatched him. Then there was complete confusion as the two of them were tumbled about in the churning interior of the node tower. Mox and his hancho became part of the jet stream that shot across the diameter.

The young recruit finally was able to grab onto something fixed and, realizing it was one the scaffolding legs, climbed up onto a platform. Crates were floating all over the place. Since the fluid was rising at an extremely rapid pace he continued to scramble up the scaffolding, twice slipping back inside the liquid. As he climbed, he noticed several other workers climbing as well. It was almost easier to let the rising liquid carry him up. Finally reaching the top, Mox climbed out and saw a half dozen other workers soaked to the bone that were bent over in various positions panting their lungs out.

The diving hancho was prone on the floor with his mask and hood detached trying to catch his breath. Mox pulled his hood off as well (his mask had been lost) and walked over to where the hancho was. He was terrified what the leader might say. Yet as he walked up, to his surprise the hancho looked up at him and suddenly broke into laughter.

"Mox, you're all right." he said between bursts of laughter, "You should have seen the look on your face when you got pulled in!"

Mox was confused and it must have showed on his face, because the hancho got up onto his feet and put his arm around his shoulders.

He said, "That wasn't your fault, it couldn't possibly have been avoided. The quakes this time are going to be major, and we thought from the start that we would probably have to drop this tower and recalculate the buoyancy of the entire sector. You did a hell of a good job out there -- better than any new recruit I've ever seen. If you like, you can be on my team."

The swimmer thrash tide was coming and an event of major significance that he didn't understand was about to happen. Mox had grown up in the narrow confines of *The Continent* -- the wide-open Plasma had tested his sanity. Yet there was something about that deep, dark unknown that attracted him. It was calling for him. He smiled and without hesitation replied, "Yes!"

But the hancho's expression changed. The older man began to look down into the hole with a confused look on his face. Mox turned around and was startled to see that all those crates he had seen floating on the surface were boxes made of an unknown ageless alloy -- they were products of Those Who Went Before, and the young diver could see more of them spewing out of the torn gap deep below, popping up to the surface one by one.

"The tower -- it has a double wall with a hidden chamber!" the hancho said.

Mox realized it was so. The mini cylindrical volume was not a shrunken version of the buoyancy towers after all, but had hidden that cache of ancient cases around its perimeter. They had been pulled into the chamber, tumbled about, and were spewed out into the interior of the tower along with all those sleek and shiny containers.

Just then a higher officer came rushing in with several lieutenants, "What have we got here?"

"I think they're coffins," a soaked salvager from across the chamber suggested.

Coffins! Mox held his breath as he looked over the floating items, and realized they were the right size and proportion. The chamber must have been a crypt, where the fleeing ancients laid to rest those of their number that could not accompany them -- remains from that elusive race that had never been seen before, who had suddenly vanished?

"Okay get back to work," the officer ordered, "we'll get the experts in on this one."

The crews began to clean up the genba and move the equipment. Salvage teams worked on sealing the passageways and stripping everything useful they could, and demolition crews carefully placed their charges to prepare to sink the tower. Later in the wake period a group of university technicians arrived and began to document the mini tower. Mox was put to work as part of a chain gang carrying the shiny coffins to a safer place. They had to hurry -- the thrash tide had just cleared the horizon, and they needed to find someplace to hunker down when the quake hit. But the quake wasn't really in his thoughts just then. Carrying away those ancient coffins his heart pounded as he thought about what they might find inside -- would they see multiple limbs, or some monstrous thing no one could have imagined? Finally several trips later the oblong boxes were safely out of the way. A series of muffled explosions sounded behind him, and in his mind's eye he could see the entire broken tower slide into the salty liquid and sink into the bottomless void -- no longer a dead weight on the precious buoyancy loads. He looked ahead and could see one of the cases open and the specialists standing around with puzzled looks on their faces. As Mox approached he could see tattered cloth and glimpses of bones, but was not able to get a good view at first because of the number of bystanders. The dead had always left him nervous, and under normal circumstances he would not have gotten anywhere near the place. However, the draw was too intriguing, and again he knew *he had to see*. Mox pushed his way through the crowd fully expecting to be shocked at what lie in the coffin, but as he emerged from between two hefty salvagers he was suddenly disappointed at what he saw. There in the box was a human skeleton, dressed in what might have been a nice suit. It was obvious -- Those Who Went Before were just as human as he.

CHAPTER 5

At that very moment Salvage Lord Ruk paused high on the balcony of his apartments overlooking Capital Hex of the central business district. A small entourage of attendants crowding the sitting room behind him went through reports on the progress of the various teams.

"Some of the towers in the university district have been reinforced, but the bridges to Ukiyo are still being worked on." Advisor Two reported.

Ruk nodded but continued looking out at the tiers of richly landscaped angular balconies terracing down to the plaza below. Multiple streams of rainwater seeped in from somewhere behind and converged into small waterfalls on the balconies.

Advisor Two continued, "Even if the bridges survive, I'm afraid the power system will be in shambles."

Ruk's eyes traced bundles of tubes and ducts attached to the walls and ceiling of the plaza. Crude half pipes sloshed fresh water along to the cisterns, and air ducts fed to scoops that borrowed from the fury of the storm outside and channeled air pressure to run turbines, pumps, generators, laundries, printing presses, elevators, and any number of other local machinery. The Salvage Lord considered how they conserved energy as much as they could, using air pressure for pumping Plasma high into tanks during the sleep period, and then drawing off that potential later when there was a greater need. But the image of crumpled pipes and severed cables wouldn't leave his mind. The lights may go out and lives could be lost.

"Aren't the crews bracing the ducts?" Ruk turned and faced the advisor.

"Whenever they can, but there just isn't enough material to go around."

Shortages -- *it always boiled down to a lack of resources*, Ruk thought. How would the old ones have handled this?

Down below, Ruk could see that some of the administrative staff from the lower-level offices were strapping down artifacts in the exhibits. In one corner of the plaza a stack of various containers of ancient date had been arranged to display how Those Who Went Before preserved things. Ruk reflected on the recent revelation as runners came in from the perimeter informing them that the mysterious ancient race may not have been the god-like, multi-armed invincibles his people had imagined. Some of the containers were of a metal alloy and were in fine condition, while at the other end of the spectrum rotten cases and worn resin barrels showed the effects of time. It seemed to be a popular exhibit, especially since it was believed that the well-preserved metallic containers were the oldest of them all. In another corner a huge, carefully polished mechanical contraption (polished in spite of the rust) was mounted on top of a platform. No one had any clue of its original function, but as recently as a few hundred seasons before it had been used to grind hard fungi spores into flour. Scattered on the floor around the installation were several minor machines, also of dubious origins. Workmen were busy tightening up special straps to protect moving parts for when the quake struck.

Ruk turned again, "The vaults -- are they secure?" He thought about the precious heritage from Those Who Went

Before, two ancient capsules packed with artifacts, records, and data crystals that still hadn't been deciphered.

"Yes sir, they've been isolated at the university."

The ancient predecessors of their city fascinated the citizens. Theories went back and forth endlessly about where Those Who Went Before came from and why they went away. Could their disappearance have been related to the thrash tides?

The Salvage Lord asked, "What is the latest from out there?"

All the attendants looked at each other nervously. Ruk saw a few misty eyes of those who had sons or daughters serving on the fleets.

Advisor Two explained, "After that last report there's been no contact. The tide is almost upon us, sir."

Ruk looked over to the side where Spats the communications officer had donned head phones. The officer, listening intently for any incoming clicks, looked up and shook his head, and everyone lowered their gaze dejectedly. They had been through this before, but Ruk had never seen this much fear in his officers. He thought back -- the thrash tide had always passed silently by at a distance. Nor could he remember ever reading about swimmers so near the city, even during the great quake of Nux's time.

Ruk worried about *The Continent.* Even in the best of times, each new wake period his survey crews found more weakened structure that had to be listed on the work roster. Each season parts of the perimeter had to be either dismantled or severed to preserve the stability of the rest of their city. But all their efforts only prolonged the inevitable -- that at some time in the future their tentative foothold would whittle away to nothing. The Salvage Lord vainly sought for an answer.

Suddenly Spats perked up and waved his hands to get everyone's attention.

"What is it? Did someone get through?" Vreg the recorder asked.

Spats held up his forefinger pleading patience, and the room went quiet. Every eye was upon him as he picked up a writing instrument and began interpreting a series of incoming clicks. The tension in the air became almost palpable as the group waited to hear the message. After several pages of notes, the officer laid down the writer and looked up with a smile on his face. Ruk knew it was both good news and bad.

"One of our local stations intercepted a message from the fleet." Spats related, "A survey pod sent us an update -- the hunting is going fine, and the fleet doesn't appear to be affected by any quakes, just tossed around a bit by the tide. They're really close now."

It was the same as in past seasons -- whatever forces accompanying the swimmers in the tide didn't seem to influence the small craft, except for compass navigation.

Spats added, "There's something else, sir. I couldn't quite get it, but the message said something about a massive bulge of Plasma."

Ruk's eyes widened, and the others in the group showed confused expressions. "What does that mean?" he asked.

But the com officer seemed at a loss and all he could do was shrug, "They said they would bring the data when the fleet returns."

"What about the tide location? Do we have an update on arrival estimates?"

Spats frowned, "The swimmers just broke the horizon. We don't have much time."

"Lord Ruk, we should sound the alarm." Advisor Two whispered from behind.

Ruk spun around and said, "Yes -- take care of it Two."

The officer turned and swiftly left the apartment.

A short time later a klaxon sounded and Ruk watched the administration staff and citizens in the plaza below scramble for cover. He turned away from the balcony one last time and led the staff to an inner room that had been specially prepared. They each found a spot by the wall and hunkered down.

"I hope my girls are alright." Ruk heard one of the men say.

Another replied, "Don't worry, they all know what to do."

Off in the distance, there was a creaking sound as hundreds of resin beams strained against each other. The sound multiplied and echoed through *The Continent.* Ruk heard a loud pop, and a woman nearby let out an astonished scream. In what seemed like slow motion, Ruk began feeling a vibration that came through the floor and entered his body through his legs. Suddenly, the entire world was wrenched sideways and the floor was jerked out from under him. From the corner of his eye he could see limbs of the others flailing about as they, too were knocked around. From his vantage, the floor seemed to attack him from all sides as his body was shaken like a rag doll.

A terrible thunder exploded nearby, and then echoed over and over again through distant halls. There was a sound of liquid rushing through a narrow opening into some chamber. Screams and cries for help could be heard. Somewhere a woman was silenced in mid-scream by a sickening crunch. Farther away still a male voice began yelling and tapered down to disappear with a gurgle.

Ruk didn't know how long the quake lasted. It seemed to go on and on without end. Gradually, as the tremors receded, Ruk began to get his bearings and realized that he was lying prone on the deck with his back to the outer room. Between him and the wall was a jumble of bodies and limbs that seemed to represent several of his downed attendants. One of the men began to stir and slowly rose up in a pushup position, only to fall again in exhaustion.

The Continent was still. Gone were the usual sounds of life and busy shop attendants. In their place were a myriad of new sounds. The messy splatter of raw rainwater could be heard from various places, some near, some farther away. Nearby a woman was sobbing silently, and a low moan could be heard from a distant passageway. The greatest noise however was the howling of wind. It was the kind of wind that had a fierceness of the Outside storms.

"Lord Ruk! Are you alright?" a voice came from somewhere behind him, outside of his field-of-view.

Ruk tried to move his right arm which was pinned under him but couldn't. He looked in the direction of the plaza and observed that the balcony he had been leaning on only moments before must have collapsed and sheared off, for from his view could be seen only the naked edge with no rail. Beyond the edge, he noticed streams of water falling from the roof where rain seeped through gaps in the structure.

"Are you all right Lord Ruk?" again the voice asked.

It was one of his junior advisors, Advisor Three, who was sitting cross-legged between Ruk and the edge of the balcony, holding his right hand to his forehead.

Ruk pushed himself up with his left hand, feeling stabs of pain as his dangling right arm dislodged from where it had been resting. "I think I'm all right, but my right arm is in pain."

Advisor Three removed the hand from his forehead to reveal a nasty-looking gash and pointed toward Ruk's hurt arm. "That arm doesn't look too good. It appears to be broken, Sir."

Ruk replied, "You don't look too good yourself, Advisor Three. You'd better keep pressure on that head of yours."

Ruk got into a sitting position and tried to look around without disturbing his bad arm. The rest of his attendants, four in all, were scattered across the floor. Most of them were beginning to stir and stretch their limbs, nursing a hurt here and a bruise there. The Salvage Lord scooted himself toward the nearest staff member and did what he could with his good arm to treat his colleagues.

Soon a dazed Advisor Two shuffled in from beyond, "The elevator lift is gone. There's a gaping hole in its place. The only way to get down from here is over the edge."

A moment later Advisor Two was dressing Ruk's arm, and Vreg sat on the floor nursing an injured leg. The other officers stood in a circle and waited for the Salvage Lord to call out assignments.

"Spats, make an appearance at the command center and tell them we are on our way. Try to set up correspondence with the other lords."

The communications officer gathered up his headphones and equipment and left.

Ruk knew Advisor Three was eager to go check his girls, so he turned to the younger officer and said, "Three, do a quick survey of the local district, and gather together as many salvage team hanchos as you can find."

He watched the younger man adjust the bandage on his head and quickly retreat down the corridor.

Turning to the others he said, "One and Two, help me carry Vreg down."

With his hurt arm Ruk was useless, so Advisors One and Two grinned at each other as they lifted Ruk and the recorder one by one over the edge and lowered them to the balcony below. Two eager shopkeepers who operated a restaurant nearby lent a hand and helped the small group reach the command center at the bottom-most level. When Ruk and the recorder were safe in the hands of the administrative staff, the two advisors set off on various other errands.

The command center consisted of a large diamond-shaped room. Mounted on a massive circular table in the middle of the room was a map of the entire floating city stretching from one side to the other. Around the table, staffers would use long poles to reposition icons that represented actual personnel and pod locations. It was clear that the quake had scrambled the positions, for the majority of the icons were bunched up to one side. The staffers began replacing the icons as reports came in from streams of messengers verifying actual locations.

Around the table were the chairs of the lords, some of which were already filled by their owners. The lords could look down on the map and council with each other across the table. Ruk seated himself at his own seat, all fixed up with his arm in a sling. Advisor Two had returned, and the recorder, waiting his turn for examination by one of the medic teams, was jotting down information dictated to him.

It wasn't long before most of the lords had assembled and the command center became quite animated. Many were deep in discussion, assisting with tidbits of information their own intelligence networks had collected. This was particularly true of the admirals in the pod fleets, where they could obtain unique information that was not available to the salvage teams. Many of the pod fleets were being recalled, and every spare vessel was being employed to inspect the under surface of *The Continent*.

During the wake periods that followed, occasional tremors would interrupt the operation. Workers would look up from their tasks and hold onto something solid or dive under a table while waiting for the motion to cease. Ruk noted with regret that the incoming reports painted a bleak picture. The main quake had seriously compromised the structure in many districts and left whole sections unstable. Until they could begin to repair the damage and bring stability, punctured buoyancy tanks that were slowly taking on Plasma would gain weight and cause strain and tremors in a chain reaction. As parts of *The Continent* structure gained weight and lost buoyancy, more towers could shear away and cause tremors.

Of more immediate concern, it was found that casualties were quite numerous. In the administrative plaza alone there were four known deaths and many injuries. One of the first things on the list had been to identify wounded and dead, where special teams of trained medics from the doctor's guild roamed from place to place trying to tackle that overwhelming task. Staff members were teetering between relief and heartbreak as news about their families began to trickle in. In a few cases, when it was thought that their absence would not affect the operation, some staff members whose neighborhood had been hit particularly hard were allowed to go home to attend to personal tragedy.

Three wake periods later Ruk was reeling because of some news brought in by one of the pod crews. Advisor One brought in his own son who had related a fantastic tale of using the new sonar to follow a massive, mysterious thing that traveled deep below the Plasma.

"I don't know what it was," The boy shrugged, "But we followed it as it passed the city and continued onward. It got very close -- perhaps within a hundred nodelengths from the perimeter."

Ruk, interviewing the young man asked, "What did it look like?"

"We couldn't tell because of the swimmers in the tide. But it must have some power to create the bulge."

Again Ruk's eyes widened, "What do you mean by 'bulge'?"

A veteran pod officer who was standing nearby explained, "We observed the entire surface of Mother's Plasma rise up and bulge over the top of the thrash tide."

The Salvage Lord was skeptical, "The storms are always causing mounds and waves to form as the surface is violently chopped by the winds."

The submarine officer shook his head, "This was no wave, sir. It formed a gigantic mound that stretched from horizon to horizon."

"And why has no one ever reported this in past seasons?"

The veteran pilot answered, "We've never had sonar before, sir -- we've always been occupied down below with the swimmers. No one has ever dared to venture over the top of the thrash tide."

The Salvage Lord was astounded. Whoever heard of such a strange thing!

Ruk finally got all the lords together and briefed them on the situation. "The relationship between quakes and the tide of swimmers may be only coincidental -- the thrash tide drags along something deep below the Plasma."

A Manufacturing Lord asked, "What causes the quakes? Has the thing been passing by every time the thrash tide has been spotted?"

"Notice how this time the swimmers filled the waters immediately nearby our city? How often does that happen?"

One of the admirals spoke up, "Most seasons the swimmers are spotted quite a distance away and migrate out of range. We have to send the hunting fleets far out to sea. The last time the swimmers were this close was in Nux's era."

Some of the lords were becoming alarmed. Could it be that there really was some unknown force out there? Was there a malicious entity wandering around in the dark? He looked around the room and saw fear in their eyes as each one was imagining some unknown faceless horror in the terrible deep.

Ruk continued, "Relax -- there must be some logical reason for this. Since the tide usually passes by way out on the horizon the quakes are small. But this time it was too close."

"But how can there be something so large? What is it, and how can we protect ourselves from it?" Near one of the apexes of the diamond-shaped room, President Nirk commented.

"We don't know. But solve one problem and you may solve the other." Ruk attempted to summarize the state of *The Continent* for the rest of the lords, "It appears that there is a large swath of particularly severe structural damage. This area separates *The Continent* into two zones which are fairly intact."

One of the pod fleet admirals asked, "What do you mean by severe? How severe?"

"Well, as you know, this disaster is the worst on record we have ever experienced. There has never been a quake this strong or damage this extensive. This was not some little neighborhood of the perimeter that failed and slid off into the Plasma. This is the kind of thing that may split *The Continent* in pieces. No one has ever seen anything like this before."

The admiral queried, "Will it be possible to repair the breaches, or will the two intact zones need to be severed from each other?"

Ruk turned back to the map, "Unfortunately, this whole area that is quite intact will have to be separated from the main city because of significant damage occurring here, and here. The engineers have almost given their guarantee that leaving it attached would completely destabilize this whole sector and cause further quakes."

Jirt, one of the Manufacturing Lords, had a scowl on his face, "That's all residential."

Lord Ruk stared at Jirt for an instant. The two men did not get along because Jirt advocated dropping the whole perimeter so they could concentrate their salvage resources on the heavily populated core districts, and Ruk didn't agree with that.

"We'll have time to evacuate everyone. We think we can make repairs enough to hold on a temporary basis. The old deserted Defender districts in the perimeter are intact," Ruk swept the long rod that was serving as a pointer all the way across the map and indicated an area of *The Continent* directly opposite the residential area and continued, "so we can relocate some of the families there. The area needs to be cleaned up a bit, but at least it's sound."

The numerous lords sitting around the table were quiet for a few moments as they considered the possibilities. President Nirk spoke up, "Do you think this is a solution? And how does this solve the problem with the thrash tide?"

Ruk hesitated. Nirk's question brought back that age old, ongoing debate of what the real solution was. He shrugged and replied, "This is certainly the best interim solution we can think of."

President Nirk seemed irritated, "We are looking for a permanent solution. A permanent goal is what this people needs. Can we tell our people that that could be the end of their worries?"

"The only permanent solution is to centralize our people and jettison the perimeter once and for all." Jirt jumped in with confidence. "Doesn't this disaster prove what we have been saying?"

Many of the lords nodded in agreement. Ruk noted that the same group rallied around the man as they had always done in the past. They called themselves the 'Pros' -- a gang of meddlesome cowards who only cared about their own wealth and shortsighted gain. But this time even some of the neutral or undecided lords appeared to be wavering over to Jirt's direction.

President Nirk asked Ruk point blank, "What do you say to that, Lord Ruk? What do you think is the permanent solution?"

Several of the lords who agreed with keeping the vast ruin of the perimeter for future growth and resource management -- the 'Cons' -- encouraged Ruk with their eyes. The Pros only glared at him.

Ruk turned and faced Jirt, "Lord Jirt, I understand your position and agree that under the circumstances it might seem appealing. But I do not agree that this disaster could possibly prove that the Pros are advocating a permanent solution. On the contrary, this only shows that we are losing. Perhaps Lord Jirt's solution will give us another twenty seasons. Perhaps even fifty or a hundred. But what then? What happens when the structure weakens then? What happens when our children's children experience their great quake? What happens when there are no more deserted parts of *The Continent* to evacuate to? Will they draw straws and choose who gets to ride on the piece that still floats? Also, who's to say that our population will stay the same several seasons from now? Will we need to regulate the size of families so that we don't tax our static infrastructures and fixed-walled spaces?"

Ruk turned and faced Nirk and continued, "It's even worse -- my experts tell me we may not even have a few seasons. My people have tracked the statistical data of the thrash tide location over many seasons. The trend shows that the next time the tide comes it will probably pass directly below us. If from a hundred nodelengths away this thing can cause towers to crumble, what can it do if we are right on top of it? "

Lord Jirt shook his fist at Ruk, "And another sobering thought -- what of the myths about a massive Creature of the Deep passing underneath? Could some entity passing below fail to notice something as large as *The Continent*? If you would have trimmed the fat seasons ago, do you think this tragedy would have happened?"

"There's no use arguing whether it could have been prevented or not by cutting off the perimeter. Whatever we do only prolongs the inevitable. But are we strong enough to face the real permanent solution?"

Nirk seemed a little puzzled, "Lord Ruk, what do you mean by a 'real' permanent solution?"

This was what was going through Ruk's head at that moment: what would *The Continent* do if the inevitable suddenly were upon them? What about a few seasons hence when the thrash tide passed close enough to pull entire districts under? What was that gigantic thing traveling deep below the swarm of fish -- was there indeed a monster out there that could tear their precious city apart? What if they could no longer be where they had always been? First of all, where would they go? As far as Ruk knew, the oceans stretched forever in all directions. And if the problem of 'where' was solved the second problem that remained was 'what'. If only *The Continent* inhabitants departed, they would be as good as dead. How would they continue their work and their technology? Ruk thought of the indispensable bulk of machines in the manufacturing districts, stores of food and products from the business districts, and personal belongings from the residential districts. They would have to devise a way to uproot a thousand seasons of culture and technology and replant it in an unfamiliar location and make it work. The last problem was 'how'. There certainly was not enough of a pod fleet to carry all the inhabitants of *The Continent* at once. If all their machines, factories, culture, and learning had to be accommodated as well, it would pose an insurmountable task.

Lord Ruk tensed a little and cast his eyes over the entire governing body. He thought about how the quake had put them in the predicament that un-repairable swaths of destruction hopelessly separated intact districts. He considered that by conventional wisdom it would not be possible to keep them both as separate floating islands, since the storms would probably bring them together against each other as battering rams. Ruk looked down at the map and let his eyes trace the outline of that isolated group of towers they would be forced to let loose. It was a small neighborhood -- left to drift it would surely come back to haunt them unless they sunk it, or...

Suddenly he had a flash of inspiration. Maybe there was a way! That small part of the massive city structure was small enough to tow! *It was now or never*, he thought.

He addressed the group, "President Nirk, Lord Jirt, my distinguished colleagues and administrative staff, one solution will overcome both challenges. The only 'real' permanent solution is that we must leave *The Continent* permanently!"

CHAPTER 6

Mox sat exhausted with his back against the wall, peering at the small procession of citizens crossing the floor of the well-lit node. His comrades were the same way, sprawled out wherever there was a smooth place on the floor. They were all suited up and still dripping from the last assignment.

What a whirlwind experience it had been since he started as a greenhorn! First Mox had been drafted into the work teams, then the quake hit sending *The Continent* into turmoil, and finally the most massive repair movement in history had been mobilized. He was no greenhorn any more. Mox could not think straight or pin down any of that big blur of memory. All he could do was to stare blankly at the passing settlers, who were evacuating unstable sectors in *The Continent* with loads and bundles of belongings. They were all working in haste, knowing more quakes could occur if they didn't jettison those bad sections soon. And some of the citizens were worrying about the rumors that the thrash tide might be caused by some kind of huge creature after all, on its way back to smash their city.

A group of children emerged from the tunnel to his left. The young ones were all fidgeting and looking about in every direction but the one their guardians wanted them to. As soon as each child exited the passage, they would undoubtedly fan out in some other tangent than the single file they had been walking in. Eyes full of curiosity, they filled the room looking at all the tools and equipment stacked against the walls, as well as the resting men between them. The leaders tried to herd them all together in vain.

Two little boys walked up to Mox. One pointed his finger and said to the other, "Hey there's a diver!" Then he leaned over and asked, "Are you a diver?"

Mox just looked at the boy for a moment and then answered, "Yes."

The other boy walked up beside his friend and asked, "Have you been swimming in the Plasma? You're all wet!"

Before Mox could say anything, other children started gathering and asking questions. Since his comrades were either asleep or unresponsive, Mox seemed to draw their attention. Questions like "Have you been fighting corpuscles?" and "My pop's a diver, too." and "Is it dark down there?" began coming at him in a barrage.

Three little girls began touching his suit, asking, "what's this?" about every little instrument and strap they could get their hands on.

Mox looked over to his hancho, who was faking sleep but had one eye open watching the scene with a smirk on his face. Mox straightened up and forced himself to be a little more animated. He loved children and wasn't about to let this opportunity pass without playing with them. After all, in his mind touching those carefree little hearts was the best way to relieve stress.

He looked them all over with a big smile on his face and explained, "We've been up topside!"

"Wow, up in the storms?"

"Yes, up in the storms. It's raining out there you know." Mox singled out a particularly bright young girl to do the explaining to.

One child asked, "Are there corpuscles up there?" at the same time another blurted out, "I think it's dangerous out there."

"No there are no corpuscles topside but it's still dangerous. You see, the storms are made up of scary winds that can take even grownups away." Mox answered, trying to play down the actual degree of exactly how dangerous so the kids wouldn't have bad dreams. In his mind's eye he could see one of the other divers struggling at the end of a tether pulled horizontal by the winds, trying to do a patch job. Another fragment of memory put Mox on the end of a tether trying to do the same thing.

"My papa says people don't go topside. Why you go there?"

"We don't like to, but we've got to fix *The Continent*," Mox started to explain, but the children's guardians came to round them up.

"Say good-bye to the nice diver." One of the adults said among waves of hands and receding little bodies.

After talking with the kids, Mox was feeling better already. They could be called to do another job anytime, but he tried not to think about that now. He looked around him and noticed that the rest of the dive team was coming around. It was getting close to mealtime and most of the men probably wanted to have full stomachs before another assignment came.

At a time when there was a long gap in the stream of citizens, suddenly five tall black-haired beauties shouldering backpacks exited the passage. Immediately they all turned to face in Mox's direction. Mox was tired but couldn't help but smile a little. None of the women smiled back, but each one proceeded to step on his outstretched toe as they walked by. Without flinching or looking back, they all continued across the node and entered the tunnel beyond.

Mox, embarrassed, looked at the other guys and realized they were all staring at him in disbelief.

The hancho, who had also observed the little incident with the children couldn't help but comment, "My, aren't you popular today!"

Another of his seniors shook his head and blurted out, "You little green bean. What have you got that we ain't got?"

"The kid's a flirt! Introduce one to me."

Mox just shrugged it off with a lie, "Oh it's nothing. I get that all the time."

Just then a messenger came by with an assignment. Even though they hadn't had time to eat a thing, it was back to business as usual. This time the job was inside for a change. They were to patch up a potential leak in one of the passageways along the settler's moving route.

"All right men, saddle up!" the hancho ordered. "We change into work clothes for this one."

One of the divers named Mel, with whom he had gotten particularly close, lifted Mox's pack and helped him put it on. Mox reciprocated and all the men moved into a nearby room to change. It was a relief to get out of those wetsuits. For the last season and a half, six out of ten sleep periods were spent suited up in some forgotten corner of some genba.

Mox and his colleagues had been stationed in what had become known as the war zone after the quake hit. The war zone was a wide swath of heavily damaged structure that split *The Continent* in two. As a whole the area was hopeless and couldn't be saved, but the crews had been employed doing minimal maintenance until the citizens resettled the intact neighborhoods on both sides. The goal was to make two separate communities and split *The Continent* into two floating structures, the smaller of which would be called '*The Island*'.

Lord Ruk's plan went beyond that of course -- *The Island* was small enough to be towed. It was his intention to tow *The Island* somewhere for the purpose of experimental settlement. With the extensive damage in the war zone, it was either execute this plan or sink *The Island* to dispose of potential junk that could eventually bang up against the perimeter of *The Continent*.

Mox had been thinking about the human skeleton they had found, which put Those Who Went Before in a whole new light. Again the thought crossed his mind -- how had the wise ones lived and maintained the city? As he worked he tried to imagine an ideal state where some technology did the work of shoring up the walls and all were happy and content.

Mox and the others moved to their new positions on the settler path. Taking care to move out of the way every time a group of citizens went by, they wound their way to a tunnel that had a badly fractured end. Settlers would come to the spot and stop, wondering if it was safe to cross. Some of the fissures had been filled in, but the rest remained gaping holes up to two or three handwidths wide. Wind and rain were tearing at the opening making all kinds of racket. Still, the break was sheltered for the most part so it was really only a matter of plugging them up enough so that the settlers could pass in ease. Two of the men went to fetch some bricks of resin and other materials. Mox and Mel were assigned the job of removing loose debris from the openings, and otherwise making sure the new material had a firm, clean surface to bond to.

It was Mel who brought up a point that Mox hadn't considered, "Why do you suppose Those Who Went Before tucked all their things away in vaults?"

Mel was also a fanatic about old things and was a good sounding board for different ideas. Mox thought about it as he lay down in the passageway, leaving enough room for the settlers to pass, and put his head next to the hole as he picked away at the loose material. Suddenly he heard giggling in the hallway from the direction of *The Island*. He looked up just in time to see those five beautiful girls coming back for another load. Hoping the girls didn't see him, Mox stuck his entire head through the hole and hid his face. Too late! Each of the girls walked by and reached down to slap him on the bottom. The last one even took the time to swat both buttocks! As before they kept walking without saying a word, as if nothing had happened. Mox was turning red as he realized how silly he must have looked with his head in that hole and his rear-end sticking up. He pulled his head out of the hole and looked up to notice all his teammates staring at him in disbelief again. A couple of the men were laughing.

"What!? What are you looking at?" Mox looked back and forth between them.

"How'd you get them to do that?" Mel asked.

Mox shyly fibbed, "Oh, I dunno. Girls just can't resist me, I guess."

"Get out of here! How come we've never seen girls act that way around you before?"

"Well, we've never been around the public before." Mox snickered inside.

They finished the patch-up job in less than a wake period. Since the repair was mostly cosmetic and didn't need to have structural integrity, they were able to finish it in less than half the time it would normally have taken. All the men retired to a nearby node and Mox was sent to tell the work dispatcher that they had finished. The work dispatcher was on *The Island*. Since Lord Ruk's headquarters was being moved there, all work operations were being coordinated from a temporary dispatcher office.

Mox thought about Mel's comment as he moved along the passage in a good trot, passing the slow-moving settlers whenever he got a chance. Occasionally he passed other work crews like his own doing their individual assignments. He went through node after node stacked with repair materials and moving crates. *Here we are, stockpiling our food and goods*, he thought. Was there some parallel with Those Who Went Before? As he approached *The Island*, the number of work crews increased. On such border areas the crews were doing hard-core structural shoring, not the light maintenance stuff going on in the war zone. Once inside the border however, the number of crews were less and the number of busy settlers and technicians increased dramatically. Mox had glimpses of special installations being set up in some of the chambers, and stores of crates being stacked in others. He had been told that new portable, modular machinery was being developed that could fit into cargo pods. They were almost like seeds, having the ability to be planted or installed anywhere on a moment's notice and brought into full working order within a wake period. There were supposedly all kinds of machines prepared in that manner, especially ones from the manufacturing sectors. The settlers were also busy setting up an entirely independent community within the boundaries of *The Island.* To this end, they were already functioning as a unit, going through gaming simulations to find flaws in their economies and getting necessary support from the main city.

Everything his people did was out in the open not in some sealed chamber, but he couldn't help but thinking there was some clue to the motivations of Those Who Went Before. What was it about those stacked crates that made him think about those ancient occupants?

Mox made his report to the dispatcher and headed back to the team with another assignment. One of the nodes along the passageway was flooded, with a fence around an open pit above a pool of Plasma. Settlers were getting nervous walking through that node. The team was to patch the tower below Plasma line and work in conjunction with a pump crew to bring the tower to full buoyancy. Finally they were to build a floor over the open pit.

He reached his crew just as the sleep period was about to begin. The team was instructed to start the job early the next wake period, so they had plenty of time to rest. When Mox handed over the orders to the hancho, he turned toward the wall hoping to get something to eat and relax with his reading. Suddenly, coming back with another load, those five girls came walking back from *The Continent*!

Oh no, I've got to get out of here, Mox thought, but it was too late. He was standing against a wall and there was nowhere to retreat to. On top of that, his colleagues also saw the women and were watching to see what would happen. Mox's face started turning red as the girls began to get closer. With no apparent emotion on their faces, one by one they came up to

Mox and planted a big kiss on different parts of his face, the last one landing on his lips! Mox's face was quite red to start with but each one of those girls left bright red kiss marks all over his face. As before, each of the girls continued on their way as if nothing had happened.

At first Mox's teammates were dumbfounded and didn't know what to say. Then they noticed the kiss marks on his face (which Mox seemed oblivious to) and burst out laughing. Mox turned away from everyone in embarrassment and continued with his meal preparation. He heated up a container of spore soup with chopped swimmers and sat with his back against one of the curved node walls. Mox's intent was just to watch people as they walked by (the stream of settlers was getting fewer and fewer as the sleep period started), and enjoy his meal. A woman walked by the point where Mox was sitting. She looked at him briefly and quickly turned away trying to suppress a laugh. Mox wondered why a perfect stranger would act that way towards him. It took five more passers by giving him strange looks before Mox realized there was something wrong with his face. The rest of the guys on his team, who had been watching the interaction between him and the passersby, busted out laughing again when they saw his embarrassment.

The men were somewhat rested when they got to work early the next wake period. They relocated their equipment to the node in question and gathered to get an assignment of responsibilities from the hancho. The entire team suited up and rigged a ladder of sorts to provide access in and out of the Plasma pool. A pumping team arrived soon thereafter and began setting up their equipment as well.

Mox and Mel were assigned to dive some of the flooded sub-Plasma tunnels and patch their leaks. The nodes themselves had been surveyed shortly after the quake, but connected passageways had been passed over due to a lack of manpower. Mox chose to do a feet-first leap from the edge of the pool, while holding onto his mask to keep it from getting dislodged. As he entered the Plasma his body was momentarily engulfed in the usual cloud of small bubbles and lukewarm liquid. Mox twisted his body around and peered down into the darkness below. There were outlines of two dark shapes below, swimming around in the depths. For a moment Mox felt a surge of panic until he realized that those were members of his own team. Depending on how big the holes were to the outside, the amoeba-like corpuscles could have found access and might be roaming about. Two stabs of light from the divers' torches shot back and forth across the flooded chamber and occasionally hit one of the walls. The two divers below reached a deck of sorts and began crisscrossing the bottom. Their torches illuminated a dark, ragged hole punched into the deck. Mox watched them as they approached the hole and disappeared into its depths.

As Mox turned up from watching the divers, Mel splashed in next to him and gave him the okay sign. They both began to descend together, switching on their lamps as they went. They soon reached the deck Mox had seen the other divers land on. The two of them hovered above the deck for a few moments and shone their torches over the area. Debris churned up by the previous two was swirling around in the liquid, but not enough to obscure what lay on the floor. Over against one of the walls there were several box-shaped objects stacked on the deck. Swinging his torch around the other way, Mox saw two chairs facing toward the center of the node hall, as if they were waiting for someone to sit on them. Many other small objects were scattered across the floor. This space had been occupied quite recently! Someone had used this sub-Plasma level for storage and living space. Families had lived and breathed here, perhaps to suddenly find their home flooding after the great quake.

Mox shined his torch over the ragged hole he had seen the other divers disappear into moments before. Perhaps Plasma had come bubbling up through that hole from some rent in the tower wall down below. Across the node hall, several dark holes marked entrances of tunnels leading into the blackness. Mox swung his torch around and counted a total of four passageways around the perimeter of the room. His companion slowly swam for one of the tunnels and Mox headed for another. As he reached the opening, he turned his head in the direction of his companion and the two nodded to each other before entering the respective passages.

The floor of the tunnel was littered with small objects that appeared to be personal possessions of the former occupants: pots, pans, silverware, and an occasional piece of furniture. Other objects littered the top of the tunnel, floating up as high as they could until blocked by the ceiling of the passage. Hairbrushes, crates, small containers, and other personal effects jumbled together and dispersed from the current generated by Mox's movements through the liquid.

Mox swam on, carefully observing the walls for any signs of cracking. The debris seemed to increase the farther in he got. It became necessary to dodge around large floating crates and jumbled piles of furniture. Somewhere close to where the tunnel should have run into another node, the passage was so choked with debris that Mox couldn't pass through at all. Holding the torch, he stretched his arm out and wedged it through a jumble of chairs, aiming it out straight. Walls beyond to the right and left, and in the middle -- darkness. Yes, the passage continued, and it was his responsibility to check it all out.

He attempted to pull his arm back through the gap, but to his dismay a piece of debris tore through the tether of the torch and caused him to drop it beyond. As the torch settled to the floor, it must have switched off, for the entire tunnel was enclosed in complete darkness.

Mox was mortified. He turned around and looked back the way he had come in and saw a faint oval at the mouth of the tunnel, but blobs of junk and debris shifted around to occasionally conceal it. What if those blobs were corpuscles swimming this way? Something bumped into his back and made him jump. He spun around and blindly began swimming away from the thing, but all he ended up doing was to stir up the floating debris and get tangled in darkness. Calm down!

Mox fought his uncontrolled feelings and attempted to get a reign on himself. He must get that torch!

Mox began to make a mental picture of the tunnel from what he remembered having seen before losing the light. There was that jumble of chairs with a gap along the wall. Would it be possible to enlarge a hole enough to squeeze through? He began feeling his way back to the choke of debris and located the gap through which he had lost the torch. It was pitch black, but he could keep a mental image of the objects and work from there. He began to pull at the chairs and locate loose pieces. It wasn't long before some of the junk around the gap started breaking loose at his prying. Mox took a big tug at one piece and in the process looked back down the tunnel. Something was swimming there! The gap widened a little and he dove through the opening.

In a panic he started feeling around in the dark for the torch. There seemed to be some tattered folds of fabric floating around. In between the strips of fabric Mox felt a soft, mushy substance clinging to hard rods or sticks. It was there that Mox felt the back end of the torch, buried in the mush and folds of cloth. He reached down and pulled at the torch and realized that it was still switched on; only the lighted end had been completely enclosed by the folds of cloth. In the instant he began to pull up the torch, his mind began interpreting the nature of the material the torchlight illuminated. Cloth from clothes, a gray-whitish mushy substance enclosing a hard white structure -- a corpse!

That very instant, Mox was staring at a blank-eyed, mostly decomposed human head only handwidths from his face. Mox went into a panic and jumped backward. He twisted about and flailed his arms trying to get away from that grisly monstrosity. The torch was firmly welded in his hand this time as its beam swept back up the wall and flooded the whole area with light. In the struggle Mox spun around and faced upward, moving toward the ceiling in a quick motion. He let out a gasp under his mask, for there were more bodies floating at the ceiling, with decomposed faces staring down at him. In those frenzied moments Mox thought he could see dozens of corpses floating along the top of the tunnel on and on into the darkness beyond. He pushed off the bodies and attempted to get away, get away! But they seemed to be closing in on him. As he kicked and struggled, parts of the corpses began to tear off and float around inside the tunnel or sink to the bottom. He screamed!

Mox didn't know how he made it back through that gap in the debris blocking the passage. He couldn't remember swimming along the tunnel back to the submerged node hall. The next thing he remembered was thrashing about at the top of the pool with three other divers trying to get him to calm down.

Mox whipped off his mask and breathlessly called out, "There ... there's bodies all over ... over the place! A whole family ... or something!"

One of the divers got him to stop flailing about, "OK, we'll check it out. Just calm down."

Just then Mox's companion Mel broke the surface in a hurry. He popped his mask off and in the same breathless voice Mox used, cried out, "There's a whole group of trapped corpses down there!" It was he who had intercepted Mox and helped him out of the tunnel. He had gone back to see what had spooked him so.

The rest of that wake period was a hectic one. The other divers had found the leak on lower levels (just as Mox had supposed) and began patching it so the pumping team could do their work. A medic team was called in, but since they had no diving experience the grisly job of pulling out the bodies would have been left to the divers, or wait until the place had been drained. None of the divers were trained to handle such things. The pumping team was afraid body parts and debris would start floating to the surface and gum up their equipment. Finally it was decided to just seal off the tunnel and let the bodies rest in peace in their liquid tomb.

Mox was allowed to sit out for a while and recover himself, but by the middle of the wake period, hancho ordered him back down to help with the patchwork. It was for his own good: if he faced his fears and conquered them right off he would get over it quicker. He got back to the dive a little paranoid, peering at dark holes and doing his best to stay away from the tunnel.

The crew took the rest of that wake period to finish plugging the tunnel tomb. The hancho decided to give the men a good rest and didn't push them during the sleep period. And the next wake period had only two men down on the actual patch job and the rest of them were playing around in the pool. Since the place was secured against corpuscles, none of them were suited up and they even had the pumping team stripped down to the waist splashing around in a game with them. Such was a favorite past time of all the citizens of *The Continent*. Some of the settlers passing by would be nervous about the open pit, but most of them would pause and happily watch the men. Occasionally one or two of them would strip down and join them for a while.

Mox was thoroughly enjoying himself, splashing around in the pool. They had a small floating ball with them that one of the men carried for just such an occasion, and were split up into the traditional three teams. He and Mel had begun a conversation about Those Who Went Before while they swatted the ball around.

"I think the vaults were needed to protect the artifacts from something. They must have been too cumbersome to use as closets." Mel pointed out as the two of them waited for the ball to come close.

Mox wondered if the vaults could have been an ideal way to protect against quakes.

"I don't think so -- somehow I can't imagine Those Who Went Before having to deal with quakes." Mel countered, and Mox agreed.

"What did your grandfather say about how the vaults were placed?" Mel asked.

Just then Mox caught the ball and was about to shoot up out of the liquid and make a dynamic motion pass to Mel when he noticed from the corner of his eyes some onlookers beginning to jump in. The rest of the men had settled down suddenly and were all treading Plasma, looking in the direction of the newcomers. Mox canceled his intended pass and turned around to look at the newcomers. It was those five girls! They were stripping their clothes down to their undergarments, taking those incredibly shapely bodies over to the edge of the pool, and diving in. Of course it was common for men and women alike to swim together in public in their undergarments, but having five beauties do so all at once was a sight to see! They all swam over to where Mox was treading Plasma and proceeded to dunk him one by one. Unlike the last encounters, this time each of the girls said, "Come see our new apartment, Mox." and proceeded to push him under. By the time the last one left, Mox was gasping for breath. Each of the girls calmly climbed out of the Plasma, dressed, and continued on their way.

The other men had all been laughing, but became quite silent when the girls actually spoke to him. "Did you hear that? They're inviting him to their apartment even! What ever happened to all those dreams about a girl with golden hair?" Mel said, referring to a mythical goddess.

Mox only blushed.

Many wake periods later the team was lightheartedly walking along the passage toward *The Island*. A messenger had brought good news and they were all excitedly discussing the new developments. The pod fleets had been sent out to explore distant regions of ocean using repeater nets to maintain contact with *The Continent*. One of the pods had actually found something -- a vast solid barrier or platform out in the storms.

"What do they mean by 'barrier'?" Mox asked.

The hancho shrugged and said, "I think they tried to sail around it but it just keeps going like a never-ending wall."

Mox tried to imagine a barrier that even the submarines couldn't get around, but all he could picture were buoyant node towers and crisscrossing bridges. He couldn't fathom anything radically different from *The Continent.*

The hancho continued, "Maybe we could visit it, or even move there. I wonder how it reacts to thrash tides and quakes?"

Regardless of the details, *The Island* with its settlers now had a destination, which until then no one had ever hoped to find.

Most of the work crews had been retired from maintenance and were put to work getting *The Island* ready for the long trip. They were about to blow the connection with the main city. Many citizens had been about saying good-byes to those they would leave behind. The crew would soon be able to go to their new homes for the first time since the disaster had struck. Their families had moved to *The Island* along with the rest of the settlers. The rushed nature of their job had kept many of them from even seeing their families since the quake.

Again Mox and Mel were discussing the vaults of Those Who Went Before. Mox had thought back on all the stories Grandpa had told, and the two of them were trying to figure out the reason for the vaults.

“All three vaults were lined up in a chamber with lots of other machines or installations. No one knows what the other stuff was because it was lost.” Mox recalled.

Mel considered, “It probably wasn’t a library or storehouse, because it would be difficult to access things that way.”

The two men sat silent for a while, going over in their minds the different possibilities. Their own people stored crates and machines out in the open, and simply braced the chamber to guard against quakes -- again Mox couldn’t help thinking there was a connection somewhere.

“I’ve got an idea. Think back to the beginning, when Nux first found them.” Mel suggested.

Suddenly it hit Mox -- he knew why the ancient race used vaults. "There was a war! They were hiding the artifacts from someone else."

"Exactly! That's why they sealed the chamber. Those Who Went Before must have hidden their most precious things from some unknown enemy."

The connection with his own people was that Those Who Went Before had stockpiled important items because of an impending upheaval in their community. But that only opened up another mystery. If the ancient ones had hidden their things away, why didn't they fetch them again when they left?

Without warning, from the direction of *The Island*, the five beautiful girls came walking through the tunnel carrying wide flat boxes. Mox thought, *oh no, here we go again!* He attempted to hide his face. Again it was too late. It seemed as though they knew where he was and came directly to him.

One of the girls stopped in front of him and within earshot of all the men said, "Mox, Mom sent some cakes along for you and your team." Then all the girls set down the boxes and went back to where they came from.

"'Mom'? What's this 'Mom' stuff?" Mel asked.

"Oh, didn't I say? Those girls are all my sisters." Mox replied.

CHAPTER 7

The landing dock in Pod Bay Three was quite crowded. The drone of chattering voices engaging in small talk was almost overwhelming. From one corner of the bay a mother's voice could be heard giving advice to her son something like, "Don't forget to scrub behind your ears and change your undies every wake period!" In another direction, a young girl wrapped herself around one of the young men and said, "Oh, I'm going to miss you. Be careful and come back to me safe!" An older man's voice cautioned his children, "Now you listen to your mother and do what she says." Anywhere one looked, groups of citizens and crewmembers were deep in conversation and greeting.

The numbers were so great that the docks couldn't hold everyone adequately. Ix noticed a couple of times that people got pushed off the edge into the Plasma. They would laugh and paddle around a little, but would never really pause in their conversation with those who were still standing. Above the tops of all the adults, dozens of young boys were in an elevated position engaged in their own conversation. They were sitting atop pods tied up at the docks. It was one of those rare occasions when they could freely come and touch those machines they always dreamed about.

Beyond the boys, a great wall arched overhead. Bay Three was one of the larger ones, mostly hexagonal in shape. When they refitted *The Island* they literally had to carve Bay Three out of the existing triangular pattern and patch up the seams. The walls showed horizontal scars of former floors giving hints to bygone levels. Each of the six apexes sported stubs of passageways at each level that had been removed. Most of the stubs had been plugged, but a few were still open to the node towers beyond. If the crowds below weren't enough, young women crowding against the handrails at the mouths of those high openings raised the overall noise level. They were calling out to the work crews below who were about to leave on a historic expedition.

All the commotion reminded Ix of the send-off party and good-byes that had characterized the sealing of the last passageway bridging *The Island* and *The Continent* before the final separation took place. Crowds of citizens embraced each other, giving warm farewells, and returned back behind the 'safe' line while crews sealed off the tunnels. Last minute interfamily marriages had taken place where daughters and sons were given and received in tears. Ix sent off one of his sisters to a neighboring lord who was to stay in *The Continent*. It was a sad time for the family, for they knew that perhaps they would never see her again. A series of well-timed explosions had ripped along the line of the war zone dividing *The Island* from *The Continent* and forever separated the two.

Ix looked across the hall where lines of uniformed men with standard issue backpacks were standing at attention about to enter the pods. They were all Lord Ruk's crews. One of the men looked back at Ix and gave him a slight nod. It was Mox. Ix had just left his twin brother on that dock moments before as they said their own good-byes, barely given enough time for a quick embrace, and had made his way back to where his own pod was waiting. Both of them were to be members of the expedition, but since Ix was stationed on a smaller vessel none of the diving crews would be able to ride with them. Theirs was a minor role in the expedition anyway, and unlike Mox they would not directly take part in the first landing. Ix's vessel would simply function as a repeater in a long communication chain stretching back to *The Island.*

Their mission was to attempt a landing! For many wake periods pods had gone back and forth between *The Island* and those strange massive structures so far away. They had surveyed many hundreds of nodelengths of perimeter but still had no clue as to how large they actually were. One thing was clear, the size of *The Continent* paled in comparison. Until now, the senchos explored the structures using visual and sonar, so an understanding of their nature remained incomplete. On this expedition, they would actually reach out and touch.

After a while the small talk in the pod bay ceased and there was a great hush in the crowd. Ix looked out across the bay and saw that Mox's line was moving: they had begun to board their carrier pods. Certainly Ix's sencho would come soon and order them to board as well. He watched as the line Mox was in disappeared into the open airlock hatch. When the last man had entered safely, a dock crew closed the hatch and tried its seal. Then in a matter of moments the pod had drifted out away from the dock and had begun to dive. Lines of men continued to enter into the other carrier pods that one by one took their leave. Why wasn't Ix's pod leaving as well?

The boys who had been playing on top of the pod got down one by one and left the dock area. Ix saw the communications officer of his own pod nearby and walked up to him.

"Does anyone know what's going on? Why aren't we leaving yet?" Ix asked.

Smash had a puzzled look on his face also and turned to look at the navigator who was approaching them from a different direction.

Seeing both of the men looking his way, Mag stammered, "I'm not sure. There must have been a change of plans. The other relay ships have already left."

Smash shook his head. "Maybe we're being dropped from the expedition roster!"

"I don't think so. If that were the case Sencho would have told us sooner."

The men watched some of the last remaining pods sink below the surface. The farewell crowd began to disperse, leaving the men and dock crews mostly to themselves. Only their pod remained. The rest of the crew came straggling in from various directions. Except for Sencho and the pilot, they were all there and ready to go. Why weren't they leaving yet?

Ix decided to do a quick external check of the thrusters while he still had a chance. In its docked state, the craft's thrusters were only a few handwidths under the surface. He climbed up a ladder onto a hydro-dynamically shaped upper deck. There was just a simple pipe handrail surrounding the deck, for the only time anyone stood upon it was at times like this when the vehicle was at dock. As he strode across to the other side, Ix looked around and noticed crumbled remains of snack cakes the boys had left when they had been playing their games. The crumbs would wash away easily and dissolve as soon as they dove beneath the surface so there was no need to be concerned with them clotting up the thrusters. Ix reached the far edge of the deck and looked down into the clear liquid to make a quick visual inspection of the submerged thrusters. There was something different about them that he couldn't quite put his finger on: they looked cleaner and newer than he had remembered. Ix climbed down in order to make a closer inspection. Sure enough, the old thrusters had been completely replaced with more robust looking new engines Ix had not seen before. The steering mechanisms were also new -- why would their vessel be fitted with such sophisticated equipment? Ix gave a quick glance and saw that the other thruster had been refitted the same way, so he made his way back to the dock convinced that their boat was specially rigged for some important mission.

The reason soon made itself clear. It wasn't long before a small group of people entered the pod bay. Ix could see

Sencho and the pilot and two others. As they approached closer, Sencho called out, "At your stations on the double, we'll be leaving shortly! We've been designated as the command ship."

Ix just stared and couldn't believe his eyes. He knew the other two men who were going to be fellow passengers -- Advisor One and an assistant from Lord Ruk's staff. Papa on his own boat! Ix wasn't sure he liked the idea of having his own father along, especially as the expedition commander. Lord Ruk himself was a very gentle man with incredible intelligence. He was not too charismatic, but in his silent way was able to motivate his senior officers with his overpowering logic and resourcefulness. His staff, including Ix's father, was devoted to him to the end. Advisor One on the other hand was so strong-willed and confident that one glare from his eyes alone would get any man moving with healthy fear. Ix and Mox had to live with that all their lives. In their teenage years they had fought and clashed with papa. Now that they had each moved away and were on their own, they realized that they had also picked up that old streak of strong will. Just the thought of having to live with papa in those tight quarters was enough to drive him crazy.

"Hello son. How has the work been coming along?" Papa put his hand on Ix's shoulder as soon as he had gotten close enough to reach it.

"Everything is fine, sir." Ix gave a formal reply.

"You've developed quite a reputation, son. Your discovery of *Mother's Heart* has not gone unnoticed."

Ix had returned from the hunt and found the citizenry exchanging all sorts of rumors -- the mysterious readings Ix had seen deep below the thrash tide had suddenly become a 'creature'. But the more sophisticated folks were beginning to refer to the unknown thing as *'Mother's Heart'*. Ix wasn't sure what to think. His curiosity was piqued, and he had spent most of his leave time researching the thrash tide. More than anything he wanted to go down there and get a better look.

But the tide had already passed, so his curiosity would have to wait.

The rest of the crew had entered the pod with Sencho and began the warm-up sequence for the various instruments. Papa and his advisors followed, with Ix and Hord the pilot bringing up the rear. As soon as Ix entered the submarine he noticed small canisters of food completely covering the entire floor of the corridor two layers deep -- he had to stoop to make his way to the control cabin without bumping his head on the ceiling pipes (Ix later learned they would eat their way down to the floor). Extra supplies and equipment had been loaded while the men were on leave, preparing their vessel for a long journey as the command ship. They had even loaded papa's personal effects as well. Papa and the other man went directly to the guest cabin as if they had been living there already.

Ix moved his way to the control cabin and observed the departure sequence. As the craft slowly descended below the surface, the pilot switched on the spotlights and put the ship on a trajectory that would pass through the gate into open sea. Very little light filtered down under the belly of *The Island.* The spotlights illuminated parts of the massive floating foundations, revealing surfaces rough from ragged growths. Tiny swimmers could be seen darting in and out of the plants, but some of the swimmers seemed to lose their way and drift away from the wall -- evidence that *The Island* was in motion. As they cleared the bottom of the deep towers they caught a momentary glimpse of one of the massive low-velocity thrusters installed into the foundations. The large propeller blades moved slowly, but created a vortex that seemed to capture small drifting fragments of discarded trash that somehow had fallen away from the walls. Briefly, Ix thought there was something about the collection of flotsam and jetsam that he should remember -- something that had to do with the thrash tide …

Hord guided their craft into a power turn at a descending angle. Below them, the spotlights of two other pods could be seen as they hovered in a holding pattern. One of them carried the admiral in charge of maritime operations, and the other was an escort. As for the larger transport pods, Ix had no clue as to their whereabouts. Once their submarine reached open Plasma Hord accelerated up to full speed and fell into formation with the other two pods.

Smash began communication with distant vessels in the fleet. "C22, what's your position?" Papa would call out and Smash would tap out the messages precisely as they were stated. Sencho set up several charts that they used to track the positions of each craft.

"We're coming on the first checkpoint." Smash interpreted a series of clicking noises.

Advisor One asked, "Which relay is waiting here?"

"R6, sir," the communications officer continued, "they're in position now."

Ix understood that a relay submarine up ahead designated as 'R6' had stopped and would remain a stationary link in the communication chain. He began looking out the pilot's dome and side ports to search for it on visual, since their own course would take them right past it. Looking ahead, occasional bright specks of suspended particles moved into the path of their spotlight beams and glittered with the intense light. However, one particular point seemed to hold steady, and as Ix fixated on it the shadowy outlines of the relay pod became apparent. They approached the other vessel with great speed and it was suddenly upon them. In an instant Ix had a clear picture of the streamlined silhouette, and just as suddenly as they had come upon the vessel, they whizzed by and it disappeared behind them. Advisor One sent off a quick greeting and continued with a conversation with the admiral. As they passed, Ix could see small floating particles get caught up in their trail, and he remembered his earlier thought about the flotsam and jetsam caught in the thruster propellers. Why did he have the feeling it was important and related to the thrash tide?

Over the next few wake periods the crew watched relay pod after relay pod take their position in the chain. After they passed the fourth relay ship, they experienced a problem that took a quarter of a wake period to fix. The command flotilla came upon one of the larger transport pods drifting still in the Plasma. Hord slowly maneuvered up to within viewing distance and the crew watched as three divers set about repairing a faulty jet. The larger transports were of a different design than the smaller pod Ix was stationed on. Where the smaller vessels had four external thrusters that could be rotated for maneuverability, the larger pods had internal ducts that directed streams of Plasma through jets. There were intakes located near the front of the craft that took on Plasma, and once the streams went through the jets they could be redirected through any number of output openings for propulsion and steering.

Ix peered through the view port as several divers exited the other submarine and swam along its hull. As he watched, he sensed someone walk up next to him and knew it was his father.

"Walk me through this, son. How do they make deep water repairs?" papa asked.

Ix briefly glanced over at his father before returning his gaze out the view port. The two of them watched as three more divers emerged from the airlock of the other vessel.

Ix began, "The first group is security. They'll keep away corpuscles as the technicians do their repairs."

The biggest difficulty with the internal jets was clogging. Repairing internal thrusters from the outside was no simple matter, for it required dry access to some of the mechanisms.

"In the open ocean they'll need to employ a portable dry dock that's extremely tricky to install." Ix explained.

"What's a 'dry dock'?"

The two of them watched as one of the technician divers swam up to a repair access panel and flattened himself against the hull. The other two divers unrolled a thick blanket and slapped it against the hull, pushing the edges up against the smooth surface to form a bubble around the technician.

Ix answered, "It's a dry place to work. Once that blanket is sealed, he can create a pocket of air."

The two technician assistants proceeded to peel away an outer layer that exposed the thick, clear blanket to the Plasma. Ix and his father could make out the figure of the person inside through the clear substance.

"There are valves underneath that he can use to draw out the liquid and fill that bubble with air." Ix pointed.

As he spoke the bubble began to expand and they could see the waterline move down as the liquid was vacated. The clear material of the bubble began to harden as soon as it was exposed to the Plasma, and soon the technician was enclosed in a cramped but dry working environment. Those watching from the smaller pod could clearly observe the technician as he removed the access panel and proceeded to do the repairs. The air on the inside gave the bubble a silvery color, but portable lights illuminating the work area made it visible from the outside.

Since Ix had never been able to find time to get qualified for diving he had never actually gone through the dry dock training. His little submarine of course didn't need dry dock as the larger pods occasionally required. Ix saw his father looking on in fascination as the diver technician worked.

"On a job like this it's imperative that the technician has all his tools and replacement parts prepared in advance," Ix noted, "there's no way to pass anything through into the bubble once it has hardened."

Ix had heard of stories where the procedure had to be done twice because some rookie hadn't prepared well. It was unheard of for veteran diver technicians to do the job twice.

Watching the repair job, the men became completely oblivious to the security divers that had been swimming about with corpuscle prods. Suddenly one of the divers came up from below and put his face up to the view port, causing the men to jump. Ix looked at that face which was partially obscured by hood and mask, and immediately recognized those eyes.

"It's Mox! That's Mox's transport." Ix waved at his brother before the latter swam away.

The father and son shifted their attention back to the technician in the dry dock bubble who was just finishing up with the repairs. The two valves were reversed and the bubble began to fill with Plasma again.

Ix explained, "He's got to wait until the fluid pressure inside the bubble matches the surrounding ocean before he can get out."

As soon as the bubble was completely filled, the technician turned around and with his back to the hull, he simply kicked it away from the craft to break the seal. Since the shell was hardened it was now useless and they let it sink into the depths. The diving crews re-entered the pod and within moments they were underway again. As he watched the discarded shell sink, suddenly Ix thought he understood the connection with the thrash tide. What if the movement of a billion-thrashing fish created a vortex that could drag along something behind it? Perhaps a vortex strong enough could carry a swirl of objects large and solid seeming to give them the phantom readings they took during the hunting expedition. Or, he had a darker thought, was there something larger that caught all those swimmers in *its* vortex?

Ix felt he might have solved another piece of the puzzle regarding that mysterious thing deep below the thrash tide. There was something disquieting about the revelation, but still he had high spirits. He followed the mission progress with an excitement he rarely felt. However, after a while it was apparent that the repair event they had watched was insufficient. Though they didn't attempt another external repair, the command flotilla caught up with the same transport vessel several more times as they attempted to get stalled jets running again. The three smaller pods would slow down a little and wait for the large craft to get going again. It wasn't until the sixth relay ship deployed that the sencho reported the jets were finally operating steadily, though with less than optimum performance.

It wasn't as though Mox's transport was the only one with problems. Most of the transports needed minor repairs of some sort, but never enough to delay the command group as the one had. The small escort pod completely lost one of its thrusters at one point. Luckily it was near to where they were to meet up with the fifth relay pod, so the officers on board the escort transferred over to the relay ship and the two vessels traded missions. The crippled pod became the relay, with all the time in the world at their disposal to repair the damaged thruster.

Though the problems experienced by the pod fleet were far from out of the ordinary, Ix was quite amazed that their own pod experienced no problems at all. With the new metal joints and overhauled thrusters, Ix was just along for the ride. He got much more sleep this mission than he had since he began his tour. It wasn't until after the seventh and final relay ship deployed itself that things started picking up again. He was startled to wakefulness by a message from one of the crewmen calling all hands to the control cabin. As he staggered down the corridor he could hear excited chatter of the men and his father barking orders to Smash.

"The transports are waiting at the rendezvous point, sir." the communications officer interpreted the clicks sounding through the hull.

The navigator spit out, "I've got them on the scope."

"It's a big bay thirty-eight nodes across and about fifty-two long," the communications officer added, receiving a report from the other pods.

"Have the admiral direct three of the transports to conduct a survey of the structure, and have the other two do wave studies and hydrology analysis." Advisor One directed Smash.

"We're entering the bay, sir." Mag sounded out measurements from a sonar device. "We're heading between two points approximately thirty-two nodes apart. The structures go too deep beyond our range. It's like nothing I've ever seen before!"

Excitement welled up inside as Ix understood what was happening. Out in the gloom were strange structures -- towers, or something -- no one had ever even known existed. Instinctively Ix looked out first one side port and then the other to no avail -- whatever they were, the 'towers' were outside of visual range. It took another two wake periods to assimilate all the data and gather the fleet into one location. From the bits and pieces Ix was able to put together, it appeared that the fleet was in only one inlet of many along a wall of unfathomable length that no one could find the end of.

It was the beginning of another sleep period so very little light filtered down from above. Advisor One and the senior officers had all swum over to one of the larger submarines where they were arguing about a landing. Ix and the rest of the crew could only wait to find out what the plan would be. Most of the men retired to the lounge to play a few games as they often did in their spare time. In the control cabin all the lights had been extinguished except those necessary for the operation of the vessel. Ix entered the cabin and sat at the navigator's post and looked out the view port at the other vessels. All the other pods had bright parking lights piercing the darkness and were scattered about in no specific formation. It was beautiful, like jewels mounted to a velvety background. Ix could see divers making their way from craft to craft, crisscrossing back and forth on various errands.

I was like old times when he and Mox would go deep below Plasma line in *The Continent* and stare out the thick pressure windows for long periods of time, pondering about what might lie way out in the void. They had occasionally seen pods from those view ports, and had wondered what sort of tasks the machines had been working on. He missed his brother and the times they would imagine mysteries and adventures out in the eternal green expanse.

Ix wasn't sure when it was that he noticed two divers crossing the void between them and the fleet of transports. The two silhouettes grew closer and were coming toward their own pod. Could it have been the sencho and papa? Ix went over to the sencho's station and switched on the spotlight. A searing beam of light stretched out from somewhere overhead and extended well out into the void. He fingered the controls and they moved easily, intuitively raking the beam back and forth a little before getting his aim right at the men. He only flashed them for a moment and turned the beam away from their eyes for courtesy's sake. The design of the suits gave away the fact that the men were from Lord Ruk's diving crews, perhaps coming with a personal message. Ix waited until they came directly in front of the view port before switching off the spotlight. The two men swam around to the side out of view, in the direction of the airlock.

When the two divers had entered the lock and opened the inner hatch, Ix and the crewman on duty, named Sal, were there to meet them. It was Mox!

In halting breaths Mox struggled out a greeting. "Hey, Ix." ...pant, pant... "How is everything?"

"I'm doing great, brother! How'd you get over here?"

"We got permission to come over from my hancho. He knew you and papa were on this pod so he let me come as long as I found a buddy to come with me. This is Mel."

Ix helped Mox remove the most cumbersome parts of his suit. Both Mel and Sal were staring at them both. One of them finally said, "You guys are twins! You have the exact same face."

Since there was not enough room for all of them in the lounge, Mox and Mel followed Sal back into the control cabin while Ix went to the lounge to pick up a few hot drinks. When he got back to the control cabin, all three of the other men were looking out the spherical view port at the beautifully lit jewels in the void. Ix was intending to switch on a light but decided against it as he handed the other three their drinks.

"This is incredible!" Mox said without turning his head.

"You sailors have so much extra room to breathe. Can you take this baby anywhere for a spin?" Mel asked.

Sal immediately fingered the controls and powered up the thrusters. They moved forward and then made a wide turn to the left that took them back to where they started (or near enough so).

"Ix, this is just like we used to play when we were kids! You are so lucky. I'd do anything to pilot one of these!"

The two of them spent time philosophizing while staring out at the jewels drifting in the void. Mox told about the insights he gained about Grandpa Nux and Those Who Went Before, and Ix described the new things he had learned about the thrash tide and whatever thing that was being dragged along by billions of fish.

Mox began, "I think Those Who Went Before were our ancestors."

"Interesting. But I thought they had gone away." Ix wondered.

"I don't know for sure, but it seems as though they hid their things in the vaults because there was a war or something. They wanted to keep their prized possessions away from the invaders."

The brothers looked at each other for a few moments, both in deep thought.

"There are rumors of a Creature of the Deep that could devour the city." Mox changed the subject.

Ix shook his head, "It travels at a constant rate of speed in a perfectly straight line."

"You mean it doesn't behave like a swimmer?"

Ix nodded, "Whatever it is, it's huge -- much larger than both *The Island* and *The Continent* put together. And I don't think it's a creature, it's something else -- something even stranger."

The two of them stared at each other in excitement, fueling each other's imaginations like old times.

Ix continued, "They say next season that thing may pass by shallow enough to reach with a submarine! We may be able to descend below the thrash tide and pay it a visit, Mox." He didn't add the strangest thing of all, how the entire surface of the ocean seemed to rise up in a great mound, with their submarine poised near the apex. Ix shook it off -- he couldn't even explain it to himself.

With Sal's guidance each of them tested the controls. They all stayed up late into the sleep period. By the time Mox and Mel had to swim back to their transport it was almost waking time. They had all taken turns piloting the craft all over the place, and had made several very wide loops around the whole fleet. A few times the Pilot and some of the other men came forward between games and gave some pointers to the beginners. Ix thought it must have been because they were all in this strange exciting place and were feeling a little high, but he was sure he felt closer to his crewmates than he ever felt before. It was one incredible rip-roaring party where he and Mox were experiencing a dream come true. Ix sent his brother off, watched them cross the void with a helping beam of light and collapsed on his bunk in an immobile heap. It did not occur to him that he might never see his brother again.

It was only half way through the next wake period when Ix was back at his station. Sencho and Advisor One had returned and were making preparations to penetrate the wall and perhaps make a landing.

Hord took the controls and powered up the thrusters. The craft lurched forward and began traveling at a good clip. Ix looked out the view port and watched the sparkling particles whiz by. Quite a bit of light was filtering down, much more than he had ever noticed before. Instead of a greenish hue, the Plasma was a stunning bluish color. The bluish hue suddenly got darker as a massive shadow loomed up ahead. The pilot slowed the thrusters to a crawl and eased in close until suddenly it was right in front of them -- an alien obstacle of immense proportions.

But Ix didn't exactly understand what he was looking at. The surface couldn't have been part of a node tower. He imagined in his mind an undulating wall surface shaped by haphazard bundles of standing columns and numerous gaps, like a great porous barrier. He tried to analyze this new structure objectively, but having grown up in the uniform layout of *The Continent* he couldn't help making comparisons. The rest of the wake period the small flotilla passed back and forth, peeping and prodding, trying to collect data about the nature of the strange structure. The porous nature of the wall would almost allow one to navigate into the gaps, but there were few places where a large enough passage presented itself. It was a whole wake period later when Mag the navigator indicated that he had found something of interest. A gap large enough for the pods to pass through showed up on their screens. Ix's father gave the order to proceed into the opening.

Advisor One turned to the trackers and asked, "Are we still clear ahead?"

"Everything's fine sir. There's quite a void back there."

The small craft drifted into the opening and was soon engulfed in darkness. The space was so vast that illumination from their puny headlights only disappeared in the void. Immediately sencho switched on the spotlights and sent a beam cutting through the Plasma. The beam struck the far wall of the void and illuminated a thin cylindrical column formation stretching up and down into the darkness. It appeared to be similar to the rough structures observed on the outside. Sencho swept the beam along the far wall and illuminated column after column of varying diameter cylindrical formation, all rough and erratically shaped, extending deep below out of sight. More and more columns were behind each other in greater densities until they appeared tightly packed in the darkest corners. Above them, the cylindrical formations widened out and melded together in places to form a ceiling. In other places the columns penetrated silvery barriers that apparently were air pockets.

The crew craned their necks upward as the spotlights swept back and forth, illuminating the underside of the calm water surface.

"Would you take a look at that!" Advisor One commented.

"Take her up, Pilot." sencho ordered.

The pilot looked for a good spot and took the vessel toward a large expanse of smooth Plasma overhead. The silvery surface became a wide ceiling and suddenly the craft broke through the calm surface into a dark cavity.

For a while no one moved, as water poured down from above off the upper deck over the spherical cockpit window. When the last runnels of liquid decreased to nothing, an alien landscape opened up before their eyes. Two of the crew rushed to the airlock with torches in hand, with Ix and Advisor One right on their heels. The hatch opened to a thick blackness. Immediately a burst of odd-scented air and strange sounds hit them from the outside. All the men jumped back in astonishment at a frightening noise. An inhuman moaning could be heard from far away, echoing along narrow passages and voids to where they were. At times the moan almost approached words of some human whispering long, drawn out warnings to unwary expedition members.

"Who's out there?" One of the men looked back at the rest wide-eyed and nervous.

"Maybe this is a place of death where ghosts and corpuscles dwell!" said another.

Ix was initially as shocked as the rest, but quickly hypothesized a cause for the noise. "No, it sounds like wind blowing through narrow spaces, like a natural pipe organ of sorts."

The two crewmen switched on their hand torches and directed the beams into the darkness. The beams swept across calm liquid and illuminated an occasional column piercing the surface from below. One by one the small group stepped out onto the dock skirt and climbed the ladder to the deck on top. They spent quite a long time crisscrossing that deck, looking first at the formations on one side and then the other. The void above Plasma level was similar to that below, with the tops of the irregular column formations melding together to form a tight roof over their heads. The presence of calm liquid was quite heartening. They could almost see an air cavity such as this become a pod bay for their new home if it weren't for the spooky moaning noises. Unfortunately, though the liquid void below was fairly wide, the air cavity itself was quite small and wouldn't accommodate more than a few pods.

"Sir, there's a message coming in." The communications officer stuck his head out and shouted up from the airlock to Advisor One. "C22 and several other vessels have followed us in. Please advise."

Ix's father hesitated only a moment before returning, "Have them explore the cavity and report. Isn't there a place we can park the pods, and get out and walk around?"

"Right away sir!" The officer ducked back inside the hatch.

Ix stood toward the rear of the craft and eyed a pair of nearby column formations. They didn't appear to be artificial at all, but some sort of gigantic biological growth.

Ix turned to his father, "Papa, I think the formations are natural. Maybe there aren't any decks."

Advisor One walked over to where Ix stood. He pointed his light toward the nearest and squinted his eyes in detailed scrutiny. "They appear to be made of some fibrous material. We ought to get some samples of it."

At that moment the communications officer stuck his head out of the airlock hatch again. "Advisor One! C22 reports something of interest that needs your attention."

"I'll be there presently." Ix's father motioned to the others to follow and made his way to the ladder and airlock.

The men entered the ship and battened down the airlock hatches. Immediately Advisor One headed for the sencho's table and sat down. Smash began rattling off the interpretation of the clicking sounds as soon as they came.

"Looking toward the interior, the formations are not so dense but continue in a scattered pattern. There may even be clearings to allow navigation through them in some places." the other submarine reported.

Advisor One asked the sencho of the other vessel, "Does there appear to be any places where the roof is higher than the level of the Plasma, such that it forms an air cavity?"

"Yes sir, I believe so, but cannot tell very much from here." Smash paused for a moment and continued the interpretation, *"Sir, there's something else farther in..."*

"What is it man?"

"... there seems to be columns of light!"

Columns of light! What strange wonder have they found this time? Ix wondered about it and began to feel a little frustrated at not being able to see what those men were trying to describe. The communications officer began again. *"They're somewhat obscured by the formations, but it looks like light shining through the Plasma from above."*

Advisor One ordered, "Send in T04 and T12 to investigate. Have one of the teams in T12 suit up and prepare specimen canisters. C22 hold your position until we arrive." Ix was quite sure T12 was Mox's vessel. Mox was going to see those columns of light first!

Hord fingered the controls and initiated the dive sequence. Thousands of tiny bubbles of air flushed out of the ballast tanks bathed the outside of the view ports. As the pod slid beneath the surface, Ix noticed a shadowy motion just outside of the radius of illumination of the headlights. Again and again shadows flitted across the view port. Suddenly one came into clear view -- a corpuscle. There were hundreds of them swarming about. They were safe, of course, tucked inside their electrified nests, but the thought of having so many of the amoeba-like predators about always made one nervous. It was almost as if the pod had invaded their territory and they had come to chase the vessel away.

Clicking noises continued to reverberate through the hull. Smash began to translate some of the intercourse occurring between C22, T04, and T12.

"Looks like we're at a dead-end. We'll try the third passage."

"Take a look at the light!"

"Have you ever seen so many corpuscles?"

"T12, travel along the inside of the wall a distance to get around that cluster."

Pilot guided their own craft deep into the cavity to rendezvous with the others. But what first had begun as communications of excited crews happily exploring an alien landscape soon turned to tragedy. Transport 12 started having troubles again.

Smash translated, *"This is T12. We're drifting. I think we have a problem. We're losing buoyancy control!"*

Losing buoyancy control was a major problem. Still, as long as the problem wasn't too severe, it was easy to keep the thrusters powered up to provide lift. Ix was getting worried, and by the looks of the others, it was obvious that they were worried as well. Ix peered out the nearest view port and could imagine dark clouds brewing in the depths. The thought of a great creature below struck him with terror -- maybe these growths were more sinister than they had imagined…

A message was overheard from the admiral, *"Power out of it. Use your jets!"*

Again from T12, *"Sir, our jets are having trouble again. We're getting intermittent response."*

Advisor One was alarmed. Frantically he began spewing out commands. "C22, have T04 get a tow on T12. Get them out of there!" The admiral could also be heard sending out a barrage of similar commands.

"Sir, we can't see them! They're somewhere in these growths."

There was a long pause, and then T04 reported, *"Admiral, we see them now. They're too deep! We can't get to them."*

T12 came on again, *"We have major collapse of two ballast chambers. The hull is beginning to buckle! Airlock failure..."*

There was another gap in the clicking.

To the horror of all, the next message came from the escort pod, *"Sir, they're gone! They're gone!"*

Advisor One queried back to the man, "What's wrong? C22 what's happened?"

"There are bodies all over the place. They're being consumed alive..." The clicks stopped for a brief moment and then

resumed. *"Sir, T12 was charting passage along the wall. She began sinking and must have passed into the Mineral Strata. She just imploded, Sir! There's just twisted wreckage and bodies all over the place. Corpuscles are mopping up..."*

Ix's heart jumped into his throat. T12! The dark clouds billowed up from below, haunting his imagination. Mox, what happened? Are you alright? As if in answer, the communication continued, *"There's nothing left, sir! It's so horrible! They're all dead! They're all gone!"*

CHAPTER 8

Blujic shouldered her backpack and dragged herself into the corridor. She was totally exhausted down to the tips of her toes. Somehow she managed to make it to the stairway and crawl to the top. A persistent whirring noise had followed her from the machine room and Blujic barely had enough energy to turn her head and watch a legged automaton mop up the muddy mess she had smeared on the floor and stairs with her passing. It barely occurred to her that her whole left leg was dripping with the stuff.

The automaton followed her all the way to the showers. Blujic hadn't noticed the stares she had gotten from the Wardens she had passed. She also hadn't known the flurry of excitement that had been present before she had arrived. It wasn't until Blujic had partly revived in the massaging warmth of the showers that she began to notice others hurrying back and forth in front of her stall in an unnatural way. What could it be?

She began to think about the past few days. It had been the first time she had gone outside in the Flesh overnight. She had carefully packed food and a blanket and had set out on foot. How many times had she gone out now? Twenty?

Thirty? She tried to think back and count but couldn't get her mind to work that precisely. All of her secret little excursions seemed to meld together into a single blur. Except this one. She had seen the *Origin* with her own eyes in the Flesh! Off in the distance it had appeared just as it had when she was in the rocker.

She knew the territory around their home pretty well now. Much of the natural landscape was the same as the Database with only a few exceptions. She had carefully visited nearby forests in the rocker and noted all the details. The next day she would go out in the Flesh and verify if the place was really as it appeared in the Database. In almost all cases things were pretty close. All unnatural or man-made things were non-existent in the Flesh, and she was sure animals were carefully contrived loops or sequences. Blujic never saw an animal on her Flesh excursions, including those wonderful cuddlers. Another thing she noticed was that weather was carefully controlled -- though there appeared to be constant clear skies in the Database, the Flesh was often messy and rainy.

Blujic thought she had figured out how the Database was renewed. She was convinced it was through the Mappers. 'Mapper' was the name Blujic gave to the self-propelled hovering devices that systematically crisscrossed the countryside high in the sky. It was hard to understand the nature of the devices, partly because of their high speed, and partly because she purposely hid from them whenever she saw them coming in the distance. She had no desire to attract attention from other Wardens.

Blujic was just finishing up with her shower when Miss Pollic rushed by. Miss Pollic did a double take and backtracked to Blujic's stall.

"Miss Blujic, where've you been? Have you heard the news?" Miss Pollic asked.

"What news?"

Miss Pollic looked excited as she changed her stance into one of someone intending to stay awhile. "The Inmates have boats that travel under the Plasma!"

Inmates! Blujic had had more than a few run-ins with them in the Flesh. It seemed as though she constantly had to hide from them at some time or other to avoid getting detected. The whole reason she didn't go all the way to the *Origin* this trip was because a whole army of Inmates was camped between it and her. She had turned back before reaching her goal and had even been detected and pursued for a while. Memories of splashing through swamps and whip lashing foliage came back in full clarity.

Inmates in boats? Blujic looked surprised, "What are you talking about?"

Miss Pollic started to explain; "Some of the Wardens were diving in the deep lakes and saw Inmates in submarines! Maybe they'll be able to get into our deep ports!"

Deep ports were extensions of the city that pierced the ground crust and opened up directly onto the great liquid expanses underneath them. The liquid expanses were linked to the lakes and even to the stormy oceans. There were many gathering spots at the deep ports, and Wardens often liked to go to there to dive around and play. Miss Pollic's concern about the Inmates being able to invade using submarines must be on everyone's minds, for there were no protections at all down below as there was on the surface. Of course that was only in the Database! None of the other Wardens knew the truth about how safe they really were, because deep ports probably didn't even exist. For all Blujic knew, maybe the liquid expanses didn't exist. Blujic could not help but think that any such submarines were also cleverly crafted loops thought up to make a wildcard appearance for the sake of excitement. Maybe their grandfathers fashioned them as a surprise gift.

Blujic dryly asked, "How do you know they're Inmates and not just automatons or someone's invention?"

"Automatons never go outside, you silly!" Miss Pollic began.

Yeah, right, If you only knew, thought Blujic, recalling the Mappers.

Miss Pollic continued, "And besides, some of them have come ashore at the lakes and have started to do battle with the land Inmates!"

CHAPTER 9

Several wake periods after the tragic T12 incident Ix found himself in a position he could not have imagined in his wildest dreams. He cowered with his back to the massive bole of the column-shaped growth and faced skyward with his eyes closed, gasping for breath. To his left Mag, in obvious pain, sat clutching a shaft that protruded from an open wound in his upper arm. The navigator was also trying to catch his breath after their exhaustive run. Between Ix and Mag, Sencho lay prone and unconscious on his stomach, his body wrapped in bloody strips of cloth.

There they were, fugitives from an unimaginable battle in a strange, alien landscape. Who could have known that above those placid caverns violence lay waiting?

Ix turned to his companion and observed his condition. Seeing the navigator struggle with the broken-off projectile, Ix stepped over Sencho's body and gently reached for the other man's wounded arm to verify that the arrow had cleared the arteries.

"Grit your teeth, man." Ix whispered between breaths.

Without warning Ix quickly pulled the shaft out and tossed it on the ground. Mag started to let out a cry, but Ix covered his mouth with his other hand and muffled it.

"Shhh! You've got to bear it. Don't make a sound!" Ix glared at him.

Slowly he removed his hand from the other's mouth after satisfying himself that the man would keep silent. Ix pulled out a hardened resin canister and poured liquid over the raw wound. It burned a little, but the look on the navigator's face showed that it must have been soothing to a certain extent. Ix got a wad of cloth and soaked it in the liquid. After applying it to the wound he began wrapping the arm with more strips of cloth, using the same technique he had used on the Sencho earlier. Mag got a far-away look in his eyes and began to teeter so Ix had him lean over and place his head between his legs.

The field dressings were the best he could do with what he had on hand. He leaned down and picked up the broken projectile shaft he had discarded earlier. There was a nasty barb on the business end, which was soaked in the navigator's blood -- perhaps pulling it out had caused more damage than leaving it in. Ix couldn't be sure what the barb or shaft was made of, but it was clear that the projectile had only one deadly purpose. Those barbarians had no other desire than to kill them all. Ix thought Advisor One would want to see the weapon, so he wiped off the blood and carefully slipped it into a pocket on his pack.

For the time being they had lost their pursuers and had a few moments to spare. Ix thought it was appropriate to give the medicine applied to the navigator's wound some time to take effect. Having caught his breath, he looked around at the small clearing they had settled down in. The deck in these parts was quite uneven, with soft plush growths of bright green moss covering most everything. He had never seen anything like it before. Even the columns had moss growing up one side. Nothing seemed to be in any order, no elements lined up at all. The ragged edges and uneven surfaces didn't appear to have been made by anyone, but might have resulted from the huge growths gone unchecked for seasons untold. The place where they sat was depressed a little from the surrounding area, defined by the huge boles of four great column growths. There was even a little rise all around the low spot, like a levee or ridge. Ix suspected it was a scar formed in the deck when one of the giant growths had fallen or decayed eons before. A moss-covered lumpy ridge extending off to his right may have been remains of the column fallen to the deck.

Looking straight up, Ix could see higher than he ever thought possible. The columns rose up and up and all but disappeared into ragged green growths far above them. In that chaotic canopy was one of the strangest things of all. Startlingly bright beams of light pierced the rough ceiling occasionally, striking on whatever lie in their path. All the beams were perfectly parallel. Ix couldn't explain exactly where the beams were coming from, only that there appeared to be an exceptionally bright source of light way up high. Whenever one of those beams happened to strike his face, he could feel the warmth and detect the source that must have been many nodelengths away. One could not look directly at the source for longer than an instant, for the brightness was greater than any light element Ix had ever beheld, and he was sure he would go blind if he weren't careful. One thing was sure: the parallel beams striking on the bright green carpet stretching between thousands of column growths was the most beautiful thing he had ever seen.

Ix thought about the first time he had seen the beams of light. It was back in those spooky submarine caverns. After Mox's transport had imploded in deep Plasma and everyone on board lost, the vessel carrying Ix and his father had cruised through the area sometime after the accident. Ix couldn't help but weep as he had seen remains of the wreckage clinging to the rough surfaces of the columns and floating in pockets below the ceiling above them. Corpuscles had been slowly picking away at the debris and capturing fragments of wreckage. The sight of those terrible half-transparent bodies with flowing streaks of red had awakened within Ix that old inbred fear. He couldn't bear the thought that one of those monsters could have devoured his brother! Ix was sure he had seen a tear in his father's eye as they passed through that morbid scene. Advisor One wouldn't show his true feelings, and a tear had been the only sign of the torture his father must have been going through. They searched for any hint that there might have been survivors but to no avail. Advisor One had ordered the expedition to continue as planned. As Ix had spotted the hideous creatures, he had begun to hatch an idea that somehow related to the thrash tide. Why did he get the feeling the corpuscles could be related to a billion-thrashing fish?

Everyone's spirits had been down. The spotlights illuminating across column after column in that dark liquid void had had a haunting effect, and occasionally a corpuscle would appear in the headlights for an instant and startle the crew. Sencho kept asking the navigator about the depth, obviously worried that the craft might go too deep. Ix had caught himself checking out the gauges himself, going back time and again to assure himself that they were working properly. Whenever Hord had steered the craft to go under low outcroppings, Ix had tensed and wondered if they were getting too deep.

Ix couldn't be sure when he had started noticing that the utter blackness outside wasn't quite so complete. He had begun looking upward and seeing irregular circles of silvery green, which was the underside of the surface of the Plasma. The circles were holes in the ceiling, opening up to who-knows-where. The ambient light filtering down gave a strange beauty to the scene, and the crewmembers were glad to take their minds off of the transport accident.

After rounding a sequence of columns, suddenly Ix had seen them: thin beams of strong light shining through some of the larger holes up above. They had all been parallel and so crisp, shining down into the depths. Ix hadn't known whether to be afraid or to cry for joy. Certainly there was nothing intimidating about the phenomenon, but he kept trying to discover where such a powerful source could be. It was almost as if the ghosts of the dead transport were riding up into brilliant glory. The other men in the crew must have felt the same as he, for the rest of the wake period had proved to be less stressful and full of energetic conversation.

Two of the other transports had arrived earlier and were suspended stationary in the Plasma. They were being bathed in beams of light. A flood of clicks had burst upon them as Ix's craft powered into sight and Smash had rushed to interpret the messages. Even from the sound of the clicks Ix had sensed a heightening of the spirits. There was something peaceful about the play of light on the minute particles suspended in the liquid, glittering away as if touched by some warm energy. And Ix had felt he was on the verge of another significant discovery about the nature of that massive thing hiding below the thrash tide. The evil, terrifying darkness billowing up in his mind from below seemed to be dispelled by those beams. But the idea of the corpuscles would not leave his mind. He had wondered -- what could the connection be?

Coming back to the present, Ix saw the same thing happening above that beautiful carpet of green. He still couldn't guess where the light fixture could be mounted. The beams seemed to strike a fine mist or mostly transparent vapor and give a similar effect. The air was so fresh and he loved to breath it in. There was certainly no need of respirators here! With his back against that rough natural column, Ix renewed his determination that he would someday live in this place even if he had to fight the barbarians a hundred times more!

In the upper world there was no strange moaning as there had been in those submarine air pockets. Instead, a sort of hissing noise could be heard. It was almost as though air was being sucked into small openings or moving through narrow passageways. Ix hadn't had time to explore the source of the sounds, but was sure they were coming from higher up on the columns. For the moment, Ix listened to the nearest hissing sound and attempted to find out where it could have been coming from.

Suddenly Ix heard footsteps beyond the mound. He slowly moved away from his resting spot and hugged the side of the rise. Working his way to the top, he peeked between two protruding growths in the direction from which the noise came. There was a runner out there, almost doubled over, zigzagging over the uneven deck. A salvager! As the runner got closer Ix looked for any signs of pursuit by the barbarian warriors. Satisfied that there were none, Ix proceeded to flag the man down. The salvager was running almost entirely on adrenaline and nearly passed Ix altogether. Initially he was startled, but after recognizing the technician he was overcome with relief to the point of collapse.

The salvager labored between breaths, "Oh, I'm so glad to see you!" and promptly passed out.

Ix looked around one more time to check for pursuers then pulled the man behind the rise to safety. Laying the salvager on a comfortable bed of moss, Ix looked him over. He immediately recognized the man as the big diver that was one of Mox's fellow recruits. The salvager had several wounds on his shoulders that had been treated and bandaged, but he was bleeding badly from a stomach wound. With all the patients lying around, Ix was thankful he himself had gotten through and hadn't received a scratch. Without further ado he fixed another wound.

After bedding down the salvager, Ix checked up on Sencho and Mag. Sencho was breathing lightly but was still unconscious. The wounds on his back and head needed better dressing, but Ix had nothing to work with. The navigator seemed a little groggy so Ix had him lie down as well, side by side with the other two in the bottom of the depression.

Ix noticed that the crisp beams of light changed their angle as the wake period progressed. The source seemed to move so slowly across the top of the canopy that consciously one could not tell, except that it was apparent that after a while the light patterns had shifted to a different surface. As the angle got shallower and shallower the number of beams decreased, as did their intensity. Observing them for an extended period of time, Ix suddenly realized that it was getting late and the sleep period was approaching. Soon the beams disappeared altogether and the overall ambiance of the entire scene began to wane.

The hissing sounds also seemed to change intensity. Taking care to stay well hidden from any observers, Ix stood up and crossed the depression to the huge bole on the opposite side. That particular column growth was a little unusual. The ridge was piled up higher there, and he was sure it would be possible to reach higher up the column than would normally be possible, just by standing at the top. Also, starting from a single base, the column split into two about twenty armlengths up, leaving a pair of columns and a notch or saddle. If he could look closer at the column, perhaps he could find the source of the hissing. It might even be possible to climb up to the notch as well. Ix carefully made his way up the ridge and hugged the base of the column. Immediately above him the sound of air passing through a narrow opening assaulted his ears. Feeling with his hands, Ix discovered a small opening in the face of the column. He could see the hole faintly, but only if he looked carefully. As he had thought, there was a weak suction force when he covered the hole with his palm. The hole was sucking in air!

Looking closer, Ix saw other holes here and there in the surface of the column. He was convinced he could use them as a ladder to climb up to the notch. Perhaps he could make his way up there at the beginning of the next wake period and watch out for the enemy. Since it was getting dark, Ix decided to retire with the rest of his patients.

Settling down in a bed of moss, Ix began considering the route they would have to take to get back to the pod rendezvous point. When Ix's pod had came out into the open area bathed in columns of light, three carriers and the C22 command vessel were already waiting. Above them, the silvery under surface of the Plasma had been calm and smooth, opening up to larger bodies of liquid. One of the bodies had been large enough to function as a port of sorts for their little fleet, so Advisor One had directed C22 and T04 to surface and report. Ix had watched as the two crafts broke the smooth silvery surface and powered over to the shore.

The report from C22 had come back in a steady stream of clicks, *"The shore is sheer in some places but generally is thin at Plasma level, and thickening up the farther away from the shore you get. We'll have to find an appropriate landing spot."*

Accordingly, Ix had watched C22 move along the shore a ways before it stopped.

"It's hard to describe the scene here. There appears to be a blanket of green growth covering a deck as far as the eye can see. It's nothing like The Continent's *deck. As a rule the floor is open instead of enclosed like* The Continent. *The columns we see under the Plasma continue up above as well, higher that anything I've ever seen before. The view is magnificent!"*

The officer on C22 had attempted to describe the very terrain Ix was now hiding in, tending his three patients. For all of them, having been born and bred in the confines of *The Continent*, trying to describe such a strikingly beautiful place was quite a task. The salvage crews from T04 had organized several landing teams and became the first people from *The Continent* to set foot on the new deck. It was quite a historical moment for them.

In time, all five vessels landed. Only one carrier had remained below with the admiral's flagship (they were keeping communications open with *The Island*). Each person to view the magnificent scenery for the first time had been awestruck. And Ix had walked around the beautiful mossy deck with nothing but corpuscles in his head -- he was sure there was a clue to the mysterious vortex in the thrash tide. The command team had set up a base camp in that soft moss and the entire expedition team was quite happy and content. The expedition had appeared to be an overwhelming success.

Ix sat up for a moment and tried to get his bearings. It was now almost completely dark, well into the sleep period.

He turned his head slightly to the right and imagined the way they should follow. *The base camp should be in that direction*, he thought. But with no regular triangular features he began to lose his convictions. He lay back down and pondered about the base camp -- how good it would be to feel safe again. Somewhere in his train of thought Ix succumbed to sleep.

"Ix! Ix, wake up!" A rude voice intruded into his peaceful slumber.

Ix felt an arm shaking him. Almost instantly he awoke and looked up at Mag. It was still dark in the middle of the sleep period so he could not see too well, but there was enough ambient light to pick up the movement of shadows. Ix could see the big salvager was also awake, leaning over the still unconscious Sencho.

"What is it?" Ix asked, but he already knew the answer before the navigator said a thing.

"The barbarians are coming! They're on the hunt again, this time in the dark."

Ix could hear the drums beating away in the distance. The rhythm grew stronger by the moment. Immediately Ix shot up and climbed the ridge behind them. Between the columns in the distance a wall of fiery torches waved back and forth as an army marched to war. Along with the drums was a low guttural chant or song. In both directions an unwavering wall of masculinity pressed forth. Chills ran up and down his spine as he tried to think. With such a great army they would be overwhelmed! Even the base camp didn't have a chance, especially since they had no weapons! Somehow they had to be warned.

The drums grew steadily closer and Ix could see the torches were only a few nodelengths away. There was only one thing they could do. They would have to send a runner to the base camp while someone stayed behind to keep the enemy occupied. Quickly Ix half ran and half slid down the slope to where the others were waiting. The big salvager had lifted Sencho up on his shoulders, careful not to disrupt any of his wounds.

Ix turned to the salvager and asked, "How is your stomach?"

"A little sore, but I'll be all right"

"Can you make a run for it?"

The big man shrugged as if Sencho's body was just a light jacket lying across his shoulders. "Sure. Let's go."

Ix asked again, "Can you run carrying him? Do you know where the base camp is?"

"Certainly."

Mag didn't look quite as good. Even though he had lighter wounds, he was of a slighter build and wasn't much used to physical punishment. He had his wits when he woke Ix, but seemed a little delirious now. There was only one person who could stay and try to hold the barbarians off.

Ix turned back to the salvager, "Take these guys and run. Now! Tell Advisor One what we saw and make sure he gets out quickly."

The salvager attempted to argue but soon found it pointless. He finally agreed and was up over the ridge with the navigator in tow. Ix watched them run along the deck toward the direction of the base camp. As soon as they were out of sight, Ix got to work. He knew his time for death may be up, and it wasn't going to be easy. They'd have to take him in a fight before he would go down. Ix was going to use every bit of strategy he could devise to both keep their attention and avoid getting killed. Direct exposure to the enemy projectiles would never work, so he must use wits to try to outsmart them. If he died, he knew it would be worth it if only the others reached safety.

The drums and guttural singing brought back to mind the events of the last few wake periods. It had been decided to use the base camp as the beginnings of a small colony and to expand from there. The teams from one of the carriers had put together a smaller party to map the territory toward the coast of the great ocean from which they had come, and those from another transport had moved inland. The diver crews from the third carrier had remained at the base camp and dove the local ponds and lakes. Sencho had saddled up his crew and gone inland. They would survey a series of triangular sectors each somewhat approximating the area enclosed by node towers in *The Continent.* Having surveyed *The Continent* for generations, the people had perfected a coding which allowed them to record detailed information about materials, installations, and surface conditions in the triangular areas and easily transmit the data without having to heavily rely on some portable media. The conditions were quite different in this new environment, but once a new set of notations had been devised, the blocking off of triangular areas and the sequence of advancement came quite natural. Sencho's team would sink a transmitter down one of the holes opening up to the caverns below and transmit away. The whole party would then move on to the next sector and repeat the whole process.

Since the triangles were not innately present or clearly marked as they were in *The Continent*, there was initial confusion as to how to retain accuracy. It was finally decided to use a marker system, where small brightly colored resin spikes were driven into the fibers of the deck to pinpoint the location of the triangle vertices. That was of course only if there was no column growth at that spot.

Ix and the technician from the transport had been the only technicians in the inland exploration party. It had been their job to carry the transmitter equipment, set up the power sources, and insert the long poles into appropriate sinkholes. Finding the right spot was no easy task, for considerations had to be given to structural support for the poles without exceeding available cable length. The two usually traveled with the communications officer from the transport so he could be free to use the equipment at will.

One of the mysteries Ix could not understand was about the corpuscles. Whenever he constructed the transmitter pole and had lowered it into the Plasma, he could see unusually large numbers of them flowing about in the depths below. They would approach the equipment but would back off when they encountered the weak electrical current running through the pole. What Ix could not understand was why the corpuscles did not climb out of the Plasma as they did in *The Continent*? Did they dislike the rough ground material? What if the creatures were only attracted to artificial objects? A peculiar thing about them was that they tended to prowl about collecting things, which they would surround with their amoeba-like bodies. Once an object was captured, some internal process would coat it with a layer of Ferro-rich substance -- the longer it stayed in the creature's gullet the more coats it would get. Ix's people called such objects 'corpuscle pearls' and they were very rare. He had seen multi-coated cups and dishes that collectors would sell for a high price, apparently having spent many seasons in the innards of one of the monsters. Again the thought had nagged at him -- somewhere there was a connection with the thrash tide. It was one of those problems he would ponder if there were not more pressing matters to consider.

Unfortunately a more pressing matter had come up. Four salvagers had just finished laying out a triangle and were intent on driving a colored spike into the deck. The small clearing had had multiple beams of light striking the columns and deck in the area. Suddenly the four men had noticed shadows moving in to block the areas of illumination immediately in the area of the spike. Simultaneously all four of them had looked up in alarm. There on a small hill, silhouetted in the beams had stood two figures. The sight of the figures was shocking. Though they were blinded somewhat by the beams, the men could see their terrible appearance. They had hardened plates on their chests and upper legs, jointed in the form of some scales like a sea creature. The figures had helmets that were also jointed, leaving only a narrow slit through which they could see. Long strands of hair-like fibers flowed out of the helmets. One of the figures had braided the strands while the other had left them wild and flowing in the wind. The parts of the body that the plates did not conceal were fully covered with some flexible material. All the plates and the flexible material were dyed blood red. Even the hair-like fibers were red, and silhouetted in the light as they were gave the appearance of blazing flames. The figures had arrays of strange-looking objects attached to their backs. There were a series of shafts with tufts of thin translucent fins arranged in a fan over one shoulder. Later they were to understand that those shafts were projectiles that the barbarians were able to accurately propel over long distances with the help of spring-loaded launchers.

For many moments the two parties had stared at each other, each no doubt equally startled by the appearance of the other. The salvagers had been quite intimidated by the terrible appearance, and thinking in retrospect, Ix was positive the barbarians had been sizing up their foe. It was one of the barbarians who had made the first move. He had reached over his shoulder in one fluid motion and took one of the shafts. The salvagers had looked on with curiosity, wondering what the stranger was doing. They had had no clue that their lives were in imminent danger. The barbarian fitted the shaft to his launcher and had let the bolt go into the chest of one of the men. The fatally wounded salvager had fallen backwards with the force of the impact, sprawling spread-eagle on the deck. The other three salvagers had stared in disbelief. By the time the idea of escape had finally registered, the barbarian had already taken another shaft and had downed a second man. The last two salvagers then fled for their lives. As one was able to duck behind a column he saw the third man go down with a projectile in his back. The survivor had run in a panic with all his might to try to catch up with the rest of the surveying party. He made it, giving a detailed report to an astonished expedition party, but Ix noted that that same man had been killed in the slaughter that followed.

Sencho, Hord, and all of the salvager hanchos had gotten together and had thought that it might have been possible to somehow make a defense. The entire party had readied themselves and the hanchos sent out a small team to hunt for the two strangers. Ix had helped the communications officer relay the information about the incident to the base camp and the admiral's vessel. The first time Ix had heard the war drums and chanting was shortly after that. The entire inland survey party had been scattered over five or six nodelengths of territory, hiding behind columns and hills or wherever they could find a place to take a stand. A faint rhythmic sound broke the typical rush of wind through the growth and the always-constant hissing noise. With every passing moment the beat grew louder and each of the men had strained to see what the sound could have been. Soon the guttural chanting could be heard, singing in time with the drums. Between the farthest columns appeared movement, and the men braced themselves for possible conflict. The movement turned into a wall of terrible blood red stained warriors looking ready to devour everything in their path. In front of the army two men ran for their lives -- the last two members of the hunting party the hanchos had sent out. First one man, and then the other went down as projectiles hit true.

The marching army was loading their launchers and firing at will in fluid, trained motions. Though supposedly well hidden, Ix had observed the other technician tumble down from the crown of a hill with a shaft protruding from one eye. Ix had watched in horror as one salvager went down after another. Sencho came up running and gave the order to retreat back to the base camp as fast as possible. Ix had abandoned the transmitter and had followed Sencho, along with Mag and some other members of their pod crew. In that terrible flight all of them had gone down except for the three of them, and Sencho was badly wounded. The barbarians were expert in their craft, and those from *The Continent* who had tried to resist had been mowed down without mercy.

Standing there in that mossy depression, Ix knew that the terrible foe was coming again. As far as he could tell, Sencho, Mag, the big salvager and he were the only survivors of the entire inland surveying party.

Ix looked out toward the chanting army. He could see silhouettes of figures now as they marched to the drums. He hurriedly picked up fallen rods and outgrowths that had broken off the columns high in the upper canopy. He carried them over to the base of the split column and went back for more. After his second load, he strapped the whole bunch onto his backpack with flexible webbing and proceeded to feel the surface of the great bole for the intake holes he had found earlier. One by one he thrust his hands into the holes and lifted himself higher, making his way up to the saddle between the two massive columns.

Just when he was only a few armlengths from the notch, Ix heard footsteps below him. At first he was startled and thought the barbarians had already found him and were at that moment taking aim. But when he looked down Ix saw a familiar figure looking up at him: the navigator! Doing as Ix had done, Mag followed him up the massive bole. Without saying a word Ix turned back around and continued the rest of the way up to the saddle. From below, the notch looked as though it was flat on top, or at least slightly concave upward in a natural transition radius from one massive column to the next. Not so, as Ix was to find out, for he slid waist deep into a pool of liquid. What the nature of that liquid was, or whether it was filthy or clean never crossed his mind. Once having found a firm footing he proceeded to unload the bundle of rods and stack them off to the side against one of the columns. From this vantage, the great boles protected two sides and two sides were open. The navigator soon made it to the saddle and slid into the pool beside Ix.

"What are you doing back here? You were supposed to go with Sencho and the salvager!" Ix railed on the other man.

"I made sure he was headed in the right direction then prevailed upon him to let me come back and join you."

"Well, you keep your head down. I've got an idea." Ix took a thick rod into his hand and peered over the edge. "When I throw this, start yelling and screaming as loud as you can."

The marchers were right below them now, singing that terrible war song. Ix had confidence that he could pick off a target with the object, and be pretty accurate at that. He and Mox had both been marksmen in the throwing competitions back at *The Continent.* However, how much damage the object would cause with all the plate armor protecting those barbarians was debatable.

The bulk of the army marched past their perch without detecting them. Ix was a little surprised at that, and concluded that the barbarians were making a general detailed ground sweep and didn't really know whether there was anyone actually there to find. Behind the front line, a few stragglers casually marched along, singing out in a different tune than the others. Ix rose up, took careful aim, and threw the thick rod with all his might. Immediately after letting go of the first one, Ix had another in his hand and was aiming at another straggler. Mag let out a tremendous yell right as the first rod hit one of the barbarians squarely on the side of the head. Ix couldn't tell whether it was the force of the impact or the startled reaction from the navigator's yell that knocked the barbarian down. The warriors in front broke ranks in disarray and confusion.

"Take this you bastard butcher!" Ix yelled at the top of his lungs as he let another rod sail.

A few more thrown rods hit true and all hell broke loose. Between the flying rods and the shouting from Ix and the navigator, the confusion reigned much longer than Ix would have thought. To top it all off, some of the barbarians began clubbing each other and fighting among themselves. The thought occurred to Ix that they might not have even known what hit them, but were naturally high strung and ready for a fight. The warriors Ix had labeled stragglers were the ones who finally brought order to the group. It was clear that they were the leaders of sorts, and had some measure of power or influence over the others.

One or two of the leaders finally caught on that all the commotion was coming from the same place. They started making arm motions at the unruly crowd and using deputies to bring them all together. From nearby and off in the distance, torch-bearing warriors came in closer and closer and began forming loose groups around the giant bole.

Oh great! *I could have just let them walk by and get on with my life*, thought Ix, but he knew that attracting their attention was the only way to give the other men enough time to escape.

A few of the barbarians got their act together enough to launch some projectiles at them. At that point Ix and the navigator kept their heads down to avoid becoming easy targets. Crouching down low in the pool they were able to completely hide behind the substance of the column and protect themselves from enemy fire. Ix knew it wouldn't do much good, but only prolong the inevitable. As soon as one or two of those barbarians climbed up after them they were as good as dead.

With their heads low Ix and the navigator listened to the commotion below. The warriors were milling around and grunting to each other in what must have been their language. Occasionally some angry voices could be heard along with scuffling and the sound of heavy blows on those hardened plates of armor. Presently the commotion died down. Grunts and whispers were silenced and not even the sound of many warriors milling about could be heard. There was only the ever present hissing of the suction holes in the column boles.

"Onhui do luk luk yeo!" came a deep voice up from below.

Ix had no idea what the voice was saying. Neither of the men made any response, but Ix got the largest of the rods he had gathered and readied it to be used as a club.

"Onhui do luk luk yeo!" again the same voice called up from below.

This time Ix draped the end of the club with some strips of cloth and used it to toss them into the air. The response was both immediate and terrible. From both exposed directions over two-dozen projectiles hit the cloth and nailed it to the column. Ix noted that six of the projectiles were so accurate that they vied for the same exact spot to the point of splitting the arrow before it! On the other hand most of the shafts had quite a bit of scatter and ranged from close to way off.

So, there are six marksmen out there, he thought.

Ix took a couple of the rods and tossed them out into the crowd one after another without exposing himself. As he had thought, the first one got six hits before it passed from his view, but the second one got none at all. Ix deduced that they hadn't had time to reload their launchers before the second object flew.

"Onhui do luk luk yeo!" came the voice again.

Ix was determined to prolong the confrontation as long as possible. He readied the club and prepared himself to beat every barbarian that climbed up that column after them. Both men were quite excited and were unable to sleep any of the rest of the sleep period. Ix stirred at every sound and expected one of those blood-red stained armor heads to pop up at any moment. To the men's surprise, though they heard the warriors moving about below, the expected confrontation never came.

When the light returned the next wake period the men found they had been sitting in a sparkling clear pool of fresh warm water. They made a meal of some fungus growths on the side of the column (the same type growths that could also be found in *The Continent*) and continued their wait. Ix let his mind wander as he tried to think about corpuscles, and what it could be that had some connection with the thrash tide. Was it their indefinite form? Corpuscles were known to divide into two separate animals, and smaller ones sometimes combined to make a larger creature.

Somehow Ix thought he might be getting closer, but there was no time to give it more thought. At long last the men finally heard scuffling noises that could only have been the sound of someone climbing the column below. Ix took a chance and made an assumption that they wouldn't fire if one of their own were near the target. He held up the club with another strip of cloth draped over the end and got no reaction. Slowly Ix peeked over the edge and saw fifteen or twenty warriors staring up at him. Since none of them had his weapon drawn, Ix looked over the edge and sure enough, a red clad barbarian was slowly trying to climb the base. Still, something seemed quite odd about his movements as if he were hesitant to climb. Ix crouched back down and readied his club, preparing himself for the instant that head popped up over the edge. The navigator also got out a rod with his good arm and waited behind Ix.

A red helmet peeked up over the top. Ix stood up suddenly and whacked that head as hard as he could. The first blow only seemed to graze the helmet but Ix hit home a couple of good ones after that. Each time the club impacted the barbarian's head was jerked to the side but was protected by the heavy plating: he kept on climbing. Ix wished he had a more significant weapon with a little more weight to it, for the club just seemed to be irritating the warrior if anything. Then Ix stood up straight. He would have been an easy target to any of the enemy had they readied their weapons. Ix took the club and swung with all his might, this time aiming up toward the lofty green canopy rather than down. The helmet came off and went soaring through the air, only to fall back into their little pond. The thought that came to Ix as he brought that club back for another blow to that unprotected barbarian face was the emotion he read in the eyes of his enemy.

Ix didn't know if his final blow killed or wounded the warrior, for he ducked down low again soon after his enemy plummeted to the deck below. Ix sat back and fished the helmet out of the pool. It was made of metal strips, pounded into shape by a thousand blows of a hammer against a mold and fastened together like scales. The strips were stained red on the outside but worn bare on the inside. Bare metal -- the sight of it connected the thought that had intrigued him regarding the corpuscles and the thrash tide. What if enough of the predators merged together to make a huge monster? If there was a giant corpuscle, it might have enough pearl steel to create a magnetic field large enough to get their compass needles going wild. Was there a gigantic corpuscle lingering about under the thrash tide?

"The barbarians are afraid of heights." Ix suddenly realized. "If we can stay high and out of their line of fire we might be able to get out of this mess."

The barbarians were afraid to climb up after them. They would probably lay siege for many wake periods in a row but it must have taken a lot of courage and coaxing from fellows to even think about trying to climb up after them. *Well, now*, Ix thought, *there might be an even playing field after all.* Ix and Mag had a chance of not only surviving but perhaps escaping as well.

Mag replied, "Can we keep climbing up those holes in the columns?"

"That's a possibility. Perhaps we can climb all the way up into that canopy growth and pass from column to column."

"I don't think we can do it." Mag observed. "Climbing up the outside will expose us to those projectiles."

"Yes, but what if we were to do it in the dark?" Ix countered.

"That might just work. What will we do once we get to the top? We don't know what that canopy growth is like."

"Well, what are our choices otherwise?" Ix pointed out.

The only thing left to do was wait. Ix worried about hypothermia because they had to crouch down in the pool, but since the water was quite warm they got by without a problem. If there was some other weapon that could flush them out, the barbarians never used it. They just seemed intent on laying the siege and taking their time. Ix and the navigator spent the rest of the wake period snacking on the fungus and talking about this and that.

When it started to get dark again the troubles began. Not only had the numbers of warriors increased, but also several groups of them had built campfires quite near their perch. The fires were no trivial matter: Ix could see the flames licking the air even in his hiding position, illuminating the entire area. There would be no way to climb those columns without being seen. Ix couldn't say how they could keep those fires from burning a hole in the deck. At first he thought they were planning on burning them out of the notch by setting fire to the surrounding area, but when the warriors below began singing and entertaining each other Ix knew it was just one of those male bonding things that must occur in any culture no matter how refined or savage.

Ix and the navigator were disappointed at first, thinking that their plan had been permanently stalled. Nevertheless it didn't take long before Ix had an idea that would work those bon fires to their advantage.

Ix turned to Mag, "Do you have any baku juice?"

Baku juice was the liquid Ix had used to treat the wounds of his patients. The people of *The Continent* used it as a medicine at times, and some even drank it, relishing its strong burning and intoxicating effect. Regardless of how it was used or abused, the liquid was quite flammable. Mag pulled out a canister full of the juice and handed it to Ix. Ix also pulled out his own canister, which had been half depleted already. He took the heaviest bottle and hefted it in his hand as he looked out over the edge at the fires.

He explained to Mag, "See this fire over here and the one beyond? If this works we'll have a few moments to slip into the darkness. Get ready to run after the second one goes!"

Ix took the half empty bottle and gave it a toss. As planned, it landed right in the middle of the nearest fire. Ix watched only a moment or so before ducking his head. The warriors suddenly grew silent and looked around, trying to find a culprit. One instant they were calmly sitting or standing around, and in the next instant a tremendous blast sent up a huge fireball. Ix got up and looked over in that direction and saw that the explosion had completely snuffed out the bonfire proper and a dozen or so screaming figures were fighting to put fires out of their clothes. The warriors sitting around the fire beyond were all calmly looking at the commotion at the neighboring campfire.

Ix gave the second bottle a good throw, and landed it in the next fire. As with the first, the warriors seemed confused at first wondering what had fallen in their fire, then suddenly a big explosion ripped away at the group. Burning bodies flew in all directions. Again the fire was extinguished by the blast. Now there was no illumination on that side of the column upon which Ix and the navigator were hiding. Quickly, the two of them scaled down the side. Warriors from the other side rushed past the gigantic bole to see what had happened, and passed Ix and Mag without noticing them.

The two made a mad dash in the opposite direction from where the explosions had occurred. Ix had calculated that the simple-minded brutes would all gather to the scene and leave the way open for escape. Still, he carried along his trusty club just in case. In his calculations he was almost entirely correct, except for one big warrior that appeared out of nowhere and blocked their path. Ix didn't stop but braced himself with everything he had to impact the barbarian with full force. The collision knocked him back a little, winning Ix just enough time to bring the club up from below and send the other's helmet flying. This time it was Mag who finished him off, getting in a good whack across the face before the helmet even hit the deck. The barbarian didn't have a chance.

Ix and Mag ran with all their might and never looked back.

CHAPTER 10

It was the same dream over and over again -- suiting up in the airlock, readying the specimen canisters, and watching the Plasma rise degree by painful degree. Then the world splits asunder and there are thousands -- no! -- Millions, of bubbles. Bubbles can carry one away. Rise with the bubbles higher and higher. They come together and flow, oozing this way and that. Those hideous streaks of red change direction and reroute themselves. Get away! Get away! The corpuscles come again and again and again. Jab at them and they keep coming. Push at them and they try to take your hand. Many men are swimming away. A body is consumed and the flesh dissolves off the bones right before your eyes -- a morbid skeleton that keeps coming with oozing flesh working those borrowed bones to swim faster and faster. Must get away! Up and out of the Plasma! Back away from the edge and up against the wall! It's all a muddle. What's happening to me?!

Suddenly everything is clear. There is darkness all around except for the mouth of the cavern up ahead. Two terrible men are coming, for their silhouettes are clearly visible against the cavern mouth. They walk closer. All their clothes are red. They have red scales that clank with a hollow sound every time they brush up against each other. They peer through narrow slits with eyes that desire to see death. Their hair is a blazing flame. They've come to kill me!

It's all perfectly clear. Two terrible men are standing in a cavern. They raise their weapons. They take aim. They're aiming at me!

Those Who Went Before come swooping in. Their pod rises on thrusters, not in the Plasma but in the air! A silver metal hatch opens. From the hatch a kindly old grandfather emerges. Two swift strokes of blazing lightning and the terrible men are cut down. I'm saved!

"Have you come to take me away with the fathers?" I ask.

The grandfatherly gentleman reaches out his hand. "You would live forever? Not now, my young friend, later. But just remember this: it's all One Eternal Round."

Everything fades away. The dream is over.

****

A young man found himself wandering through growths of moss. He was purposefully going over 'there', somehow knowing that it was the right way. Why was he going over 'there'? He could not remember. How did he get here and from whence had he come? He could not remember that either. The surface he walked on was not even and smooth as he was accustomed to, but had ups and downs and ridges and valleys. What was he accustomed to? Somehow that memory fled him too. The hundreds of tall columns that surrounded him seemed different also, but he could not explain why. Since he had nothing better to do, the young man just followed his instincts and kept walking, wondering at all the strange sights along the way.

He suddenly realized that he had no respirator on and fumbled with his clothing. It was gone! He would suffocate in the thin air! But as he breathed he felt the satisfaction of filled lungs and the taste of air cleaner than any he had ever tasted before.

The pathway he followed had several sets of footprints going both ways. The young man paused for a moment and kneeled down to study the footprints. Obviously standard issue diver's boots like his own left them. Diver's boots? The young man sized his own boots up with the footprint and found a perfect match. Had he walked this way before, or did everyone wear the same size shoe? He couldn't remember walking this way.

The young man followed the path to a large crevice in the side of a rise. The crevice opened up to a wide darkened tunnel. Off the top of his head the young man thought it shouldn't be wise to enter a tunnel without a light, but somehow he knew it was the right way to go. Timidly, the young man entered the tunnel. After going in several armlengths he paused to let his eyes adjust to the dim light. On his left was a somewhat vertical wall that stretched ahead into the darkness. The ceiling slowly came into focus and extended in a gradual arch that decreased in height, the floor bowing up from below to meet it. Up ahead the tunnel was not as dark as he had first thought. It opened up into a large natural room or chamber that had multiple holes in the ceiling that let light filter down. The wall on his left continued all the way to the back, but the floor narrowed and became a beach for a great subterranean lake that stretched out of sight. The great chamber had numerous columns connecting the ceiling to the beach and also standing in the lake.

Arriving at the beach, the young man looked around. This was the cavern of his dreams. He remembered his dream. There were fearful creatures swimming around in the depths of the lake. Walking to the edge, the young man peered into the Plasma illuminated by beams of light shining in from the ceiling. An occasional flicker of movement down below confirmed what he already somehow knew. Walking along the beach, the young man remembered things. *In the dream, two terrible men fell over there*, he thought. But looking down the beach he could see no one. As he thought about it, the dream was filled with too many things that didn't make sense. Perhaps he had imagined the two men and the flying vessel.

The young man suddenly felt very uncomfortable and needed to get outside. There was something at the end of the beach that he didn't want to see. What it was he could not remember. The young man turned around and went back out. As he walked out of the cavern, his hands went to the instruments on his chest and he realized that he had had a torch all along. Still, no matter of tools would have convinced him to reenter that cave.

This time he walked the same path going the opposite direction. He walked between the columns and over the uneven, mossy deck. The young man walked past the footprints and the spot where he had become aware of himself. He walked all the way to where the columns ended and stopped. There were no more columns. There were no more columns! For dozens of nodelengths there was nothing but open deck! He had never seen anything like this before. From under the cover of the columned canopy he peered out at the great open space. What could the ceiling be? The young man looked up and saw wispy white splotches and occasional small sharp white shapes against a rich blue background. He could not quite grasp as to how high it was, or where and how it connected to the deck.

Out there in the open, the deck was covered with soft green tufts. The young man nervously left the safety of the canopy and walked out of the shadows and onto the green tufts. He immediately felt warmth on his neck, since his hood was slung back. It was very warm and peaceful. Nevertheless he could not get his bearings; there was nothing to hedge up the way to his right and left. He could go anywhere and not bump into obstacles and walls. Momentarily he was overcome with feelings of agoraphobia and fell to the deck. He closed his eyes and hugged the deck until the feelings of confusion passed.

The young man thought he had felt this way before. Memories of being suspended in unfathomable deepness came haunting him. What had he been doing there? Somehow he felt that he had overcome his fear and had grown to love the deepness. If that were the case he could do it here as well. Slowly he opened his eyes and raised himself to his feet. The openness was still strange, but as long as he kept his eyes going back to the deck whenever he started to get confused, he felt he could handle it. And the openness had a certain appeal to it. It held a similar sort of freedom as he had felt in the deep. Feeling confident, the young man started to run in circles until...

He saw the light!

A large orb of unspeakable brightness hung from the ceiling above the spot where he had exited the columned canopy. He could not look at the orb for anything longer than an instant or the brightness would cause him pain. Each time he looked away, an image of the orb would remain ingrained in his head, only after blinking several times would the image start to lose strength. The orb did not remain fixed above the columns, but moved as he moved. This was so with the entire ceiling also, which gave him the impression of a brilliant light fixture attached to a vast blue and white dome. The dome was a vast room within which the columned canopy and open deck lay. The orb seemed to be the source of illumination and warmth in the vast room.

The young man basked in the light and warmth of the orb. He rolled around in the soft green tufts and watched the blue and white ceiling. He counted six small white shapes scattered over the dome. Though the orb and other shapes appeared to be stationary, the soft white wisps he had noticed previously did not stay put but moved slowly across the ceiling. As he watched their slow progress he began to notice that they appeared to take on the form of objects he knew or had vague memories of: a person kneeling, a pod, a smiling face, etcetera.

Watching the wisps had a hypnotic effect. He spent great amounts of time feeling the peaceful warmth and watching the wisps go by. The young man found himself drifting off to sleep and felt safe and secure under the watchful eye of the orb. It was much later in the wake period after waking from one of his little naps that he began to notice that the orb and other shapes did change their positions. Where the orb had been in one place when he had first seen it, it was now all the way across the dome. The six small shapes had also changed their arrangement, with three of them grouped together in one place and the others in totally new locations from before.

The young man sat up on the soft green surface and looked around. With the orb in a new location, he was disoriented and could not tell from where it was that he entered the vast open space in the first place. He had been so taken by the novelty of the open deck that he had not noticed what lie on the edge and beyond the space. With nothing to block his view he could see incredible distances! The columned canopy bordered the open space on two sides. He could clearly see the huge columns extending up into the rough green growths and tapering out at the top. The surface was mostly flat where he sat, and the deck rose higher and higher at the ends of the vast open area to form huge ridges or hills almost equaling the height of the canopy. The ridges were bare except for the plush carpet of soft green tufts.

The ridges intrigued the young man. He had seen changes in elevation and unevenness in the deck between the columns, but these massive obstacles were a wonder that piqued his curiosity. A dozen questions entered his mind. Could the ridges be holding up the dome? What lie on the other side of the ridges? The young man stood up and began traversing the open space toward one of the ridges. It took a while to climb the hill, resting as he went. Each time he stopped he turned around and looked down at the vast open space. As he gained a higher and higher perspective, the field looked smaller and smaller since he was able to view both ends at once. The feelings of agoraphobia intensified at times so that he had to concentrate only on his feet and the surfaces immediately within his reach. Still, the distances were so immense that it hardly made any difference whether a feature was a few nodelengths away or several hundred. He found it difficult to fathom that a speck in the shadow of the distant columned canopy was actually a significantly sized object and not merely a speck. Another thing he noticed was that the apparent top of the canopy was merely a small version of what appeared to lay beyond in the distance: a massive wall of columns shrouded in mist slowly came into view the higher he climbed. Almost invisible in its most distant parts due to haze, the wall stretched from one side of the dome to the other. It was a breathtaking view to say the least.

The young man found his way to the top of the ridge. Fighting his agoraphobia, he found he could see fairly far in all directions. The open space that had seemed so vast was now merely a small field in a network of many fields. The columned canopies covered much of what he saw, but a significant part of the endless deck consisted of rolling hills and valleys. On the opposite side of the ridge from the direction he had climbed, a massive peaked hill towered in the distance above the nearby canopy. Between that peaked hill and the ridge upon which he stood was a valley ten times more vast than the first open space!

On the valley floor hugging the base of the hill was a series of small lakes that had irregular shapes. In the middle a great linear lake, almost perfectly straight, stretched from one end of the valley to the other. Though the incredible distant scenery kept his attention for a long time, it was the massive object that was located at the end of the valley that finally captured the young man's curiosity. At the far termination of the linear lake, a huge hemisphere protruded from out of the ground. There were cracks and rents, with moss or some other plants attached to its side, and the material was unmistakable -- metal. It was as if a huge metallic ball had rolled along soft mud and finally sunk into it, the depression left behind having filled up with liquid. On the backside, the fibrous material of the deck had built up to form a small ridge, perhaps displaced by the settling of the massive sphere. The ridge had long since covered with the soft green tufts.

Still struggling with his agoraphobia, the young man immediately rushed down the hill toward the hemisphere. The slope was a little steep, so much so that the fibrous material showed through the green cover in places. More than once the combination of steep slope, light-headedness, and protruding growths sent him stumbling to the deck. Adding to the poor footing, the bright orb had moved so far along the overhead dome that the hillside became cast in shadow. Reaching the bottom of the hill, the young man could not see the orb at all, and the entire overhead dome had started to lose its brightness. He carefully skirted his way around the odd-shaped lakes until he came to the edge of the linear body of water.

As the young man began to walk along the length of the lake, he noticed that the small shapes on the overhead dome were getting brighter, and that the whitish puffs were starting to turn bright yellow and orange. Incredible! The dome looked as though some painter had taken a gigantic brush and had spread the colors at will, decorating the expanse for his delight. Walking next to the lake, the beautiful overhead scenery reflected almost as a gigantic mirror. Awestruck, the young man continued his journey towards the metal hemisphere, watching the overhead dome get darker and darker. There was a gradation from one side of the ceiling to the other, ranging from deep to light blue. The small shapes turned a brilliant white against the dark blue background, and several small sparkles of light began to appear in the darker areas of the dome.

Soon the entire dome was black and the whole ceiling was studded with sparkling points of light. The young man was overwhelmed with the beauty of it all. It was getting late, well into the sleep period, and he had to find some enclosure. His journey had been exhausting and his body craved sleep. The only option was to make haste to the metal hemisphere and perhaps find some shelter at its base. He felt an acute need to have walls around him once again, even if it were only on one or two sides.

Even though it was dark, the brilliant shapes in the dome ceiling provided illumination of sorts. Where there had been six shapes before, only four remained visible, the others having moved behind the darkly silhouetted hills and canopy. The eerie light cast onto the deck was enough to pick out a trail to the hemisphere.

The gigantic dome loomed out of the darkness before him. As he approached it he could make out large expanses of unbroken metal, interrupted by growths and occasional dark rents. Up close, the smooth skin retained a near perfect curve in a few places, but in general appeared to be somewhat crumpled. It was difficult to find a spot where he could approach the curved wall too closely, for the fibrous deck was quite uneven, leaving a liquid-filled moat. The young man skirted the base of the massive structure, at times splashing through dark pools and stumbling over low banks. He approached the wall where he could, dragging his hand over its surface as he searched for an opening large enough for a man to enter. At length he worked his way around the back where the ridges had been thrown up when the sphere had come to a rest (or so it seemed to him). In place of a moat, the deck material was instead banked against the curved metal wall higher up the hemisphere. It was at the top of one of the banks where the young man finally found a tear in the metal skin large enough to enter. The rent was quite narrow and ran diagonally fairly high up the curved surface. The fibrous material of the valley floor had filled the space behind the metal skin leaving a level path at the top of the bank leading into the bowels of the hemisphere.

The young man stood with both hands on each side of the ragged opening and peered inside. The torn curved skin appeared to be supported by some metal structure. About three armlengths inside the outer skin there was an inner curved wall, where the metal structure members formed a complicated web that zigzagged back and forth in the gap between the two walls. The inner wall was also torn, opening up into darkness.

What could the hemisphere structure be? Who built it and where are they now? The young man couldn't bring himself to enter into the dark interior, but since his body was craving sleep he found a moss-covered level place between the outer and inner walls and lay down with his head facing to the outside. He fell asleep wondering about the strange hemisphere and watching the incredible twinkling lights way up above.

He dreamed of things he remembered. He dreamed about the cavern and the two red bad men, about Those Who Went Before and that terrible thing at the end of the subterranean beach. That terrible thing!

The young man woke with a start. The vast ceiling way above was a bright blue color again, contrasted against the dark ragged edge of the tear. White wisps moved across the opening as they traveled across that expansive blue dome. It must have been halfway through the wake period already. With his eyes the young man followed the tear down its length and focused on the green-carpeted hills in the distance. The tear framed a slice of that new wide world he had discovered. He turned his head around the other way and peered into the darkness of the interior of the hemisphere. With the increase of light he could barely make out shadows and silhouettes of geometric objects, but could not discover what they could be.

Suddenly he noticed a dreadful smell. Thinking that it was coming from the interior of that strange structure, he craned his neck and took deep whiffs of the interior air. Though a little musty, there was nothing wrong with that air. Again the smell assaulted his nostrils. Could it be inside the cavity he had slept in? The young man stood up and sniffed around, peering through the web of structural members as far as he could see. Nothing. Then -- something. Following the smell, he turned his head to the side and discovered it was coming from himself!

"Boy, I've got to take a bath!" he said out loud.

The young man exited from the torn metal wall and climbed down the green-carpeted bank. There were plenty of lakes and pools in the valley; perhaps he could find one to take a swim in. Sheltered between two banks not far from the tear, he discovered a small pond that was shallow enough for a man to stand in without getting deeper than his neck. What's more, there were no connections with the seas or openings through which corpuscles could swim in and spoil the fun. The pond was not salty Plasma but fresh water! Happily the young man dove into the water and began peeling off his suit and undergarments layer by layer. As one layer would come off, he would scrub it inside and out, rubbing it with a handful of course moss, and then lay it out on the side of the bank facing that brilliant orb. Soon he was completely naked and proceeded to wash himself. Feeling refreshed he splashed around a bit and began to climb out of the water. At first he intended to put his diving suit on right away, but the warmth of the shining orb and the wonderful feeling of being clean and fresh got to him, and he decided to lie out on the deck himself. Feeling a little agoraphobic on top of his nakedness, he found a spot that was partially surrounded by waist high shrubs and low berms. He lay down on his back and put his arms over his eyes to shield his face from the orb and promptly relaxed.

Slipping in and out of lazy slumber, the young man thought he heard women singing in his dreams. No, it was the voice of a girl. She was singing to him. The young man opened his eyes and lazily watched the white wisps form shapes as he listened to the beautiful song.

Beautiful song! There was someone singing and he was naked! The young man looked around but could not see where the singing was coming from due to the shrubs. Slowly he raised himself up and peeked over the top of the growths. There, sitting on the bank with her feet soaking in the water was a girl with golden hair. Golden hair! That was impossible -- all girls had jet-black hair. He had to get his clothes; where were his clothes?

Suddenly the young man knew he had a real problem. His diving suit was still lying out on the bank on the other side of Golden Hair!

CHAPTER 11

"So what you're saying is that the thrash tide will be shallower -- *Mother's Heart* will be approaching the surface?" Lord Ruk rubbed his chin as he peered out the plate resin window built into the wall of his office. The plaza below was bustling with activity normal for a late wake period, with workers doing last moment errands before they headed home for the sleep period.

"The technicians have gone over their calculations several times. They're sure it will happen during the next season," replied Advisor Three who was calmly sitting at Ruk's small meeting table.

"We're talking about the *Heart* and not just the thrash tide?"

Advisor Three nodded his head. "Well, we can't know that for sure, we don't even know what that thing is. But that's what they are saying. I have some reports here that seem to verify it."

Advisor Three pulled out some papers from his case and laid them on the table. Ruk walked over and picked up the papers and began leafing through them. As far as he knew, it was the first time any such thing had ever happened.

Ruk asked, "Will it be shallow enough to send a pod down?"

"It looks too deep for the resin pods, but a steel hulled vessel may be able to make it."

"What do you suppose we could learn from getting close to it?" Ruk was in deep thought and began going down a list of questions.

"Well, no one really knows. Some of the crews believe the old stories about a massive Creature of the Deep. Many of the technicians suggest that it may be where the corpuscles reside. Who knows what's down there!"

"I wonder if we can discover anything about Those Who Went Before?"

"That's not very likely. Those Who Went Before were most likely up against the same barriers we are," Advisor Three suggested, "the crush threshold."

"It might be worth our while to send in an expedition. I'll get Advisor Two started on a feasibility study. First we should prepare some deep Plasma beacons, and see if we can get one to catch on the thing." Ruk seemed quite excited about the possibilities of approaching the Heart. He paused for a long while before turning to the next subject on the list.

"What's the latest word about the sonar interpreters?" Ruk asked.

Advisor Three pulled out another set of papers and began shuffling through them. Finding the right one, he quickly looked over the text and briefed himself before replying. "It looks as though they've been doing some experiments with sending and receiving voice messages."

Ruk's eyes widened. He quickly turned to squarely face Advisor Three and exclaimed, "Voices over sonar! How successful have they been?"

"I'm not sure, Sir. They were scheduled to do the experiments the last wake period and I haven't been back to see how things went."

"Make sure you keep up on that one. When can you get out there again?" Ruk asked.

"I'll be going out there the next wake period." Advisor Three put up a mental picture of the sonar lab and refreshed in his mind its location on the perimeter of *The Island*.

"And the landing party? What's the latest word from Advisor One and the landing party?" Ruk fingered the next item on his list.

"Not much to add that you don't already know. After discovering those air tubes inside each of the column formations, it was apparent that the growths were hollow -- sometimes there is enough space for a man to climb through. Now getting up and down from the platform forts is a breeze. The barbarians have set up a camp down below, but as long as no one exposes himself they appear to be safe for the time being. They're pretty resourceful those barbarians, as you know. They find new ways to confront our people all the time. I wouldn't be surprised if they figure out some way to overrun the platforms."

Ruk asked about some minor points he wanted clarified, "Have they found out a way to communicate with the barbarians?"

"No, Sir, any attempt to communicate has been met with hostility."

"What about the subterranean cavities. How is the survey coming along?" Ruk worried about how they would actually colonize the great structures if they couldn't even move heavy equipment from *The Island* to their new home. From all indications, using the air-filled cavities as temporary bases of operation might be to their advantage.

"There are two command pods and one carrier working on the survey, Lord Ruk. That makes six diving teams altogether. They're a little short on men, I'm afraid."

"Yes, that battle with the barbarians."

Advisor Three continued, "Advisor One has stayed put at the platforms according to your orders, Sir."

"Fine, keep me posted. If we're serious about making a colony work we'll have to solve that problem. Is there anything else?"

"No Sir."

Lord Ruk was about to walk out of the room, but quickly turned and added, "One more thing. About *The Continent* - have we gotten any more communications from them?"

"No Sir. There were a few reports of contention between the tech lords at the university and the Manufacturing Lords. It seems as though a new movement has begun called the 'Prisoners'. They believe *The Continent* was once a prison, and that our people descended from the prisoners. But all communications have abruptly stopped."

CHAPTER 12

Ix peeked through the slits in the stockade with the greatest of caution. If any one of those terrible barbarians below had so much as a fingerwidth of a target they would certainly fire off dozens of bolts. He quickly took in the scene below and ducked down again. With his back to the stockade, he went over in his mind the layout of the land and the placement of the enemy. Having gone on sentry duty many wake periods in a row now, just glancing down and accurately judging enemy numbers and activity was almost a matter of mechanical repetition. Since the barbarians were not known to climb the column formations, the expedition members were now fairly secure as long as they stayed behind the stockades of their lofty platform forts.

It had been many wake periods since that dreadful experience with the survey party. Ix and the navigator had returned to find the camp almost completely evacuated, with only the command pod standing by. As soon as the two of them came bolting out of the undergrowths, one of Advisor One's assistants helped them on board and they cast off. They were only a few armlengths away from the shore, still scrambling over the top of the hull when those terrible drums had sounded through the column growths. Ix had glanced up and seen dozens of red-clad barbarians running toward them, readying their projectile weapons. At that point the pod had begun the dive sequence immediately. The men had jammed into the airlock and closed the hatch, but not before a considerable amount of Plasma had flowed in around the edges.

Advisor One had been visibly relieved. It occurred to Ix that after having lost one son he had purposely waited longer than was prudent for Ix's return. The big salvager (who Ix heard later was named Oke) had been there, and sencho was bedded down. Their reports had painted a hopeless picture that Ix and Mag probably would not get out of there alive, but Advisor One had waited just the same. To their joy they found Hord the pilot alive and well, but were saddened by the news that Smash, Sal, and all the other members of the crew had been killed. Sencho also passed away only two wake periods later. Overall the battle had been a terrible loss and the numbers of men in the teams that had participated in the survey party had been greatly reduced. Still, owing to their sacrifice the rest of the expedition members had been warned and were evacuated.

The expedition vessels had regrouped in a subterranean cavity, where the thick crust that formed the deck uplifted out of the Plasma to form a spacious air pocket. Though scattered with the massive boles of the column formations, the cavity had had plenty of room to port all their vessels. Many of the men had been crying for their lost crewmates and friends. For two wake periods afterwards they had remained in port and had held a mourning period, during which time the leaders had gotten together and discussed the status of the expedition. Ix and the others were called several times to give their accounts of the battle, and relay what they had learned. As soon as the mourning period had ended, the crews had been put to work constructing floating docks in the cavity. Portable corpuscle nets were stretched between columns and a semi secure base had been established. They were all lucky to be alive.

Ix was awakened from his daydreaming by another guard who had come to relieve him. He quickly rose to his feet and made his way back to report. To get from the outer stockade where he had performed his guard duty to the central command platform he had to cross a maze of catwalks and footbridges. There were close to a dozen or so platform stockades, each built around the massive boles of the huge column formations. Constructed of the same material as the columns, the round platforms were well shielded from below.

Ix made his way across a catwalk bridge. It was triangular in section, with one side of the triangle forming the floor and the other two sides meeting overhead. Diagonal braces zigzagged along on both sides of the entire length to form a huge three-dimensional truss. Every rod used in its structure was held together by rope lashings. Two crewmen were working on this one, replacing some of the shielding matter that had broken loose. The barbarians below had developed a heckling tactic, where one of their marksmen would launch a sharp projectile and strike the bindings of the shielding. Their purpose was to try to weaken the lashings. The severed bindings would then unravel a little at a time when jostling occurred during normal foot traffic along the bridge. If the bindings were not replaced quickly, the shielding would be compromised and the men exposed to fire.

Ix wandered through several platforms and across as many footbridges before he finally arrived at the central command platform. Other men were coming and going, and there was a large crowd waiting to talk to the officer in charge of intelligence reports. Ix took a seat on one of the crudely formed benches that lined the stockade wall and waited his turn. Just as he sat down, a man walking by stumbled and nearly fell in Ix's lap. He quickly recovered himself and went on his way after apologizing. Having tripped and stumbled himself countless times in the last few wake periods, Ix knew it was the uneven floor that was to blame. Long lengths of rod harvested from the fibrous material of the column formations had been split in two with the halves turned upward in an attempt to make a flat surface. Since the splitting process was at the mercy of the direction of the grain in the material itself, the surface wasn't entirely flat but left edges and ridges turned up all over the place. Their dwelling wasn't exactly the most comfortable, but at least it was safe.

Ix's eyes followed the line made by the slats of deck material all the way until they ran into the massive column itself. The side he was sitting on happened to be the side that opened onto the riser shaft. When Ix and the navigator had reported about the breathing holes in the column faces, a couple of the other technicians who were specialists in plant biology went and did some studies of their own. Riding with patrols during the dark sleep periods, they would surface on remote lakes and spend a few moments here and there measuring and cataloging column characteristics. One thing they discovered was that the columns consisted of bundles of fibrous materials growing together to form the walls of a tube. Surrounded by thick walls of structural material, some tubes were quite large in diameter -- up to two armlengths across! Knowing Ix and the navigator had been safe up high during the survey battle, it was Advisor One who first thought of the idea of boring into one of the column formations in their cavity port and seeing if the tubes could be used as a way to climb high above the enemy. The riser shaft on the command platform was one of those tubes that had been transformed into a crude counterweighted elevator. Each of the dozen or so column formations that supported their forts had at least one shaft that was used as either an elevator or had a ladder built into it. Now the expedition members were not only safe above the ground, they also had secure routes to their cavity port below the moss-covered deck.

Ix turned to see that the intelligence officer had come. As he had done so many times before, he reported the numbers and locations of the barbarians below his lookout area. It was very typical, and the numbers of the enemy were not unusual. Ix finished and was about to return to his quarters when the officer stopped him.

"Ix, can you spare some of your rest period? I'm in a crunch looking for volunteers to help bring in some more building material. The barbarians have wreaked havoc on the left side and all of the repair crews are having a rough time keeping up with the shield repair."

They had come up with names for four cardinal directions. Looking ocean ward was the 'ocean' side, with 'inland' direction behind. The other two cardinal directions were 'left side' and 'right side'. Some of the best marksmen of the barbarians seemed to be out on the left side, or at least those savages were more active in heckling the expedition.

Ix replied, "I suppose I can help for a while. Our pod is due to go out on an after dark survey trip so I should get some sleep later on."

"No problem." the officer began, then called over his shoulder to a large character standing behind him in the shadows over by the wall, "Hey here's your fourth hand!"

The large man stepped into the light. It was the big fellow that had been with them during the survey battle. "How are you, Ix?" he asked. Oke had been left an orphan when his entire diving team had been killed during the battle. He had been reassigned to another diving team, which were all busy maintaining the forts in plainclothes when they were not on duty at the port.

"Fine. I see you have recovered well."

The two of them headed ocean side and crossed two bridges. Another pair of volunteers waited there at the stockade wall. Oke pointed to some tools that had been adapted for material gathering: saws, spike cleats, rope, and axes. Each of the men donned a set of cleats and the rest of the tools were split among them. The big man led them to the nearest riser shaft and entered. The opening was rough and narrow, having been hacked and carved away by manual labor. The hacking of the opening had at first caused the area directly above the hole to become weak and unhealthy, but the mineral and moisture-bearing veins that had been temporarily severed had naturally rerouted themselves and the fibrous material was heading for recovery. The raw edges of the carved-out passage were recovering as well, much as a wound heals itself on the human body. The passage led horizontally for a couple of armlengths before it intersected with the vertical tube. The shaft was another couple of armlengths across. Directly above the opening, block and tackle had been anchored to the fibrous wall, with rope dangling into the darkness below.

The big man didn't go down in the direction of the port but started climbing. Anchored to the wall every few handwidths or so was a ladder rung which had been fashioned out of the same fibrous material that the column formations were made of. All the expedition members were enamored with the material because of its strength and ease of use. It was truly a convenient building material.

Ix and the rest of the men followed Oke up the ladder. The climb was long and arduous. Fortunately, the tube narrowed slightly as they got higher and the men were able to lean with their backs against the rear wall of the shaft to rest. Unfortunately it got narrower and narrower until it was difficult to bend their knees without hitting them on the next step. Just when Ix thought he could go no farther they came across another opening to the outside. This passage was shorter than the one below due to the thinner tube wall. The passage opened up onto a platform that had been built in a crotch where the column growth split into several separate branches. The branches all continued upward, but gradually fanned out away from each other. In addition to the thicker branches like the one they just emerged from, numerous thin branches also split off in various places, some of them no thicker than a man' s arm. It was these small branches that they were to harvest and bring with them back to the stronghold decks below.

Ix was overwhelmed by the beauty and overcome by the height. He had never imagined it was possible for people to get so high. He thought back on a theory of his about different inhospitable strata with man sandwiched between. This peaceful environment didn't fit into those crushing depths below or the raging storms above. He couldn't imagine a mythical Creature of the Deep or thrash tide terrorizing this idyllic landscape with quakes and tremors.

In the vicinity of the platform many of the thinner branches had been harvested already. Oke instructed them that they should only take every other branch that was of a certain size, and leave the rest. The biology technicians had warned them that the column growths were living things and that there may be a point past which they can no longer heal themselves. The four men worked in pairs, belaying each other in turns as they climbed up from one crotch to another. They finally reached a spot that hadn't been picked over and set about to work. Since Ix had no experience at material harvesting, he hugged close to one of the big branches and belayed for the big diver as he went about doing his job. First Oke would attach an anchor through the base of the branch and tie a line to it, then he would saw off the branch below the anchor. After sawing part way through, the weight of the branch would cause it to sag until it snapped off with a loud crack. He would reel in the dangling branch and cut it into manageable lengths before collecting them into a bundle that he tucked into the crotch of two larger branches.

All Ix could do to help was to belay his partner as he climbed out to spine-tingling overhangs, and watch the man work. It was when Oke had completed the second branch that Ix began to notice something strange. There was a glint of light behind a knot of branches as if some metallic object were caught there. Ix stared at the object but could not see it clearly enough to discover what it was. Sometime after he began paying attention to it, he was startled when it moved. Ever so slowly the object crept over to one side and passed behind a large branch. Ix followed the object's last trajectory with his eyes and sure enough, it emerged from the other side and came to a rest a little ways above the spot where his partner was working. Though it was still mostly obscured, Ix could see that parts of it were cylindrical in shape with complicated objects attached. It was definitely metal.

Suddenly the object emerged from its hiding place and floated out over the great void between column growths, to stop only a couple of armlengths or so behind the big diver. It floated in the air without any support at all! Ix didn't know what to do. He had never seen such a thing before. He just stared wide-eyed at the floating machine and watched as some of its parts telescoped in and out or spun around in some complicated way.

Without warning a loud clap sounded as a blinding arc shot from the front of the machine, erratically zigzagging through the air, and struck the big diver in the back. Ix was so startled he almost dropped the rope. Fortunately he did not, for Oke cried out and lost his hold on the branch to fall helpless. Ix frantically brought the rope down between his legs to prevent it from reeling out due to the weight of the man. He wondered what would happen next and cautiously refrained from moving. The floating machine remained motionless with various attached devices telescoping, spinning, or whirring. After a moment or two the other two workers climbed over to where they were to see what all the commotion was about. Seeing the big diver doubled over dangling at the end of the rope with the strange machine floating motionless out over the void the two could do nothing but stare wide-eyed at the scene. Then as suddenly as it had appeared, the machine spun around and was off with blinding speeds.

The three men looked at each other with curious expressions. As soon as they got their wits together they went to work trying to get the big diver to a safe place. The man had temporarily lost consciousness but began stirring again, moaning with pain. Ix and the other two succeeded in lowering him to the platform below them and began examining his wounds. Oke's clothes had burn marks surrounding a ragged hole, and the exposed skin was already developing blisters. They quickly dressed the wounds and helped him enter the riser shaft. He recovered enough to climb down by himself, but Ix tied a rope around his waist just in case. The three managed to get him safely to the stronghold deck below.

When they arrived at the fort, crowds of men were gathered along the stockade, intently peering through peepholes at some scene outside. Ix left Oke in the hands of the other two and went to see what had grabbed their attention.

"What are you guys watching?" he asked the nearest man.

The man backed away from his peep hole for a moment and turned to see who had asked. He said, "There are strange floating machines hovering out yonder" and turned back to the hole. Ix found a hole for himself and looked out between the great column formations. It only took a moment before he was able to spot two of the same machines that had attacked the diver earlier.

Ix said loudly in a voice everyone could hear, "Those things are lethal! One of them just attacked one of our men!"

The whole crowd turned almost in unison to stare at the four.

"This man needs medical attention. He's been badly burned."

Needless to say, Ix never got the sleep he had hoped for before his survey trip. They escorted Oke to the command platform and Ix spent the rest of the time describing what he had seen and making detailed reports. More and more of the strange machines were being spotted out among the column growths, but there was only the one incident of actual attack. The whole fort was put on the alert and men were required to keep weapons handy. They had a team of men distilling baku juice and constructing small bombs with fuses that could be lit on a moment's notice. The bombs were distributed throughout the stronghold.

About the time Ix usually rested in the sleep period, he found himself descending the riser shaft to the port cavity. The natural tube of the riser shaft presumably continued to who knows what depth, but a small platform had been constructed over the hole at dock level. Ix emerged out onto the dock and strode over to their pod.

Their assignment was to explore the underside of the floating crust, and survey any cavities that they might find. *The Island* was fast approaching on its slow course through the stormy seas and Lord Ruk was hoping to look into the possibility of using the cavity ports and lofty fort constructions as permanent colonies for the rest of their people.

The Pilot and navigator were with him as well, and one of the smaller diving teams had been assigned to fill in for the missing crewmembers. Hord had been promoted to sencho. Ix could not get used to calling him by the title 'sencho', so he ended up just saying 'Pilot Sencho'. Even though he dreaded working through the sleep period, the fact that there were only three original crew members left meant that Ix would be fit into the piloting assignment rotation. Ix grinned inside as he thought how the unusualness of the events associated with the expedition had opened up a door he thought he would never be able to enter. He was going to enjoy being a pilot! The diving team had been given the assignment to perform the survey activities, so the three crewmen needed to double and triple up on their onboard responsibilities.

When everyone had boarded, Mag and Pilot Sencho were doing their best to cover the communications seat, which left the first piloting assignment to Ix. Though he was looking forward to the assignment he approached the pilot chair with apprehension. His only experience at piloting had been in open Plasma, without any docks or column formations to run into. As he passed the navigator's seat, he noticed the dials were starting to disagree with each other. It gave him a start -- that was a sure sign the thrash tide was approaching the neighborhood somewhere below them. With the needles unreliable he would have to guide the craft mostly with dead reckoning following the Pilot Sencho's experienced hand.

Recalling the thrash tide, there was something about his recent experience helping Oke gather construction material that triggered his memory. Ix sat down in the chair and fastened the webbing over himself, deep in thought. Pilot Sencho walked him through the steps, and Ix succeeded in firing up the thrusters. What connection could there possibly be between Oke and the thrash tide? Oke had been doubled over on the end of a rope as he waited for his companions to get him over to a safe spot on the column growth. Quakes -- it had to do with quakes, and the thrash tide.

Very slowly, Ix jockeyed the thrusters in such a way as to shimmy away from the dock a few armlengths. So-far-so-good. Pilot Sencho gave the order to dive, and Ix opened up the ballast valves until they had sunk below the surface.

The commander ordered, "Shut those valves quickly or we'll sink faster than a piece of metal!"

Ix shut the valves, but did not quite get it right and the craft listed slightly to one side.

"Compensate, compensate!" Pilot Sencho called out from behind.

For an instant Ix hesitated, not knowing whether to flush Plasma from the heavy side, or open the valve on the light side.

Hord sensed his indecision and explained, "The choice is yours, Ix. One or the other will do the trick. The thing you will have to worry about is whether the decision brings equilibrium or not. You may have to readjust later."

Ix chose to let out a bit of air from the lighter side. The craft began sinking ever so slowly so he went back the other way and slightly lightened up the ballast tanks. Since Pilot Sencho was waiting for the go-ahead from the port crew (they were parting the corpuscle netting), Ix had plenty of time to get the equilibrium right. When the order finally came, Ix simply used the hand sticks and pedals as he had learned for roll, pitch, and yaw and slowly powered the craft into a shallow dive toward the opening in the netting. With all the obstacles around that could be collided with Ix felt a little nervous, but he was doing a better job than he thought he would. He looked down into the depths between the long roots of the columns and thought about the thrash tide, and whatever the massive thing was that traveled below it. *You're down there somewhere*, he thought, *what are you*? Ix found himself veering off to the left toward a column and corrected the vessel a little too quickly, jostling the crew around a bit.

"Sorry!" he apologized, but went on to do the same thing several times more.

Quakes. Quakes and thrash tide and Oke… Suddenly it became clear. A body supported by a single point would tend to bend. The quakes were not caused by something ramming the foundations -- they were simply the result of the massive structure of *The Continent* riding over the bulge! If the Plasma ocean mounded up so tightly, of course the center of the floating structure would be supported, but the edges would tend to sag, producing tremendous stress.

Ix was ecstatic about this new revelation as the Pilot Sencho guided them toward the region they were assigned to survey, which was ocean side from the base. He was painfully aware that the region was where Mox had lost his life. They worked their way over to the left side edge of the region and began mapping all the air pockets and cavities. Pilot Sencho only had Ix surface in the cavities that appeared high and wide enough for the big transport pods to port. They approached some of the lesser pockets, but at Hord's discretion they moved on. Ix started feeling more confidence as he got better and better at piloting. After surveying six cavities, the commander relieved Ix and had him take a nap.

Ix slept for a while and then wandered back into the bridge. They had discovered an unusually large cavity and Pilot Sencho was bringing the vessel to the surface. Ix moved just behind him in the bubble cockpit to watch the ascent. They broke the surface and spun the craft around to get a preliminary view of the space. This particular cavity was quite unusual. It was long and wide and instead of merely being a blister in the thick crust, there appeared to be some sort of natural shelf or beach running the entire length of the cavern. The place was a natural for a good port.

The diving team rushed up on deck with Ix in tow. The team hancho operated the spotlights and swept them back and forth along the shelf as Hord drew the craft closer. At the last instant Pilot swung the pod sideways and it glided gently to the beach. Ix released a couple of stakes from their clips and hopped onto the natural shelf. He and one of the divers kept the fore and aft pod tethers taught until the stakes could be driven into the soft material of the beach for anchorage.

While Ix was busy with the stakes, the other divers disembarked and fanned out to start the survey. "Hey look at this!" One of them was pointing his torch down not far from the anchorage.

The rest of the men came running, and Ix followed to see what the man had found. There were footprints. Ix noted the unmistakable pattern of diver's boots!

"Are you sure one of us didn't step here?" the hancho asked.

The diver who discovered the prints shone his torch up and down the beach and said, "No, it couldn't have been us. These prints track back and forth up there and back here as well."

Just then Pilot Sencho climbed down off the pod and made his way over to where the men were gathered. Ix asked, "Has this place been surveyed already? There are diver tracks over here."

"This is the first time any of our men have come to this region." the commander replied.

Nevertheless after studying the footprints, Pilot Sencho had to admit that some team must have been there before them. He made the decision to survey the cavity anyway, since it was their responsibility to cover every promising place in the region. Duplicate reports were none of his concern. Pilot Sencho climbed back on deck with the dive team hancho and set up a survey command center. The rest of the dive team, including Ix, split up to do a preparatory search of the cavern.

Since Ix was not qualified as a diver, he was selected to explore the shelf to the left. One of the divers went to the right, and the rest of the men dove into the Plasma.

Ix took his torch and followed the diver footprints. The shelf was quite wide, varying from perhaps four to ten armlengths. To his left was open Plasma, and a vertical wall bound the right. Ix approached the end of the cavity, but the shelf ran into a natural tunnel of sorts. Continuing along the tunnel, Ix discovered what seemed to be a spot where the tunnel opened up wide with leaves and foliage drooping down from above. He stood under the leaves and shone his torch ahead. There were massive boles of the column formations and moss-covered deck in between. The diver's tracks continued out into the darkness. When Ix shone his torch upward to discover the height of the place he realized the columns continued to a tremendous height without any ceiling to be found. He was topside again -- the tunnel had connected the cavern with the surface.

Just then he heard screaming from behind him. Ix turned and rushed back down the tunnel along the shelf, past where the pod was anchored and on to the other end where the second man had gone to explore. The screaming had died down, and when he passed the pod he noticed that both Pilot Sencho and the hancho had also gone there to see what was the matter.

As he ran he could see beams from the torches flashing back and forth along the shelf. Ix approached the scene with caution. What could have set the man screaming like that? There was a terrible smell that he instinctively knew: the smell of death. Had corpuscles finally come ashore, against what everyone had assumed? With that thought Ix shied away from the Plasma edge and hugged the wall. Looking ahead, he could see the other's beams illuminate objects lined up along the wall. He was still too far away to make out what they were.

All of a sudden his light beam struck the figure of a man sitting up against the wall only armlengths in front of him. His heart pounded as he realized that the man was wearing the blood-red armor of the barbarians. Long red-dyed hair flowed down his shoulders. Ix jumped back and held his torch squarely on the figure, waiting for an inevitable attack. The barbarian didn't move. His head was slung down with his chin on his chest, such that only the wild shock of blood-red hair could be seen. Was he asleep? Ix moved closer a footstep at a time until he stood directly in front of the barbarian. When nothing happened he reached down and grabbed a handful of red hair, intending to lift the head up so that he may see the man's face.

The thing that happened next caused Ix to cry out in shock. The hair came away in clumps and exposed a white surface of bare bone. The entire head came loose from the body and rolled to Ix's feet: a gray-white skull staring up at him with those empty sockets. Ix backed away and almost fell into the Plasma. He just stood there on the edge for a long time afraid to move a muscle.

The next thing he realized was that Hord had his arm around his shoulder and was walking him back to the scene. Ix braced himself for the gory sight.

Pilot Sencho soothingly said, "Ix, stay with me boy. I need you to stay with me. Calm down and let's get this over with."

The two of them walked back over to where the fallen barbarian corpse leaned against the wall. Pilot Sencho shone his torch to the right and revealed another dead barbarian in full armor, his mostly decomposed eye sockets peering out from under a blood-red helmet. Pilot Sencho pointed to the barbarian's chest.

"You see that? Aren't those the same burn marks your big diver friend got from the floating machines?" he asked.

Ix looked at the burn marks that had pierced the armor. "Yes, it looks the same."

Pilot Sencho gently walked Ix farther along the wall. There were more figures leaned against the wall. Ix held back a gasp as he realized that each of the skeletons had on standard diver's suits! The corpses were riddled with barbarian's arrows, and their suits were torn in some places.

"Now take a look at this." Pilot Sencho said as he guided Ix to a small spit at the very end of the shelf. Another decomposed corpse lay there, next to the remains of a campfire. The corpse had a dark stained bandage around the forehead of the skull, and the suit was torn badly on the leg and an arm, but there were no arrows. "This guy was alive for a while and must have died from that head injury. By the looks of things, there's still one of our guys wandering around out there alive! What do you think Ix? You think a survey team got ambushed here?"

Ix did not answer. He had moved to the side of the dead diver and was inspecting the nametag above the right breast. Tears came to his eyes.

Pilot Sencho went over and kneeled down beside him. "What's the matter?"

Ix waited a long time and finally answered, "This was no survey team. This was a diving team from the wrecked transport!"

Pilot Sencho looked confused. "Why do you say that? No one could have gotten out of there alive!"

Ix pointed to the dead man and the nametag, tears welling up in his eyes, "That's my twin brother Mox!"

CHAPTER 13

Blujic sat on a small lump of ground with her feet dangling in the clear fresh water pond. She was so thrilled to have finally made it to the *Origin* in the Flesh that she forgot all about the wild experiences evading the Inmates. This valley was so peaceful and sacred that all her troubles seemed to melt away in insignificance. She knew she would feel this way before ever setting eyes on the place. After having visited the *Origin* so many hundreds of times in the rocker, she expected the Flesh to be so much more exquisite. Even the Inmates held the valley in reverence and seemed to have some taboo about entering it. Blujic never felt so safe and secure in her entire life.

Blujic looked back over her shoulder at the curved rise of the *Origin*. She wanted to take her time here and look in every nook and cranny. Even if the Database locked out entry into its interior, she could not imagine being precluded from enjoying its most secret inner parts now.

In the excitement of the moment, Blujic began singing a song. It was an old song, with many verses. She knew it well, and some of her favorite verses inspired her as they did all Wardens. Blujic wasn't exactly proud of her voice, but being out here in the Flesh she felt no inhibitions at singing out loud, a thing she would never have done in front of anyone. Blujic got quite caught up in the song.

It wasn't until she had gotten halfway through the seventh verse that she had the distinct impression that she was being watched. Someone else was here! Blujic abruptly stopped singing and froze. The feeling was a little spooky. What if some of the Inmates had come? Slowly her eyes panned the far banks of the pond, searching for any sign of movement.

Then she heard a sound coming from directly behind her! It could have been the sound of a footfall a few armlengths back. Blujic was frozen with fear. Should she make a mad dash and try to run for it? She wanted to turn around and see what was behind her so bad it hurt. Still, perhaps the intruder hadn't seen her and any sudden movement on her part would bring their attention to her. She heard another footstep, and another. It sounded like someone tiptoeing, trying to mask the sound of passage.

It seemed like she sat there frozen for eons until she couldn't stand it anymore. In one swift motion Blujic stood up and spun around to face the intruder. Shock! There was a completely naked young man not ten armlengths away, with all his natural equipment hanging out in the breeze for anyone to see. The man was facing to her left in the classic tiptoe stance, partly bent over with arms winging out to the sides for balance. Obviously he was trying to pass behind her without being detected. Blujic brought both of her palms to her cheeks and screamed with all her might. The scream startled the man, and he jumped up with a genuinely embarrassed look on his face: the look of having gotten caught doing something extremely shameful. The young man in turn let out a yell of surprise.

Blujic and the young man faced each other and screamed and yelled.

Suddenly the young man started running towards her! Blujic was so startled that she couldn't scream anymore. All she could do was stand there with her palms plastered against her face and watch him approach, natural equipment flapping back and forth and all. The man veered around her and headed straight for the pond. Blujic turned as he passed and watched him take a big dive into the water, his great big white-bleached buttocks completely exposed until the moment the water enclosed them. The young man swam with all his might until he reached an outcropping on the far side and disappeared behind it.

Blujic didn't know what to think. She stood there wide eyed for a long time, watching the outcropping with her palms still pressed against her cheeks framing her mouth and chin. She had never seen a naked man before. What was he doing out here? Blujic finally sat back down on the lump, still looking out towards the outcropping. She had to sort out her feelings and the events of the past few moments. One thing was sure, she no longer felt threatened by some unknown intruder. In fact, she almost felt like a monster for putting that poor young man through such an embarrassing experience. Blujic remembered that instant when the young man had had that fearful look on his face. But who was he? He certainly didn't look like an Inmate. He was tall and dark with jet-black hair and almond eyes. All she could think of were those eyes widening in that instant of discovery. No Warden had features like that. She had never heard of anyone who looked like that. All in all he seemed quite young and even handsome. Blujic guessed his age to be similar to hers if not slightly older. Why would a naked young man be tiptoeing around?

Though keeping one eye on the outcropping, Blujic started looking around for some hint as to what the young man might have been up to. It was then that she noticed the clothes spread out neatly to dry in the sun. Perhaps the young man had been bathing and washing his clothes. Blujic tried to work out a scenario that fit the facts. First the man had been alone and had found a peaceful private place to bathe. He washed his clothes and laid them out to dry, then went to bathe himself. Suddenly a girl unexpectedly comes along and he has to hide. Blujic looked over at the growths that were in the opposite direction from where the young man was heading when they had startled each other. He must have been hiding over there. Continuing with the scenario, Blujic mused that the young man must have waited patiently and had decided that the girl would never stop singing, so he would have to sneak over and get his clothes behind her back. There! That seemed reasonable enough. It didn't answer the question of where he had come from, but it seemed like a plausible explanation for why he had been out there naked.

Blujic made a quick glance over to the outcropping. Seeing that the young man was still hiding, she strode over to where the clothes were laid out. She picked up one of the now dry garments and felt it in her hands. The material felt very smooth and well made. There was none of the crudeness of the Inmate's clothes. Blujic stroked the material and held it up to her cheek as she turned to look toward the outcropping. Maybe he was a strong and gentle man! The more she thought about it, the more she felt badly at having embarrassed him. Blujic promptly sat down on the ground and began folding the clothes. The largest garment was thick and of a strange appearance. There was a series of pockets that contained instruments of some sort and tiny metal studs woven into the fabric. Blujic sang as she worked, and somehow didn't feel self-conscious about her voice anymore. Once or twice she looked up toward the outcropping and spied the young man's dark head peeking at her over the top. He would immediately duck down again when he noticed that she was looking. Blujic smiled inside and purposely resisted the temptation to look up. *He's looking at me*, she thought.

When the clothes were all neatly folded, Blujic took the pile in her arms and strode down to the water's edge. Looking toward the outcropping, she confirmed that the young man was still hiding.

"Hello! I have your clothes here!" Blujic called out toward the outcropping.

She waited a while but there was no response.

Again she called out, "I'm sorry to have embarrassed you! Here's your clothes all folded up nice!"

Again there was no response. Then it dawned on her that he was probably still embarrassed and would continue hiding while she was still looking. Quickly Blujic looked around and spotted the growths that she had seen earlier, that she had surmised was the place he had been hiding. She took the neatly folded pile of clothes around to the other side of the growths and set it down in the grass. Then she walked back around and sat down on the lump. She crossed her legs and propped up her chin on her elbow and faced away from the outcropping and growths. After a long while she noticed out of the corner of her eye something moving in the middle of the pond. He was swimming across to where she had put the pile of clothes. Blujic turned and peeked toward the pond and saw the young man's head bobbing up and down, his arms moving in clean strong strokes at a surprising speed. He *is* strong! She quickly turned back away before he could see that she was looking at him and started singing again. Out of the corner of her eye she saw him get out of the water and jump behind the growths. She could see glimpses of him behind the growths as he rushed to throw his clothes on. While he was dressing she dared to peek over in that direction a few times, but was otherwise careful to act as though she was looking around at the scenery.

By the time she had gotten to the end of the song, she noticed that there was no more movement on the other side of the growths and was sure that he was watching her. She straightened her back a little and started combing her long blonde hair, starting in on another song. She didn't feel herself to be overly attractive, but wasn't ashamed of her looks either. She suddenly had the strongest urge to be as beautiful as she could possibly be.

After a while Blujic got a thought. She took off her backpack and pulled out some manufactured chocolate bars. She didn't have too much food left, but thought that if she could offer some to the young man, perhaps they could become friends or something. Blujic's heart swelled at the idea, and she promptly walked over near the bushes.

"Hello sir. I have some food here. Do you want some?" She held up the bars where she knew he could see them.

Since there was no immediate response, Blujic removed one of the bars from its wrapper and started eating it. Between bites she said, "See, it's really good! Here's one for you, too."

There was a stirring in the bushes and reluctantly the young man emerged. Blujic backed over to the lump and sat down, still holding out the manufactured chocolate toward him. Shyly, the young man followed her and sat down on the ground a few armlengths away. Blujic leaned over and handed him the chocolate. The young man would not look up at first so she could not get a good look at his face. He bowed his head and first tasted the chocolate before eagerly devouring it in no time.

"My name's Blujic. I'm a Warden."

There was no response so Blujic continued to talk.

"We always use the rockers to go everywhere, but I like being in the Flesh. This is my first time here. Do you live here?"

She looked up at the man and for an instant he looked at her. He blushed and looked away. In that instant Blujic remembered those eyes as he had stood there naked and recalled his appearance then. She blushed herself.

Blujic waited only a moment or so before continuing, "I love this place. The *Origin* is so peaceful and quiet. Are there any others like you here?"

The young man finished the chocolate but continued to sit there, sometimes giving quick glances in Blujic's direction. He seemed to be at ease and the embarrassment was wearing off.

Blujic uncharacteristically began to ramble on about many things, "I got away from the Inmates coming here. Are you an Inmate? You sure don't look like an Inmate. You look really nice and civilized compared to those savages. What's it like inside the *Origin*? Can I go inside, too? Do you know if there are any cute little animals around?"

Sometime during Blujic's monologue, the young man attempted to say something. At first Blujic didn't hear it so she continued to talk. When the young man repeated the words, Blujic stopped and give him her full attention.

"Saki no fudo mata eeto dekiru kai?" he said.

"What did you say?"

"Saki no kureta fudo mada havu no kai?"

Blujic looked puzzled, "I don't understand what you are saying. Is that Inmate speech?"

The young man held up the wrapper of the chocolate and pointed to it. He said, "disu disu!"

"Oh, you're asking if there is any more?"

Blujic reached for her pack and dumped the contents on the ground. There was one other block of manufactured food (not chocolate), a blanket, and a few small personal effects. The young man picked up the block of food and looked at it, gave it a sniff, and put it back down. He was obviously disappointed.

"I'm sorry. I didn't intend to be out here this long. I still don't know what I'll do tomorrow for food. I don't know what I'll do on my way back." Blujic made the motion of eating while pointing at the young man, shrugged her shoulders and said, "Do you have any food?"

He answered an unintelligible, "Boku mo havu na." and shrugged his shoulders as well.

The young man stood up and looked around. He started gathering branches of shrubs and dried moss. Blujic watched him do his work and smiled. After having obtained an armful, he came back and stood in front of her.

"disu ike nan mo ne-e. Obadea nara fudo gozaru."

He walked off and trudged over the bank that protected the little freshwater pond. Blujic had no idea what he was saying, but followed him over the rise. He led her to the shore of one of the large Plasma lakes. The young man proceeded to arrange the matter he had collected into a circle and used a technique to suspend it off the flammable ground surface. He then began to light it on fire. Blujic watched, fascinated at his skill. Soon there was a small fire going, and the man went to gather up more chunks of bare ground and branches. After he had made several trips he stacked the wood on the ground and turned to Blujic.

"Kimi, hi wo yare." He said, but she could not understand what he meant.

The young man picked up a chunk and tossed it on the fire, then motioned for Blujic to do the same. Blujic started to pick up piece after piece and add it to the fire until he stopped her, waving his hand back and forth in a clear 'no'. Then he took one branch and put it on the fire, after which he sat back on his heels and folded his arms as though he were waiting. Then he added another and exaggerated the fact that he was waiting again.

"Oh, I see! You want me to put one on just now and then!" Blujic was ecstatic at having understood what he was saying.

The young man motioned 'yes, you're right' and immediately jumped up and dove into the Plasma lake. Blujic was a little surprised, and began to get somewhat concerned. The Plasma lakes had fearsome creatures swimming in them and she wasn't sure if the young man knew that or not. What if he were killed? Blujic had just met a wonderful friend and she couldn't bear to lose him so soon. She periodically put a piece of wood on the fire, but continuously paced back and forth on the shore looking down into the depths. As the time grew longer, she began to worry that he perhaps had drowned. No one could stay under Plasma that long in the Flesh! Blujic sat down cross-legged by the fire and started to cry. It was all so pointless! Though she had just met him that afternoon, oh how she wanted to see that boy again!

Blujic was startled when something touched her shoulder. She looked up and wiped the tears from her eyes. The young man was back safe! He reached out and touched her cheek with his fingertips, a look of concern on his face.

When she smiled at him he smiled back and pointed to several swimmers he had caught in the depths. Blujic suddenly realized that this was his world and that he had been diving for food that he wanted to share with her.

The late afternoon sun was beginning to set. In Blujic's grief she had let the fire go down to coals so the young man spent the next few moments building it up again. He took the swimmers, gutted them, impaled them through the mouth with a straight stick, and drove the stick into the ground at an angle in order to get as much exposure to the heat of the fire. Blujic watched him as he worked. Every once in a while he would look up at her and smile, whereupon she would smile back at him.

By the time the swimmers were ready, the sun had already gone behind the hills. It was getting dark and lonely out on that valley floor, but Blujic felt wonderful in those beautiful settings. The colorful sunset reflected off the surface of the Plasma and a slight breeze was blowing. The faint light of the flames illuminated the young man's face as he taught her how to eat the swimmer by holding onto its tail with one hand and the stick with the other. She gave it a try and found the taste to be naturally salty and quite wonderful. Both of them ate their fill.

It had been an exhausting day and Blujic was quite happy. In the light of the moons she began to sing a song for the young man. He listened to her sing and appeared enthralled by her voice. As she went through several verses, he picked up on the tune and began humming along with her and swaying with the rhythm. When she finished her song he started singing one of his own and they both entertained each other for quite some time. The young man appeared interested in the first song she had been singing when she had caught him naked by the fresh water pond. He hummed a few notes of it for her as if to request her to sing it again and again. Blujic happily obliged and by the end of the evening had almost taught him some of the phrases in her favorite verses.

It was getting late and there were only three moons out. Blujic began to worry about where she would sleep. It would be too much to ask the young man to stay with his family or people or whatever (for some reason she assumed that he lived inside the *Origin*). They developed a simple sign language between them, and she told him she had to go by pointing at her own self and motioning toward the hill in the darkness. He shrugged his shoulders, which was their universal question sign, and she interpreted him as asking why she had to go. She put both of her palms together and pressed her head against them in mock sleep, which he appeared to understand. It took a while, but she managed to communicate to him that she would be back tomorrow. When he understood that she would be back he smiled and nodded his head. She waved good-bye and trudged into the darkness.

Blujic didn't go far. She skirted around the lakes at the floor of the valley and found a small knoll from which she could view the fire. She lay down in the plush grass and pulled the blanket over her body. She turned over on her side and fell asleep watching the young man pace around the flames.

The next morning Blujic woke up with a peaceful feeling in her heart. Though she couldn't remember the details, she was sure she had dreamed about the young man the night before, and the dreams had been pleasant. Blujic quickly folded up her blanket and stuffed it in her pack. After making sure no one was around she went down to the water's edge (it was a similar fresh water pond to the one they had been at yesterday), and bathed herself as quickly as she could manage. She used the reflection of the smooth water surface as a mirror and fixed her hair up nice. When she knew things were just right, she got her things and headed over to the first pond.

From the top of the bank Blujic could see the entire pond, as well as the massive wall of the *Origin* beyond. Since she could not see the young man anywhere, she smiled and headed back over to the lump of ground matter she had sat on yesterday and began singing his favorite song again. This time she faced the *Origin* instead of the pond. Sure enough, it didn't take long before the young man came stumbling down from the *Origin* and walked to her side. He smiled at her as she sang and she smiled back. He listened intently to her voice and hummed along in places. When she finally finished, the young man held his hand out to her. She welcomed his touch, and reached out to grasp his hand. The young man sat on the ground beside her and they held each other's hands for a long time without saying a thing, looking into each other's faces. She had never touched a boy before in the Flesh.

Blujic studied his face intently. There was nothing unattractive about it at all. Everything about him pleased her. She reached out with her free hand and followed her fingers along his brow and down the side of his face. He ran his fingers through her hair and seemed to admire it greatly. The young man smiled at her once more and looked out over the pond, his arm still resting on her shoulder.

Blujic remembered the last bar of manufactured food and brought it out from her backpack. After she had peeled away the wrapper, the two of them took turns taking bites out of it. The young man wasn't nearly as excited about the food bar as he had been about the chocolate, but he ate it nevertheless. Blujic couldn't blame him, since she wasn't too crazy about the stuff, either. She had brought only the blocks she had thought were the best tasting, or that would give her quick energy in her travels.

Blujic looked at the boy and said, "My name is Blujic."

The young man just looked back at her with a puzzled look on his face.

"Me. Blujic. Blujic." she continuously pointed at her own chest and repeated her name.

The young man also pointed at her chest and asked, "Blujic?".

"Yes, Blujic. What is your name?" Blujic pointed to him.

"Boku, boku oboen ne." instead of pointing at his own chest, he pointed at his nose when indicating himself.

"You're Boku? Can I call you Boku?"

"Dame dame! Boku to iu wa-do wa namae ja ne." the young man emphatically waved his arms to the negative. He then pointed to his head and shrugged his shoulders several times. "Oboen ne. Oboen ne da yo."

Blujic was a little puzzled at first but finally realized what he was saying. "You don't remember your name? Well, what shall I call you?"

The young man must have had some kind of accident. She had heard of this thing before, where Wardens in the Flesh had thought they were still in the rockers and had accidentally fallen and bumped their heads. They would forget things like their names for a while and then remember everything later. Blujic motioned to him and made it clear that she was trying to think of something to call him, until he remembered his name. She propped her elbow up on her knee and rested her chin on the palm of her hand. She looked out over the pond in contemplation. The young man also looked out on the lake apparently deep in thought.

"Blujic." he said.

"Yes?" she turned to face him.

"Boku, 'Future' to sei shi-te. Future, Future ga gudo." he pointed to his nose as he repeated it several times.

Blujic countered, "But 'Future' is not a name." She wondered where he had come up with such a word, not knowing her language, then she realized that he was repeating one of the phrases he had learned from the verses of the song. Perhaps 'Future' would be all right. After all, it was only until he remembered his real name. 'Future' had a bright and positive ring to it as well.

"All right, from now on I'll call you 'Future'!"

The young man smiled at her and said, "Future, Future" over and over again.

After a while Future stood up and walked over to the bank. He proceeded to take off his outer garment, which was thick and dark in color. Blujic was a little alarmed at first and remembered back to their little run-in yesterday. She was soon put at ease when he folded the outer garment, set it on the grass, and walked over to the shore with his inner garments still on. Calmly Future dove into the pond. Blujic watched him for a while, noting that he was a natural in the water. She herself had dived the lakes and oceans many times, but always in the rockers. The closest she had come to swimming in the Flesh was wading through waist deep swamps trying to elude pursuing Inmates.

"Blujic, come!" Future called out to her with one of the simple phrases he had learned.

"No, I don't really know how to swim!"

"Come, come!" he persistently called.

Finally Blujic gave in, only on condition that he held her hand and didn't play any pranks. She calmly waded into the water and reached out to grasp his hand. Suddenly he pulled her off her feet and cradled her body in his arms. Blujic let out a gasp and held on to him for dear life. Future carried her through the water, careful to make sure she felt secure and unafraid. After a while he let her legs drop to the bottom while keeping one firm arm around her waist. There really weren't many deep spots in the pond, so Blujic quickly grew in confidence. Soon the two were splashing about, frolicking in the water having the best of times. Future taught her some of the rudimentary steps for skillful swimming and had her practice staying afloat without touching the bottom. Since Blujic had dove in the rockers before, she had none of the natural fear children usually have of large bodies of water, because she knew the submarine world was just as beautiful and scenic and natural as that above the surface (though the sub plasma scenery in the Database was probably fake).

Blujic and Future swam well into the afternoon and had a wonderful time enjoying each other's company. The two of them climbed out of the water all waterlogged and lay side-by-side panting in the grass. They both looked up at the sky and watched the clouds blow lazily by. There were five moons visible, their irregular shapes showing crisply against the deep blue sky. Future studied the sky intently for quite a while with a puzzled look on his face.

"Sheering wa do yatte horudo appu shi-te aru kai?" Future suddenly asked. The first word could have been 'sheering' in Blujic's own language except that the 'r' was heavily rolled.

Blujic shrugged her shoulders indicating that she didn't have the slightest idea what he was trying to ask.

Future took hold of her hand and helped her stand up. He led her to a place where there was no grass and the ground material had worn down into fine particles. Future took a stick and began drawing pictures in the dust. He drew a wide horizontal line that rose at the ends. On the line he drew little pictures that Blujic immediately recognized as representing a forest, the *Origin*, and lakes. The horizontal line was the ground! Next Future drew a wide arc from the left side all the way over to the right side that put the ground, forest, *Origin*, and lakes under a big bubble. On the arc he drew a symbol that Blujic assumed meant the sun, since there were rays of light shining down from it.

Future took the stick and pointed at the ground, "Dekki."

He next pointed at the arc and said, "Sheering."

Finally he circled the area where the arc and ground line met and asked, "Do yatte horudo appu shi-te aru kai?"

Blujic thought for a moment and suddenly realized she understood part of what Future had said. She couldn't believe her ears at first, since some of the words in his language sounded so similar to those in hers. She happily exclaimed, "'Dekki'. That must mean 'deck'! And 'sheering' means 'ceiling'!"

The rest of what he appeared to be asking eluded her for a long time. First of all, even though he was referring to the arc as the ceiling, she thought he was only referring to it metaphorically, such as 'cloud cover' or 'wall of water'. When she finally realized that he was literally thinking that it was a ceiling she was able to put the pieces together and understand the whole question. It sounded incredible, but perhaps it was possible that there could be someone so ignorant as to think that the sky was a literal ceiling. She certainly wouldn't have put it past the Inmates, but Future seemed a little more civilized than that.

"Are you asking how the sky is held up?"

"So! horudo appu, horudo appu!"

"'Horudo appu' means 'hold up'! My how some of our words sound so similar. No, the sky isn't held up by the ground." Blujic replied. Then she took the stick from his hand and began to doctor up the picture a bit. She erased the arc and walked several paces away to draw a circle that she wanted to represent the sun. She drew rays of light as he had, and then drew five other shapes for moons in various places and distances from the ground line. Finally she drew some puffs not too far above the ground that signified clouds. To cap it off, Blujic took Future's hand and walked him over to each symbol, pointing to the actual object in the sky before indicating to the one etched in the dust. At that she made fists and propped them against her waist, extending her elbows outward in a how-about-that stance.

Future stared at the new picture for a long time. He took the stick from Blujic and walked over to the sun symbol, and then proceeded to draw another arc even bigger than the first, enclosing all the shapes. Before he could finish Blujic came over, took the stick away, and crossed out the arc.

"There's no ceiling, Future. No sheering." Blujic used his pronunciation to drive the point home.

Future seemed confused and made indications that without a ceiling, the sun and moons would fall down to the deck. Blujic thought hard and tried to think of a way to explain gravity and orbits, but just couldn't. Finally she settled on a compromise. She picked up a large chunk of ground matter and threw it into the water. The fibrous material floated on the surface and Blujic put the tips of her fingers together and simulated wave action with her arms. The principle wasn't exactly correct, but maybe he would get closer to understanding the truth if he believed that the moons were floating. Future seemed tentatively satisfied with that answer.

The two of them spent the rest of the afternoon talking about all sorts of things and teaching each other words in their respective languages. It was amazing how many of their words had a similar ring to them, and how parts of the languages were so completely foreign. 'eeto' was the same as 'eat', 'fudo' was the same as 'food', and Blujic identified dozens of other parallels. One of the biggest differences in the two languages appeared to be the order of the grammar. Future's language seemed to put the verb last and often left out the subject altogether.

Future built a fire by the Plasma lake and did another late afternoon dive for swimmers. This time Blujic knew he was in little danger of drowning, because he explained to her how his diver's suit worked with built-in gills and all. Future also explained the protection against the horrible creatures that oozed around in the Plasma depths. Blujic waited patiently on the shore, tending the fire and looking forward to his return. The sun set once again leaving a spectacular splash of colors in the sky. Blujic felt warm inside and was almost overwhelmed with the beauty of evening.

Future took much longer than he had the previous night, and it was already getting fairly dark by the time he made his exit from the water. Blujic was a little startled at his approach this time. As the spectacular colors of the sky faded and left only a faint reflection on the surface of the Plasma, Blujic suddenly noticed streaks of bright light coming up from the depths. Looking closer, the streaks took on the appearance of a beam, which erratically swept back and forth, illuminating growths and formations under the Plasma. Blujic followed the beam to a submerged outcropping, behind which the source seemed to be hidden. Presently the source, in the form of a very bright point of light, emerged from behind the outcropping and continued to sweep erratically across the bottom formations. The source of light got closer to where Blujic was waiting on the shore, and finally broke the surface only a few armlengths away. It was Future brandishing a portable torch that was probably a piece of equipment that had been included in the instruments of his diver's suit.

This time Future had caught some of the same type of swimmers as before, but brought up some new types as well. He explained that the new type could only be caught after dark, which is why he was so late getting back. Future prepared all the fish as before, and Blujic helped set them in front of the fire. The two of them sat back and enjoyed the fire, waiting for the swimmers to cook, turning the impaled creatures to get even exposure.

Blujic looked up at the moons and stars in the night sky. Five moons were still there, but three of them had grouped together in a tight knot on the horizon forming a triangle. Blujic gasped as she saw the group of three, and realized that Mother herself was eclipsing them as a set! Each moon had a circular bite taken out of it, which singly would not have been noticeable, but together clearly defined the circular form of Mother's shadow. Such a sight was extremely rare, and Blujic thought how appropriate it was for it to have occurred on this night that was so exciting in so many other ways. The wonder of the eclipse must have showed on her face, for Future followed her line of sight and looked at the moons as well. He was astonished at the sight, for the circle of the shadow indirectly hinted at a fourth shape in the set. Blujic found a clear space by the fire that was covered with dust and took a stick to draw with. First she drew the same diagram they had drawn that afternoon, with the ground line and the objects in the sky. Then she took the ground line and looped it all the way around the bottom of the picture and joined it at the other end, such that it made a circle. Then she made an arrow indicating that the sun had moved to the other side, and redrew the three moons in such a way as to simulate a shadow falling on them.

Future was completely confused. Blujic presumed that the possibility of Mother not being forever flat had never occurred to him. She used all sorts of methods to try to get him to understand, including taking a spherical chunk of ground matter and using her fingers to walk all over (and under) it. She knew exactly what he was thinking, that things on the bottom of such an object would fall down. Somehow she felt he was able to understand at least portions of what she was saying, including the part of the shadow, but whether he was actually buying it she did not know. The roundness of Mother seemed to be hard for him to swallow.

Just when Blujic thought the magic of the moment couldn't be better, a bright light appeared on the horizon and moved slowly and steadily upward in the sky. The *Destiny*!

"Blujic! Sore wa?" Future asked as he pointed toward the moving light.

"That's the *Destiny*! The Wardens came from the *Origin* and will return to the *Destiny*."

The mainstream belief was that Warden's spirits would go there after death, but a certain movement claimed that the Warden race would actually remove from Mother's surface and fly up to the *Destiny*. Blujic had tried several times to journey there while in the rocker. She had flown higher and higher until she looked back and saw Mother as a tiny bubble. Ahead, the *Destiny* was still a bright spot of light. She had feared that she would get lost in the nothingness and not be able to return so she always turned back.

As they had done the previous evening, Future and Blujic enjoyed a wonderful dinner. Future requested his favorite song and he sang some for her. They spent a lot of time learning each other's words, for each of them was eager to be able to communicate with the other without any handicap. During the whole time they held hands and thoroughly enjoyed each other's company.

Blujic got up and danced around the fire. Future was mesmerized by her beautiful figure and the way she leapt and sang. Suddenly he reached out and grabbed her arm and pulled her to him. He didn't quite put his arms around her, but the momentum of him pulling her close to him brought their faces together for an instant, and he kissed her tenderly on the lips. Wow! All sorts of fireworks exploded inside Blujic that she had never felt before. Was this love? She had never been in love before so she couldn't say, but whatever it was, her feelings overwhelmed her and she backed away blushing. From several armlengths away, she stopped and looked back at the young man. Who was he? Why did he affect her so? What were these new feelings she was experiencing? Blujic fell into confusion. She picked up her pack and ran off into the darkness, leaving him standing alone in the pool of illumination generated by the fire.

Blujic curled up on a soft grassy spot and pulled the blanket over her head. She regretted having run away. She wondered what Future thought of her now, after having behaved so childishly. She began feeling a little self-pity, saying to herself how unattractive and foolish she was. The feelings persisted until she slipped into a deep sleep.

Sometime during the night it began to rain. Half asleep, Blujic attempted to use the blanket for protection, until it became soaked through. The persistence of the rain brought her to full wakefulness, whereupon she realized she had to find better shelter. Not far from where she had bedded down, Blujic found some bushes with mostly bare branches and enough space to sit, so she stretched the blanket over the top in the form of a tent. The arrangement kept most of the direct rain off her, but wherever the blanket sagged between branches the liquid seeped through and dripped down like a torrent. Blujic put her back against the trunk and squeezed herself between the pouring leaks in a vain attempt to get comfortable. A miserable battle continued into the night: first she would find a good position and attempt to relax, then the rivulets would shift on top of her and start her squirming again. Somewhere in all that hellish mess she managed to fall asleep once again.

She was flying through the air. She collapsed into a tree, which enveloped her in its branches. Her momentum pulled the branches from the tree. When she tried to get herself untangled the leaves and branches closed in tighter. She couldn't see beyond the leaves. They were shutting out all the light. She was falling into the lake and she couldn't get untangled or manage to see beyond the leaves. She would hit the water soon! The water began to splash around her.

"Blujic!" a voice was calling her.

"Blujic, come!"

Blujic looked around in confusion. It was dark. She sneezed twice and struggled to figure out where she was. She was in reality tangled up in the branches and leaves, sloshing around in the water. She had to get fresh air! Somehow she was able to crawl out from under the bushes and pull her way to freedom. It was dark and rainy so she still couldn't be sure about where she was. Her nose was runny and she sneezed every time she turned her head. Blujic tried to stand up but vertigo spun the world beneath her and she collapsed.

"Blujic, come!" again the voice. It was Future!

"Future..." she weakly replied.

Strong hands reached behind her neck and under her legs. Future lifted her up and began to carry her somewhere. Blujic was still confused and sneezed three times in a row. The rain was pouring down on her face so she repeatedly wiped the moisture from her eyes with her hand. The whole world seemed to be spinning.

"Blujic sreep!" Future said, and somehow she understood it to mean 'sleep' even though it wasn't one of the words they had learned.

Blujic held onto him tightly. With the world spinning she could do nothing but close her eyes and pray. The journey didn't seem too long, although Blujic wasn't in any condition to judge time or distance. All she knew was that one moment they were out in the storm and the next he was laying her down in a dry place by a warm fire. She vaguely remembered looking up and smiling at Future before the whole world spun around and faded into blackness.

CHAPTER 14

Chief Warden Korric stepped into a rocker. After mounting the harness to her tactile suit she gave the command to fire up. The rocker frame slowly dematerialized and she found herself standing on the personal launch station surrounded by a sea of translucent eggs. A slight extension of the body sent her floating into the air above the tops of the other rockers. Below her, figures were barely visible doing various acrobatic feats inside their own cocoon-like spaces. She floated over the bubbles in the direction the markers indicated and entered a long darkened corridor. Ahead there was a light that continued to grow until it became the mouth of the tunnel. Korric emerged onto the apron in broad daylight.

From her right and left a man and woman immediately sped to her side. The man was Secretary Sarnic who was chief officer in charge of physical facilities and the woman was Secretary Kammoc, the leader of the Prison Guard Corps. Trailing behind were three others: Korric's personal assistant, Advisor Herrec, and two staff members. There were several critical issues on the day's agenda, and they all involved the two secretaries.

The small group drifted away from the apron. Korric looked up toward the city skyline. The bright sunlight glinted off the towers of the crystal city in a dazzling display. Many Wardens were out doing their business, crisscrossing the skies between the towers. There seemed to be more out than usual. Korric touched a panel on her harness and faint red bounding boxes only visible to her appeared around many of those flying about. Those were the real ones. Chief Warden Korric didn't have the luxury of playing games with the Database today: she needed to know who was real and who was not. At close range, the bounding boxes had a few lines of text attached, which included the person's name and occupation. With a touch of her control panel, she could choose the content of the displayed information, getting as detailed or thorough as circumstances required. It was privilege of rank.

The group headed toward the Department of Physical Facilities. That was Sarnic's department. Korric thought it best to get that issue out of the way first since it didn't have anything directly to do with Warden security. At the most, she gave it until midmorning, by which time she hoped to assign a lower ranked deputy to the problem.

"It seems that there's been a few breaches in the city perimeter." Secretary Sarnic began.

Korric looked alarmed and almost stopped in midair. "I thought this was an internal affair that had nothing to do with the Inmates!"

Sarnic defended himself, "Internal yes, no one has entered from the outside. It's a Warden. A young Warden has been leaving the facilities in the Flesh."

"Oh, another Flesh explorer huh? Get one of those every generation or so." Korric was obviously relieved.

Secretary Kammoc chimed in from the other side, "Do they come back alive? Will we need to send out a rescue squad?"

Sarnic answered, "That has all depended on how far they wander. Most of the Flesh explorers we have records of have just looked around outside, well within the security perimeter."

Korric added, "As I recall it wasn't too many seasons ago when we found one of them living in the mouth of a ventilation tunnel. Had collected all sorts of stuff the Flesh kickers like. As far as I know it's all down there still."

The group flew in silence for a few moments.

Korric remembered that Secretary Kammoc's comment about the rescue squad was still up in the air. "How about this one. Has she wandered far?"

"Well, we're not sure. She's been doing a pretty good job at avoiding our scouts. Some of my people say they've seen her outside the security perimeter but they always seem to lose her."

Korric added, "Has anyone talked to her yet?"

It wasn't as though she was advocating reprimand or detention. Any Warden was free to come and go as they please as long as they lived by the Warden code: defend fellow Wardens and protect Inmates from injustices. It was beyond her why anyone would want to be too involved with the Flesh anyway. She herself had had only one Flesh kick when she was a young girl, and had found it distasteful. After all, anything they needed or wanted could be simulated with much less effort than actually constructing it. As long as the physical needs were met, why not live one's life in ease? Well, to each their own. Korric was only worried that they might have to allocate some manpower for a search and rescue effort when that other issue of Warden security was pressing.

Sarnic just shrugged and said, "Well, just look at what we have on her. We'll follow your lead."

The group came into view of their destination. The Department of Physical Facilities was a structure floating entirely above the ground, connected only by thin wisps of bridges to two neighboring core towers. Of course Korric knew most of it wasn't real, nor were any of the activities contained therein. Perhaps none of it was real. It was just another part of the fabulous graphic user interface developed by the Wardens over the generations to interact with the Database and their physical environment. The real nature of the city was not common knowledge among the Wardens and perhaps no one knew it all. Every person knew just enough to function in their occupation and little else. Of course if someone searched, the information wouldn't be withheld, it's just that no one asked. Those few who discovered bits of the truth usually kept silent, either because they were extremely disappointed and wanted to forget about it, or more likely, because the other Wardens would laugh them to shame.

They alighted on the reception apron and followed Secretary Sarnic past security. An aesthetically designed corridor took them to the center atrium of the building, which let the sunlight in at all times of the day via the use of huge mirror arrays with solar tracking coding loops. The atrium also served as the vertical circulation of the building. Workers were floating up and down the high space intent on their various errands. Korric noted that most of the workers had faint red bounding boxes around them indicating that they were not formed entities pulled up from the Database. The few that had no bounding boxes she assumed to be virtual experts and messengers on the way to their next assignment.

They followed the Secretary as he gestured his body into a slow upward drift. Korric thought that the man was purposely setting a slow pace to show off his department that was decidedly functioning well and in good order. The lower levels of the building were devoted to remote agriculture and food production. Korric could plainly see the Wardens in their workstations, manipulating some remote automaton that was doing the real work in the Flesh (or what they assumed to be the Flesh --- there was no way of knowing for sure). Remote farmers would plant, tend, and harvest their crops of soybean and cornucopia meat, which would be hauled by remote shippers to mobile processing plants operated by remote food specialists. Since the food actually showed up in their cafeteria Korric assumed that the whole system was actually operating smoothly in the Flesh. Many Wardens had the impression that automatons were autonomous but in actuality there was nothing autonomous about anything in the crystal city: somewhere there were real people driving them. Even the virtual experts were not capable of handling sophisticated jobs and always had to work under the supervision of a real Warden.

Above the agriculture and food production section was facility manufacture and repair. Whenever a Warden operating a remote automaton detected any slowness of reaction or faulty readings, they would report the problem to manufacture and repair. The repair section had automatons that specialized in maintenance. The workers there would remotely collect the faulty device and attempt to repair or replace it if necessary. Of course it was their machines that were doing the actual work in the Flesh. The repair team also had to repair each other's automatons from time to time as they broke down as well. There was often a need to replace old equipment with new equipment. This fell under the jurisdiction of the manufacturing section. Manufacturing usually made use of recycled materials, but there was also a need for raw materials. In these cases, the raw materials were synthesized remotely in one of the manufacturing section's three matter synthesizers, using regular ground matter. However, matter synthesis was extremely costly and usually drained up to 70% to 80% of all the power available in crystal city for many days at a time, so it was only performed as a last resort. Also, synthesized materials were almost always inferior to natural materials and tended to break down or fail early in their life cycle depending on how sophisticated the compound. (That was another problem on Korric's mind that needed periodic attention, since the Wardens were losing their ability to produce reliable machines: the older long functioning ones were slowly being replaced by newer cheap imitations.)

The group's destination was the upper levels: operations and maintenance. Secretary Sarnic led them past clusters of workstations to a conference room prepared in the back. The conference room was glass walled and appeared to cantilever away from the main building giving a magnificent view of the crystal palaces. There were five of Sarnic's workers already seated there, waiting for Chief Warden Korric's arrival. An usher showed the new arrivals to their seats. He had no bounding box around him so Korric assumed him to be a virtual expert assigned with the task of determining optimum seating arrangements for the numbers and ranks of officers in attendance.

When they were all settled, Secretary Sarnic introduced each of the workers from his department. Since Korric had been reading the resumes attached to their bounding boxes the introduction was unnecessary, but it was all part of formalities.

One of the Workers was an under deputy assigned specifically to the case at hand. She had gathered the other workers together after her research confirmed that they were all witnesses to the supposed breach in the crystal city's system. There were two remote maintenance operators, a remote cartographer, and a remote janitor. The under deputy activated a two-dimensional wall display that projected a photograph of a young woman.

"This is Miss Blujic, a young art student." the under deputy began in a formal tone (she was slightly nervous in the presence of so many ranking officers), "Miss Blujic has apparently been leaving the facility in the Flesh. Our records indicate that she may have breached the system several times as indicated by this chart."

The photograph was replaced by a list of incidents, including dates, times, durations, and sources. The number was somewhere approaching thirty! Korric and several others gasped as they had not realized the magnitude of the breaches. In Korric's memory, the Flesh explorers went out only a half dozen or so times before they either abandoned the Flesh kick or were killed by some mishap. The one exception in memory was the Flesh explorer who lived a few seasons in the mouth of the ventilation tunnel.

The under deputy continued, "We have no definite proof of many of the breaches, except for the fact that duration suggests that a breach was made."

Korric spoke up, "What do you mean by that?"

The under deputy explained, "We have witnesses that see her pass through the ventilation tunnel and return several days later. During that time we check the tunnel and she is not there, leaving us to believe that she has left the facility. In support of this, there is no record of her logging on to the Database during these times. I have called two representatives from maintenance working in the machine room below the rocker port."

She indicated to one of the maintenance workers and the picture on the display changed. It was a two-dimensional moving image of Blujic walking through the machine room, as seen from the camera eyes of an automaton. The young girl avoided other automatons working in the area and slipped into the darkness beyond some of the installations.

One of the remote maintenance workers explained, "I testify that this is a record taken on one of my shifts in the machine room."

Immediately another video came up, showing Blujic wandering through the machine room from a different angle. The second maintenance worker testified, "I testify that this video was taken by the automaton I operated while I was on duty in the machine room."

The under deputy thanked the two workers and brought up an image of a map. She pointed to two red dots and said, "We have reason to believe that Miss Blujic has visited each of these two areas. This spot is on the outer edge of our security perimeter. The cartography department spotted her here."

On cue from the under deputy, the remote cartographer began to describe a video that replaced the map. She explained how the mapper first used laser rangefinders to paint a 3D contour of the area, followed by infrared, visible, ultraviolet, radar, and spectrometer scans to create a rich data file.

The cartographer continued, "Next the automaton moves to a new position and the entire sequence is repeated. I am filtering out some of the data so it won't be too confusing."

The rich image was immediately toned down a bit as the filters took effect. When the new scanned sequences started to display over the old ones, a picture began to appear with startling clarity. The image was oddly distorted as one might expect a full panorama of stereo three-dimensional information squeezed into a limited two-dimensional frame. The center of the image was looking directly down toward the forest floor, while the outer edges the view was looking straight up toward the tops of the same trees in a fish-eye lens effect.

"This is an image from the day in question." the cartographer explained, "When this data is collected it is analyzed and then sent to the central data banks for comparison with the Database. At that point it is either all or partially used to update the Database or stored for future reference."

Chief Warden Korric was growing impatient, "What is your point, young man?"

"Well, its this." the cartographer caused the center of focus of the fish-eye to move within the setting, making the trunks of nearby trees loom into the center and slide past. "When we detect objects which weren't there before we investigate further. That way we can follow the migration of the Inmates, or trace the movement of one particular Inmate for that matter. We can even create loops within the Database approximating the behavior of real Inmates in the Flesh."

The focus of the fish-eye came to a stop with the horizon just above center. The cartographer zoomed in the image more and more until it became evident that there was a figure there crouched between the trees. Increasing the zoom several more steps filled the entire screen with the image of the person, who was looking squarely in the direction of the camera: Miss Blujic.

"When we went to investigate there was no trace of her. She might know how to fool even the spectrometer and radar sensors, which wouldn't be too hard, I might add." the cartographer concluded.

The under deputy put the map back up and pointed to another spot. Korric recognized the area of the map as being quite near the *Origin*, though between it and the crystal city. Had they spotted Miss Blujic there also?

"This other area we have no direct proof of, but we have assumed that Miss Blujic has visited beyond the security perimeter in this area because of certain evidence that has been collected." the under deputy explained. "For this reason I have invited a remote janitor as a witness. Sir, if you please."

As the man stood up Korric wondered. What could a remote janitor possibly have anything to do with all this? Visions of janitor automatons wandering around the *Origin* just didn't connect. Of all the workers in attendance, this man had her curiosity piqued the most. As she thought, a new video image came up on the screen. The image was taken from low to the floor, perhaps only a few handwidths high. The automaton recording the video was moving along a corridor within the Warden facility. There was a trail of ooze and slime that had been left on the floor by someone that the automaton was busy cleaning up. The video scene reached an intersection in the corridor and proceeded to turn the bend. There in front of the camera was Blujic, half her body caked in mud and filth, dragging along exhausted. The young woman fought her way up a flight of stairs, depositing mud on every step. The automaton followed along doing its job. The video sequence ended.

The remote janitor explained, "I testify that this video was taken by the automaton I was operating on this day. The refuse left behind by Miss Blujic was taken to a lab and analyzed."

The under deputy chimed in, "And the substance has been pinpointed to this particular area where a unique swamp environment exists, not too far from the *Origin*."

****

Korric was deep in thought. The group headed toward the Department of Security, except for Secretary Sarnic who had remained with his department. The Blujic case was indeed interesting and she wanted to stay up on it. She would have taken the time to interview the young woman that evening had it not been for the fact that the girl was at that very moment nowhere to be found, presumably away from the crystal palaces on another Flesh kick. At any rate Korric left one of her staff members behind to put together a detailed report. The Chief Warden only hoped that the girl would make it back safe again, wherever she was.

As intriguing as the Blujic case was, Korric forced herself to switch gears to more important matters. A new Inmate group equipped with submarines had invaded their lakes and forests. The Wardens had observed them from afar and were shocked at what they saw. The new group were physically different than any Inmate they were familiar with. They had jet-black hair and many of them had narrow almond eyes. One of the most alarming developments was that they were at war with the native Inmates and seemed to be holding their own. The new group's success had nothing to do with war skill or strength, but was entirely based on strategy and technology. These were no savages like the locals. The fact that they had a higher technology threatened their security like nothing the Wardens had ever seen.

The new group was able to move freely under the Plasma even among the corpuscle monsters. The Warden's security perimeter was only effective on the land. What if these newcomers discovered their deep ports? They would be able to walk right in and no one could stop them. Of course Korric wasn't sure that the deep ports actually existed in the Flesh. She even hoped that they didn't exist for security's sake. Still, she had to take measures just in case. With these latest developments, the Chief Warden had to think more and more like a Flesh explorer.

The group arrived at the Department of Security and were ushered to the command center of the Prison Guard Corps. The command center consisted of rows and rows of workstations exclusively for the use of commissioned officers to command the forces assigned to them. Korric and Advisor Herrec were each taken to empty workstations and were given some instruction to brush up on their operation.

The workstation was simply a framework surrounding a seat. In front of the seat were displays and simple controls. Korric stretched her fingers as she moved her hands into place over the control pad. It had been a long time since her training days at the academy and she was more than a little eager to get down to business. Immediately after getting seated the workstation powered up. The control center scenery around her disappeared and was replaced by the inside of a hangar, where many flying machines sat waiting for use. She was inside one of the machines, and to her right she could see Advisor Herrec and Secretary Kammoc readying their own machines. The workstation had transformed itself into what amounted to be a virtual rocker of sorts. Suddenly it occurred to Korric: she was actually in the Flesh in a rocker somewhere in the physical Warden facility. Now she was in that rocker, and virtually inside another rocker! For a brief instant confusion reigned and she wondered, what if the Flesh was actually another rocker? But dispelled the thought quickly.

Korric raised her flying machine off the pavement. From the higher vantage, the Chief Warden saw that though there were many machines in waiting, the hangar was nearly empty. Korric switched the appearance control from working mode to Flesh mode. Each of the machines below visually transformed into compact spheres, with racks of thrusters, cameras, sensors, and weapons arrays attached. This was the actual appearance of the guard automatons in the Flesh, and the hangar scene was the actual remote appearance of the automaton base facility. Sitting in the workstation, she was now connected in real time to a real guard automaton in the Flesh, seeing what its cameras saw, and reading what its sensors detected. Feeling the Flesh mode a little too sterile for her taste, she switched the appearance control back to working mode and watched the automatons visually transform back into human-piloted flying machines.

Advisor Herrec and Kammoc lifted off shortly after Korric, along with three attendant fighters. A low, horizontal hangar door slowly opened in front of them as the six aircraft hovered over the tops of the off-duty machines. Leading out, one of the attendant fighters moved slowly toward the opening and paused outside. Korric and the other craft followed, carefully maneuvering to be clear of the structure and each other. They emerged to find themselves on an open plain with shallow rolling hills. Looking behind her, the Chief Warden saw that the hangar structure was disguised as a low hill itself, and one had to actually see the hangar door open to realize that it was artificial.

The six flying machines regrouped and fell into a formation of sorts, with the three fighters forming a triangle and the three less-experienced officers doing their best to stay in the middle of it. The machines were not very fast, and only slightly exceeded the speed a Warden might fly through the Database using only a rocker. Still, the idea of being inside a flying machine was a novel one for Korric so it seemed as though they were speeding across the landscape. The terrain underneath turned into forest, and the aircraft kept above the lower canopy. Older, larger trees towered above them here and there, but were sparse enough to allow them to keep formation. The Secretary briefed them on the way.

"The invaders have holed up in crude forts high above the forest floor. Though the Inmate armies lay siege to them day and night, the newcomers don't even budge. We believe they've bored shafts down the trunks of the trees and are using the shafts to move safely between the forts and the deep lakes."

Korric posed the question that had been nagging her ever since the invaders were first spotted, "Any idea about where they came from?"

The Secretary replied, "We have no idea. There is no record of any such peoples anywhere in the Database."

The next question was also on her mind, "Do we really know they are real? What if our ancestors played a trick on us for our entertainment? They could have been programmed into remote corners of the Database many generations ago and are just surfacing now."

"It's true that we haven't been able to bring up profiles on any of them. They register blank like virtual experts. But so do all the Inmates for that matter." The Secretary was referring to the function that displayed bounding boxes around real people. The function only worked when the person was logged onto the Database in a rocker. "Still, they show up on infrared and spectrometer readings."

Korric shook her head, "You know those readings can be programmed in as well. The stream transmitted from the automatons can be merged before we even see the data. Clever Wardens have done it before."

Korric would have said more, but the lead flying machine slowed, bringing the small squadron of aircraft to a crawling hover above a clearing. One by one they dipped below the canopy and regrouped among the massive boles of the forest giants. In their immediate vicinity the forest looked normal at first, but Korric began to detect other flying machines here and there, deftly hidden behind tree trunks and clumps of foliage. It took a while longer for her to spot the invader's forts, quite a ways in the distance. The forts were constructed from branches and ground matter and looked like large growths on the tree trunks. Thin-shielded catwalks stretched from tree to tree connecting the bulbous cantilevered strongholds. It certainly didn't look like something a high technology race would construct! Seeing the condition of the invader's stronghold, Korric had much more confidence that their cleanup operation would be a success.

"Are the Guard in place?" the Chief Warden asked.

"Ready and waiting your order." the Secretary replied.

"Have you contacted the Inmates? Is Tsrok-Gwor willing to work with us on this one?" Tsrok-Gwor was the Inmate chief. Though there was standing animosity between the Inmates and the Wardens, there was some cooperation. After all, it was the Warden's responsibility to keep the Inmates fed and out of trouble.

"Very reluctant, but he's with us. They hate these guys!"

Korric looked over the target area. Figures could barely be seen walking back and forth along the catwalks. The dozen or so bulbous growths attached to the massive tree trunks seemed so vulnerable. On the ground below, red-dyed Inmate armies congregated in camps, waiting for some opportunity to strike. From Korric's vantage, hundreds of Warden flying machines could be seen, their pilots itching to go. Korric almost felt ashamed at the obvious overkill. She was at the height of her confidence.

Just then Advisor Herrec, who had said nothing all day calmly shattered the mood. "It'll never work."

Korric couldn't believe her ears. "What are you talking about? Do you know something I don't know?"

"No, I just have a bad feeling about this one. Remember, all our weapons are designed for crowd control. Our prods don't even have enough voltage to kill a man. We have nothing like the weapons the ancients had that could lay waste to entire regions."

Korric was still confident, but now began to worry. Advisor Herrec's judgment was sound. She had trusted the advisor's feelings many times and had acted upon them. Never had he given her any reason to doubt. Still, it was just a feeling or a hunch, and not some piece of hard evidence. After all, the Wardens obviously had the advantage!

Korric led an attack. Her machine moved swiftly around the massive boles and approached the enemy. This was a swift surprise strike before the main force would be cut loose. She had only eleven fighters with her, the mission being to isolate one of the towers and sever two connecting bridges if possible. Her squadron came quickly within battle range and Korric was so close she could see the almond eyes and jet-black hair of the men standing on the catwalk. The enemy launched a projectile directly at her. Even though Korric had no time to react, her machine instantaneously lurched to one side and successfully avoided the object. Behind and to her right, she saw the projectile impact upon the ground and explode in a ball of flame. Korric sped forward and sent two bolts of pure electricity down the man's throat. The poor man writhed for a moment or two then turned away to flee. Losing his footing he slid off the bridge and crashed through the thin shielding to fall to his death. Inmates swarmed around the man's body, contributing a few stabs here and there to make sure.

Two other men that were standing on the catwalk also started to run toward the nearest stockade. Three of Korric's fighters gave chase, their arcs making contact. Another pair of fighters approached the bridge and began sawing at key structural members with remote manipulators. The bridge suddenly crashed sending the two men tumbling to the ground with their fellow. Two other fighters began working on the remaining catwalk while Korric lead a small number to attack the stockade itself. They entered with no problem at all, sending arc after arc after the fleeing enemy. Arc-shocked men would collapse to the floor and get back up again screaming in terror. Some jumped to their deaths but the majority escaped through a tunnel chiseled into the tree trunk. The whole operation lasted only a few moments: mission accomplished!

Regrouping her fighters, Korric exited the stockade. The enemy was gathering in force and sending out more and more projectiles. Not one projectile ever came close to hitting one of the Warden's machines.

Korric gave the order for the overall attack, and headed for another bulbous stockade to join in the battle. With arcs flying all over the place, the invaders could do nothing but hide. Most of them were escaping through the tunnels. As she watched one of the black-haired men duck into the opening, Korric got an idea. If it were possible to follow them down and actually board their submarines, they could rid themselves of the enemy for good. Acting on the idea, Korric ordered three fighters to follow her into the tunnel. The tunnel started out horizontal, but immediately dropped off into a shaft of indeterminate depth. As Korric proceeded along, she realized that the dimensions of her craft in working mode was actually larger than the width of the tunnel, so a strange automatic scaling effect was reducing the apparent size in order to fit. The scaling effect gave the impression that the tunnel was much larger than it actually was. Since the actual automaton she was remotely operating fit into the tunnel without scraping the walls, Korric didn't worry about the effect.

The Chief Warden switched on her headlight and began to sink slowly down the shaft. A long ladder had been built into one wall, but there were hanging ropes or cables that Korric assumed had been used for lifting things. In a moment of inspiration, Korric used her manipulators and sliced cleanly through the ropes in one sweep. A whoosh sound resulted, followed by a crash and scream from below. Korric's machine gave readings that another opening was below her. The opening came in on visual a moment later and she slowed her descent. Normal human instinct told her that it was a natural spot for an ambush. She decided to leap through the opening suddenly, sending off bolts in all directions. Her prediction was correct, as the machine reflexively dodged twice to avoid flying objects. The rain of bolts cleared the enemy from the immediate vicinity of the tunnel and allowed the other three fighters to exit with her.

The space they came into was a subterranean cavern of sorts, with massive root structures of the trees penetrating the roof and disappearing into a pool of water below. A floating dock had been constructed and several dozen of the enemy were backed up against the other end, frantically trying to enter one of their machines -- a submarine! Korric could not tell the exact nature of the craft since the crowd mostly obscured it. The Chief Warden moved forward slowly. Several of the enemy continued to throw things to no avail. Moving within range, Korric let loose a solitary arc into the crowd. Several men screamed and dove into the Plasma. Flanked by the other fighters, Korric cut loose. Men began falling onto the deck, into the water, or struggling to board their craft. Several dozen men were reduced to only six or seven in a matter of moments.

Korric moved in to finish off the rest. Suddenly a large man stood forward in front of the bunch and put his hands on his hips in a defiant gesture. He was dressed differently than the others, having on a black suit and hood with bulging goggles covering his eyes. Korric sent off a bolt at dead center to the man's chest. Nothing happened. She sent out more arcs but there was no effect -- the man didn't budge.

Frantically Korric deployed a manipulator and aimed for the man's neck. The black-clad man calmly reached out with his left hand, grabbed the manipulator arm, and forcefully pulled the automaton closer to him. With one swift swing, the man cocked his other arm back and let it go right for Korric's cameras. He punched out her lights!

The entire scene went black. Korric found herself sitting at the workstation with void data being projected around her. The void screen faded and she was in the command center at the Department of Security. The Chief Warden looked around her in confusion. From the other end of the long line of workstations a young Warden came rushing toward her.

"What happened?" she asked, "I was just about to win the battle!"

The young man politely said, "Chief Warden Korric, your automaton has been rendered inoperable from unknown causes."

CHAPTER 15

A complicated web of metal beams zigzagged back and forth in a narrow space between two curved metal walls. Patches of soft, plush moss bunched up on the level area at the bottom and even collected on the walls and across the tops of the beams. Hundreds of bundled wires, conduits, and junction boxes in various stages of deterioration emerged from the clumps of moss and followed the narrow space up into the darkness overhead.

Waking up groggily, Blujic wondered where she was. The conduits and junction boxes brought to mind the machine room in the lower level of her Warden home, but the corrosion and fungus didn't seem to fit with that sterile environment. The illumination was not too strong, so she thought she was back in the forest. Were her eyes playing tricks on her? She sleepily tried to think back and remember how she had gotten there. Was it in the course of being pursued by the Inmates? No, she had gotten away from them cleanly. The Inmates didn't seem quite as strange and barbaric as she had first assumed, at least not all of them. She had met Future. Oh Future!

The thought of Future made her start. In one smooth motion Blujic rolled over to face in the opposite direction from when she woke up. There were no trees anywhere to be seen, though there were moss-covered surfaces abound. This was no forest!

Blujic sat up, careful not to bump her head on a beam. The illumination was coming from an opening that began at ground level and extended fairly high up the curve of the wall. From where she sat it was difficult to see for sure, but Blujic could tell that the edges of the opening were uneven and ragged. The substance that formed the walls had been torn at some time in the past, leaving crumpled ridges of bare metal. The exposed parts were glistening with moisture and Blujic noticed dripping water in places. *It must be raining outside*, she thought.

Directly in front of her on the ground in the narrow space, Blujic saw the remains of a campfire. There were stacks of wood and ground matter to one side, carefully organized according to size. On top of the wood stacks were articles of clothing that appeared to have been carefully laid out to face the now non-existent fire as if to dry them out. Blujic suddenly realized that they were her clothes! She looked down at herself and saw that she was modestly covered, but not with her own clothes. She was wearing the coveralls that she had seen Future put on just under his diving suit. The thought made her blush. Had Future changed her out of the wet clothes? Blujic blushed again as she imagined Future's probing hands on her body. The shock of the thought got her thinking again about how she had gotten there. Yes, Future had brought her there and had sat her in front of the fire, but her fleeting delirious memories suggested that Future had offered her his coveralls and had gone outside while she changed herself. Future had been a perfect gentleman. Blujic also remembered Future nursing her and hand feeding her during her delirious waking moments. How long had she been sick? She could not tell, but only held the fabric of the coveralls close to her as she realized they were his, and that warmed her heart.

Having solved the question of how she got there, Blujic suddenly realized where she was. The curve of the torn wall suggested the inside of a sphere. The *Origin* -- Blujic was inside the *Origin*! She was there in the Flesh at the place where the Wardens worshipped and held sacred above all other places. She had heard stories about the *Origin* all her life. As soon as she was old enough to mount a rocker she had come with her parents. There were hundreds of stories about famous Wardens coming to pay their respects at the *Origin* before going off and doing heroic deeds. The oldest stories told how the Wardens had come out of the *Origin* to build the crystal city.

The excitement welled up inside her as she thought about the opportunity to explore the *Origin* in the Flesh. Blujic tried to imagine where the little moss-covered camping spot could be in relation to the entire dome of the *Origin*. It seemed to her that she was sitting in the interstitial space between parallel inner and outer dome walls, filled with zigzag cross bracing. The only light came in through the torn outer dome skin, so the diagonal bracing pattern faded away in the darkness on all sides of her. The light illuminated a tall patch of the inner dome, and Blujic could see more rips in the crumpled wall surface deeper inside. She peered through the hole hoping to get a glimpse of the interior and thought she could barely detect the outlines of massive rounded objects and geometrical shapes.

Just then there was a stirring noise over near the opening. Blujic had a sudden stab of fear as she looked to see what could be making the noise. There had been other stories about the *Origin* as well, such as it being a tomb. Perhaps there were ghosts and spirits wandering these dark corridors! Blujic looked around quickly and began to imagine spooks hiding in every recess and corner. Suddenly she was not quite as excited about exploring as she had been earlier. At that moment a person walked in from the outside, dripping with moisture. Blujic was startled at first, but felt relieved when she saw that it was Future carrying a catch of swimmers.

Blujic realized how hungry she was as she cried out, "Future, I'm so glad to see you!"

Future had kneeled down to set the swimmers near the stacks of fuel and looked up when she called. "Ah Blujic! Kimi wa betah na no?" He paused and quickly corrected himself, "You feel betah?"

"Oh yes! I feel so much better now. Thank you so much."

Future excitedly reached over and held up the swimmers, "Look Blujic! Sakana wo kachi shita yo!"

"You kachi some swimmers!" Blujic let her hands come together in a single clap as she looked proudly at his catch.

Future was smiling as he set about to build a fire. Occasionally he looked up at Blujic, an unusual excitement filling his eyes. Blujic guessed that he had been nursing her for days perhaps and was relieved to see her well again. Future had the fire going and swimmers skewered in no time. He came around and sat down next to her and stared into the flames. Blujic stole a glance at the young man's face. Who was he? Perhaps he was just camping here. There was no family or others here as she had briefly suspected earlier. Future had lost his memory and was wandering the countryside on his own, alone. Was he indeed an Inmate from some tribe she hadn't heard of? Suddenly Blujic remembered hearing Miss Tarroc and Miss Pollic talking about Inmates having submarine vessels. There had been quite a stir back at the Warden home but Blujic had been too caught up with her Flesh kick to pay much notice. Was Future from a new Inmate tribe that used submarine vessels? At home in the Plasma where even the corpuscle monsters dwell, it was apparent that Future must have grown up in such an environment.

There was another big question on her mind. What was she going to do with him now? She would have to be going back to her home soon. Should she just leave him here? He was at home anywhere, it seemed, so there was no need to worry about that. After all, who knows how long Future had been staying here before she came. Still, the biggest thing on her mind was the warmth she felt toward this gentle black-haired youth. She was in love with him! As he watched the fire, Blujic reached up and put one hand behind his neck and used her other hand to turn his head toward her. He was facing her now, and both of her arms encircled his neck. For what seemed like an eternity they stared into each other's eyes. Blujic was drinking in those eyes and savoring every moment. She pulled his face to her and closed her eyes as she followed his lead. He kissed her, first lightly and then with more vigor. Blujic was stunned at the warmth that filled her heart as the man she loved was holding her. She had never kissed anyone before in her life, but kissing this strange Inmate seemed so natural to her. Suddenly Blujic became aware of some incredibly powerful feelings inside and was alarmed at their intensity. She pushed away from him and moved several handwidths away. Seeing the hurt look on his face, Blujic reached out and warmly grabbed his hand but for the moment made no attempt to move closer to him.

The two of them ate the swimmers in silence, each wondering about the strange tension between them.

Out of the blue Future asked a question, "Blujic, dis you home?" He motioned to the space around them.

At first Blujic didn't understand what he was asking. Did he want her to make this her home, or was he saying something completely different?

Future must have read the confusion on her face, for he quickly attempted to rephrase the question, "Blujic, is here you home?"

Blujic was caught off guard. She had been thinking all along that Future lived here with his family or something, when actually he had just wandered in. All along he had been thinking that the *Origin* was her home.

"No, this is not my home. This is the *Origin*." She explained.

"Here wa home janai nara, donna place na no?" It took a while to get the question across, but Blujic finally understood him to be asking what sort of place this was. Future seemed every bit as curious about the *Origin* as she was.

"This is where the Wardens came from. You know Wardens?"

"Future not know Wardens. What is Wardens?"

"The Wardens are the overseers. I am a Warden, too. We watch the Inmates and maintain the Database." It was a mouthful and it took a lot of explaining to get past the language barrier. Unfortunately much of it went by without being understood. Blujic paused for a moment or two before adding, "You are an Inmate, Future. Your ancestors were prisoners."

She regretted having said such a thing after it was too late, and made a grimace. However, after explaining the word 'ancestor', Future seemed quite excited and flooded her with questions. Blujic was relieved that the 'prisoner' part slipped by him for the moment.

"You know my ancestors? Who are my ancestors? Where ancestors from?" Future excitedly spouted out.

Blujic was taken aback and didn't know quite what to say. Mustering up some courage, she began to think of every good characteristic she knew of that the Inmates possessed. Unfortunately there weren't many. "Your ancestors were quite resourceful and very strong. They always did their own thing."

"Future ancestors also from here? From *Origin*?"

Inmates from the *Origin*? Blujic had never thought about that before. All she could do was shrug. She began, "Well, I ... I don't ..." and left off without finishing.

"You know inside, Blujic? Future look inside now." Future proceeded to pull out the portable torch from his diving suit.

Blujic suddenly realized that Future wanted to look deeper into the structure than they could see with the natural light streaming in through the ragged opening. She didn't know whether to feel excited or afraid. If she would have examined her own feelings a few days earlier she would have jumped at the opportunity to look around inside the *Origin*.

Now that she was here and had remembered some of the ghost stories she was not quite sure she wanted to go prowling around in the dark. To tell the truth, she hadn't known what to expect inside the *Origin*. Just sitting there, looking at the corroded machinery and deteriorating walls gave her more and more a feeling of something long dead and gone. Still, when Future rose and began to peer into the darkness, Blujic used a diagonal strut for support to nurse her body into a standing position and followed along.

Future switched on the torch and pointed it toward the inner tear in the wall. Most of the smoke from the fire escaped out the opening to the outside, but enough of it remained in the air such that the light beam illuminated particles all along its path. They stood at the opening and peered inside while Future aimed the beam through the hole. Beyond, the light picked out a corroded metal framework enclosing the remains of some unintelligible pieces of machinery.

He shined the light to the right and left and the sweep of the beam showed a row of massive tanks lined up in each direction as far as the beam could reach. Beyond the tanks and machinery was a massive impenetrable wall that had no apparent entrance.

Future would have stepped through to get a closer look, but as he shined the light downward Blujic gasped as the beam disappeared into a bottomless abyss. Between them and the row of tanks was an unbridgeable gulf dozens of armlengths deep.

From their current vantage Blujic could see that the row of tanks appeared to trace out a massive curved line closely approaching the radius of the inside of the great dome itself. She suspected that if they were to climb down into the hole and walk around the line of tanks that they would eventually find themselves at the place they started, having gone full circle around the inside of the dome. The secret of the *Origin* must lie beyond that wall of tanks! She had learned from a very young age that the Wardens had come out of the *Origin* into this world. No one ever told her who had built it or why it was here in the first place. How could they have just come out of here without first getting inside? She hoped she would be able to find the answers to all the questions that no one seemed able to answer.

Future suddenly turned around and began using the zigzag struts in the narrow gap above the camping spot as a scaffolding to climb upward. Blujic watched for a while then began to follow him up into the darkness. When the light from the rent below no longer illuminated their way, he periodically shone the torch down to her to light the hand and foot holds. But after a while she detected that the structure was so regular that she could climb more out of rhythm much as one would climb a ladder. The climb was vertical at the beginning, but Blujic soon realized that they were gradually moving diagonally as they followed the curve of the sphere upward. Soon it became easier to crawl along the shallow slope of the inner plates than to grasp the struts. She would have preferred to stand and walk, but there was only enough headroom to crouch or creep along on all fours.

Crawling along in the dark, Blujic suddenly ran into Future's rear end.

"Blujic, look!" Future said and promptly turned out the lamp.

To Blujic it first appeared that they were in complete darkness, but after a few moments her eyes adjusted and she realized that there was a faint light ahead. She could see all the zigzag struts around her. They were still on a slope but were fast approaching the top of the sphere. Future and Blujic resumed crawling without turning on the torch. The light grew brighter as they went along. Passing one strut, suddenly she spied a brilliant point up ahead. As she approached, the point grew wider and wider and revealed itself to be a patch of ceiling: the ceiling plates above their heads were no longer metal but consisted of a thick clear or translucent substance that let in some sunlight. Blujic could not tell which: clear or translucent. If the plates had been clear before, all the seasons of mineral build-up had frosted their surfaces to the point of translucency. The whole ceiling in this area appeared to be part of a sophisticated light and shading oculus covering the crown of the dome. Cankered hinges and mechanical motors attached to the triangular structure were frozen in place from a thousand seasons of neglect.

Blujic and Future reached the top of the dome. As they moved along, one or two spots showed through to a deep blue sky. *Ah, the storms have passed*, she thought. Beams of sunlight shone through to strike the dark, moss-covered material upon which they crawled. It was at this point that Blujic made a startling discovery. The slick material upon which they crouched was not metal either. As she looked down to where the beams of sunlight struck that surface, her eyes adjusted to focus upon an object illuminated ten or so armlengths away, beneath the floor! They were traversing across plates of a pure transparent material. Blujic swept away some of the dust and moss that had built up over the seasons. A vast chamber underneath the dome came into focus. She could not make out any detail, but enough beams of sunlight reached those far away surfaces to paint the picture of a space of incredible size. Blujic nervously moved from the center of one of the clear plates to the nearest side beam.

After having crossed the top of the dome Future continued to lead her down the other side of the curve. When the angle started getting a little steeper there was a marked change in the floor material, and it was no longer possible to crawl forward; they had to sidle sideways with their feet leading the way. They had reached the line where the floor and ceiling panels were once again metal plates as before. The spaces beyond that line were decidedly darker and didn't have any of the sunlight penetration. Blujic knew they had climbed up from such dark recesses, but after having gotten used to the dimly lit attic, the downward climb awaiting them held little attraction.

"Blujic, koko de wait shite kudasai." Future had paused and was looking back at her.

Blujic was relieved that he was asking her to stay put at the line dividing the clear plates from the metal ones. Future set off on his own, traveling along the dividing line searching for something. Moments later he returned and continued along the line in the opposite direction. Blujic sat squarely on one of the metal plates and positioned herself over the beam that divided it from the transparent surface. She cleaned away most of the dust on the clear plate and peered down into the massive cavity. Beams of sunlight created isolated spots on far away surfaces. She could barely make out a tower of sorts that she assumed to be in the direct center of the vast space. The tower stretched up to almost touch the dome ceiling upon which she crouched. At the base of the tower there were various structures of sorts which she could hardly discern at all, except for the fact that the smattering beams of sunlight provided pinpricks for her eyes to focus upon. Down there was the answer to where her people came from! Blujic had an excited feeling in her breast that she was about to make a wonderful discovery.

"Blujic, come!" she heard Future's voice faintly from the direction he had disappeared moments before.

"Future where are you?"

Future's excited reply came back, "I found door!"

Blujic hurried along the line that separated the metal plates from the clear ones. The line appeared to follow a contour that wrapped around the entire dome at the same level. As she moved along she began to notice an unusual brightness ahead. She saw that a little ways upslope there appeared to be a large opening in the translucent ceiling plates that let in raw sunlight. The clear plates had been carefully removed in eons past and were shoved to the side. Scattered near the opening were corroded metallic containers, boxes, and coils of cable and wire. Blujic looked for Future there but could not see him anywhere. She made her way to the opening and picked over the objects that lay there. Disintegrating lumps had provided substance that tufts of grass could take root in over the seasons. Containers were neatly stacked over to one side, as if waiting for removal. Pointing upward toward the blue sky a rusted makeshift derrick extended a few armlengths out the hole above her. Several lengths of tangled cable were tied off to the derrick above.

Blujic stood up straight and poked her head and shoulders out of the opening and felt the fresh breeze. Because of the massive curve of the dome she could not see the green hills and lakes where she and Future had played days before, but some of the hills beyond and the great forests on the horizon were plainly visible. Wisps of clouds drifted across a serene sky. On the dome surface around her vines had taken root and every nook and cranny had protruding tufts of grass. On the down slope side, remnants of a rope ladder and strands of cable slung down the side of the dome.

Blujic ducked back down into the hole. Looking around she finally saw Future's torch shining from down slope through the zigzag beams. She crawled in his direction and finally made out his figure in the dim light. Future sensed her approach and steadied the lamp pointing to a spot off to one side, and turned to watch her. He sat with his legs slightly coiled beneath him and even though he continued to watch her steadily, his entire body seemed to be pointing in the direction the torch beam indicated. As she got closer, she was able to make out a hole in the floor into which the beam disappeared. It was a regular shaped circular hatch or door that had been opened to stand vertically on heavily oxidized hinges, connecting the narrow interstitial attic space in which they crawled with the dark interior. A way into the core of the *Origin*!

Blujic's heart beat with excitement as she peered into the hole. It was a small chamber, perhaps only three or so armlengths across. There were decaying consoles with corroded conduits lining the walls, and a row of lockers lining the floor deck. Some of the locker doors were ajar, revealing strange tools and disintegrating machinery. There was something quite strange about the placement of the consoles and locker doors. The orientation was unnatural. Blujic could not imagine working in a room like this: it would be difficult to work and have to access the tools from the locker under foot. Also, the consoles were attached to the wall when it would have seemed more natural to be mounted to the floor.

With Future holding the torch, Blujic swallowed her fear and slowly lowered herself down into the chamber. Her feet lit upon one of the closed locker doors and moved to the side. Momentarily Future leaped in one smooth motion and landed on the same locker door as Blujic had stood.

She was quite frightened now. It seemed as though all the ghost stories she had heard as a child came back to haunt her at once. Perhaps it was the man-sized hatches and objects that gave her the feeling that the place was occupied by the dead. The spirits that had protected this inner sanctum had been disturbed and now sought revenge. Future swept the beam up the wall. The light illuminated deep columns with multiple canisters and tanks tucked in between. The ghostly white spherical tanks and neatly arrayed pipes made her gasp as she imagined skulls and bones of dead creatures. A hatch on one wall was hinged on the bottom and opened toward them to form a shelf about waist high. Tattered strips of fabric that were remnants of some decayed object spilled down from a locker above and partially obscured the open hatch. There was darkness beyond.

The two of them stood side by side and stared through the hatch. Blujic tried to get her bearings and concluded that the hatch opened onto the vastness of the big chamber she had seen from above. Future, waving aside the tattered remnants hanging from above, climbed up on the shelf and backed out of the hatch. The level of the floor on the other side was lower than he had thought, for a confused look crossed his face as he struggled to find a firm place to plant his feet. Finally he stood on the surface beyond, the shelf coming all the way up to his chin.

Future shone the torch back into the hatch and said, "Come now, Future help Blujic."

Blujic hurried toward the hatch and got up onto the hinged door shelf. The container propped under the door let out a cracking noise. Suddenly the rusted hinges gave and container collapsed spilling Blujic onto the floor. She reached up and grabbed at anything she could in order to break her fall, and got a fist full of the tattered remnants hanging from above. But the fabric strands dragged along the thing they had been attached to which had hidden in that dark locker -- all she could see was a silhouette of a horrible creature that leaped down upon her with limbs flailing! Blujic screamed from the bottom of her lungs.

She struggled with all her might to get free of the creature that seemed to weigh down upon her. The more she kicked the more her feet seemed to become restrained. The light from Future's torch illuminated the ceiling behind leaving only the dark outline of a hideous head and large limbs. Blujic fainted.

When she came to, Future had her in his arms holding her tightly and consoling her, "Blujic, daijobu dayo. You OK, you OK."

She looked up and saw that she was still in that small chamber. The torch was sitting on one of the consoles pointing to the far wall. Clinging to him she peeked around and looked for the monster that had attacked her. In the dim light of the indirect torchlight, she gasped as she saw the figure of a man sitting on the floor with his back against the wall. The man had a fearsome bulbous head with a reflective surface that mirrored the room. Blujic did a double take. That was no head! He was wearing a helmet with bulky clothes that were in tatters. The helmet was attached to the clothes with a metal ring, leaving no gap between it and the shoulders. The suit had a harness of sorts with various pockets and corroded devices and tools attached. The man remained still and unmoving. Feeling safe in Future's arms, Blujic turned squarely to face the man. The mirrored helmet was intimidating; she was not able to see the man's face or eyes. It was like a large Cyclops monster she had heard about in fiction stories.

"Sore wa karappo no fuku dake dayo, Blujic. It only empty clothes!" Future explained.

"Are you sure? It looks like there's someone inside there to me."

Future got up and went over to the side of the sitting man. In a quick motion he flipped at the side of the helmet and the mirrored faceplate moved back, in its place there was a perfectly clear bubble that revealed a completely empty interior. It was just a person's empty suit that had been stashed up in that hole. She had pulled the suit down out of its resting place purely on accident.

Blujic regained her composure and they started over. Future went first and climbed out the hatch. Blujic followed, passing the spooky suit as she backed out the hatch. Future held her waist and gently allowed her feet to settle to the smooth floor. When they were both there crouching below the open hatch, Blujic realized that there was actually quite a bit of light filtering down from above. The ceiling was a vast geodesic dome of varying degrees of translucency. It was a dirty translucency, caused by thousands of seasons of dust build-up on the clear plates. Here and there were darker spots where presumably some thick moss had taken root, contrasted by completely clear areas still remaining that allowed pure sunlight to filter down in beams.

The floor upon which they crouched had a shallow slope and was actually a ledge of sorts that appeared to run the entire circumference of the vast domed space. The ledge was continuous even under the small antechamber from which they had just emerged, which now appeared as a large box affixed to the ceiling and floating a good armlength above the floor. Right at the edge of the ledge on which they sat, a pipe framework extended out horizontally over the vast space, like a handrail on its side.

Future turned to her and said, "Let's find way go down!"

The two of them began crawling along the deck. There was quite a bit of dust build-up and the smooth surface seemed a little slippery. They almost had to consciously keep from sliding down the slope to the pipe framework. It occurred to Blujic that something seemed odd. The webbed plates on the wall could have been put to better use here on this floor. At least they wouldn't be slipping around. Another thing: the builders should have installed that pipe framework standing vertically on the edge rather than hanging out over the space. Then it could work as a handrail for people walking along the ledge.

Ahead Future had come upon another open hatch in the floor. It was another long rectangular one with rounded corners, extending sideways almost the entire width of the ledge. The door had been opened downward and now hung into a dark space on corroded hinges. Blujic noticed that lengths of cable had been tied to the pipe frame, and disappeared into the dark hole below.

It occurred to Blujic that she and Future must have been retracing the route taken by her ancestors so many generations ago. In her mind she envisioned Wardens climbing the cables and making their way out of this hatch. Gallant men turned to give the women and children a hand. They dragged along bags of personal effects and slipped and slid along the sloped ledge to the raised antechamber. The men handed bags and bundles to others waiting inside that hatch below which the suit had hidden, and in turn lifted the luggage up through the circular hatch into the narrow attic space between inner and outer plates. Some of the valiant fathers erected a crane to help lower themselves and their belongings to the ground while others worked on removing ceiling plates. They chose the translucent panels because they must have been easier to remove than the metals ones. But where did they come from? Why did they leave?

Blujic was afraid of the darkness down that hole, but her curiosity was too strong. The two of them peered down the opening as Future shone the light in. About ten armlengths below was a floor with another hatch leading lower into the darkness. The intermediate chamber was quite strange. From their vantage, it looked as though the whole room was on its side! Mounted to the wall in a line above each other from floor to ceiling were four chairs facing consoles. Blujic could imagine people walking on the wall, sitting on the chairs and working at the consoles. But what had been the floor was now a wall.

Blujic and Future looked at each other in bewilderment. "Future think Warden ancestors totemo strange!" he voiced the thought that both of them had felt.

"Well, the *Origin* is mysterious. Who knows why it's built this way."

Future used the cables to support himself as he climbed down the line of chairs. When he reached the bottom, Blujic tossed down the torch and followed him down quickly. She backed against the wall, and tried to imagine how anyone could use the room on its side. She thought back at the way the antechamber seemed so strange and realized that it, too was oriented on its side. The handrail above also appeared to be on its side. Suddenly the realization hit her that the orientation of the rectangular hatches was just normal doors on their sides. Of all the confusing things! Why would anyone build something on its side? Did some cataclysmic event knock over the *Origin*, forcing the inhabitants to leave?

Blujic's curiosity was burning stronger than ever. She quickly tore the light from Future. Using the dangling cables she leaped through the open door in the floor, down the two or so armlengths to an even lower floor. Future followed tight on her heels. The lower space was a corridor of sorts, oriented on its side. Doors could be seen opening off the corridor above and below, in what would have been the walls but were now the ceiling and floor. The corridor was curved. In both directions the corridor disappeared around the curve into darkness, probably following the big radius of the drum. Had it been oriented properly there would have been plenty of headroom, but on its side they had to crouch a bit to keep from bumping their heads. Blujic began approaching the nearest door in the floor and attempted to open it. Finding it locked, she moved on to the next one. The second door was also jammed shut. She tried a door in the ceiling and succeeded in opening it. The light showed another room on its side, with banks of machinery mounted to the wall and a jumble of loose junk piled up where it had fallen. Blujic backed off and continued down the corridor trying each door on the way.

She began to suspect something even stranger than rooms on their side. The thought was so strange that she had not a clue as to how to answer it. With Future in tow she finally found a door in the floor that could be opened. Shining the light inside, she saw that it opened onto a stairway that was oriented sideways. She climbed down the stair on what used to be its risers and perched at the 'top of the stair' as she found a former corridor now turned into a bottomless pit, too deep to jump or climb down.

The two of them went back and searched some of the other rooms until they found some strong wires that didn't seem too decayed. Future tied the wires to the stair handrail and tossed the coils down into the pit. He showed Blujic how to set herself up for a rappel by wrapping the lines under the arm, across the back, under the buttocks, and hold on tight in the crotch before descending himself into the darkness. Blujic was right after him on her own wire. She descended in total darkness. Soon after she left the stairway, the entire corridor lit up below her as Future turned on his torch. She detected doorways in the walls as she slid past, some of them open and gaping darkness.

Taking it slowly, she paused the descent long enough to take a peek downward. Future was dangling below her, shining the lamp into every door that was open. Momentarily he pulled to one side and shone the light directly below. She had a clear view to the bottom, which was quite a ways down. It was only an instant before Future brought the lamp back up again, but in that instant the sight she saw turned her stomach. She screamed and closed her eyes holding tight to the wire. No matter how hard she tried the image of a skeleton rib cage and skull with black gaping eyes glaring back up at her would not go away! She couldn't go down there! Blujic was breathing heavily and in a panic. No way to go up and no chance at going down, she froze with the wire gripped tightly in her crotch.

"Blujic, come down!" Future called from below.

Blujic didn't answer.

"Blujic, Future help you. Hurry come down." he pleaded. Blujic could feel him tugging at her wire trying to get her attention.

"I... I can't!" Blujic managed to squeak out an answer.

"Hayaku kurunda! Blujic come shite yo!"

She couldn't bear to look down to see him. Was he standing near those bones? Without warning she felt her wire give a little, and she fell for an instant before jerking to a halt. Perhaps some of the outside covering of the wire failed and the insulation layers or inner cable still held. Whatever it was, she knew the wire could fail entirely at any moment now.

"Blujic, use cable Future use!" he called up from below.

Blujic opened her eyes and looked around for the other wire. When she spotted it she reached one of her feet over to try to hook onto it to no avail. She used her head to lock her own wire into position and freed her upper hand. Carefully she used the free hand to reach over to the dangling wire. Before she could reach it her own wire gave again and sent her into a panic. She closed her eyes and frantically held on with all her might. Seeing that she was still hanging, she tried once again to reach over and grab the other wire. This time she succeeded and wrapped it several times around her wrist.

As she prepared to shift her weight over to the other wire her own line gave out completely. All of her weight was suddenly resting on those few coils wrapped around her wrist. The severed line came down on top of her as she struggled to kick it free. Now that she didn't need to grasp her old line at the crotch, she had another free hand that she used to hold on. Her foot bumped into a doorjamb and provided just enough of a ledge for her to rest all of her weight.

Carefully Blujic reset the rappel. She looked downward and realized Future was not standing at the bottom after all, but waited inside an open doorway not far below her own perch. Slowly forcing herself to rappel down, Blujic somehow managed to make it that far and he helped pull her inside. Feeling relieved and coughing up a storm she let Future hold her and calm her. They sat back against the former floor of the room and Future prepared a snack out of some tasty fungi that he was used to eating. The room they had entered was lined with cabinets and had a ship ladder attached to the back wall. Since the room was on its side the ship ladder had no purpose for them for they could just walk up to the former ceiling. It took Future a while to pry the hatch open, however. Blujic just sat back and fondly watched him. They had managed to jam shut the door through which they had come, so she avoided thinking about the skeleton at the bottom of the pit.

The ceiling hatch opened onto a wall near the bottom of the vast domed space. Once again they emerged into the naturally lit space and had no pressing need to use the torch. Blujic had thought it dreadfully dark when she had been crawling across the top of the dome, but now that she was down there she found she could see quite well. And what a startling place it was! As soon as they emerged from the hatch the tower she had detected earlier loomed above them from the exact middle of the space. There were several structures built into it with suspended rooms and cantilevered tubes protruding along its height. The very tip of the tower had a miniature geodesic dome that was only a few armlengths below the domed ceiling itself. Blujic could see the various shades of dirty translucency in the dome panels. She gasped in surprise as she was able to pick out the path they had taken when they had crossed the dome earlier in the day. The clear panels had been partially scraped clean of dust when they crawled across them. Blujic saw the point where she had realized she was crawling over transparent panels and had scooted over to the side beam. In contrast, Future's path barreled straight through across the top of the dome. She took a quick glance down at herself and grimaced when she realized all that dust was now on her clothes.

Scanning upward again, trying not to think of how filthy they had become, she noticed there was a particularly bright spot in the ceiling where a large amount of sunlight was streaming through. Blujic noted that it was probably the opening where the makeshift crane poked up into the sky. She could barely see the shadows of the stacked containers and lumps of grassy decayed material. A little way down from there was the antechamber affixed to the roof through which they had come. It looked quite small from where she was now. Blujic also noticed another antechamber directly opposite on the underside of the dome.

Blujic and Future climbed down a series of ledges to make their way to the center tower. As they were leaving the vicinity of the hatch, she noticed a hastily painted cross above the opening. When she looked around she saw other hatches, some of which had the same cross symbol painted above them. Blujic remembered the skeleton and the bottom of the well and thought that perhaps the cross was a symbol of death. She shivered as she thought that perhaps each one of those crosses marked a tomb. Why? Why was there so much death here so long ago? Why did the Wardens have to leave their home?

As they stood with their backs to the tower structure, part of the answer seemed obvious. Everything was on its side. Nothing was oriented in a way that could be livable by normal people. Blujic remembered the buckled triangular outer framework and torn outer skin and wondered what kind of tragedy struck here so long ago. Was the *Origin* oriented differently so long ago and suddenly tipped on its side? No, she didn't think so. The thing she suspected that was the strangest thing of all was confirmed right here before her eyes. No manner of reorienting this world would set the spaces right! Blujic looked up at the antechamber high above and the sloped ledge with the pipe handrail. It was a handrail for a deck on its side. That deck, and the series of decks that stepped up to the very base of the tower at which they stood, at one time had people standing on them. There were plazas and places to plant trees and set tables. Everything was now on its side, with broken and decaying jumbles of junk bunched up where they slid.

That handrail was continuous all around the vast space and she could imagine someone jogging along it only to return right back to where they had started. The thing that was the strangest of all Blujic had no answer for. It was not only that the decks and rooms were on their side, but that these people lived on the inside surface of a cylinder!

CHAPTER 16

On their way back to the outpost, Ix couldn't help but think about the fate of his brother as he piloted the pod through a maze of column roots. They had identified all of the bodies, and one name turned up missing -- Mox's pal named Mel. Was the diver out there somewhere, lost in that strange world? Ix found it hard to concentrate on his job. The Pilot Sencho was giving him directions mostly via dead reckoning since Mag couldn't make heads or tails out of his needles. Instead, the navigator was clumsily manning the communications post since they had not found anyone experienced to replace their late colleague Smash.

A flurry of clicks brought Ix out of his thoughts and he was conscious of Mag scrambling to decode the message. Pilot Sencho also listened intently since Mag was known to let some of the speedier sequences slip through the crack. Ix looked back briefly and saw a strange expression come over the commander's face.

As the clicks died down, Hord looked over and gave the terse command, "Ix, turn around. We're heading out to sea!"

Ix immediately set the thrusters to do an about face around a particularly large column formation as the Pilot

Sencho continued, "We're going to do an underwater rendezvous with a pod departing from *The Island.* Ix, you have a new mission -- you're transferring over!"

The next wake period they met up with the other pod. Ix was on pilot duty again so he had a front row seat behind the hemispherical transparent cockpit as they approached the other craft. He noted that the vessel was of an older type, with a thick steel hull that had the strength to resist fluid pressures much deeper than their own hardened resin hull.

He was curious about what sort of mission it was that had to go to all the trouble of getting him out to an open-Plasma rendezvous. As he adjusted the valves into a neutral buoyancy drift mode a few dozen armlengths from the other pod, Ix asked, "How do I get over there?"

Pilot Sencho replied, "You suit up like everyone else."

Ix was ecstatic, "You mean I dive in open Plasma?"

Hord nodded, indicating desperate times called for desperate measures.

Ix took in the novel experience with great interest -- donning the loaner suit, checking the equipment, standing in the airlock accompanied by two veteran divers as the Plasma level slowly rose, waiting for the inside to equalize pressure with the outside, and finally opening the outer door into the void. He carefully followed the others out, trying to reign in any uncomfortable feelings that so easily beset those who were raised from birth in *The Continent* when thrust out for the first time into the boundless Plasma. Looking about, he could see fearsome shapes oozing just at the edge of visual range, and imagined the monsters closing in. The swim over to the airlock of the other pod was short, and they met divers from that vessel hanging around just outside to help him get safely inside. As soon as the handover was complete, Ix acknowledged his previous companions with sign language and saw them swim back to their own pod. He began having feelings of homesickness already, in spite of the excitement.

Inside the airlock, which was larger than that of his own vessel, the two divers helped him remove the mask. It was then that one of the divers began to stare at him in disbelief.

"What?" Ix asked, wondering what could be the matter.

The diver, whom Ix had not met before, replied, "We heard you were dead!"

"I've never been dead. Um, I mean, I'm alive as ever."

Then it dawned on Ix that the diver may have been referring to his twin brother Mox. He introduced himself and explained that he was a twin.

"Oh! Mox was on my dive team back before the big quake and I got transferred," the diver explained.

Ix removed the diving suit and was shown to his quarters so he could change before meeting the rest of the crew. He discovered that Advisor Two of Lord Ruk's staff was on board, and was invited to an interview with him.

"Your father told me about the sonar soundings and measurements the last time you went out with the hunting expeditions."

Ix responded, "Yes, ours was the first installation of the sonar equipment -- we kind of stumbled around a bit I'm afraid."

Advisor Two asked curiously, "We've heard about how you observed some strange effect at the surface?"

Ix was at a loss. What had he seen? It was too strange to describe. "I don't know how to say it, except that the surface of the entire ocean seemed to mound upward over the thrash tide."

Advisor Two stared at Ix for a while, still in deep thought. Suddenly he said, "We're going down to study *Mother's Heart.* We've dropped a deep-water beacon and it stopped sinking before the crush depth. The technicians think whatever is down there will be passing close enough to the surface for us to reach down, and perhaps touch it..."

Ix was shocked. That strange set of readings had been on his mind from the time he made his first trip. Now he had been chosen to come along on an unprecedented mission to go down there and look for it. He smiled nervously as he thought about all the wild stories that had been circulating since that eventful hunting expedition. What would they find? What could be so large and yet be carried along by a billion-thrashing fish?

As soon as all the divers buttoned up their respective craft, the vessels parted and went on their way. Ix heard a clumsy farewell as Mag clicked out a message to him from somewhere out there. *You stupid* ..., an embarrassed Ix thought, but wiped away a tear from his eye.

****

The old steel-hulled submarines didn't have a cockpit bubble, but consisted of a row of seats facing outward toward a row of portholes. Their crush depth was rated much deeper than the common resin hulls, but some of the larger contrivances for visibility had to be sacrificed. In the background they could hear the clicking communications of other vessels out on the periphery, presumably those in the hunter fleets from *The Island* and perhaps even from *The Continent.* Ix strained his neck as if it would improve the view out of the small window. They could see the churning wave strata above, and small particles drifted by as the vessel moved forward. Below them an endless expanse of thrashing fish extended to the underwater horizon out of their visibility range. Some of the crew appeared nervous, not knowing what to expect, or whether they would find themselves surrounded by the billions of swimming creatures.

Ix looked over to Advisor Two and saw that the officer was peering back at him. An understanding passed between them and they continued to look at each other as the older man voiced a request, "Admiral, I'd like to cross the thrash tide right over the middle and take some measurements."

The admiral had an archaic name 'Suihiro' with easy-to-pronounce syllables that meant 'wide waters'. It sounded like something from way back in the olden days, unlike the current trend the Technicians followed of naming their children with tongue-twisting syllables. As the admiral relayed the order to his crew, Ix worked his way over to the console and tried to understand the readout. Compass needles were spinning wildly and sure enough, off to the side the bulge pattern was barely visible in the small screens -- if he didn't know already that something was amiss he would have dismissed the readings as noise.

Ix watched the strange effect materialize on the scopes, and called over Advisor Two. "See how this curve is shaped here and here? A normal flat surface wouldn't have these patterns. The entire Plasma surface is bulging up out there."

As they approached the point directly over the top of the thrash tide, the effect became more pronounced. Looking out the view ports, it was difficult to discern because of the myopic tunnel vision those ports afforded, but a careful study revealed they were indeed hovering at the dome of a massive uplift many nodelengths across. Ix and the senior officer looked at each other from their respective view ports and shrugged. Ix wished they had the wide view that could have been possible from the hemispherical resin pod cockpits. The submarine crossed the bulge several times taking measurements until Advisor Two was satisfied. By the end of the wake period they found themselves drifting near the apex of the bulge, slowly tracking the progress of the thrash tide below, wondering how they would be able to get down below the cloud of swimmers.

"What if we just dove into the lot of them?" Ix tossed out.

The crewmembers were nervous at the thought. No one had ever gone *inside* the thrash tide before. Wouldn't the fish interfere with navigation and clog up the thrusters?

"Hold on," the admiral began, "remind me how you determined that shape down below wasn't just a solid mass of swimmers."

Ix explained how the sonar readings around the edge of the thrash tide had a rough ambiguity, even when the fish swam in tight formation, "We got a hard edge down below -- it's definitely solid, sir."

Advisor Two considered, "Ix, think back when you first detected the thing down there. Were you on top of the thrash tide?"

"No, I think we were still approaching the swimmers. We hadn't even found the thrash tide yet. If I recall correctly, our first thought was that a branch of swimmers had somehow reached underneath us and it scared the whole lot of us, thinking that we might somehow find ourselves surrounded."

Advisor Two continued, "If so, perhaps there weren't any fish between your vessel and the *Heart.* We have to approach it from the side."

Admiral Suihiro nodded his consent, and got the craft headed away from the center. Quite a bit later, when the shimmering carpet below them began to fall away, the navigator directed the craft to get clear and start the descent. The craft plunged deeper as the seething creatures glistened off to the side. The light began to fade and their cabin lights went down, replaced by a crimson glow. After a while all they could see were the particles illuminated by the paths of light made by their headlights.

"Anything down there?" asked the pod's sencho.

"Sir, the sonar shows some faint reading. I can't make it out very well." the navigator reported.

Looking toward the officer, Ix watched the needles erratically jump from bearing to bearing. The scopes showed the same echo down below that he had seen on his first trip. He was anxious and more than a little afraid, as was probably every person on the vessel. What could be down there? All the theories about freak phenomena that got swimmers together every few seasons raced through his mind. Maybe the thrashing fish got so dense that they began to work en masse, as a single entity. Or perhaps the old legend about a massive, malevolent creature was true -- what if it didn't want to be disturbed?

The communications officer interrupted his thoughts, "It seems like we're fairly close to that beacon now, sir."

Ix put his face closer to the porthole and peered down below, as if the beacon were close enough to observe. Again he thought he saw those evil clouds billowing up from the depths, but there was just blackness. If a creature waited down there it could not be seen. Even the fish were gone -- Ix felt utterly alone in the void, deeper than he had ever gone before.

"There's something down there all right! It's enormous!" said one of the men seated by the scopes.

Ix glanced over to the sonar unit and saw the sharp, crisp patterns all over the bottom of the screens. *Wait,* he thought, *do we really want to rush into this?* The descent continued a lot longer than he would have thought, which prolonged a mixed sense of dread and curiosity. He began to get a little worried when there was a sudden groaning in the metal hull. He looked up in alarm at Admiral Suihiro and saw the older man intently staring out the viewport, sweat beaded on his face. Ix nervously looked around the tight cabin, at the rivet heads hiding behind pipes, conduits, and junction boxes, as if by will power alone he could keep them from failing. The men nearby all had frightful countenances as each of them gazed out into the darkness at imagined monsters.

"What is that?" one of the men in the bow said in a hoarse voice.

Ix turned back to his own window and stared out into the void, trying in vain to see some sort of shape or discoloration on that black canvas.

A woman in the front called out as well, "I see something too!"

Ix felt the ship change heading slightly as the pilot veered to starboard. The spotlight beam illuminated some shadowy silhouette ahead and to the left. Momentarily the vibration of the pod's thrusters slackened and the forward motion slowed. He kept his eyes on the thing as the pod approached. The young technician subconsciously recoiled -- it was right out there, and they had no place to hide! Was it moving? No, he did not think so. The shape was not entirely clear, but it appeared to be long and thin, extending up from some unknown depths like a stiff tentacle. Ix could see that the top of the dark outline was about even with his view port. As the pod crept forward, the object resolved out of the darkness. It was artificial -- a brown-crusted rod with corroded boxes and other objects attached.

Ix was confused -- a *machine*?

The pod got closer, drifted to within four or so armlengths of it and hovered for a while, circling slowly.

"What do you suppose it is?" one of the men asked.

The pilot began to let the craft sink gradually. The growth-covered surface of the rod moved past the portholes a handwidth at a time. The rod became a tall pole-like cylinder with rusted frame structures hanging from its sides. Ix could only guess their purpose and stare in amazement -- how could the thrash tide buoy something artificial? Unfortunately things would only get worse -- he never would have imagined the scene that followed.

"Large body below us on starboard side." the navigator was feeding instructions to the pilot, who was skillfully working the thrusters and ballast controls.

The men held their breath waiting to see a glimpse of whatever gigantic thing passed below. Ix stared across the cabin and tried to paint a picture of what lie beyond those small circles of reveal. The distance from the rusted pole structure increased as the pilot powered away. Suddenly a large shape loomed from below just at the edge of the spotlight illumination. A massive broken cylindrical object, tipped at an angle on its side, revealed itself out of the deep darkness. As the spotlight swept across it, the men let out a gasp. Whatever was the nature of the object could not be seen, for it was buried in the familiar partly transparent ooze with the flowing red veins. Corpuscles -- he remembered back to his corpuscle theory, about the pearl steel and a nightmare of suspended monstrosity drawn along by the thrash tide. Fear gripped his insides, and he waited for some gigantic appendage to come up from the depths and enclose their small vessel.

The pod continued its descent along one side of the cylinder -- very slowly. The cankered pole visible from his porthole disappeared totally from view, fading into the dark haze. The pilot slowly backed away from the cylinder to allow them to get a better view. The light beam moved sideways and illuminated large chunks protruding out from its walls at even intervals around the circumference. Something about the shape and placement of the protrusions seemed familiar, even though they were crawling with corpuscles.

"*The Continent*! Pieces of *The Continent*!" someone yelled.

The cylinder was a sunken node tower from *The Continent*, with broken off passage tubes. Sometime in the distant past, a portion must have broken off and sunk, and the hideous morphing creature caught it. But the seething mass was not floating on it's own -- it was only the tip of something larger that Ix could not see clearly, even while the submarine continued to descend into the depths.

"Approaching something!" the navigator called out. "We have multiple hard surfaces below, Sir!"

The view out the window ports moved past the broken node tower. Ix began to make out that it was resting on a jumble of segments of other towers, interspersed with bare shards of cankered metal, reaching up like teeth from below. Again he was puzzled -- was it a giant corpuscle, or not? Large broken fragments of pearl steel like that would require amoeba tendrils that stretched many nodelengths through open Plasma to keep them buoyed up, but Ix could see no such thing -- the hideous predators seemed to be small, coming and going and swimming about like any other sea creature.

The sweep of the spotlight gave them glimpses of large objects just beyond their range of vision. The admiral called out from Ix's left, "The sonar gave us an underwater field of rubble? Take us toward those shadows."

The pod eased to a standstill as the motors changed their thrust vector. The craft began moving parallel with the bottom, along a course that would take them towards the large shapes in the distance. Ix began to see piles of torn metal plates, beams and gnarled wreckage heaped up high in some places and dipped low in others. The pilot occasionally shifted directions in a power turn that barely missed misshapen towers or distorted frames. Strange structures swept by only armlengths from Ix's window, with those eerie heaps of torn debris as a backdrop. More than a few times their craft crept by remains of *The Continent*, with sunken node towers and occasional corpuscles. Other than that, nothing was recognizable. Indeed it was like a vast landscape of wreckage and rubble, suspended out in the middle of the ocean.

"Is this the Creature?" Someone asked.

Advisor Two called to the sencho, "Have we located that beacon yet?"

The sencho checked with his crew and called back, "We're close, but not yet."

The eerie landscape seemed endless. Ix momentarily caught a glimpse of something familiar: the ruptured hull of a sunken pod sitting on top of the heap. It was an older type, perhaps from several generations earlier. Once or twice he saw vague outlines and remains of larger vessels he couldn't recognize. Was it all refuse from *The Continent*? Did a thousand seasons of trash and junk end up here in a vortex dragged along by the thrash tide?

Near the peak of a shredded metal heap they found the beacon. It was hanging from a twisted metal frame high above the rusted shards, caught on some protrusion. Advisor Two explained that some technicians had dropped several of them into the depths of the Plasma and listened until they were all silenced but this one. For some reason only this device had hitched a ride and saved itself from the crushing depths.

Suddenly Ix had an interesting thought. Did *everything* find it's way to this trash heap? With all the pieces of *The Continent* lying around, was it possible they might catch a glimpse of the fabled Third Vault of old Grandpa Nux's era? Wouldn't that make this expedition worthwhile! Unfortunately, there was no hint of the Third Vault the rest of the trip. After checking the beacon's condition, the craft moved on again through the strange landscape.

The pod entered an unusually wide rift and he couldn't see the bottom or the other side, even though the navigator hinted that the heaps continued up ahead. That hole -- what if the jumble of rubble collected together in the vortex? Might they be able to dive down through and see open water underneath all this? However, Ix reasoned, if they had found themselves in a vortex wouldn't there be microcurrents? Somehow the idea of giant heaps of junk drawn along by thrashing fish didn't add up.

He suggested to the admiral, "Let's survey the bottom of this rift. Maybe all this metal is piled on top of something."

The admiral agreed and passed an order on to the sencho. The pod came to a stop and lurched forward and down at an almost uncomfortable angle. The spotlight beam stretched into the depths. Ix could see more and more particulates suspended outside as they sailed through the Mineral Strata. It wasn't long before a dark surface came into view. The pod stopped and hovered for a bit as they all peered out their ports. The surface seemed gnarled and twisted, but caked in a layer of growths and extended in all directions past the ranges of the spotlight beams.

"Sir, I'm having trouble maintaining stability!" the pilot exclaimed, "There appears to be strong currents or something pushing us against the surface!"

Ix could hear the thrusters screaming as if they were heading out at full speed, except that the pod was standing still. Were they fighting currents of a powerful vortex? Somehow Ix didn't think so.

"It's magnetic," the vessel's technician explained, "somewhere down below that surface is a powerful magnetic field."

Ix immediately knew the man was correct. Underneath them was a magnetic field powerful enough to knock out their compasses from far away, from over the horizon, perhaps extending its field by lining up the iron atoms dissolved in the Mineral Strata. Their submarine had a steel hull and would be drawn to that source.

The mystery only deepened as he realized that most of his assumptions were wrong -- there was no giant corpuscle and no evidence of a vortex. The thrash tide didn't seem strong enough to carry anything heavy. Instead, it appeared that billions of fish just seemed to follow a mysterious junk heap as it moved through the ocean. And how that junk heap maintained its course Ix had no idea.

"Back off slightly. Without losing control, can you hover along the bottom for a while?" the sencho asked the pilot.

The pilot acknowledged and began to power the pod in a parallel track with the bottom. The thrusters continued to scream. As the spotlight's circle of illumination swept across, more and more rubble and shards of torn metal accumulated. For a long distance the wreckage continued. Then there was something else -- Ix could not be sure, but he thought he detected a slight ridge. The pod continued on as if no one else had noticed it.

"Sencho, back up a bit!" Ix called out.

The pilot worked the thrusters hard and eventually got them back to where he had seen the hump. "There! There's a rise down there."

A smooth expanse seemed to push out of the wreckage around it, as if something very large were buried in the heaps. Ix thought that perhaps it was made of unblemished metal, with only a superficial layer of growths attached.

Advisor Two also seemed intrigued, "Let's follow it."

The others began to see the ridge as well and the pilot aimed the craft slightly to the starboard side. As they continued along, the ridge became more pronounced and the pilot was able to ease off on the thrusters a bit as they rose above the field of metal shards. The smooth object formed a perfectly straight line that continued for dozens and dozens of nodelengths. Suddenly the men in the bow began talking excitedly and the pilot swerved to one side. The ridge rose to form a low platform with a pipe structure towering vertically up into the Plasma. As they passed, Ix could make out pieces of cankered machinery and other objects attached to the structure. They had no time to rest before another obstacle loomed out of the darkness. The ridge increased in height at an alarming rate, forming a massive wall that gracefully curved upward in artificial precision.

It was at that time that they made the most alarming discovery of all. A series of darkened circles penetrated the wall in neat horizontal rows. As the pod slowly moved past, Ix watched those circles come and go only armlengths from his own view port. He stepped back shocked! He swept his head back and forth and observed the row of men in front of the row of view ports. The likeness was too uncanny -- a row of circles on this side looking onto a row of dark circles across the way. They were approximately the same size, and similarly spaced. It all became suddenly clear: that wall beyond was part of a vessel of sorts. Could it have been the remains of a conning tower to a ship of massive proportions; a submarine so huge its upper deck had just taken almost a quarter of a wake period to cross? Ix suddenly imagined dead men in that other ship looking back at them and was filled with terror.

They passed the conning tower and continued to cross the harsh vastness of the sunken hull in silence. The piles of debris scattered about on the smooth surface increased again, and shards of torn metal created peaks and valleys too deep to penetrate. Soon the navigator indicated that the massive, ghostly landscape was sinking and that it would be too deep to follow. Their mission was approaching the end. But now the mystery was as deep as ever -- *Mother's Heart* was apparently a massive vessel moving on an unknown course, large enough to swallow *The Continent* many times over. It had the power to shake the floating city to its foundations, and its deck was piled high with the bones and remains of a long-dead civilization. Was it a wreck crewed by ghosts from the nether world? Somehow the reality struck more fear into the hearts of the men than the legend of a creature ever had.

CHAPTER 17

Future and Blujic took one last break before making the final push. Blujic chose the crest of a hill, where an interesting depression hid their presence from any curious eyes below. There was a strange formation in the middle of the depression which could have made them invisible from above as well, should the need arise. It was obvious that Blujic had hid herself in the hole many times before, and was merely being a creature of habit.

They had left the forest behind them at the end of the last wake period (or day), around the time Blujic called dusk, where the wonderful great light in the sky (the sun, as Blujic would say) faded away beyond the horizon. 'Forest' was the word Blujic used to describe the vast stretches of deck 'ground' where the column formations 'trees' filled the landscape. They had been journeying for three sleep periods or 'nights' now, and Blujic was sure they were close to their destination. Nighttime travel was safest, it seems. Both the Inmates and the mechanical guards were easier to ditch that way.

Future looked up in the sky. There were no clouds at all to mask his view of the stars and moons. He saw the gleaming point that Blujic called the *Destiny*, slowly moving down from the azimuth where he had been visually tracking it since it peeped up over the horizon. It was all so fantastic! To think that a calm and serene place such as this existed beyond the raging storms! Future was still confused about the scale of things -- was this calm an island in the universe of chaos, or were the storms and violent waves enclosed by the calm? Of course, underneath the great waves was the calm deep...

That was another thing -- try though he may, Future still could not remember who he was. He saw passages and node towers in his mind's eye, beat upon by massive waves, and somehow knew that that was his home. But how did he get to this dream world? What was that lonely, storm swept place he had grown up in? Would he ever be able to get back? Even with all the wonderful things in this place, Future felt a little homesick for something. Still, nothing could compare to that beautiful golden-haired princess Blujic. It was as if he had been dreaming about her all his life and suddenly she is there right in front of him. This was indeed a dream world.

"It's right over there!" that golden-haired dream girl lay prone on the ground, peeking over the edge of the depression, "See that dark shape between those two hills?"

"It look like other hill to me." Future answered in his still rough approximation of Blujic's language.

"That's it nonetheless. Let's go!"

Blujic jumped up and started to run down the hill, Future hot on her heels. They passed through a narrow grass covered valley and climbed up through the pass between the two hills Blujic pointed out earlier. The mound that was their destination could be seen more clearly, but there was one more low-rise between it and them. Blujic scampered up the rise and paused on its crest, capturing the moonlight in her golden hair. Future admired the sight.

"Come on, we're almost there!" She turned and motioned to him without having the slightest inkling that he had been watching her.

Future climbed the rise and put his arms around her waist. She turned fully toward him and they embraced for a few moments. Blujic tenderly broke away, still keeping an arm locked in with his, and faced down the hill. There was a grassy valley, and beyond that the destination: Blujic's home. It rose like a grass-covered hill, but on close scrutiny Future could see that it had a regular shape to it. The structure was vaguely pyramidal shape, with grassy tiers cascading down the sides. At the base, a cave or opening gaped out of the hill. The two of them took their time and strolled down into the valley. Blujic headed straight for the cave, and parting the vines and leaves partially covering the opening, disappeared within.

When Future followed, he found himself in a rectangular passage of sorts. The floor was strewn with a variety of articles, neatly stacked in some places and recklessly scattered in others, as if someone had spent a long time meticulously collecting things. Deeper along the tunnel a metal grille stretched across the passage from wall to wall.

Future felt a wave of relief. Though he was thoroughly enjoying himself in this new environment, the uneven surfaces, erratic placement, and unordered growths were foreign to him. The passageway was much closer to his own home than any place he'd seen so far on this trip except the inside of the *Origin*.

Blujic lay down on a soft surface and began to get comfortable. "Future, get some sleep. We have to get up real early before anyone else gets up."

Future complied gladly, almost not waiting to find a suitable spot before collapsing in a heap on the floor.

The next wake period (or day) Blujic shook him awake. Future sat up disoriented at first, and slowly looked around. It was still dark outside. She led him to the grille wall and began to unfasten the lock mechanism of a gate that Future had not noticed the previous night.

"Remember what I said about logon?"

Future was thoughtful for a moment as if trying to remember a difficult sequence, "First say nothing when Blujic talk to machine, then close door after Blujic leave so red light go on."

"What about the harness? How do you connect the harness?"

Future described the elaborate process that Blujic had painstakingly rehearsed to him over and over again: mount the platform, connect the harness, leaping, turning, and waiting for her at the rocker port landing apron. What it all meant he was not sure, and felt a little uneasy about whether he could remember it or not. Blujic had been thorough in her descriptions, but with his infantile grasp of the language, and not having seen any of the things before, he hoped he had not missed anything important.

Blujic succeeded in opening the gate and slipped through. Future followed after her and entered a narrow space with three huge fan blades lined up from wall to wall. Only one of them was rotating, drawing air from the outside into the interior. Blujic paused in front of one of the motionless fans and prepared to slip between the blades into the space beyond. Suddenly a loud clap sounded from the vicinity of the hub and the fan started rotating without notice. Blujic jumped back momentarily startled. She looked back at Future and shrugged her shoulders, then moved on to the next stationary fan blade.

Passing through to the other side, Future found himself in a long darkened corridor. The only light filtered through the fan blades from the outside, which created an eerie flickering effect. The girl led him into the darkness. When it became too dark to see anything at all, they moved toward the wall and began feeling their way along its length.

Perhaps they turned corners in the dark (he couldn't be sure). Future soon found himself in a room full of machines with many points of colored lights. Most of the lights were steady, but some of them flashed on and off. Blujic had told him about the machine room and mobile automatons. As they passed through the chamber Future wondered which one of the devices was a mobile automaton, for none of them seemed to be moving.

"The automatons are all asleep." Blujic explained. "It's still very early, you know."

They moved through a door on the opposite side of the machine room and entered an artificially lit corridor.

"Cover your head with this." Blujic pulled out a strip of cloth from her backpack and tossed it to Future.

He caught it easily and made it into a hood of sorts. Blujic led the way through a series of corridors and up several flights of stairs. They emerged into another passage lined with small doors. Toward the other end of the long volume a solitary figure was walking toward them.

"Don't let anyone see your face!" Blujic whispered under her breath.

Future turned away from the stranger and made as if he were looking at one of the doors on the wall, with the cloth covering his head. The person passed by and turned into a side corridor. Blujic walked a few paces away and stood in front of one of the small doors.

"This one's empty. Come on!" she said, and turned to open the panel.

Future climbed inside when she motioned to him, and turned to close the door as he had rehearsed.

Blujic stopped him, "Wait! Lock the door but don't put on the harness yet. I'm going to get some food for us!"

"Good idea. I very hungry!"

Future closed the door and fiddled with the controls until the red light went on. He turned around and sat on the floor with his back to the panel, waiting for Blujic to return. The small compartment was very cramped, just barely high enough for a man to stand. His legs were stretched out as far as they could, but still bumped against the far wall. On closer inspection, Future realized that to one side was a small platform that must have been the lift Blujic had told him about. He cast his eyes about and found the controls that operated the lift and went over in his mind what he must do after she started the logon sequence. Next he found the locker that had several items of clothing hanging inside, and chose one that would probably fit his frame. 'Tactile suits' was what Blujic had called them. He stripped his diving suit and hung it up in the locker, then carefully put on the tactile clothing.

Only moments passed before there was a knock on the door. Future opened up and Blujic tossed some wrapped packages inside.

"Eat these. Hurry!" she whispered, "I'll be right outside when you're finished."

Future recognized the strange packaged food that Blujic had had with her on that first day that they met. The food somehow brought back the memory of when he stood before her naked and embarrassed. He had to let out a little laugh. He quickly opened the packages one at a time and devoured them with the energy of a hungry soul. Some of the packages were not really to his liking, but a few were quite wonderful. Blujic had thrown in his favorite chocolate which made him smile again. When he finished he opened the door and called out to Blujic.

"I'm finished. What we do next?"

"Wait a moment!" she spit out quickly and positioned herself in front of the door.

Future heard the sound of footsteps walking down the corridor and waited until they passed. A few moments later she stuck her head inside the small compartment.

"I hope this will work. I've never logged on twice at the same time before. Future, stay completely silent while I do the logon." She reached up inside and placed her palm on a plate on the wall at about shoulder level and started mumbling a series of numbers. A light flashed on and she pulled back away.

"OK Future, you're on. Don't forget how to connect the harness! I'll see you on the apron."

She shut the door and Future again secured it until the red light came on. He turned to the rear of the compartment and stood squarely on the lift platform. He was elated when the lift actually began to rise as Blujic had said. The lift pushed up through a darkened hole in the ceiling. His head emerged into what looked like the interior of a faintly lit, semi-transparent sphere. He could not be sure what lay beyond the thin wall, but thought he saw the shapes of other spheres and unknown machinery.

When the lift stopped rising, he found himself in the exact middle of the sphere. Future looked around at his surroundings carefully, trying to associate the different objects with what he understood from Blujic's explanation. Nothing was what he had imagined it to be. After some contemplation he located what he thought must have been the harness, suspended between structural supports. He backed into the harness and plugged in the various bare connectors and pipes in receptacles that were built into the suit, and donned the soft helmet and goggles as Blujic had said. Finally, he fitted the mask with its multiple hoses to his face.

Suddenly the structural supports, cables, and inside of the sphere faded away. He stood sandwiched in between three great eggs, with nowhere to exit. Future reached out his hand and felt the wall of the nearest egg. What a strange sensation. It was almost as if there was some very soft surface there that yielded to pressure, yet visually his hand did not seem to depress the surface. When he walked over to the other eggs, the bottoms of his feet felt similar, as if he were walking through powdery sand or yielding fungus. In fact, he found it difficult to get anywhere at all. How would he be able to get out of here?

Future looked up then and saw a flashing circle immediately above his head and remembered. Blujic had said that light markers would guide him out, and that he must use the various techniques of leaping and twisting to affect navigation. Future jumped up toward the flashing circle and flew upward. He slowly rose above the tops of the great eggs and saw that he was hovering above a great sea of the spherical structures. There did not seem to be any danger of falling.

Most of the eggs were darkened, but here and there was a strangely lit one that had some dancing figure behind the semi-transparent skin.

Future continued to rise and soon bumped up against a soft ceiling. When he looked around, he saw that the blinking circle was no longer above him anymore. Instead, a series of squares lit up in sequence in a path that seemed to begin only a few armlengths from his face and ended some distance away in the horizontal direction. He watched the squares light up in sequential perspective, starting with the one near him and ending with the last one on the end. Obviously the squares were pointing the way for him to go.

Future began struggling with the different hand motions and body twists that Blujic had taught him, but only succeeded in setting himself on a slow sideways drift. He began to worry that perhaps he would lose sight of the lighted path, but to his surprise the path moved sideways along with him, adjusting its direction along the way. Future continued struggling and was able to shift his direction by degree, but the overall drift was still sideways to the direction he wanted to go. He soon found himself approaching the edge of the sea of eggs and was not surprised when he finally made contact with another soft surface where the wall should have been. The wall brought his drift to a stop, and the ever-present lighted pathway continued to point off into the darkness.

Future tried kicking against the soft wall, but to his surprise did not get an intuitive reaction. Where he thought that he had pushed himself in the direction the path was indicating, the result was that he began moving sideways again. In frustration, he began swimming in the direction the path indicated, as if he were under the great deep. Though not as maneuverable as his powerful strokes propelled him under the Plasma, the swimming motion did seem to have the desired effect -- he began moving in the right direction.

As he floated along, the pathway guided him into a tunnel and changed directions. He managed to awkwardly change directions without bumping into any more walls, but the progress was painfully slow. Now that he knew the basics of simple navigation, Future began to experiment with his strokes in order to get more power out of them. By the time he emerged out onto the apron, he had improved quite a bit.

The view came in degrees. As he slowly emerged out of the tunnel, nothing could have prepared him for what he was about to see. The sun had still not arisen yet, but the sky was starting to brighten. There, framed in the predawn moments, was the most breathtaking light show Future had ever seen. Fantastic structures were all lit up, floating above the ground. They were like great crystal jewels suspended in clear liquid.

Future lighted on the elusively soft surface of the apron and paused in shock. The idea of lighted crystal jewels suspended in clear liquid brought back a memory from his past. He remembered seeing a fleet of great vessels congregated in the darkness of the deep, each lit up like jewels. Future caught hold on that thought and milked it as far as he possibly could. If he could only remember something about that fleet, he might be able to discover something about his past. In his mind's eye, the scene was perfectly clear. He was swimming through the Plasma toward the third vessel on the right. That pod was the one that carried he and his friends. They were going to discover a new world. They wanted to find a new home that was free of the massive waves and storms that continually beat upon them, where they could live in peace.

What was that vessel? T12! T12 was the name of the craft. And he remembered a name -- 'Mel'. Was that his name, or the name of someone he knew? When Future tried to remember more, something about T12 that was so horrible loomed just beyond the reach of his memory. His link with the past snapped and he could remember no more. Still, he was closer to finding about his origins than before. The vision of that fleet of submarines stayed clear, even as he beheld this new scene of the wonderfully lit floating structures.

A figure moved up to his left. It was Blujic. Excitedly, Future pointed out at the crystal city and smiled.

"Blujic, I remember some things! This wonderful Blujic city remind me of my life!"

Blujic only looked at him wide-eyed and in shock. Future didn't understand why she would be shocked, thinking that if anything she would be pleased.

"Blujic, what wrong?" he asked.

Blujic recovered from her startled expression and explained, "Future, we have to do something about this. The Database thinks that you are I! You look just like me!"

Future looked down at himself and was in turn shocked. There protruding from his chest underneath the tactile suit were two nicely shaped breasts, covered with flowing strands of golden hair! He reached up and felt his chest and his hand passed right through the mounded fabric. Closing his eyes, his chest felt as it always had, flat and muscular. It was some kind of illusion.

"Blujic! How could this have happened?" quite concerned, Future called out in a panic.

"Let me tell you a little about the Database," Blujic began, "Everything you see here is wonderful, but none of it is real. Right now you are still back in the spherical rocker. Reach up and take off your helmet for a moment and see."

Future reached up and pulled off the goggles. Sure enough, though some colors were projected on the semi-transparent walls, he was indeed still in the sphere, hooked up to the harness. Blujic was nowhere to be seen. He replaced the goggles and Blujic reappeared with that startlingly real crystal city backdrop. He repeated that motion several times, on off, on off, just to get a feel for what was real and what was not.

"There is a whole world inside here that is all illusion, modeled somewhat after the real world. We can explore this world with amazing speeds, and enjoy far-away places without having to actually go there. This is where I grew up!" Blujic explained.

Future wasn't at all sure how to take the revelation. That he was enthralled, there was no doubt. He could play around in an environment like this and do dangerous things without getting hurt. He could fly and go explore places with tremendous freedom. Still, it wasn't real. When it came down to it, this Database (as Blujic called it) could only be a temporary place to play.

"Come here. Let's get you fixed up." Blujic motioned for him to turn around and stand still.

Voicing strange commands, Blujic began to move her hands all over his virtual Blujic body and change the appearance of certain places. On his feet, Blujic formed smart looking boots. She kept the breasts, explaining that it would be a better disguise, but somehow toned them down a bit.

"Can't have you attracting any attention. Especially from your own eyes!" she explained while she laughed.

When Blujic finished, the virtual Future was still a blonde-haired girl, but with shorter limbs and general volume reduction he could easily pass for a child. During the entire exercise Future observed the crystal city as it slowly emerged out of the predawn twilight. There were a few figures flying around in the distance, but as a whole the city seemed asleep. More than once other Wardens emerged from the tunnel and flew off on their own business. At those times He and Blujic acted as though they were busy at some activity and tried their best to hide the half-changed disguise work.

"Are they real people?" Future asked.

Blujic shrugged and replied, "I'm not sure if all of them are, but I know that some of them are."

"Future confused. How do Blujic know which is real? I feel real and illusion is mixed."

"So do I, Future, so do I." Blujic began, then quickly added, "I like real the best. That way I was able to meet you!"

Future looked up in the virtual sky and saw three of the moons. "I still don't understand 'orbit'," he said.

Blujic paused and looked with him up at the three shapes. She thought for a bit then proceeded out of thin air to create a small sphere with a string attached. She held the string in one hand and swung the ball in a circle over her head. Similar to the effect it would have in the Flesh, the sphere tried to fly off but was kept in the tight circle by the force of the string.

"The cord represents 'gravity', like a giant magnet. We can't see it, but it keeps us all from flying off into space." she explained.

Space? Future assumed it was the void beyond the ball of the planet -- the ultimate serene strata. "What powers the moons -- how they move?" Future continued to look up at the shapes.

"There are no motors. It's all a perfect balance in free-fall. The moon falls toward the world, but still tries to fly straight out into space. The force causing it to fall balances with the force trying to fling it away, so it moves in steady circles forever."

Future recalled playing with magnets and seeing the invisible force attract metal objects from a short distance away. So 'gravity' held them up there as they made circular trips around their world -- it was all so fantastic.

With the disguise complete, Blujic proceeded to show him around. At first he was hesitant, not willing to make the leap off the apron that would send him flying in some direction. Future was amazed at how fast and how precise Blujic was able to move and maneuver. With a little coaxing, she succeeded in getting him into the air and learning new tricks and techniques. He found that it was similar to swimming in a lot of ways, but completely different. He remembered back when he had to give Blujic swimming lessons how he thought it odd that she should kick a certain way, or reach out counter intuitively. Now that he watched her fly, he saw the same kicks and reaches and realized that she had been trying to move through the liquid media the best way she knew how. Future was beginning to experience her world and found he imitated those same kicks and reaches, finding them to be most effective in navigation.

As they flew side-by-side, some Wardens would approach them and call out a greeting, "Hello Miss Blujic. Teaching children navigation tricks today?"

Blujic would turn to Future and say under her breath, "That's my friend so-and-so. Good disguise eh? Now I can teach you all day and you don't have to hide."

But the happy-go-lucky feeling was soon replaced by worry. Future went off by himself to a far tower, always under the watchful eye of Blujic. As he alighted on a grand cantilevered balcony of one of the core towers, a woman approached him and began making a few comments.

"Hello Miss Blujic. I see you're masquerading as a child today. How clever and unique. You have a lot of unique interests don't you, such as sneaking outside in the Flesh. Let's talk about it sometime."

Future just stayed where he was and didn't know what to say. If he spoke he might reveal his heavy accent and cause suspicion. But how had the woman mistaken him for Blujic? It was almost as if the woman could see Future's virtual Blujic body as it was before it had been altered in disguise.

When Future only stared back at her and didn't answer, the woman got an oddly suspicious look on her face, shrugged, and turned away to enter the core tower.

As soon as the woman had gone, Future immediately flew back to where Blujic was waiting and told her about the incident.

"What woman was that?" she asked.

"The woman also have golden hair, but is much older than Blujic. She already go away so Future can't show you."

Blujic grilled him, "You sure she called you 'Blujic'? How could she have made such a connection? Does she have some way of seeing logons, I wonder?"

From that point Blujic seemed to get a little paranoid. She backed up against the wall and continually looked this way and that to see if anyone was looking. For a long time she just stood there deep in thought with a worried look on her face. Finally she said, "Future, let's get out of the crystal city. I'll show you places I went when I was a little girl."

At first Future was confused. Did she mean that they should go back in and get out of the harnesses and fantastic rocker machines? But Blujic headed in the opposite direction for that. She took off and flew toward the distant green horizon. Future leaped up and followed her, excitement welling in his heart. He thought, perhaps it is possible to view the countryside as well. Perhaps they can search for clues as to where he came from.

In no time their flight paths took them beyond the bounds of the city, over rolling green hills. Blujic seemed to have some destination in mind, so Future was content at just following along. The scenery below turned into forest, and they flew above the tops of the younger trees. Up ahead, the massive older giants towered out of sight. The view was wonderful. Future never would have imagined that it could have been possible to view the environment from this perspective. He soaked up every scene with avid curiosity.

"Come with me!" Blujic excitedly called out.

She flew up and up, higher and higher. Future followed and soon they were approaching the tops of even the giants. The sky above slowly faded from a deep blue into a light gray. The world below got smaller and smaller, and soon both horizons started caving in to the middle to form a huge green bubble. They continued to rise and the bubble shrank in size to a small sphere.

Blujic stopped and turned around, "This is out-of-bounds for the Database. The machines that do the mapping don't reach this far, so it just remains gray forever and ever. You remember those flying machines we saw in the Flesh? Those are Mappers."

Future thought for a moment and then said, "In crystal city I remember about my home in ocean. Can we find my home in Database?"

"The Mappers can't go out in the storms. We can see some of the oceans but most of it is gray. We can swim in the Database, too, but everything is fake, even the corpuscles."

Future lingered there in the gray for a while, somewhat downtrodden. He had really hoped that this wonderful Database thing would help him find out where he came from.

At length they zoomed back straight down, the green sphere growing at a dizzying speed, and found themselves above the canopy of the younger trees again.

Continuing on, Future could see other Wardens flying in the distance. Blujic seemed quite worried and would zigzag their course to avoid others as much as possible. Future had the impression that if it weren't for the others flying here and about, they might have arrived sooner at whatever destination she was leading them toward. As they flew on, there seemed to be one place that had an extra amount of commotion. Wardens were flying in hordes above a certain spot in the forest. Future could see fliers dipping below the canopy and coming back up again. By the look on Blujic's face, he could tell that she was extremely curious about the gathering, but was holding it in for safety's sake. Instead of yielding to her curiosity, she led them the long way around. As soon as they passed that crowd, the numbers of Wardens they saw dropped off dramatically. Soon there was not a soul to be seen.

Blujic dropped down into the trees and Future followed. They flew along the deck at tremendous speeds, giving Future a thrill he had never known before. The mossy hills and ground sped by in a blur only armlengths below him, and the massive boles of trees swished by on either side. Indeed, they had to constantly maneuver in order to keep from running into them.

Future watched Blujic and followed suit. At one point, an unusually large number of young thin trees grew together in a small area. Blujic headed right for them, and to his surprise, she made no attempt to avoid running into them. Her body passed right through the trees as if they weren't even there. Future did not have the courage to follow her directly, but raised his altitude in such a way that he passed between only the higher growths, and safely cleared the majority far below. After seeing what Blujic had done, he decided to experiment by holding out one arm and whacking one of the thin treetops. As was expected, his hand passed right through it and he felt a strange sensation through the tactile suit, as if he had swatted a very soft, yielding object. The thought that came to mind was that his hand had just passed through a column of falling water.

They emerged from the trees into green hilly country. Nearby, a low peak poked up above some hills in such a way that seemed vaguely familiar. As they sped over the tops of the hills Future found out why: the peak stood sentry at one end of the valley where the *Origin* rested. Though he had not seen the country from such a high perspective point, the pattern of lakes and the vine covered towering half dome was unmistakable. Blujic paused and looked around, checking whether the coast was clear. As far as Future could tell, there was not a soul to be seen.

"That's strange, there's always at least one or two Wardens around. And there's no one guarding the *Origin*. I've never seen this before!" Blujic began. "This might be our lucky day."

From their high perspective the relationship between the *Origin* and the long, linear lake was quite clear. Having been inside, and knowing the structure was a half-buried sphere, it was more apparent than ever that the *Origin* must have formed the lake as it rolled along the ground and finally sunk in at it's current resting place. But that only deepened the mystery of what the *Origin* was, and how those people could have lived on the wall of the cylinder. Was it magnetic? Did the cylinder walls have 'gravity' to hold the people up? Whatever force allowed those people to live that way had long gone, unfortunately.

They approached the dome hovering just over the ground, as if they were on foot. From the upper valley side, there appeared to be some rents and cracks that he hadn't realized existed on the real *Origin*, some with young trees protruding out of them. Coming around the side, Future found the fresh water lake where he had first met Blujic, and traced the path up to where the tear scarred the side of the dome. Everything seemed just as he had remembered it, except for the tear: where the space between the inner and outer skin should have had exposed triangular structural members, Future could only see a solid surface. It was as if the virtual tear was only made to look like the real tear from a distance. The two of them went around and checked all the other openings as well, to no avail. Even the removed plate high up on the dome, which had the makeshift crane structure protruding into the sky, was only a superficial opening.

Future remembered his experience passing through the tree and began to wonder: could they pass through the surface of the dome? He couldn't restrain his curiosity, "Blujic, let's get inside *Origin* again!"

"It will never work. The *Origin* is solid with no way in."

But Future was persistent, "Nothing is solid!"

He flew off before Blujic could stop him. Deciding to take a bolder approach, Future opted for a higher speed with the intent to crash through the virtual upper dome into the massive space in the core of the *Origin*. After all, it would only feel like that tree, with a strange sensation at the beginning and then he'd be through. Just think, if he could explore by flying, he would not need ropes or cords and could explore all those impossible-to-reach places that he had wanted to see the first time around.

The dome got closer and closer. Blujic called from behind for him to stop but he wouldn't listen. Visually the signals his eyes were giving him told him he was about to have a deadly collision with the outer surface of the sphere, even though he knew otherwise. Still, his reflexes followed the more powerful imagery he had been conditioned to follow all his life, and he rolled up into a ball and cringed. The impact was completely unexpected. Though it was much similar to the soft impact he had felt when he had bumped back and forth against the walls and ceiling of the rocker port, the high speed brought a completely different reaction: an uncontrolled spinning head over heels. There was one thing for sure: he was NOT inside the dome. Other than that he lost all bearings and just spun faster and faster.

"Future!" Blujic called from somewhere (a somewhere that changed directions every instant), "Future, you have to get yourself out of it."

Future started feeling sick, but heard Blujic mention that he should throw his arms and legs out spread-eagle. Immediately giving it a try, the spinning slowed quite a bit but did not stop.

"Now you have to reach over and grab the structural supports on the rocker harness in the Flesh. It won't be easy because it's behind your back."

Future tried to keep himself as spread-eagle as possible, while reaching behind his back with one arm. The effort was quite difficult. Future's stomach couldn't take the motion and he lost his breakfast, heaving several times. Finally, trying to keep his cool despite all the undesirable things his body was uncontrollably doing, he managed to touch one of the harness supports and apply enough pressure to slow the spin to a stop.

When Future finally got his wits back, he found that he was hovering just above the surface of the vine-covered dome in the virtual world. He felt terrible. Somehow the vomit had found itself going down the right mask hose for disposal, or at least he didn't have to think about it anymore. Future just felt content to drift for a while, happy to be free of the sickening motions.

"I told you to stop! You didn't listen!" Blujic came up from behind, railing on him. "I've done that before. I already know it's useless."

Future didn't answer, but just drifted motionless with his eyes closed trying to recover from the awful vertigo. Blujic seemed to understand, and just waited for him to heal. After a while she tried a new approach.

"I know a place where we can relax. You can take all the time you need to rest." she offered.

"Blujic, can I just climb out of harness in rocker? If we actually in rocker why we must travel back?" Future asked.

"The harness won't release unless the Database has been properly reset. Believe me, I've tried that before, too, and our only alternative is to fly back to the rocker port. You're struck with rocker fright. You must get over it and face it right now."

Blujic slowly led him back along the valley floor, parallel with the long liquid-filled depression. They flew over the green hills and above the forest canopy. The movement didn't help his motion sickness any, but since he had already vomited everything up he felt he could survive. Sensitive to his situation, Blujic found a spot she had been looking for and slowly sunk down below the canopy. She floated easily just above the forest floor at a pace that Future could handle.

They hadn't gone far when Blujic suddenly stopped and turned, "Hey look! Cuddlers!"

Future followed her gaze and was quite startled by what he saw. There were three little fuzz ball creatures moving along the mossy carpet. Future had never seen such a thing before (as far as he could remember). There were little multi-legged things that lived among the fungus in the node towers, ten of which could easily dance on the tip of a man's forefinger. There were also the swimmers, which were about as large as a man's hand. He had seen small-scaled creatures from the sea, and then there were the corpuscles that could be quite small or downright huge. But never had he seen a creature such as this before. Future went down to pick one of them up and his hand passed right through it, to his dismay.

"Aren't they cute?" Blujic began, "I've always loved cuddlers ever since I was a little girl."

"This is wonderful! Little things that can walk by themselves!" Future excitedly commented.

Blujic was obviously overjoyed that he had taken an interest in something so dear to her. "Yes, too bad they're fake."

"What is fake?"

"They only exist in the Database. I've never seen any in the Flesh. There are flyers as well. We'll probably see some of them." Blujic explained.

They continued on their way with an easy pace. To Future the forest seemed to get noticeably greener and more beautiful than before. A series of small lakes and ponds dotted the forest floor. Suddenly Blujic came to a halt. She seemed visually upset as she looked around at the scenery ahead. Future pulled up to her side and saw an unexpected sight. There ahead of them was a small clearing with a beautiful lake and meadow. What was unexpected was the structure that had been built at one end of the meadow. With only a very slim base connected to the ground, the main bulk of the structure cantilevered out above them and almost seemed to hover. Future thought back on the imagery of the crystal city with its floating towers and remembered that such things were possible in the Database. The walls of the structure were of some course material that Future had never seen before. The pattern was a grayish, black / white speckle that was fashioned into blocks laid in intricate overlapping courses. In some places along the walls were slit windows. The overall layout was not square, but had some geometrical pattern Future could not discern from their present angle, with cylindrical towers at each corner. It was a magnificent structure.

"Those guys went ahead and formed a castle anyway!" Blujic angrily complained. "This was such a beautiful spot and my friends spoiled it!"

Just then a voice called out from some upper slit windows in the castle, "Miss Blujic! Hello! Hello down there!"

Future and Blujic looked up just in time to see a Warden girl emerge from a dark doorway high above them that opened onto a balcony. The Warden descended to where they were and hovered above the ground between them and the castle. Behind the girl, two more figures followed from the castle and stopped a little ways off. They were children. A little boy and a little girl, dressed in some elaborate costumes, hovered upright a few handwidths above the ground. The boy had a gold-colored metal helmet of sorts, and the girl had long flowing blonde hair. Future was quite curious. He loved children and wanted to see what they were like in Blujic's culture. Still, it would probably be too dangerous. Future, remembering that he himself was disguised as a child, decided to act the part and cowered shyly behind Blujic.

"Hello Miss Blujic. I see you are playing with children today, too. You want to play together?"

"Miss Tarroc! I thought we were going to keep this place natural! You guys formed that castle anyway."

Miss Tarroc got defensive, "Miss Blujic, we haven't even seen you for weeks now. We were going to ask you, but you were so stuck on that Flesh kick we thought you didn't care about us anymore."

Blujic looked surprised, "Has it been that long? So much has happened since then. I've found a wonderful boy I'd like you to meet."

She turned to Future as if to introduce him but checked herself. Future wondered if Miss Tarroc had caught that slip, but the girl continued on as if she didn't notice. His disguise was working well.

Miss Tarroc said, "You're not the type that would be wandering around at a time like this. I would have thought you would be over watching the war. I'd be there too if I didn't have to baby-sit!"

Blujic was surprised again, "What war?"

"You don't even know about the war? It's the one against the horrible submarine Inmates."

"What submarine Inmates?"

This time Miss Tarroc was surprised, "You don't even know about the submarine people?"

Blujic was in deep contemplation, "Miss Pollic called into the shower once and told me about invading Inmates. I guess I'd had too much on my mind to give it much thought."

Future was getting curious. Could there be people out there similar to his own who used submarines? Maybe he could find out more about his own origins if he could see or talk with those Inmates. He whispered quietly so Miss Tarroc or the other children could not hear, "Blujic, what are submarine people?"

As if to answer his question, Miss Tarroc started to explain, "These people who wear thick black suits and climb out of the Plasma have been harassing the local Inmates and fighting with our armies. They've built a stronghold up in the trees. Everyone has been watching them."

Blujic got a look on her face that Future had learned to read -- she was hiding something when she said, "Wow! Maybe we'll have to go take a look sometime, huh twinkles?" She turned momentarily to Future. "Well, we've got to go. See ya!"

"Twinkles?" Future said under his breath.

Miss Tarroc waved good-bye and watched as Blujic and Future lifted off and rose straight through the canopy. Blujic was leading quite slowly, as if she were deliberately trying to make a show that she was not in any hurry when deep inside she was busting to cut loose. As soon as they had put the canopy between them and her friend, she did race onward. Blujic knew exactly where she was going and was intending to get there fast, whether Future had motion sickness or not. She turned in flight to face Future who was struggling to keep up.

"Do you realize who those submarine people are?" she asked. "They're your people! My people the Wardens are fighting your people!"

Future was shocked, "My people?"

"Yes, Miss Tarroc described your diving suit. It must be your people. We have to go see the war to make sure."

Even though it was above the top of the canopy, Future recognized the place as soon as they got near. It was the same area where they had seen many Wardens flying around earlier. Abandoning all caution, Blujic rushed up to a group of Wardens who were busy conversing above the treetops.

"Hello, have you been following the war?" Blujic asked one of the men in the group. "Can you fill me in a little bit?"

By the look on his face it was clear that the man seemed to think the request a little odd, but he began to explain anyway. "Sure. See that tree over there that's a little higher than the others? That's the center of where the submarine people have built their forts. Right below us and surrounding the enemy are our security forces."

"Thanks." Blujic waved at the man.

"One more thing," The man called out as Blujic and Future turned to leave, "I wouldn't take any children in there if I were you. It's not a pretty sight!"

Blujic nodded and waved again, as if she was listening but had no intention to take the advice. At that point Blujic and Future sank straight down below the canopy. Scattered about in hidden corners and behind trees, hundreds of strange machines lay in wait. The machines consisted of smart-looking frames surrounding a seat and banks of controls, unknown devices, and arrays of weapons. A warden sat in each one of those machines, engaging each other in conversation and otherwise waiting for orders. Floating round and about the machines were countless Wardens who had come to watch the battles. Without exception the crowd was excitedly chattering about the event. War games were popular, but a real war would be even more entertaining. At the center of their attention, off in the distance could be seen the forts of the enemies. Like growths attached to the massive trunks of a dozen or so trees, the bulges were linked together by catwalks and bridges.

Blujic approached one of the machines and began asking the operator questions. Trying to keep calm, Blujic asked, "I've been away for several days. How has the war been going?"

"Well, we had a major offensive two days ago. We killed some of the enemy and almost drove out the rest with our prods. It was a great battle. We almost got rid of them all together!"

Blujic was trying hard to hide her dismay, and turn it around into false excitement. "Wow! Why didn't you finish them off?"

"Other submarine people came up out of the Plasma with these black suits on. It seems the suits have some type of electrodes that short out the bolts from our prods. None of our weapons have any effect on them. The guys in black came up and picked off our machines one by one with their bare hands! Now all of them have those suits on ..."

Future had been looking at the forts during the whole conversation. His people! Some of his people had been killed. Blujic's discussion faded away as he began thinking about his people. He found himself drifting toward the forts, wanting to get a better view. Some Wardens called out a warning that he shouldn't get any closer but Future ignored them. No one came to stop him so he assumed that they were just treating him like the child he appeared to be. Future could see that the forts were constructed of rough sawn planks and branches taken from the trees. As he approached the base of one of the nearest platforms, he passed over some figures hiding on the ground. Could these be his people?

Future intuitively kept himself hidden. Taking a closer look, one of the figures briefly stood up and revealed a blood-red helmet with shoulder and back plates, and a hideous mask spilling bright red fibers of hair in all directions. Future was shocked. He had seen these creatures in a dream, and knew they were up to no good. Some haunting memories seemed to be there just below the surface, trying to get out. Though he tried, Future could only remember the dream where Those Who Went Before had come to save him, and the grandfather had stepped out of that square hatch from the floating pod. These must be the Inmates.

Future saw that they were poised with strange looking contraptions consisting of bent rods and taut cables. Crossing the device was a single rod with a sharp barb aimed up at the forts. What the contraptions were for he had no idea, but intuition said that they were weapons, and the barbed ends were meant to enter human Flesh.

Future looked up at the forts. Not a soul could be seen. His people were hiding behind those timbers and were guarding themselves from the barbed weapons. What were they like? He wanted to see his people with all the passion of his soul. Keeping himself hidden from those terrible Inmates,

Future drifted up toward the bulbous structures. As his elevation increased, the angle of his perspective gave him a view over the tops of the stockade. There, pacing back and forth along a rough planked deck, were figures in black. Divers! They were wearing the same suits that he had in his possession that very instant down in the rocker compartment locker -- thick black material with an embedded network of corpuscle repellent electrodes. The divers all had black soft helmets and bulbous goggles.

On impulse, Future sank down to the deck and followed a diver along a catwalk. The diver approached one of the enclosed platforms and disappeared through a grayed out opening. He had seen that light color gray recently -- *the inside must not be mapped into the Database*, he thought, recalling what Blujic had said about the gray out-of-bounds. Future started noticing gray spots here and there in out-of-the-way corners where the mapping was incomplete.

As he hesitated on the platform edge, another diver stepped out of the gray void and startled him.

"Hey, guys! It's me. I'm back! I'm ... I ..." Future waved his arms frantically and tried to get the diver's attention, but couldn't remember his own name. He couldn't introduce himself as 'Future'!

In spite of his frantic waving and yelling, the diver continued walking as if Future wasn't even there. Future looked down at himself and remembered that he was in a child's body. No one would recognize him this way. He moved right to the middle of the passageway, putting himself in the diver's path. Not only did the diver not stop, he didn't even pause or slow down. In an instant the man collided with Future, passed right through him, and continued on his way. Future felt that strange sensation of having passed through something just on the edge of being tangible, like a column of water. Suddenly he felt like a ghost.

"They can't see you." Blujic had sneaked up nearby, "They're only animated parts of the Database and not in rockers."

Future thought for a moment and said, "Like cuddlers?"

"Just like the cuddlers, except the Mappers are capturing their movements in the Flesh in real time and updating the Database accordingly." Blujic paused for a moment and then her face went grave. "Future, we've got to go in a hurry! We must get back to the crystal city and talk to Chief Warden Korric before nightfall. They've thought up a weapon that will destroy your people right out of the forest!"

The crystal palaces were already lit up and all that remained of the sun was a bright red spark on the distant horizon. Chief Warden Korric was supposedly at that very moment commanding the armies from the Department of Security tower, according to Blujic. The two of them flew directly to the tower, and Future immediately recognized it as the building he had flown to earlier in the morning, and received the interrogation from the mysterious woman. Since the Department of Security tower wasn't cleared for general entry without permission, Blujic led Future to the main reception desk and began pleading with the desk officer on duty.

"Sir, we have to speak with Chief Warden Korric." she energetically petitioned.

"Chief Warden Korric is now quite busy. They're preparing for a major offensive against the invaders this very instant."

"That's what we have to talk to her about! The offensive must not take place!" Blujic spit out in the energy of her soul.

The desk officer was a little surprised but undaunted. "Sorry to disappoint you, but Chief Warden Korric cannot be disturbed right now, especially by sniveling girls and children!"

That was the wrong thing to say to Blujic at a time like this. She got angrier than Future had ever seen her before. "What do you mean by sniveling girl! I've got important information about security that she needs to hear!" She folded her arms and pouted, "What use is it talking to this little chirp?"

"Who are you callin' chirp!" The desk officer and Blujic got into a real verbal war, shouting insults back and forth. Future was surprised at such spirit in a woman. They were beginning to cause a scene that was attracting attention. Wardens casually floating by stopped to listen and a crowd started to form.

In the heat of the argument, a woman parted the crowd and approached the two. "What's the problem here?"

The desk officer turned and almost apologetically greeted the woman, "Oh, hello Secretary Kammoc. This young lady is insisting on talking to Chief Warden Korric even though I have orders that she not be disturbed."

Kammoc turned to Blujic and smiled, "Ah Miss Blujic, the Flesh explorer! Chief Warden Korric cannot be disturbed right now, but she certainly would like to interview you later."

Blujic pleaded, "But we have to see her now! Before she launches the big attack!"

"We? Who's we?"

Blujic motioned to Future who had been neutrally waiting off to the side. Future came immediately to her side and Kammoc's eyes widened.

The secretary first pointed at Blujic and then Future, "Miss Blujic! And Miss Blujic! What's going on here?"

Everyone was silent. Blujic smiled suddenly and said, "That is exactly what we have to explain," then she turned and yelled only fingerwidths from the desk officer's face, "TO CHIEF WARDEN KORRIC!"

Blujic and Future immediately got a pass and a full escort, led by Kammoc herself. Somehow the secretary was able to mysteriously see logons just as the woman had done earlier that morning, and recognized both Blujic and Future as having Blujic logons. As the group walked, or rather shuffled along, Blujic described some of the departments to Future. Their destination was the command center of the Prison Guard Corps, where Future saw rows and rows of the same framed machines they had seen out on the battlefield, except that in this case the machines were simpler and had translucent skins so he couldn't quite see the Warden inside. Blujic and Future were taken to a conference room deep in the heart of the command center.

Kammoc sent the others out and immediately started questioning the two, "Miss Blujic, whichever one of you is the real Miss Blujic, tell me what's going on here."

Blujic spoke right up, "I am the real Miss Blujic. Mrs. Secretary, you must get Chief Warden Korric to break off the invasion!"

"That's impossible. The Chief Warden has already taken off with the special weapons fleet. They're planning on using fire this time."

Blujic argued, "But live trees aren't flammable."

"The vicinity will be sprayed with a fine flammable mist -- one spark and the whole region will go up in smoke!"

Again Blujic protested out of desperation, "But you'll kill those people! You can't kill them -- you must stop the invasion!"

"Is there some reason why we should stop? Do you have a good reason besides just being nice to the enemy? And what does this have to do with there being two Miss Blujics?"

"I have a very good reason, but you must delay the invasion and get the Chief Warden here until I can adequately explain. If my explanation isn't reason enough, you may continue with the engagement as planned." Blujic then got a very determined look on her face. With confidence she added, "I guarantee you will never go through with it!"

Kammoc stared at Blujic for a long while before finally replying, "All right, young lady. I'll ask Chief Korric to come join us. The special fleet will stay on course, with a temporary pilot taking over her seat. You will only have until the fleet arrives at the battlefield to convince us of your argument, then she will have to take her command seat back again." Then she got up and left the room.

Future was sitting closest to the door, facing whoever would walk through that portal. Since he was actually in the rocker in the Flesh, he wasn't actually sitting, but it was a pretty good approximation of it. The seats looked quite hard but turned out to be the softest seat he had ever set his rear end on. Since Future had pretty much gotten used to the fact that some surfaces were only visually solid but could actually be passed through, and other surfaces though soft became a solid barrier, he was not surprised when the chair grabbed him and kept him from drifting down to the floor. It had been the first time during his whole rocker experience that he actually sat down instead of hovered.

After the secretary left, it was only a matter of moments before she returned again bringing a woman in tow. It was the same woman he had seen that morning. Their eyes met.

"Ah Miss Blujic, I see you're still disguised as a child. What's all this about that I should be interrupted from my command?"

Then she saw the real Blujic. Her eyes widened in surprise. Before she could say anything the real Blujic began to explain.

"You've got to stop the invasion!" she began, "I went out in the Flesh and traveled all the way to the *Origin*. I had almost entirely run out of food when I ran across someone whom I had never seen before. The man fed me and made sure I felt welcome. When I was sick and dying of a fever he nursed me back to health. On numerous occasions he put his own life on the line in order to save me. He could have taken advantage of me at any time but he was a perfect gentleman. Chief Korric, the man was from the submarine Inmates! If they are all like him, they haven't even a shadow of ill intent and would just like to be left alone!"

"They've been battling with the local Inmates. With their technology they can invade our deep ports. They are a danger to us! There's too much at stake to let some presumptions or emotion cloud our judgment." Korric was finally able to say. "If you are the real Miss Blujic, then who is this Miss Blujic?"

Before Blujic could answer, Future stood up and said, "I am from submarine people. My name is Future."

In unison both Korric and Kammoc dropped their jaws. They stood up and stared at Future like it was the end of the world. During the period of shock, Blujic quickly explained that Future had lost his memory and that they were only calling him 'Future' temporarily until he remembered his real name.

Korric didn't recover from the shock, but composed herself enough to lash out at Blujic, "Do you mean that you brought one of the enemy here inside our nest? We have one of the enemy right here in the heart of our command center!"

"Of course not! Number one he is not an enemy, and number two he is in no control center but is hooked up to a rocker. Let's get what's real and what's imaginary straight right now!"

Korric was angry, "But he is in the heart of our facility. He is within our security perimeter. A person in a rocker can control any of our machines -- for our good or for our destruction!"

Blujic was also angry, "He knows nothing about controlling machines. I know nothing about controlling machines myself! Aren't they all automatons?"

"For your information there is no such thing as an automaton. Somebody controls every machine. Every machine's eye has a person's eye behind it. But that's not important right now. Even if he can't operate our machines, he can help his people invade through the deep ports!"

Blujic narrowed her eyes and sat back. She lowered her tone and in a cool, confident voice said, "What deep ports? There are no deep ports. I know! I've been everywhere in the Flesh and I know what's there and what's not!"

Somewhere along the line Future, Korric, and Kammoc had returned to their seats. Though the conversation was mostly a dialog between Korric and Blujic, Future felt the need to step in. In an emotional flood, he said, "Please stop argue. I not enemy, I friend of Wardens. My people come from place of big wave and storm. We just want a safe place to live and have family." then his voice broke and he continued, "I love Blujic!"

Blujic turned to him and started crying, "Future, I love you too!"

Future was normally strong but now he couldn't help himself and started crying also. The two of them just bawled and bawled. Korric and Kammoc stared in disbelief. After a while the crying subsided and there was only silence as each person was deep in his or her own thoughts. Finally Korric stood up again.

"The secretary and I have to discuss this. Please excuse us for a moment." she said.

The pair exited the room leaving Blujic and Future to themselves again. Blujic reached over and grabbed Future's hand (or virtually did the closest thing to it) and said, "I think it will be all right. I sure wish we were in the Flesh now so I could give you a big hug! How did you manage those tears at just the right moment?"

"I just say what in Future heart and tears come."

The time drew longer and longer. Outside, the city was blazing with light and the sky was completely dark. Certainly the fleet with the special weapons had already arrived at the battleground. At long last Korric and the secretary returned.

Korric said, "Miss Blujic, I've postponed the invasion. This is against my better judgment but I believe both of you. I don't think Future is our enemy. But I'm wondering if we should judge a whole race on a man who has lost his memory!"

Blujic was emotional again, "Thank you so much Chief Warden!"

Korric continued, "There are some things that I want you to do. First, Miss Blujic I want you to take me in the Flesh all over the facility and teach me what you know. There has never been an age like this before, so the Chief Warden must know the difference between what's real and what's imaginary." Korric winked at Blujic. "The next thing I want to do is find out from Future everything he can remember about his people. Third, I will assign you two as ambassadors to go to the submarine Inmates and open up a dialog with them."

A few wake periods later Blujic and Future were virtually together with Chief Warden Korric again. Future had been assigned quarters in the Flesh and had been given his own logon and an introductory tour of the Warden facility. He was under guard at all times of course (both in the Flesh and in the Database), and was only shown things that were required for a person to live in the facility. He had also spent a lot of time with Korric's officers, explaining everything he could remember about his people. It wasn't much, but he was able to tell about the deteriorating condition of their city, and the constant need to make repairs against the storms. He explained that they only wanted a place where they could feel secure, and not worry about whether half their homes would fall into the Plasma next season or not.

Blujic had been whisked away and had done much the same thing, explaining about their exploration of the *Origin* and her many trips in the Flesh. She was soon scheduled to fulfill her part of the bargain and show the Chief Warden around the facility in the Flesh. In preparation for that, Korric invited Blujic and Future to a special discussion session with just the three of them and Advisor Herrec.

"There's something I want to show you." She began, "Not only is the Database a current thing, but there are archives of past events as well."

Blujic said, "I know, you've recorded some of my sneaking around through the eyes of the automatons. They told me that."

"No, there's more. Take a look at this!"

The room darkened and an illuminated screen appeared. On the screen a two dimensional video began playing. The image had no sound. A blonde man in the Warden's uniform was facing the camera and was explaining something. The video panned to the left and a row of large spheres came into view. Rockers. A door closed between the rockers and the camera, shutting off the scene. The door had a peculiar appearance, similar to what Future thought one might see on a pod where a Plasma-tight seal was desired. The camera swept away from the door and captured the same blonde Warden as before, hovering in a corridor.

After having experienced the Database for a few days, Future thought it normal to see a Warden hovering in a corridor. Still, something about the situation didn't seem right. The strange feeling got worse when the blonde man reached out to the wall and grabbed onto a handhold mounted to the wall. Handholds? Looking closer, Future noticed that the walls were lined with rows of handholds. In fact, the floor and ceiling also had handholds.

The blonde man in the video used the handholds to spin himself around in midair, and began pulling himself along the corridor. The camera moved along the corridor as well, following the man. The Warden floated to a spot where the corridor widened. Though the sweep of the camera was quick, Future thought he saw other corridors intersecting the original one, coming in not only from the sides but shafts from above and below as well. The blonde Warden propelled himself upward and entered a diagonal shaft. The camera followed soon after and captured the Warden turning himself around and propelling himself feet first up the diagonal shaft. After a few armlengths, the man used his feet as well, touching them to the handholds as he backed up the shaft.

At this point, the image seemed to fool Future. He had been thinking all along that the man was backing up a diagonal shaft, when the current image suddenly impressed on his mind that a man was simply climbing down a ladder into a vertical well. After some length, the man passed a closed hatch or door in the wall of the shaft. Moving down beside the door, he reached out sideways and grasped the locking mechanism, pushing the door open. Momentarily the Warden disappeared through the door.

As the camera followed to pass through the open door, both Future and Blujic let out a gasp. The scene was so unexpected that Future could not contain himself with excitement. There with his back to the camera, the blonde Warden stood on a deck with his hands propped on his hips. Above him, a massive long narrow structure cantilevered out over a vast space. The structure had geometric modules and other objects attached. Below the Warden, the deck upon which he stood terraced down to other decks, where others were busy and milling about. Though the immediate deck seemed flat, the wider decks lower in the terrace curved upward at the sides and framed a massive rotating geodesic window that Future and Blujic had seen before -- the *Origin* dome oculus.

The video had been taken eons before inside the *Origin*, back when it was still alive and the Warden ancestors inhabited it. Perhaps the blonde man was one of Blujic's grandfathers. In the few moments before the video ended, Future and Blujic studied the scene in amazement. Where the deck curved upward at the sides, people could be seen sitting at tables, walking among trees, and standing about, all oriented perpendicular to the part of the deck on which they stood. This meant that from the camera's vantage point, the farther one looked to the side where the deck curved up, the more diagonal it seemed they stood, until some seemed to be walking on the walls. It got worse. Continuing up around the curve, Future could see people standing / playing / working on the ceiling. These people were mysteriously living on the inside surface of a cylinder, confirming what they had witnessed in the dusty old structure.

The massive geodesic dome that Future and Blujic had crawled across only a few days earlier seemed clean and new. Many of the heavy plate shield mechanisms were cracked open at various angles letting in the scene beyond. Though they couldn't see it directly (the shield mechanisms prevented it), the sun shone in a few beams that hit in spots on the distant deck to their right. In the few moments that they watched, the beams altered their direction and traveled visibly around the perimeter, as if the sun and the world outside were spinning at the same rate as the dome. Future could see glimpses of stars outside, all fixed with reference to the geodesic dome window, but spinning from their vantage.

The video came to an end and the room lights brightened. The mesmerized Future and Blujic looked at each other in amazement. Korric said, "These 2D videos were all taken in the Flesh by automatons of the day. I have one more clip that you might be interested in before we go through some rocker archives."

Once again the lights dimmed and another video projected on the screen. The scene showed the inside of the *Origin* dome as before, but instead of the blonde man, a woman faced the camera and chattered unheard words. She looked quite bedraggled and tired, and her uniform was torn down one arm.

Though the camera stayed fairly steady, the woman seemed to dance in unison with the rotation of the massive dome behind her: she would first crouch low and move to the left, then stretch out slightly and lean to the right in a circular motion that was repeated in a cycle. When Future looked at other Wardens running around frenzied in the background, they were all doing the circular dance as well. Strangely enough, trees, chairs, tables, and other inanimate objects seemed to lean back and forth or slide across the deck in the same cycle.

Through the dome Future could see a huge, round, bluish luminous object fixed within the boundaries of the dome. Behind the bluish circle were a few pinpoints of light and other smaller luminous shapes. Suddenly outside the dome window something large passed by. Then a bright flash could be seen at one edge of the dome. In one accord, every Warden visible lost their footing and fell to the deck. The woman who had been speaking in front of the camera got slowly back on her feet, a frightened look on her face. Behind her others got to their feet as well, and began scrambling for open hatches and doors. The woman disappeared somewhere behind the camera leaving the scene completely devoid of all people.

The bluish circle outside began to grow larger. Future started to see some detail on it, picking out swirling patterns of white and green and blue. Soon the object filled the entire window. At once, all of the triangular plate shields began to move on their hinges, rotating into a shut position to cover the thick clear window panels like the closing petals of a flower. The view beyond was cut off as the last shield slammed shut.

Inside, chairs, tables and other loose objects began to slide wildly about. Sometimes the objects on one half of the vast space literally hopped up in the air above the deck as if a giant had grabbed hold of the *Origin* and shook its contents. The wild motions died down a little and the various pieces of furniture and downed trees lay somewhat still in their scattered condition. Then after a few moments the wild motions started up again and all hell broke loose. All sorts of objects flew about in no apparent pattern. The artificial lighting suddenly went out bathing the entire space in darkness.

The black screen continued. Since Korric made no move to stop the video, Future continued to watch for something else. A few moments more went by and his eyes focused on what appeared to be small specks of light. As he studied the scene he realized that a triangular pattern of faint hairline cracks of light defined where the geodesic shield plates of the oculus stood slightly ajar. The dome was no longer rotating.

Beams of light began bathing the curved decks as dark silhouettes emerged from hatches. The figures were standing at a different orientation now, with their heads pointing toward the dome as if it were a ceiling. The *Origin* had become just as Future and Blujic had found it, in that strange sideways orientation.

The video continued for a little while longer, where the camera followed groups of tired Wardens through darkened corridors and chambers. Wardens climbed up onto the ledge just below the dome where he and Blujic had first entered the massive space from the antechamber. Though the video ended there, Future imagined the tired group climbing up into the space between the inner and outer skin and removing a plate to the outside where they left the *Origin* forever.

The lights in the room brightened as Korric explained, "The Wardens watched the Inmates from high above Mother. Records show that when they left the *Origin*, they moved into mostly abandoned ground facilities and waited for rescue from those in the *Destiny*, which was the sister to the *Origin*. They brought the ground facilities out of mothball status so they could continue maintaining the Database and watching over the Inmates. Wardens still believe they will go back to the *Destiny* someday."

Blujic asked, "But why did the *Origin* fall out of the sky?"

"Who knows? I've watched that clip a dozen times and still can't make any sense out of it. How did the people walk on the walls like that? We can only attribute it to the mysterious power of the *Origin* that somehow was lost after its fall."

Chief Warden Korric continued her presentation with several short rocker archives. A rocker archive was a recording in 3D of an experience someone had in the Database. It was similar to actually navigating oneself, except that one just had to kick back and relax while the scene moved on by itself. It wasn't a tour of the Database, but a view of an archive of the Database as it had been anciently.

Korric showed a series of disjoint sequences documenting the construction of the crystal city. At first Future felt a little disoriented at not having control over where he was going. At least one can prepare oneself for changes in direction if navigation is under their own control. Still, he was able to live with that discomfort since he was temporarily relieved of the great effort required for propulsion.

One instant Future was in the room with the other three, and the next instant he found himself floating over a grassy valley, approaching the Warden complex. The facility was not fancied up as it had been in the crystal palaces, but had the same humble appearance as it did in the Flesh when Blujic first showed it to him a day or so before. Future watched as construction commenced on the first tower.

Advisor Herrec narrated as they went along, "The first Wardens started with virtually nothing. They created materials and began forming their beautiful city."

Chief Korric interrupted, "You see, Miss Blujic, we have records of the construction from scratch. Doesn't this show that the tower exists in the Flesh?"

Future spoke up, "Have you ever constructed in Flesh? This is imaginary way, not possible in Flesh. In Flesh you must obtain materials from somewhere. It takes very long time and is hard work." In spite of his explanation, Future felt that they could not understand having not experienced it themselves.

Blujic added, "Think how troublesome it is just to walk between the rockers and the showers? Lifting heavy materials is no easy thing!"

Future was surprised when Korric conceded, "I was expecting you to say something like that. Actually I have some idea of what it's like. Though we never construct things in the Flesh directly, we do work through the automatons. Often we must make repairs in the Flesh to buildings, machines, and even medical surgery on people. Obtaining materials and replacement parts, whether through natural sources, recycling, or matter synthesizing, is a major problem for us." She paused a moment and added, "So you think that this sequence is entirely imaginary?"

Neither Future nor Blujic answered since the next sequence had already started. The first tower was complete and looked pretty much as it did in the current Database. Next door, two core towers had begun construction. The archived scene moved toward one of the towers and they experienced a trip down into a subterranean excavation. The sequence became a time-lapse recording, where every few moments the pit suddenly doubled and tripled in depth. The excavation finally broke through into the deep Plasma reservoirs under the crust, and the construction of platforms and observation decks for the deep ports commenced. None of the construction workers had any diving equipment on, but were working and breathing under the liquid as if it were air.

Advisor Herrec gave another narration introducing the deep ports and Korric tailed with her own comments again. "Isn't this proof that there are indeed deep ports?" she asked.

Blujic quickly commented, "There are no core towers. The ground around there is just as pristine and untouched now as it was when our ancestors first came out of the *Origin*."

"You portray swimming and work under Plasma all wrong!" Future explained. "The liquid make so breath cannot be done without proper breathing apparatus."

"So another one goes into the imaginary category? Well, what have you got to say about this one? When you watch this, remember that 2D videos are recordings made only by automatons in the flesh." Korric smugly remarked and the sequence changed again.

This time the archive scene was sitting in a conference room much similar to the one they were currently in. Crowds of Wardens surrounded the table and a screen was prepared for 2D video presentation. The screen brightened in the archive and a video began to play. Future and the others were in their rockers, in a conference room, experiencing an archive of a similar conference room, watching an archived 2D video presentation. It was all so confusing! The 2D video scene panned around a thick, glass-walled room that could have had only one purpose: a lounge in a deep port. Swimmers swam beyond those walls, quite naturally and proper.

"So you see our dilemma. Though we have not been able to locate the original 2D video clip, we have a rocker archive of someone watching the video. Someone back then recorded their database experience, watching live 2D flesh videos!"

Blujic and Future couldn't argue that one. Future could find nothing wrong with the accuracy of the video, and Blujic obviously was at a loss of what to say. The archive vanished and they found themselves in their own conference room.

"Now if you will show me around in the Flesh, and convince me that there are no deep ports in our facility, I will be able to rest in peaceful slumber at night knowing that I made the right decision. After all, this little video clip may simply be of a deep port built at one of our automaton garages or any number of uninhabited or abandoned Warden facilities scattered all over the countryside!"

Future and Blujic stood up and got ready to go, but Korric called them back. "Wait a moment. I have one more archive that you might be interested in, Future."

Sitting back down on the virtual seats, they suddenly found themselves floating high above the countryside. There was not a tree as far as the eye could see, only grassy hills and valleys. Looking ahead on the horizon, Future saw the reflective surface of open Plasma that was a large inland lake. The sun hovered in the sky above the lake, blinding him from its bright reflection. Sitting on the lake were the silhouettes of what looked like buildings in a large city. The archive took them closer and closer. As they approached the edge of the lake, the bright sun reflections began to lose their intensity.

Suddenly Future saw what the structures were. The sight seemed so out of place that he couldn't believe his eyes. There floating on the lake was *The Continent* itself, in calm Plasma without waves or storm. The archive brought them right over the top of the node towers such that they had a very good view of what lay below. Future could not believe how new and in good condition *The Continent* seemed. The familiar maze of passage tubes, node towers, and triangular chambers stretched as far as the eye could see. The towers and chambers had something that he thought was not possible: windows. The windows overlooked terraced roof decks holding beautiful gardens. He could see figures moving about without any fear of waves or storms.

In some places huge open plazas broke the city fabric below. From as far away as he was, he could still see hundreds of figures moving back and forth in the plazas engaged in some activity. Could the figures he saw be Those Who Went Before?

The archive brought them closer to one of the plazas. As he began to see the figures more clearly, he began to feel sick to his stomach. The figures were fighting back and forth in mock combat, dressed in blood-red helmets and armor.

Korric explained, "This is the prison, those are the Inmates. They have done irreparable damage to society and had to be punished. A few seasons after this archive, many of the Inmates escaped from the prison and moved ashore. Their descendants live there to this day as you have seen. They are your cousins, Future. You have descended from prisoners. From Inmates."

It couldn't be! The secret of Those Who Went Before couldn't be this! These barbarians know nothing of harmony in 'One Eternal Round!' They couldn't have come from savage thieves and common prisoners! Future just buried his virtual head in his virtual hands and cried, "NO!"

CHAPTER 18

After the expedition to *Mother's Heart*, the steel-hulled submarine had ended up at *The Island*, where Ix had met Advisor One and they were able to have a short family leave. His father had been ferried to *The Island* by Hord and Ix's old pod crew. *The Island* was now fairly close off shore. It had become possible to move back and forth between it and the colony forts without having to use repeater vessels or the new repeater buoys. Some of the men had been granted permanent leave to go back to their salvage assignments and were replaced almost daily by new recruits from *The Island*. In fact, two of the transports had been set up as a permanent shuttle service with fixed departure and arrival times.

Ix's father had the unpleasant task of reporting to his teary-eyed mother and sisters the circumstances surrounding Mox's death. Ix described how Mox and other members of his team had survived the T12 tragedy but had met their deaths at the hands of those horrible barbarians. At least corpuscles had not consumed them. Ix told his mother about the funerary services they had held and assured her that he had taken care of Mox's remains himself. In addition to Mox's death, the family was concerned about one of the daughters who had been left behind on *The Continent* -- there were rumors of more major quakes that affected all the citizens there when the thrash tide passed through the shallows right under the floating city. Notwithstanding the unpleasantness of reliving those tragic moments of Mox's untimely end, the vacation had been quite relaxing. There was no worry about nasty heathens or the war with the machines. Ix didn't even have to worry about the monstrous waves and storms since he didn't have maintenance duty anyway. In spite of the beauty of the new habitation with its awesome column structures and mysterious lights in the ceiling dome, home was home and nothing could replace it. The narrow passages and tight spaces were a welcome sight. Even having to wear those confounded respirators in the more barren passages and tunnels brought back pleasant feelings of nostalgia.

Ix told everyone about the expedition under the thrash tide as well. Getting together with his friends, he told the story of the endless junk heap and the massive ghost submarine set on a course to who knows where. As young adults are prone to do, they spent a lot of time conjecturing as to the meaning of the discoveries. Some of the young technicians suggested that the great vessel might have been the destination of Those Who Went Before -- could they have finally found a way to escape the harsh storms and live out their civilization in peace? It was unclear whether the big derelict ship was the source of the magnetic fields or merely caught it them. Perhaps the great ship was caught by the magnetism in a vortex dragged along under the thrash tide.

One of Ix's friends had evacuated from *The Continent* just before the latest quakes hit and told about the Prisoner movement. The Prisoner concept was a popular theme that suggested the ancestors might have been part of a penal colony. What if Those Who Went Before had been prisoners trying to escape, only to find their ship caught in the great magnet designed to capture escaping inmate vessels, forever dooming them to sail the depths as a ghost crew? The young men stared wide-eyed at each other well into the sleep period as the explanations grew wilder and wilder and even began to defy the laws of physics.

Ix was unconvinced, "I don't think we came from prisoners. I think we had noble beginnings. Those Who Went Before were a great people and very industrious. We still don't know the purpose of all their machines."

"Ix, you've got to look at things more objectively. All the apartments and shops in *The Continent* have bars covering their facades! Our people have been living that way for a thousand seasons. I think the Defenders were prison guards and our ancestors the Rebel forces took over." At that moment, no one yet knew the existence of the Wardens.

Ix had heard that argument before. He thought back and tried to remember what he had learned in school about the Defenders and the Rebels in history lessons. "That wouldn't explain why there was a massive magnet OR where the great submarine came from. Didn't the Rebel forces wipe out the Defender group in a very short period of time? How could they have constructed such a magnificent thing just to catch escaped prisoners?"

The conversation had gone on and on and before anyone knew it, they had stayed up almost the entire sleep period. The questions they had started out with were still unanswered: what was the source of the magnetic fields under the thrash tide, what was the nature of the great submarine, and most of all, how could something so great and massive as the ghost ship keep from sinking into the depths, or move around at all for that matter.

Unfortunately, the vacation had been cut short. Word came that there had been peaceable contact from the enemy machines and Lord Ruk sent Advisor One and Ix back right away, with Ix having been promoted officially to pilot. As they set out on their way, a very interesting story unfolded, relayed over the new voice interpreted sonar. Evidently one of the T12 divers, perhaps Mox's friend Mel, had survived (as Ix suspected) and came walking through the barbarian camp below the forts escorted by a dozen or so of the floating enemy machines. He had called up and asked to be let in. At his side was a woman whose appearance was so startling that the barbarians paled by comparison. The woman had not been fierce-looking but had been beautiful beyond anything anyone could imagine, with long flowing golden hair.

Ix and all the men were excited. In addition to overwhelming curiosity to see what a golden-haired girl looked like, Ix hoped to find a chance to get the diver aside and ask him about Mox. As they approached the subterranean port below the forts, Ix was so excited he couldn't stand it. Helmsman duty had fallen to Hord, but Ix still had technician duties to perform when the craft landed. He worked frantically to get as much of the work finished in parallel to the docking sequence, so that only a few shutdown items were left. When Advisor One and his assistants finally were able to depart, Ix was right behind them.

As he stepped out on the floating dock, Ix breathed in the fresh air with pleasure. No need for respirators here! In the subterranean cavity the docks had been strung between the column formations, with circular decks surrounding each bole. It almost mirrored the platform-and-catwalk pattern high above. Several pods were in port, and diving crews made the place look like a school of swimmers. Ix strode over to the nearest lift in high spirits.

Though some ladders remained, most of the air tubes in the massive boles had finally been fitted with counterweighted lifts. It was not so much for convenience's sake as it was for security: the enemy machines had a hard time breaking through the platforms, especially when they were securely braced from below.

The lifts were mostly made for only one person to stand on. Portable electric winches existed but were only used for heavy cargo. Ix waited his turn in line, then stepped onto the narrow platform. Two cables coming up through the floor controlled the lift. Ix selected the proper weights that balanced out his own body weight and began 'bootstrapping' by using the cable to lift himself up hand over hand to fort level.

As soon as he stepped out on the platform, Ix went up to the nearest black-clad guard to ask directions. "Where is that T12 diver?"

The guard looked at him for an instant and burst out laughing. Ix assumed that the man mistakenly thought that Ix's real intent was to take a gander at that golden girl and he was covering up by asking about the diver. Well, maybe that was his real intent, sort of. The guard said, "Walk down that way to the third platform and ask again."

Reaching the third platform, the next guy laughed as well. He pointed across the way and said, "See that door over there? No one gets in there, though."

Ix looked over and saw that there was a guard standing right next to the door. Ix knew the man -- he was some cousin or other on his mother's side. Ix walked up and asked to see the diver.

"Hi Ix. We're not letting anyone in. Not even hanchos or senchos. But you can go in."

Wow, that was strange! Cousin or no cousin, if they're not letting in even senchos, why would they let in average technician Ix, he mused. The cousin opened the door and motioned for him to enter. *At least I'm in*, he thought.

On the other side of the door he found himself in a short corridor with two doors opening onto it. One of the rooms had stacks of equipment along the back wall but was otherwise empty. Ix approached the remaining door that was closed. He could hear muffled conversation and laughing. There was an unmistakable female voice there. As he approached the door, Ix was startled from behind as someone walked in from the outside.

It was his father. Advisor One calmly closed the door behind him. Ix fully expected to be chastised for being where he shouldn't have been, but to his surprise his father was quite amicable. He smiled and said, "Just had a briefing. So you've heard, too!"

Ix moved aside as Advisor One opened the door into the room and stepped inside. The voices stopped, and Ix could tell that the others were watching the newcomers with curiosity. Since Ix hadn't been chased out, he followed his father into the room. The first thing Ix saw was that beautiful girl sitting across the table. Long golden hair flowed down the shoulders. She was built in such a way that could make a grown man cry, perfect in every dimension. The girl had a beautiful complexion also. Instead of the flat nose and almond eyes he was used to seeing on his own people, the golden princess had a slightly higher, noble nose and big blue eyes. Those eyes captured him and he felt he could jump inside them and swim around a bit. When Ix came to his senses, he realized that the girl was staring at him in complete stunned silence. She could not take her eyes off him!

The girl opened her mouth and said something completely unintelligible, using words he had never heard before. The diver, whom Ix had seen out of the corner of his eye suddenly jumped up and cried out, "I remember! I remember!"

Ix turned and looked at the man's face and almost fell to the deck in surprise. It was Mox! Mox was alive! Ix lunged across the table and met Mox halfway between. The two of them embraced. Advisor One, tears in his eyes, came over and embraced the two of them together. For the longest time, all they could do was just stand there and cry. When they finally broke up, Mox turned to the girl and began speaking the same unintelligible gibberish she had used earlier. His words flowed with some structure, animated at times, serious otherwise, and the girl nodded with understanding.

She turned to face Ix and Advisor One and said haltingly, "My name Blujic."

Mox explained, "This is Blujic. She's one of the Wardens who live in this country. I've fallen in love with her!"

Now that the initial shock was over, Ix realized why he had been allowed in and hanchos and senchos were turned away. He was so overjoyed that his brother was still alive. But now Ix was confused. Hadn't he disposed of the remains of a diver that had Mox's name tag sewed into his diving suit? Ix looked over at the suit Mox now wore and saw that where the nametag should have been was only a tattered remnant.

"We thought you were dead. There was a skeleton that we thought was you!"

Mox had a thoughtful look on his face. "Yes, I remember now. The accident caused me to lose my memory for a long time. I couldn't remember my name or where I came from. Just seeing your faces has helped me remember again."

Ix was consumed with curiosity. "Well, what happened?"

"Mel and I were suited up and in the airlock with sample containers. Suddenly the whole wall burst in on us and I found myself spinning in the Plasma in a cloud of bubbles. I swam hard trying to right myself and was surrounded by corpuscles. I was stabbing and kicking with everything I had trying to get those monsters away from me. I found myself in a huge cavern full of _____." Mox said some word Ix had never heard before, perhaps borrowing from Blujic's language. "Some of my teammates also made it, although not in good shape. We subsisted for a while, but needed food. Since my suit was torn I couldn't dive for swimmers. I swapped suits with Mel who was wounded and fished for everyone. Then I ... I'm not sure what happened after that."

Ix stepped in, "I'm sorry about Mel -- we thought it was you. We found your friends riddled with barbarian projectile shafts. We found two dead barbarians as well."

"I found myself wandering through the _____ all by myself." Mox used another unknown word.

Mox was obviously trying to check himself every time he came across a foreign word, but wasn't too successful. At times he succeeded in substituting an equivalent, but often just used the raw expression and described its meaning. During the conversation Ix began to feel that Mox had changed. In some ways he was the same old Mox but through incredible adventures his view on things seemed different than before. Incredible was the word! Mox told of exploring a strange place called the '*Origin*' (translated from Blujic's language) where people had lived on the walls! He talked of an imaginary city where Blujic and the Wardens lived, where everyone dreamed about places together. In the dream he and Blujic had come to the fort together and had stood on the platform as ghosts before ever having seen it in reality. He talked about pictures and moving scenes that recorded the exact likeness of people and places, that could be viewed over and over at will.

"Have you hit your head, Mox?" Advisor One commented.

Mox was quite sincere, "I swear I've seen these things. I know how crazy it sounds but you must believe me!" He turned to Blujic and talked to her in her language.

Blujic had trouble communicating, but had picked up quite a few words in her association with Mox. With the energy of her soul she made an attempt to back up what Mox had said. Though Ix couldn't really understand her, one thing was sure -- she was as serious as Mox about describing the strange events they had experienced.

"Well, we'll have plenty of time for that later. What about the war?" Advisor One brought up the weightier matters.

Mox explained, "The Wardens control the machines from the imaginary city. They enter the machines from a dream and see what the machines see."

Advisor One directed his comments toward Blujic, "The machines have injured and killed a great many of our men."

"They've been afraid that we would attack them. They're afraid of our technology that we are able to move under the Plasma. Up until now, there has only been the unintelligent _____, uh, I mean Inmates or barbarians."

"Are they interested in stopping the war?" asked the advisor.

Mox continued, "Blujic and I spent much time trying to convince them to cease fighting. They have made Blujic and I into special ambassadors to try to establish peace between our peoples."

There it was -- good news! If such a thing could be true everything negative about the new country would vanish. They would be able to enjoy the wonderful scenery without having to worry about staying alive. But the optimism was short lived.

"The Wardens want peace, but we can't stay here. They have influence over the Inmate barbarians but don't control them. For our own protection we cannot stay."

Advisor One thought for a moment and asked, "What do they propose? Do they have any suggestions?"

Mox replied, "There are great protected inland seas that have little influence from the ocean storms. I've seen moving record scenes, or 'videos' taken thousands of seasons ago. It seems that *The Continent* used to float on the inland seas before it lost its anchorage and was washed out into the storms. The Wardens think that there may be remnants of the city structure that still float there. They will help us settle there if we agree."

Later Ix, Mox, and Blujic were together down below in the subterranean pod port. Advisor One had taken the Warden's proposal and had communicated the content of their conversation to Lord Ruk. A message came back immediately requesting Mox and Blujic's presence back at *The Island* itself. They were taking the flagship, so Ix and his crew were assigned to ferry them over.

Mox was ecstatic. He had great passion in his voice when he explained, "Ix, I've fallen in love with this girl. We've been through so many things together. She gave me a glimpse of her life. I've seen how she lives, how she grew up. It's all very strange and fantastic. Now I have a chance to show her my life. I can show her how hard it is for us, and why we wish to move."

Ix looked over at Blujic. The girl was smiling and quite happy, looking at all the new sights and sounds. She seemed particularly interested in the pods, enthralled with the concept that they were machines meant to carry people under the Plasma.

Ix said quietly to his brother, "She sure is beautiful. You're a lucky guy Mox."

Mox laughed, "Don't you be getting any ideas about playing switcharoo with my face!"

"Oh no, no. I'm just happy you're alive and that the silly dream of meeting a golden-haired princess came true for you."

The three of them boarded Ix's pod and made their way to the control cabin. It was only the previous wake period when Ix and his father had arrived from *The Island*, and now they were going back again already. Since Ix was on pilot duty, he headed straight for the pilot's seat and buckled the mesh into place. Mox came up beside him with a startled look on his face.

"Ix, you don't mean ..."

Ix looked up and said, "Yes, my dream came true, too. I'm a full-fledged pilot now. Drastic situations sure change tradition! Two seasons ago who would have thought that a technician would have a chance to become a pilot!"

The submarine departed, floating away from the dock and sinking straight down. Ix powered the craft through the marked channels that lead to open ocean and set a heading toward *The Island* according to the navigator's instructions.

At the shift change, Ix relinquished the helm to the Pilot Sencho and headed back to where Mox and Blujic were enjoying the seascape through a view port in the lounge. When Ix walked in they were busy jabbering away in that strange language. Immediately Mox switched into translator mode and they began talking about his experiences. All in all there was a magic in the air that Ix hadn't felt since the last time the brothers had gotten together at the beginning of the expedition, when Mox and Mel had swam across that dark gulf and they had taken turns piloting the flag ship in circles around the fleet.

"Mox, what was the imaginary city like? What was it like to dream with everyone else?"

Mox explained, "You stand in the middle of a spherical framework. Suddenly everything disappears around you and you are in the dream city. Everyone is actually in the sphere frames, but they see the city and each other in the city." He went on to explain how he had appeared as Blujic in the virtual environment, and had changed into the child disguise.

Ix laughed, "It sounds so strange!"

"It was wonderful! You could fly through the air with minimum effort. We flew higher and higher until the whole place shrunk to a little bubble below us."

Ix also gave them detailed reports about his trip to *Mother's Heart.* Mox was in turn excited to hear about the strange encounter, and went on and on about the massive submarine wreck.

"It's in orbit," Mox said in a matter-of-fact way, "the ghost ship is in orbit so it doesn't need any propulsion."

Mox tried to explain about the moons, gravity, and the spherical shape of Mother, and how objects in orbit passively balance their outward trajectory with free-fall into the planet, but didn't really understand it himself so he couldn't get the point across.

Mox continued, "The ship must be in free-fall, orbiting in circles under the sea so it doesn't fall inward."

Ix knew there had to be something wrong with that idea, but wasn't sure what. As far as he could tell, the Plasma sea was flat forever. Somehow he figured the tremendous drag of liquid on the hull of the massive vessel would eventually overcome any momentum and cause it to sink. Nevertheless he put the thought away for another time and stayed with the conversation.

Ix thought about something Mox had said earlier. He was extremely curious about whether Mox had picked up any more information about their ancestors. "You told us how you had seen the moving picture, or 'videos', of *The Continent* from thousands of seasons ago. What was it like? Could you learn anything new about Those Who Went Before?"

Suddenly Mox's countenance turned dark. Ix had inadvertently stumbled on an unpleasant topic. Mox slowly formed the words, "It was an ancient historical recording, and we were fully immersed. *The Continent* seemed new and clean and stretched as far as the eye could see. Yes, I saw Those Who Went Before, and it wasn't a pretty picture. I dread the thought!"

Ix wondered what Mox could possibly have seen that could have upset him so. The answer was completely unexpected.

Mox hung his head and continued, "*The Continent* was nothing more than a prison for common criminals. We've descended from prisoners. I saw *The Continent* inhabited by those red clad barbarians! Those Who Went Before were barbarians!"

CHAPTER 19

Barbarians! Prisoners! It was that awful topic all over again. Ix couldn't seem to get away from it. He went to his cabin and lay down on his bunk, needing some time to think. Mox and Blujic had explained a little about the relationship between the Wardens and the barbarians, whom they called 'Inmates'. The Wardens functioned as guards and overseers of the Inmates, making sure they stayed out of trouble and their families were fed. The Inmates spent their time squabbling among themselves over territory.

And the stories about *The Continent* -- the bars over apartment blocks and other hints showed that it might have been used as a prison. Now Mox was saying that he had seen ancient scenes of the Inmates living in *The Continent*, and the Wardens confirmed that it was the original prison. Could the unthinkable be true? Could they have actually descended from those rotten barbarians? Were their ancestors common criminals?

Everyone around him was starting to believe the Prisoner concept. Even Mox seemed convinced. Ix thought back on the times when things were simple. Everyone had been fired up about searching out Those Who Went Before.

It was an exciting time. Finding a new machine in some forgotten corner of *The Continent* made news. Technicians spent countless wake periods trying to discover how things worked. Ix himself had watched researchers painstakingly pass light through the ancient data crystals trying in vain to pick out some meaning from them. The ancient race had been gods almost, beyond their reach. Then there was the discovery of the skeleton in the coffin confirming that they were human, and now this. The image of Those Who Went Before seemed tarnished. Whatever happened to 'Harmony in One Eternal Round'? Was it all for nothing? Would the magic of those times fade away in the dust? Had their existence started out from insignificant heathens? Did they strive and fight with the raging oceans and incessant storms to protect some pitiful dream that was actually delusions of grandeur? Would everything just fade away as moisture evaporating in a hot blaze?

Ix sank into despair. The positive thoughts that had always excited him took a turn in the opposite direction. Life seemed to feel like a great chore. Men are born, work hard in a pool of sweat, and then die. If they wasted away all their energy and repaired and rebuilt their home would it stay forever? Or will it sink anyway? When *The Continent* was gone would anyone remember? Would anyone remember how hard he and his people toiled just to survive? Was life meant to be born and snuffed out, lasting a mere instant in the eternities? Would there be anyone there to care?

They arrived at *The Island* towards the end of the following wake period. Blujic and Mox were ecstatic. Mox was visiting his home after having been gone for a very long time, and Blujic soaked in the sights with awed wonder. Everything was new to her. From the very start, even having to put on a respirator was an adventure to be relished. She attracted stares everywhere they went.

Ix on the other hand was at an all-time low. He slunk back and walked down the corridors seeing families and children playing in the plazas and going about their business as usual. They would all die as children of prisoners. No great ones in the past to be proud of, they would have to live life on their own, trying to find their own happiness. Ix's friends who had escaped from *The Continent* before the big quake had told him about the Prisoner movement, how they lived for the moment and sought thrills and excitement. Now that they'd lost their dreams would they be reduced to seeking selfish stimulation, to get all they could before that awful last day? Would they consume baku juice to forget that awful predicament, and seek to remain in drunken bliss? Would the measure of a man's happiness become how much he possessed, or how much he was able to hedge himself from work to live in ease? Would they begin squabbling over possessions and territory? Would they become barbarians again? Or would they steal from each other and return to the life of criminals?

Mox and Blujic had their interview with Lord Ruk. While Ix sulked in dimly lit passages caught up in his depression, major decisions were made regarding the future of two races. It was decided that the Warden's offer be accepted, providing that the great inland seas were suitable for colonization. Ruk ordered a small expedition to be assembled, which was to consist of Ix's pod as the flagship, a large transport, and another small escort craft. The expedition was to set out to find a passage to the inland seas and otherwise survey the area to determine if it was suitable as a new home. Mox was appointed as special liaison to the Wardens and was to be involved in talks and negotiations regarding the new territory. As part of the assignment, he and Blujic were also to be members of the expedition and were to observe the territory with their own eyes. Advisor Two was appointed as leader of the expedition.

The small flotilla departed three wake periods later. Ix took his place at the pod controls as fulfillment of his responsibilities, but had lost all interest in the nature or purpose of the mission. For the present at least, he had become a man without dreams or ambition. Mox and Blujic eyed him with concern, but he mostly kept to himself.

A few wake periods later they had passed through the great coastal wall of the main Warden floating land mass and began charting their way through unknown waters, setting marker buoys as they went. The small fleet navigated through column formations, often backtracking to find wide enough channels. Setting the buoys was particularly easy under the column growths because they could be fixed to the roots and wouldn't drift away. On one of his off-duty times, Ix found himself in the lounge looking out into the Plasma deep, thinking those age-old thoughts of what might lie beyond the blue-green liquid. The wonderment was tainted with a negative twist however, and a glum look showed on his face.

Mox walked in and sat down beside him, "Hey brother, snap out of it!"

When Ix didn't respond right away, Mox tried a different angle. "Don't worry about the past. We have the future! Look where we can take things now that we can spend our time on something other than maintenance. Look what you can explore now that you've got pilot status!"

Ix dejectedly spoke up, "But it's all for nothing. We'll just live our lives as we always have and then pass away. No one will remember us or our experiences."

Ix turned to look at Mox and saw that he was beginning to look depressed as well. Perhaps he was remembering the awful scenes of barbarians inhabiting *The Continent.* Just then Blujic walked in and must have noticed the two sour faces.

"You brothers smile!" she said.

Mox explained, "We're just disappointed that Those Who Went Before were barbarians," but quickly switched into Blujic's language.

Blujic thought for a moment and haltingly formed the words, "Maybe not barbarians. Come from barbarian is strange idea. Barbarians have different face, different hair. Barbarians cannot think of submarine!"

Ix looked at Mox and they both shrugged at each other. Even though Blujic understood little of their language, her meaning was perfectly clear. It was an interesting idea. Ix wondered why he hadn't thought of it before. There was indeed something strange that remained about the Prisoner theory. They were two different races. And if they had descended from the barbarians, how had they come across the pod technology? It was true that living in a harsh environment could spawn inventions meant to help cope, but with all the effort their people spent on just surviving, Ix wondered if such a thing were possible. Better yet, Ix wondered if there were not a more appropriate explanation. He grabbed at that thought with all the hope of a desperate soul.

By the look on Mox's face, it appeared that his brother was thinking the same thing. Maybe he was in denial, but Ix began to feel his spirits lift already. He once again started to see the endless Plasma with his old enthusiasm: a barrier to overcome, to discover what fantastic things lay beyond. And from what Mox and Blujic had said, there were fantastic things indeed.

Somewhat back to his old ambitious self, Ix was determined to prove that horrendous Prisoner theory wrong. Armed with only a hunch, he put his energy into making the expedition a success. If they were to find the original anchoring spot of *The Continent*, perhaps more clues would present themselves.

During breaks when the three of them got together, Blujic delighted in telling them about the surface world which both Mox, and to a lesser degree Ix, had experienced. Most of the time she would have to explain a concept to Mox in her own language, and let him translate for Ix. Since translating is more an art than a fixed process, Mox often found difficulty expressing the ideas. Blujic successfully explained the concepts of 'day' and 'night', which were directly related to the position of the great light in the sky (which the twins had never imagined could have existed before the time they left on the colonization expedition).

"Isn't there a place where the land rests on the bottom?" Blujic wondered.

Ix explained, "As far as we can tell, all the land is just one great floating mass. The column growths go deeper than we can go, but doesn't the Plasma just go on forever anyway?"

Again the concept came back in a full circle. When Blujic tried to explain that the world was shaped like a spheroid, her own conception referred to things that lay within the boundaries of the Database as opposed to things that were beyond. Mox caught on and told one of Grandpa Nux's stories about an old sencho who sailed his pod under the Plasma in a straight line and eventually ended up at his starting point again, but Ix knowing about the crush threshold said he must have been going in circles just below the surface. All three of them just missed each other's point.

The expedition proceeded under the Warden's main landmass farther than any scout craft had gone before. At times the narrow channels opened up to great lakes where all three vessels surfaced in broad daylight, giving the crews a chance to stretch their legs. At other times the overhead crust continued endlessly without even a single column growth or subterranean cavity to break the expanse. The Wardens had given Mox and Blujic sketchy directions as to where they thought the inland seas might be located. Advisor Two was a little flexible in following the directions, on the one hand understanding that the location was only approximate, and on the other hand hoping to make the best of the trip and survey as much of the landmass as possible.

One wake period (or 'day' as Blujic would say) the small fleet passed through a particularly dense area of growths. On the other side of the thicket, the entire area brightened and widened into a huge body of open Plasma -- a channel of sorts. Their sonar detected another wall over eighty nodelengths beyond. Could it have been an inland sea?

Advisor Two began thinking out loud, "It appears too narrow for *The Continent* to have drifted through. Still, who knows how fast these growths fill in or spread during a thousand seasons."

Ix was piloting at the moment. He looked up through the bubble cockpit at the underside of the Plasma surface and visually confirmed the calm wave activity and said, "I recommend we get a visual on that."

After having been on the colonization expedition from the beginning, the crew had gotten used to getting 'visuals', a concept that had been unthinkable in the past. Getting visuals was the easiest way to see far away, since Plasma always had lower visibility than open air. Advisor Two ordered Ix to surface.

The craft came up in the middle of some moderate waves. From the pilot's seat, Ix could see the far green wall of column growths outside the bubble cockpit one moment, and a mountain of Plasma the next. Advisor Two, Ix, Mox, and several of the others exited the airlock and climbed to the upper deck. As soon as Ix stepped out he was assaulted by a fierce wind. Occasional gusts carried salt spray that tore at his face and ears.

Off to the port side about a nodelength away Ix saw the escort craft break the surface. Plasma trapped on their deck flowed out through openings in the rail until it fully emptied itself. Momentarily officers from the other craft made their way up on deck and Ix waved his arms in greeting.

Ix looked toward the great coastal wall. The column growths (or 'trees' as Blujic would call them) were packed in tightly and towered high in the heavy overcast sky. Instead of growing straight up however, the entire dense wall was swept back as if from the effect of being constantly assaulted by the winds. That coastal wall was so dense, Ix had learned, that the incessant storms that battered the great oceans hardly leaked any of their influence into the land mass interior. Some of the technicians had also come up with a theory that the air tubes in the massive columns created a chimney effect that helped produce high pressure areas that pushed the storms away from the Warden's land mass.

Ix allowed his eyes to follow the coastline until it brought him fully around facing in the opposite direction. He could see islands floating in the middle of the channel, drifting ever so slowly toward one shore or the other. The islands took the form of dense bundles of column formations. The coastlines on the opposite side of the channel faded out in a great gradual curve to the right.

"Look out there! I see white caps!" Mox had moved up next to Ix and was looking off to one side. "See those fingers and inlets? What do you suppose that could be floating over there?"

Ix perked up and attempted to follow Mox's gaze. The mountainous swells only a few dozen armlengths away hid the view every time their pod sunk down into a trough, but yes, there did seem to be something out there. Whitish shapes bobbed up and down with every wave. From that distance, the shapes must have been huge for the sailors to see them at all. By the direction of the waves Ix deduced the objects trapped in the inlets to be flotsam and jetsam from storms.

Mox was thinking along the same lines, "That must be debris washed in from the high seas. Ix, let's go get a closer look!"

Ix concurred. They fought their way across the deck toward Advisor Two and got the commander's permission to explore, since unnatural debris could give them a hint about where *The Continent* could have had its original anchorage. The small fleet dove down below and sped toward the coast. In a matter of moments the dark surface of the coastal wall loomed out of the murky Plasma. Ix cut the power and approached the wall slowly, paying special attention to the distances being called out by Mag. A shadow fell upon the cockpit. He looked up and saw a long dark silhouette of a massive shape bobbing up and down in the waves. Its width was about the same as the distance between the right and left thrusters of the pod, and its length could have been ten to twenty times that. Mox and the sencho squeezed at his side in an attempt to see the object while others crowded around the available view ports.

Using the sensitive trigger controls for the thrusters, Ix maneuvered around the object in an attempt to get a better view. The object was roughly cylindrical in shape, but not smooth.

"It's a log! A tree fall down." Blujic called from the rear of the cabin. Indeed, the object was merely a massive floating section of fallen column growth. The severed ends clearly revealed the round openings of exposed air tubes.

Ix sunk back down to a safer depth and proceeded into the inlet. Soon several other long silhouettes, not near as large as the first, came into view. They too were logs, bunched together in a group. Above their vessel more and more fallen trees bobbed up and down in the surf. Some were quite large, but most of them were of moderate size. Every time a wave passed the whole bunch was upset and the logs jostled with each other, some of the smaller pieces tumbling end over end in violent reaction. At length the Plasma around the pod began getting dark as if they had passed under the land mass. Ix switched on the spotlights to supplement the light that filtered down through the shifting spaces between the logs.

"There's nothing here but fallen column growths." commented Advisor Two.

The Pilot Sencho added, "Look how they cover the surface and move with the waves. I've never seen anything like it."

Ix was equally enthralled. In the environment they had come from, most floating things were dashed to bits. Certainly nothing could remain bunched up like that. He had it in his mind to indulge curiosity by gliding around under the floating carpet for only a few moments longer, then turn around and head back out again.

It was at that point that one of the spotlights illuminated something completely different. It was a large object that had protrusions like a multi-legged creature, but Ix recognized it immediately as the wreckage of a node tower that somehow had maintained its buoyancy and not come apart or sunk. Broken off tubes reached out in all directions, some stretching deep into the Plasma, their ragged, sealed ends dancing about in the surf.

The first thing that came to Ix's mind was that they had found the ancient moorage and remnants of the prison structure that the Wardens had talked about. After all, that was the purpose of their expedition, and certainly the great channel was near the inland sea. In the poor light Ix could not tell how long the wreckage had been there.

Beyond the node towers were other pieces. Empty hulks of towers and triangular chamber sections still holding pockets of air jostled each other in the waves above them. Splintered logs grinding between the large chunks were occasionally thrust under the surface. It was a spooky scene, almost as if the crew were silently treading through a field of tombs and gigantic bones. Even if the remnants were from some ancient equivalent to *The Continent*, the fact that all of the men had been born and raised in similar rooms and corridors gave them an uneasy feeling, and Ix thought back about the sunken node towers they had seen riding on the back of the ghost ship.

Ix had assumed that the tower remnants were from that ancient prison structure, but the spotlights suddenly illuminated an object that provided a chilling new possibility. Sandwiched between a large log and a node tower remnant was the gnarled wreckage of a pod. The hull was almost entirely crushed and tipped on its side, probably only kept from sinking by its starboard buoyancy tanks. A battered thruster still clung onto its mount below Plasma line with bare cables frayed out. The pod was no ancient machine. Enough identifying features remained for Ix to recognize it as a fairly recent model.

A pale-faced Advisor Two stepped toward the front of the cabin and said, "This is all wreckage from *The Continent*! This was from our city!"

The parallels between the mountains of wreckage piled on the massive ghost submarine and the floating flotsam and jetsam shook Ix in pungent clarity. There was a rumor that another quake had occurred in the great floating city and refugees were starting to trickle in who began to tell tales that painted a troubling picture. Ix was deep in thought as he fingered the thruster controls and guided the vessel on a slow path that led them farther into the inlet. The surface above them was littered with countless pieces of node tower and chamber sections that all presumably had large pockets of air. The navigator reported that the end of the inlet was coming up soon so Ix kept an eye out for the sea wall.

Suddenly a startled voice cried out from the rear of the cabin. One of the crewmen gathered at the view ports exclaimed, "Would you look at that! That looks like one of the vaults!"

Mox crowded into the bubble cockpit on Ix's right and strained to see what the crewman was looking at. Ix spun the pod around and drifted in the direction the man had indicated. Thrown in with the other flotsam and jetsam, a cylindrical object with domed ends was dwarfed by a huge log. It wasn't exactly floating: a tangle of cables caught on its attached metal framework stretched a single strand deep into the Plasma that coiled around a heavy chunk of node tower pulling it down. Waves would send the cylinder and its weighty partner drifting downward slowly where it would pause, as if it couldn't make up its mind whether to sink or float. The closer they got the more the cylinder resembled Vault One and Vault Two that had been preserved in *The Continent* since Grandpa Nux's times.

Advisor Two cried out, "No, it can't be! It finally happened!"

Mox was alarmed, "You mean *The Continent* broke up?"

"The precious artifacts just scattered on the waves. They've lost the vaults. There must be nothing left." Advisor Two repeated.

Ix and Mox looked at each other with eyes and mouths wide open. The vaults! Could *The Continent* have been destroyed in one season? Could the quakes have ripped apart the corridors, spilling precious life and treasures into the storms? Was their heritage from a thousand seasons before floating like discarded trash? Ix thought about their sister that stayed behind at *The Continent* to get married, and missed her greatly. He hoped she fared well.

The Pilot Sencho suggested, "If we're careful we can rig that thing up for towing."

Advisor Two called out to the communications officer, "Get that transport over here. I want two diving teams out there on the double!"

Ix looked at Mox again and their eyes met. Ix said under his breath, "Remember Grandpa Nux!"

Mox turned to Advisor Two and pleaded, "Sir, let me go out there! In honor of my grandfather."

"You're on Mox."

"Thank you Sir!" Mox rushed to the airlock, giving Blujic a peck on the cheek as he passed.

Blujic came up to the cockpit to watch the operation with Ix. Moments later Mox swam up to the cockpit and knocked on the thick plate from the outside. When Blujic and Ix waved back, Mox turned and headed for the vault. Soon the place was swarming with divers. Several of them were armed with corpuscle prods and set up a secure perimeter. Mox and the others proceeded to attach special ballast weights and buoyancy tanks, careful not to upset the current balance that might send the vault rising into the full force of the surf or sinking past the point of no return. The job was complete in no time, and the team cut loose the cable and entangled weight. Immediately remote tubes and hydraulics purged air from the tanks to compensate.

Hord turned and reported to Advisor Two, "We're in business!"

Advisor Two formed a sly grin on his face. He said, "Sencho, I want to open her up!"

One wake period later Ix stood back on the makeshift dock and watched the men work the cables and pulleys. The vault was already halfway out of the Plasma, supported between three column growths and a dozen or so inflatable bladders. The surface of the Plasma was smooth -- they had found a subterranean cavity away from the waves and wind. A makeshift string of light elements attached to the columns lit up the work area. All they needed to do was to get the heavy cylinder high enough so that the massive door cleared the waterline.

Ix was the resident technician, ranking above the men who served on the escort pod and transport vessel, so he had been given charge of the operation. He had calculated the probable weight of the vault and had devised the lifting procedure. His team began to anchor winches to cables strung between the column growths, and slowly raised the vault out of the Plasma.

A little past mid wake period the faint hairline crack that marked the vault door threshold had cleared the dock by a hand width. Ix had been working on the circular handle ever since it had poked above the surface. Two men had been put to work with scrubbing brushes bathing the mechanism with a special solution. Since the entire vault and door handle mechanism were made of some metal alloy that seemed impervious to corrosion, Ix had hoped that they would not have too much trouble opening it. Massive hinges to the side of the door had also been washed and scrubbed.

Ix turned to Advisor Two with a questioning expression on his face. Advisor Two nodded and Ix turned toward the hatch mechanism. He yanked at the wheel and to his delight the handle broke free on the first try. He spun the wheel several times until it stopped then tugged at the door in an attempt to open it. This time they were not so lucky. Even when two of the men joined in, the door did not budge. Ix had the cleaners bring out the special solution and start scrubbing at the faint line that defined the door. If worse came to worse, Ix considered the possibility of tethering one of the pods to a distant column and hooking on to the handle with a cable and windlass. If they had to resort to that, the force might be too much for the metal and warp it out of shape. He worked every angle in order to avoid such drastic measures.

The pair with the brushes continued scrubbing as Ix and a number of others took turns pulling at the heavy door. Perhaps the solution began to work, for the tugging started to move the door ever so slightly. The hairline turned into a ridge that widened into a tangible edge. Slowly but surely the door opened a fingerwidth at a time. When the first concentric ring of the vault door cleared the jamb a quick hissing sound came from the resulting crack as the inside and outside air equalized. The crew let out a cheer and doubled their efforts, pulling harder and scrubbing at the heavy hinges as well.

The gap expanded. Unable to restrain himself, Mox stepped in from the side and pulled out his torch, shining it into the slit opening. The crack slowly widened and other concentric circles of the vault door edge became visible one by one.

Mox, who had been busy with his torch excitedly cried out, "I see something!"

Ix and the other men who had been working the door crowded against the vault and fought for a space along the crack to peek inside. The beam of Mox's torch revealed a large metal rectangle standing in the middle of the space, surrounded by unrecognizable shapes. Knowing the interior of the vaults from his technician training days, Ix assumed the rectangle to be the end of a block of shelving that ran the length of the interior.

The men backed away and resumed the pulling and tugging. Ix stayed near the opening and thrust his arm inside, using the muscles of his back to pry at the door from the inside. In a matter of moments the door gave and suddenly swung wide open, sending the men tumbling. Ix stumbled as well, landing on his face directly in front of the open door. He immediately got up and sat on the dock. There in front of him, a perfectly round hatchway framed the darkness.

Mox moved up and lent Ix a hand, the whole time pointing his torch into the interior. The beam lit up a wide vestibule, and on the left and right the shelving blocks split the cylindrical space down the middle, defining two aisles on either side. Cargo netting spilled out from those aisles where it held back whatever items sat on the shelves. Mounds of dark matter could be seen covering the floor, but the original expanded metal decking showed through in many places.

The shapes of objects lining the back wall caught Ix's attention. He stepped over the threshold onto the expanded metal deck to get a better look, closely followed by Mox and Advisor Two. Ix inadvertently stepped on a mound of the dark material scattered on the deck and heard a crunch as his foot crushed some brittle substance. He looked down in curiosity and almost jumped back in surprise at what he saw. The moldy substance on the deck had the form of a person! Strips of decayed fabric and pieces of an old respirator were scattered about. Mox turned the beam of his torch directly on the figure and the sight almost turned Ix's stomach. A corpse lay there, partially decomposed yet remarkably well preserved in its mummified state.

Mox couldn't turn away. Ix knew that his brother was fighting within himself. He'd been through a lot -- stumbling upon that liquid tomb of corpses back at *The Continent*, startled by the human skeleton of Those Who Went Before, seeing his own team murdered right in front of his eyes, and now this. It was not something one could get used to. Still, Mox surprised him when he came out with a clear controlled voice.

"Ix, this isn't Vault One or Vault Two." he simply said.

Somehow Ix knew that already. Perhaps *The Continent* had been destroyed by a quake and perhaps not. But one thing was sure: this vault was no debris from their former home. They had come to find the ancient moorings of *The Continent* but had stumbled upon a find of much more significance -- the Third Vault!

Mox replied, "Do you remember what grandpa Nux wrote about Vault Three?"

Ix waved that aside, "I've just about got it memorized. Mox, these remains must be grandpa's hancho! He must have holed up in the Third Vault when the chamber collapsed. His hand is resting on the valves -- releasing the helium must have been his last act. The gas could have just tipped the balance to keep the vault from sinking."

Ix thought back on the times they used to sit at grandpa Nux's knees and listen to the stories. "Didn't he used to talk about some metal man or something?"

Ix and Mox looked at each other and suddenly stood up straight in unison. Behind them Advisor Two stood patiently and a dozen or so faces could be seen peering in from the perfect circle of the hatch. The twins rushed toward the back of the vestibule to view the objects stored there behind cargo netting. As Mox's torch swept among the items, the beam rested on a clear box containing some metal fabrications. The Largest fabrication looked like a hatch or door of some kind, with perfectly formed radius corners and a clear window built into the middle of it. Some strange, bold-faced characters were engraved on the hatch. There was a sign on display in front of the hatch with archaic glyphs. Ix reached back into memory and tried to piece together the meanings. "Door to the *Towa Maru*."

Mox gasped. "I've seen this before. Somehow I think I should know this but I can't remember!" Mox kept the beam centered on the hatch as if by staring at it lost layers of memory could somehow float to the surface.

"Come on Mox, your memory is all screwed up anyway. What else is here?"

Mox moved the beam farther along and illuminated the thing they had both been looking for: the metal man! The sleek, brushed metal surface was mostly whitish silver, but perfectly machined joints occasionally separated other shades indicating different alloys. In a few places was a burnished yellow-gold colored metal that Ix had never seen the likes of before. The seams and joints were perfectly formed, and there were wires and strange machines on its chest and back. The metal man seemed to be in pristine condition, untouched by the ravages of time.

Mox seemed perplexed, "Why would Those Who Went Before go to all this trouble and use such precious metal to sculpt the figure of a man when they could have built something useful?"

Ix said, "I think this is some kind of advanced clothing or suit. Look at the head – it's like a helmet or something."

Mox stared in amazement. "A suit? You mean for diving or something?"

"I guess we'll find out sooner or later."

The two of them continued on and poked around the other artifacts, which mostly consisted of metal alloy containers and other unrecognizable items. Advisor Two and some of the other men could be heard wandering through other parts of the vault.

In one of the domed ends, the twins came across a generator sprawled on the deck, still connected to cables strung down the aisle. Ix followed the cables and saw that they had been wired into a junction box under the deck. He said to Mox, "The old sencho must have powered up the ancient lights. Let's see if we can get them to work."

The old generator was worthless, so Ix called out to someone on the dock to bring down a new one. Just then Blujic came up to the vault door. During the final dramatic moments when they had finally gotten the door open she had been sleeping in her cabin on the pod. "Can I enter too?"

Mox cried out, "No Blujic, it's not a pretty sight! Stay there outside the door."

Ix worked on connecting their generator to the same junction box the old sencho had used. The pilot light lit up and the power gauge began to rise. Looking down the narrow aisles toward the end of the vault, he tried to see if there was a response from any of the ancient light fixtures, but to no avail.

Ix started to exit the vault to go find some more light elements when he almost ran into a console he had not noticed before. Protruding from the top of the console was an illuminated block that resembled one of those ancient data crystals that had been found in Vault One and Vault Two. Suddenly the entire vestibule lit up with some sort of projected image. Ix, Mox, Blujic, and a few others who happened to be near the vestibule stared in amazement at the sight. The image was of a man that floated three dimensionally in the air. Ix waved his hand and it passed right through the image like a ghost. How had the projection been sustained? Ix could not tell.

Presently the projected image of the man began to speak, with a static-filled voice booming out from all around them. The language was an archaic form of their current language, but was understood easily enough except for when the audio sputtered.

"Hello, my name is Weyn. I am protector of the records of my people, the Defenders. The Rebel forces have destroyed our people and have cornered us in this part of *The Continent.* At this very moment Defender forces are holding the line only three nodes away. I'm afraid we have little chance of surviving the conflict. We have gathered all our records together and have placed them in these three vaults. We will seal the vault chamber so the Rebel forces cannot discover their existence. The Rebels will destroy all records and our precious historical artifacts should they find them. It is my hope that should the Rebel forces succeed and kill us off that a much more responsible people may someday come along and find the vaults, to learn about their ancestors and Those Who Went Before."

Weyn continued, "We have put this holoprojection together as an introduction to the records contained in the vaults. We have set the machinery to automatically trigger as soon as a suitable power circuit has been completed, which we hope any people capable of entering the vault will be able to accomplish."

Ix felt someone pushing at his back and turned around to see that the entire crew had gathered in the aisles to see the projection. Every one of them was speechless.

Weyn continued to speak, but the sound failed altogether and all the men could do was look at each other in bewilderment. Weyn waved his hand and the display changed. A series of video images showed one after the other with curious, alien scenarios.

In one clip, a man stood beside some type of vessel that appeared to be floating in the air. The man opened a small hatch in the side of the craft. Ix immediately recognized the hatch as the artifact displayed in the clear cabinet against the vault's back wall. That vessel must have been the *Towa Maru*, but of what significance did it have to Those Who Went Before?

From Ix's side, Mox gasped, "I've seen this before! I've seen this floating pod in a dream!"

The scene changed again. There was a dark and dreary landscape with an uneven gray deck. The ceiling (or sky as Blujic would say) was completely black. The figure of a person came into view, shuffling his feet in a strange slow-motion sort of way. Ix recognized the person was wearing the same metal suit, the 'metal man' that Ix and Mox had found moments before in the vault. Next a companion moved into the projection, and both the figures apparently had their backs to the camera. As the two metallic suited figures moved along down a dusty slope, the projection showed them walk up to a wheeled vehicle of sorts, with four other figures sitting in it. The sitting figures were also in suits, but much more bulky. Ix could see buildings and other installations about, with machines swarming all over the place engaged in shoveling and pushing around ground matter, perhaps in some construction or mining operation.

The gray landscape was replaced by projections of the forest showing the floating pod moving among the trees. Two blood-red barbarians came into view, walking through the forest in full battle gear. There was some confrontation where the *Towa Maru* emanated fearfully bright beams of light. The beams struck the two men in the chest area and they fell to the ground.

Once again Mox was gasping next to Ix. "I've seen this before in a dream, too!"

Ix turned to face Mox squarely and said, "Isn't this how the Wardens do battle from the rockers?" but Mox said nothing.

Again the scene changed and pod-like vessels were floating through a black void. They all appeared as crescents, for a harsh light barely illuminated their hulls. Three of the crafts approached a fourth, and a small sphere launched out of the foremost vessel slowly crossed the void to meet it. When the sphere came within a fairly close range of the fourth craft it suddenly exploded in a blinding flash. Particles could be seen radiating out into the void, and when the flash subsided nothing remained of the vessel but a wrecked hulk.

Briefly the scene went black and Ix could hear the others stirring behind him. They had witnessed a lot of confusing images -- he only hoped that some of the technicians would be able to make sense of it after they had towed the vault back to *The Island* and tore into the records it contained.

Weyn appeared again suddenly and mouthed words no one could hear. In the projection a massive ship moved slowly and silently through the void. Ix was amazed by its size! Rows of view ports could barely be seen in the great curve of the massive metal hull. It may have been large enough to hold all the inhabitants of *The Continent* at once. Coming out of one side (Ix could not understand if the vessel was oriented upright, upside-down, or in some other position), a great appendage like a fin extended away from the main hull. Attached to the hull and fin were lattice works of thin structures that reached out into the black void.

Ix let out a gasp, "That's the great vessel at *Mother's Heart!*" He heard Advisor Two echo a similar comment.

The scene turned into a view apparently from the inside of the great ship, looking out into the black void. The curve of the ship's hull could be seen in the foreground, and a great bright spheroid commandeered the center of the projection. It was magnificent! The spheroid was a bluish hue with white textured swirls almost engulfing the entire surface. While Ix watched, several smaller vessels emerged from an opening in the great curve of the hull and slowly moved toward the massive spheroid.

As the projection continued, Ix considered what Mox had said about flying out into the gray zone in the rockers. All of a sudden it dawned on him what he was looking at. The realization seemed ridiculous. Could it be that Mother was a sphere and that they lived on the surface of it? The idea was almost as absurd as Ix and Blujic's story of people living on the inside of a cylinder!

The scene changed and the image showed *The Continent* under bright, sunny skies. Ix could not put his finger on it, but something about the structures seemed new and crisp. He had never really seen the outside of *The Continent* before, except from underneath. What he was viewing now was a completely different environment from what he knew their city to be. The node towers supported various levels of structure that gracefully cascaded down, sporting green gardens and outdoor plazas. Though the gardens were a little overgrown and neglected, the effect was fabulous.

Nestled into plazas could be seen the small vessels that Ix had seen detach from the greater ship earlier. Groups of people could be seen disembarking from the small crafts and moving about here and there. Some groups could be seen constructing or refitting parts of the existing city or servicing the vessels as they arrived. The exciting part of the image was that the people all had black hair and facial features of Ix's own people. They had not descended from those barbarians!

Suddenly the audio began working again, and Ix slapped his palms to his ears as Weyn's voice boomed out, "Our fathers came on the great ship and found *The Continent* to be an ideal hiding place. They adapted some of the smaller ships into watercraft and submarines, since their hulls had originally been designed for salvage operations in a variety of atmospheres and oceans. Our small fleets find much abundance of sea creatures in the open Plasma.

"Only ten seasons ago a group of young people began to grow restless and unsatisfied with our life here. They called themselves the Rebels and moved to deserted parts of *The Continent*. The Rebel faction started out small but grew in strength. Two seasons ago the Rebels started sneaking into the main parts of our community, stealing and plundering citizen's homes. We put together a police force called the Defenders. The confrontations escalated and the Defender forces succeeded in curbing much of the Rebel activities. Nevertheless, the Rebels were quite violent. They devised explosive weapons and rockets that terrorized our citizens. On one raid, they succeeded in setting explosives and breaking *The Continent* free from its moorings. We have been adrift ever since and have found ourselves out on the high seas at the mercy of the eternal storms.

"The Rebels have succeeded in destroying almost our entire security force. We have been herded to this forgotten corner of *The Continent* and have gathered together all those who would come along. It is only a matter of a few wake periods before our meager guards fail and they overrun this corner.

"Our genealogy has been preserved among us since the first families arrived at Mother on board the big ship. Here is the lineage of all the major families."

Lists of names and faces flashed into view. To Ix most of the names meant nothing, until a certain Rebel name was mentioned.

Mox had noticed it also and excitedly cried out, "Ix, I know that name! That's one of our grandfathers!"

As the list was read, other men in the vault also could be heard excitedly noting that one of their ancestors had been mentioned. This went on until everyone in the vault (except Blujic) had heard at least one ancestor mentioned.

The scene changed one last time. They were looking at terracing gardens in *The Continent* under blue sunny skies. Something about the scene seemed a little unreal, almost artificially derived with a cartoon feel.

Weyn concluded, "Finally, we have prepared simulations..." but the audio failed again and never returned.

The cartoon scene of *The Continent* fell as their point of view rose above the deck. The scene shifted so that they were looking straight down at *The Continent*, its triangular pattern of node towers, passage tubes and chambers clearly visible. The viewpoint continued to rise until the great city completely filled the scene and the entire perimeter could be seen. Still they continued to rise. Some of the men present gave audible reaction to the thrill sensation that could be felt in connection with the simulated journey. Soon *The Continent* became a small blight on a long winding channel that disappeared under the cover of swirling mists and clouds. Wisps of white encroached over the bay, and the entire scene shrunk by the moment as they rose higher and higher. After a while the edges of the projection began to curve in with a fisheye effect. That great water ball also reduced in size until it was no more than a bluish crescent against a black void, a pristine jewel to be cherished and protected. The magnificence of the scene was overwhelming. Ix suddenly realized how puny men were.

Ix turned to look at Mox and saw that he and Blujic were smiling and making eyes at each other. Mox said something like, "My people render the void black instead of gray!"

As the bluish crescent receded in the distance, Ix was perplexed when numerous misshapen objects could be seen floating about, some near the blue-white marble and others more distant. In the corner of the projection a bright orb came into the view as well, shining brightly against the black background. Then there was a pause. Glowing yellow ellipse paths overlaid the scene, tracing out the orbital paths of the misshapen objects. The animation showed the shapes in motion, following along the yellow ellipse paths at an ever-increasing rate.

"Those are 'moons'," Blujic provided. Ix recalled that Mox had tried to explain about the ‘moons’, and as fantastic as it seemed, he was totally confused about the strange dynamics of the shapes in space.

Mother began to spin as well, with the great circle marking the Warden's land mass centered right on the rotational axis. The scene continued to recede, and the yellow ellipse paths upon which Mother and the 'moons' traveled encircled the massive light orb that came into view.

Blujic spoke up again in her halting pronunciation, "That's 'sun' -- it bright fire in sky. Bigger ball than Mother but so far away!"

Ix considered that for a moment. With all the revelations of late, a huge ball of fire out in the void was just one more incredible mystery he had to take her word for.

Mother and the 'moons' began moving along the yellow orbit paths at a faster and faster rate. As the sun-fireball with the orbiting Mother receded even further, other orbiting specks of light appeared in the projection image, each with their respective yellow orbit paths. There were more than Ix could count, and they all appeared to be somewhat similar distances from the 'sun', some a little closer and some a little farther than Mother herself. The yellow ellipse paths varied greatly, with some of them appearing quite flattened and others approaching the shape of a perfect circle. Ix realized that it might have been a perspective problem, where the flattened ellipses were also circles that came out in front of the fireball and moved behind it on their far side. Finally a lone ellipse came into view that was quite a distance from the 'sun'. An arrow indicator pointed to a solitary speck of light resting on that last ellipse, with archaic characters for the word 'Bridgestar'.

Now Ix was confused. The projection suggested that Mother was a great spheroid whose surface faced outward into a vast void. Was this the serene strata above the turbulent boundary area that Ix had contemplated so many times? What was the significance of the Bridgestar, and why had Those Who Went Before labeled it so?

The viewpoint continued to recede until even the Bridgestar ellipse could not be seen any more and only the sun-fireball showed. A long while passed and suddenly other brilliant orbs swung into view. More and more of them crowded together so that Ix could scarcely discern which was their own 'sun'. Blujic described them as 'stars', which were more fireballs. The projection receded until the vestibule was filled with billions of tiny sparks of light. In some places the sparks were quite dense where in others they were sparse.

In one corner of the seas of sparks, a red arrow indicator appeared with the label 'Mother'. Soon another red indicator appeared fairly close to the first one labeled 'Blister'. Finally there was another pause and one last indicator appeared a much farther off -- 'Taiyo'. It was apparent that these were all places on a vast map. Ix began to paint an astounding picture in his mind of islands in the vast void -- thousands of Mother-stars out there waiting to be explored!

Suddenly the vision vanished and Ix was left standing staring at the plain inside of the vault surrounded by dozens of dumbfounded colleagues. No one said a word for the longest time. Each one of them strove to digest the flood of incredible imagery that had just assaulted their minds.

Ix couldn't help but smile -- it all came together at last.

Later in the wake period many crewmembers were sitting around on the subterranean dock with blank looks on their faces, or mechanically going about their work with their minds somewhere else. No one felt like working. Advisor Two called a meeting of the key members of the expedition as he puzzled over the meaning of what they saw.

Ix began to explain, "Those Who Went Before didn't come from Mother at all. They lived in the vast serene void beyond the storms,"

"Mother shape like ball hanging in void -- my people believe." a struggling Blujic added.

Ix, who had looked in her direction turned back to the main group and continued, "Yes, as hard to believe is it is, we reside on a huge ball of Plasma. It appears that something similar to a magnetic force causes everyone to cling to its surface and not fall off."

Blujic quickly interjected, "Gravity. We call gravity".

Advisor Two, who had been with Ix on the visit to *Mother's Heart* asked, "I'm still puzzled by the big ship; was that a submarine, or what?"

"Not a submarine, but a -- a void ship. It was a ship for crossing the serene void. Do you remember the scene where several ships faced each other, and some weapon destroyed one of them? I think Those Who Went Before were fleeing from a war in the void. They came here to hide."

Mox thought a bit and said, "But what about the Wardens? What about the *Origin*?"

Ix could see that Mox was already seeing a glimmer of what must have happened. Ix explained, "Initially we know the Wardens lived in two void ships that circled above Mother. It seems apparent that Mother was a prison colony of sorts, and Those Who Went Before thought it a perfect place to hide. They must have hidden their huge ship behind the curve of Mother where the Wardens couldn't see it, perhaps intending to leave as soon as things calmed down a bit." Ix looked around at the group and continued, "But something went wrong. The war brought down one of the Warden's void ships, and Blujic's people were forced to stay on the surface. Those Who Went Before couldn't hide much longer, nor could they leave, so they decided to scuttle their great ship to hide their whereabouts. They sunk it below the Plasma, and used their small ships to ferry everyone over to an abandoned section of the floating prison. Now the great derelict orbits the inside of the liquid spheroid, perhaps drawn along by tidal forces from the various moons."

Advisor Two chimed in, "And they converted the small ships into submarines."

Ix replied, "Yes, it must have been a challenge, since the void ships were built to hold internal pressure, and pods to withstand external pressure. But remember Weyn said the smaller ships were designed to enter a lot of environments anyway."

Mox began beaming, "I think I understand how the Wardens lived on the inside of a cylinder."

He rubbed his chin and looked around, finding a rope with a bucket on the end holding a small amount of Plasma. He held onto the rope and spun around, copying what Blujic had shown him with the ball and string, until the bucket and cable stood straight out perpendicular to his height. He held the spinning contraption above his head while he stood still, eying the group. Not a drop of water spilled, but stayed on the bottom of the bucket due to centripetal forces.

Ix explained, "Perhaps we need a magnetic field to hold us to Mother,"

Blujic corrected, "Gravity..."

But Ix continued, "Out in the void there is no such thing, so they must spin their ships to cause everyone to cling to the walls. Think of this bucket as tracing out the wall of a cylinder. If we created a cylinder large enough, and spun it fast enough, we could keep Plasma from flowing away."

Mox asked, "What about the old man, and the metallic suit?"

Ix replied, "He must have been one of the advance party, in a small void ship named *Towa Maru*. He took recorded images of Those Who Went Before as they searched desolate places in their quest for a hiding place. They must have discovered the floating forest and decided the Inmates who lived there would be too much of a risk."

Advisor Two smiled and said, "Okay, we know we didn't descend from barbarians or Inmates. Still, a mystery remains -- where did Those Who Went Before come from?"

Ix thought about that for a moment. His old questions had suddenly been answered. His recent worries about whether they had descended from the barbarians or prisoners had been settled. He started off thinking the whole of existence consisted of hard labor barely maintaining delicate volumes enclosed by inhospitable storms or crushing pressures. Ix's heart had just as suddenly been filled with a grand realization -- their heritage included the very substance of the stars themselves, which must include uncountable worlds to explore! Perhaps he didn't get the physics quite right, or perhaps there was some other explanation for the magnetic field or the ghost ship orbiting the core of their world -- they could answer those questions in time. Maybe their ancestors came from Bridgestar, or Blister, or Taiyo or perhaps even beyond. But one thing was certain -- the secret was out and Ix suspected his people would not be satisfied with the surface of their tiny world much longer. He looked up and calmly replied, "That, my friend is another story. And we will write that story ourselves, all of us!"

EPILOGUE

A young woman fiddled nervously with the collection of straps and belts that made up her restraint harness. It had only been a year galactic time since she had first filled this seat, facing the complicated banks of controls with wonder and fright. In those days they had spent their time testing and improving each of the subsystems, making sure they had built redundancy into every circuit. She had even taken short hops over the bay, where there was always that liquid safety net only a few armlengths below ready catch them should something go wrong. But today was different: there was no safety net for this trip!

The girl remembered back to when she had first sat in the simulator that looked the same in every way. She and the trainer had taken priority time slots on two of the six rockers that had been installed on *The Island.* In the past few years the Technicians had come to measure their time according to the old galactic standards given them by Those Who Went Before, and the rockers were reserved by the hour. They had sat back-to-back in that virtual machine and had soared for hours and hours over *The Island*, the crystal city, and the towering treetops. Those were the days! She could still remember the feelings of disappointment when the ten-minute warning went off indicating the end of their reserved time period. Still, though a lot of young technicians couldn't get enough of the virtual world, she had taken after her Warden mother and preferred the Flesh. Which explained why she was there in front of those real controls in the Flesh.

Well, she had always been different anyway. Ever since she had been a young tot the other children always wanted to touch her long chestnut colored hair. The 'halfling' label followed her all over *The Island.* Everyone knew her and would whisper under their breath, "There goes Mox's girl". Actually that wasn't so bad. Since her father had been appointed Advisor One, filling in after grandpa retired, and later serving as general advisor to the president, she had been in the center of instant popularity while at the same time a bit lonely. One thing could be said about living among the Wardens -- no one ever made a point to say *There goes Blujic's daughter* just on account of hair color. Those Wardens zipped around the crystal palaces with blue hair, purple hair, or whatever other thing they fancied to form themselves into. Though most of them had light-colored hair in the Flesh, such a feature had no meaning to them. The whole point was how creative you could be, or what new appearance could be contracted out of the professional formers.

Talk about creative -- an interesting relationship had developed between the Wardens and the Technicians. The Wardens were good thinkers and the Technicians were good builders, so a large amount of the commerce between them had been contracting with one another for services. This had been especially true since there was no monetary standard in existence like that which had been used in ancient times. Bartering for services seemed natural from the beginning. Uncle Ix had built two very interesting prototype machines that way. One of the machines was already in limited production: the Wardens had contracted to build a better under-Plasma remote Mapper for their Mapper fleet. Now five of them were already down there adding daily to the

Database. The Wardens were thrilled to be able to increase the Database and the Technicians used the new under plasma maps for navigation.

And how about the other prototype machine? The young woman strained against the restraint harness and looked out the small view port. There it was sitting out on the launch pad, *Bird One*: the first human piloted flying machine. Uncle had traded the sub-Plasma technology for cooperation on air thrusters and displacement jets. What an event it was when that crude three-point contraption had lifted up off the deck and had sustained a stable two armlength altitude for 57 minutes! If it weren't for the fact that one of the three jets had failed and tipped the machine sideways, they could have maintained the flight indefinitely.

Now there she was, sitting in *Bird Two*, a rock stable four-point advanced prototype with double displacement jets at each point. It had been Uncle Ix's dream to reach for the stars, and he had won her over. She looked over and nodded at her uncle, who waved back from the observation deck of the control center.

Those Who Went Before had left them a great storehouse of knowledge. The Third Vault that Papa and Uncle had rediscovered had held keys for unlocking all the secrets that Vault One and Vault Two held as well. Waves of refugees from *The Continent*, including her aunt who had stayed behind when *The Island* split away, had arrived after the great quake, bringing the two vaults intact and loaded with the treasured artifacts. Still, even with all the knowledge that they had gained, Those Who Went Before were shrouded in mystery.

Whatever the meaning of it all, Ix and Mox had awakened a dream within the entire Technician race. Even the Wardens were caught up in it, her parents having convinced them that extra-Mother exploration could expand their precious Database. *Bird Two* was another step in the right direction. It was hoped that the vessel would eventually be able to fly to the upper atmosphere where the pilots would require pressure suits and oxygen bottles, like the metallic 'metal man' environmental suit found in Vault Three that the Technicians hoped to reverse engineer. Based on the data *Bird Two* brought back, the next generation *Bird Three* would be designed with self-contained life support equipment and a pressurized cabin. Ah the wonder of it all -- and she was right there in the middle of it!

As in the simulator, she sat back-to-back with the other pilot who was commander of their small crew. The commander spoke through the microphone in Reformed Neo-Japonican that sounded in her helmet earphones, "*Pilot ready to begin liftoff sequence.*"

Neo-Japonican was the name Those Who Went Before had given their language. Since they had changed and adapted the language over the centuries, the Technicians called their own tongue 'Reformed Neo-Japonican', or 'Japonican' for short. What the term 'Japonican' meant no one knew, but suspected it to be one of the ancient languages of the galactic empire. There wasn't a name for the Warden's tongue, except for a silly phrase 'Wardenese', but there were enough similar vocabulary in both languages for them to conclude that their respective races had had some intercourse in the distant past.

The young woman also spoke up in Japonican, "Copilot ready for liftoff sequence."

A third voice from their virtual crewmember sounded as well, in Wardenese, "*Navigator ready for liftoff sequence.*"

The navigator was in a rocker somewhere in the crystal city and represented the Wardens as a Database expert. Though the two live crew members could only hear his voice, the young woman knew that he was at that moment sitting in a virtual version of the craft, seeming almost as real to him as it was for them.

One more voice sounded from the control center on *The Island.* Uncle Ix gave them permission to start the sequence. The crew went down their checklist item by item testing every control and system, sounding off as they went. It was almost a mechanical procedure that they had gone through every day for the past year, mostly ending without even firing up the engines.

Today was different however, as the young lady flipped through a series of switches that answered with a rumble vibration. The thrusters were now primed and ready for the final liftoff command.

The pilot flipped the main breaker that sent the oxygen-methane mix flowing to each of the displacement engines. With all eight jets in perfect working order, all they needed was a good spurt in the right direction to overcome the mass and momentum of the vehicle. According to the library of Those Who Went Before, Mother was a small world barely stable enough to hold together. One-fourth Gee, it said. The atmosphere was so thin they needed respirators unless there were plenty of oxygen-producing plants in the neighborhood. Technically it wouldn't take much to reach escape velocity.

The young woman was pressed back in her seat as *Bird Two* shot up into the sky. Through the view port, the wispy clouds above came at them at a tremendous speed. The pilot reduced the fuel flow to the thrusters in a braking maneuver. The craft began to slow, but not before they broke through the cottony billows of water vapor.

Bird Two slowed to a stop and just hovered there. The young woman pushed against the restraints and peered out the view port. There all around them a white powdery landscape stretched all the way to the horizon, marked only occasionally by bottomless gaps and holes. An extremely dark blue sky seemed almost unreal without a single blemish of a cloud. They had made it! They were above the clouds!

The young woman smiled as she thought, next stop -- upper atmosphere; after that, One Eternal Round with the stars!

ABOUT THE AUTHOR

A. Scott Howe is a senior engineer at NASA Jet Propulsion Laboratory and has two PhDs (in architecture and robotic construction systems). He is on the NASA development team building long-duration human habitats for deep space, and permanent outposts for the moon and Mars. He lived and worked for 13 years in Japan and 6 years in Hong Kong, and is an avid scuba diver.

Look for these other science fiction novels by A. Scott Howe:

Blister (2013)

Chronosphere (2014)

Theoloop (2021)

Replicycle / *Retrocause* (2023)

www.ingramcontent.com/pod-product-compliance
Lightning Source LLC
LaVergne TN
LVHW020657110826
845149LV00012B/2025

* 9 7 8 0 9 8 5 0 7 6 5 0 4 *